FALLEN ANGEL TRILOGY

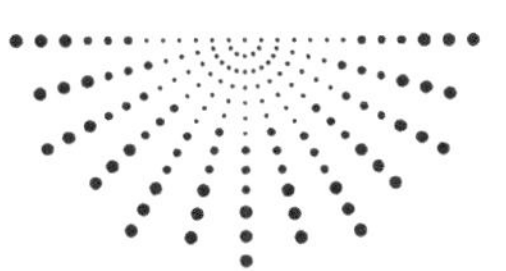

AMELIA SHAW

FALLEN ANGEL

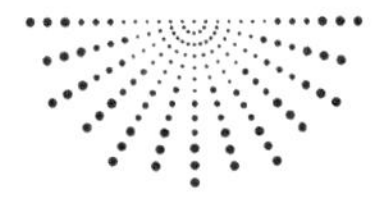

CHAPTER ONE

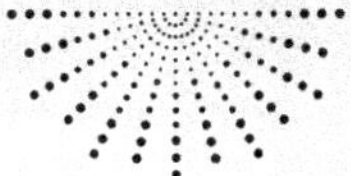

The city lay a hundred and fifty floors below, and yet I witnessed every flicker of movement as though it were mere inches in front of my face. The power of extraordinary sight. One of my many gifts from the Gods.

New York City. The city they say never slept.

And from the noise going on below, it seemed a slogan they lived by. Every other city had a moment before sunrise when everything fell quiet. The hubbub switched off, and even the humans who partied through the darkness, finally dragged themselves home to their beds. A serenity not everyone was familiar with. But it was something I could appreciate, now that I got to see it for myself.

Not New York. The police sirens still warbled their chase of drama and evil every few minutes. People tumbled in and out of diners that seemed to be perpetually open twenty-four hours. Fights broke out in street corners and women walked home at all hours in the same outfits from their evening before, makeup running down their faces, satisfied smirks touching their lips. It never stopped. If LA could have the gall to spin the lie and call themselves the "city of Angels," maybe New York should grab the title "city of Demons" and be more upfront about it. Although I sometimes wondered if LA called themselves that ironically, as though they knew it was a farce.

Three hundred and fifty years I'd watched over the humans below and the city had changed drastically in that time. But the wager going on between Heaven and Hell…that hasn't changed at all. For as long as people have existed on this planet, an Almighty being has watched over them. More than one, to be precise.

And a long time ago there was a wager made, for all the souls on Earth.

The terms and conditions had evolved over the years as Heaven began to move further ahead in score, but essentially all remained the same as it always had. The good went above, the bad went below.

And those lost souls who could be pulled either way, well…that's where I came in.

I watched as a homeless person stretched his weary legs by extending them out. He grimaced as he moved, as though the tension coiled in his body wasn't used to do such a thing. He nearly tripped a sleek man in a suit. For a moment, I thought the man was going to tell him off – as arrogant assholes did to people they saw as irrelevant – or ignore him – which everyone tended to do when it came to people they didn't want to see at all. Instead, the man stopped, handed him a five dollar bill and his coffee, and went on his way.

I frowned. The thing about New York City was that it never ceased to surprise me.

As a Fallen Angel, I fight as a soldier, for the good souls on Earth. I protect those that should be heading to Heaven when they die but are manipulated into Hell by beings who aren't meant to be here. Those fiery, evil Demons who liked to cheat the rules and control the choices made by those too weak to fight, or so important that Hell targeted them for acquisition.

Not that I'd known all of this when I'd first fallen.

I'd thought my life was over when my wings began to burn. I flinched just thinking about it, my back pinching in the memory. When it had begun, I'd believed my punishment would be absolute. I'd closed my eyes against the flickering flames and expected to never again see the light of day.

But instead, my battle had only just begun.

I wasn't sure what I preferred – a painful death or a painful life.

Tabitha had been there when I'd landed in a pile of smoke and flames. My *Angel Agent*, or so she called herself.

I'd always wondered if Tabitha had been an Angel herself. *Once upon a time… perhaps?* No one really knew what sort of being she was classified as, and no one had ever asked. What we did know, though, was that she was as immortal as I but possessed more attitude in her pinky finger than I had throughout my body.

Tabitha had found me naked, broken-hearted, and black winged over five hundred years ago. She'd taken me into her home and tended my wounds. Her house at that time had been in a parallel dimension.

When I'd recovered enough from the shock of my expulsion from Heaven, she'd explained that the only way to win myself a place back in was to fight for those souls aiming for the pearly gates. To be their champion.

Tabitha said that she'd guided many other Fallen Angels back into Heaven once they'd earned their reward. The rules, according to Tabitha, were that I had to save enough people, fulfill enough good deeds, and I would be allowed back in.

Seemed easy. Until I realized that the *enough,* though, was subjective. I'd never been given an actual number.

Well, I'd followed her guidance to the best of my abilities and three hundred and fifty years later, I remained in the land of this living limbo, having saved too many souls to count. I would like to call it unjust, but my reason for being thrust out of Heaven had been worse than most…or so they all said.

Maybe I needed to save more people than everyone else? Serve more years than the standard? I didn't know. But I had nothing else to cling to, other than the hope that one day I would finally be allowed to return home. It was the only thought that kept me sane through the unending hours, days, and decades of my Earthly service.

I had but one goal. And that kept me alive—if that's what I was.

I turned my attention back to a new scene spilling out before me. A woman walking her dog, hoodie up, dressed in baggy clothes. She walked past a construction site around even in this darkness. Her feet doubled their pace, but the workers lounging around and eating their donuts and drinking their coffee noticed and called out to her. I watched as her face pinched with embarrassment and she shook her head, muttering to herself about not walking this way again, that it would never change.

A familiar tingle coursed over my skin, rippling up my arms and down my spine like waves in a pond, starting from the center and working their way outwards.

The sun rose in the east. I could sense the warmth before it even touched my fingertips. My eyes slid shut as I turned to face the sunrise. Flashes of red, orange and yellow lit up my mind as I took a long, deep breath.

Another day, another human to save. Tabitha had already alerted me to a new female who had landed on the *list*.

The *list* was a compilation of names that held exceptional people. Humans whom Hell wanted to seduce into the fiery side. A place we did not want to lose those special people to.

And the worst part of it all was that Hell Demons did not wait for approaching death to seduce such humans. No. They weren't that kind, nor were they willing, to risk losing a soul they wanted. Instead, the Demons would torture those special beings until suicide seemed like the best way out.

Because suicide kept them from Heaven forever.

That was "suicide" in the real meaning. The English language lumped all death when you took your own life under the one banner. But there were definitely different types.

Heaven frowned on those who gave up and left a burden to others in contrast to those who sacrificed themselves for a greater good.

Because if the Demons won the battle, Earth missed out on the work of a human worthy of changing things for the better. A huge blow to our side.

The Demons had their Targets, and they were out to break the special human's will.

Enter the Fallen Angel. It was my mission to prevent such things from happening.

I didn't mind the job, actually. I would rather be home, but I liked any excuse to prevent the bastards from even thinking they won anything.

I stood up from my crouched position on a rooftop and tucked my wings in beside my body. Invisible to the human eye when needed, I could slip into anyone's life at any time.

Calm descended on me like a cloud darkening the sun as that tingle changed into something else I recognized.

There she was. My Target. And *their* Target, too.

I could feel her energy beneath me, walking amongst the crowds on the sidewalks of New York City.

Her red hair caught my eye more than anything else. The way it billowed in the breeze, untamed and beautiful. It shimmered in the rising sun as it bounced with each step she took. Such a contrast, those flowing red curls, to the modern, straightened blonde look of today. Her locks sent me back to a time when natural beauty was more highly valued than artifice.

Although the new appearances humans adopted had their moments of shocking me speechless also.

I stepped off the ledge and let my wings spread out. The blackened feathers picked up the warm, upwards drafts of wind as I floated down the silver city skyscraper. It was another reminder of my mistake, the one that ripped me from Heaven and sent me to Tabitha. I didn't know if I would ever have white wings again. Even if I served my penance, would they remain black as a warning to others as to what I had done?

My feet landed on the cement below with a solid thud and a part of me smiled as I reconnected with the Earth. There was something sacred about the ground beneath me. I'd never quite figured out the why, but there was a reason I'd fallen just outside New York. The city itself had called to me, even if it was filled with rotting humans and even worse Demons. There was always good here. It just took some time to find. I liked that. I liked the contradiction of the city.

The humans around me on the street couldn't see me. I stepped out of their way and released my hold on my invisibility, a dark-haired woman gasping as her bowed head bumped into the chest logo on my hoodie.

Her heat against my body startled my senses, but in the best way. Every nerve fiber reached out to her as though they all had their own limbs.

I longed for human contact, any contact, really. Touch. Love. Sex. But there were rules against such things, and rightly so. It stopped Angels from taking advantage of humans, and successfully tormented us even further in our punishment.

It was very effective.

"Sorry. I didn't see you there," the woman who had run into my chest muttered, as she tilted her head back to look up at me.

Her pupils dilated as she took in my massive frame and the angelic face that we of the *fallen category* were still blessed with.

I grinned at her, enjoying the briefest of connections with a human who wasn't my Target, before I turned away to walk down the street. She probably would have assumed that I was an unusually tall man. If she'd known what I really was, her long brown hair would probably turn white.

Humans didn't handle knowing there were paranormal creatures all around them very well. They preferred to believe they were the supreme creatures on the planet, so they remained firmly planted in ignorance.

As I walked, I kept my eyes on my red-headed Target in front of me. It still wasn't busy in the city, which was nice. I hated crowds. Too much intense energy and emotion made my head ache.

Humans had become so much more stressed over the decades I'd watched them—exponentially so. Technology, changes in diet and work schedules. All of it terribly destructive to their ability to rest, heal and be happy.

I slid around the people hurrying along the street and shadowed the woman I'd been assigned to protect. My gaze moved over her tiny frame from behind, taking in her lush curves and unusual fashion sense.

Well, she probably wasn't tiny, compared to most humans. But to me, she was diminutive. I was almost seven feet tall when in full Angel mode, and although I could adapt my size to suit my surroundings, it was uncomfortable to do so.

The woman—Kadie, Tabitha said her name was—didn't seem to be anything special. Not compared to the last hundred or so Targets I'd protected. She was some sort of free spirit. She did not adhere to corporate clothing styles, nor fashionable denim. She wore her hair free. Her long cotton skirt billowed around her legs as she walked. Her shoulders were bare, except for a few strands of material that clung to her skin. A wrap-around grey top bound her tiny waist and made me want to circle her with my hands and bring her close.

This was no doctor or lawyer, or even an award-winning scientist. I'd protected them for decades and I knew them well.

I mentally balked at the instant attraction I had to this woman. Despite my need for physical closeness, I'd believed my sex-drive to have died a long time ago. But as I walked, my cock stirred with desire.

Kadie glanced over her shoulder and her gaze met mine with a precision I'd never experienced with a human. Humans couldn't see me unless I wanted them to, and I'd pulled my shroud of invisibility tight around me.

But Kadie's gaze locked onto mine and a strange familiarity passed over me. Perhaps I'd known her in a past life? Saved her when she'd been in another body?

She broke the eye contact and started running, as though she sensed the danger I could present. My heartbeat picked up instantly.

The hunter in me grinned and called out with excitement. The chase was on.

I pushed some power into my legs and followed her through the gathering crowd. Then suddenly, she disappeared. Vanished into thin air.

I faltered. I looked around to see if maybe she just disappeared in the crowd.

How did she do that? Where was she?

I kept moving along the street, certain I must have only lost her for a moment. Surely, she couldn't have evaded me. Impossible.

But then I hit a corner and the sounds of the city engulfed my mind. The loud cars zoomed past and people hustled all around me. She still wasn't visible. She wasn't anywhere. My gaze darted left and right, across the street, and then I whirled around to stare back the way we'd come. Where on Earth could she be?

How was that possible? I'd never lost a Target before. Ever.

I closed my eyes and projected a message to Tabitha. *I've lost her.*

A chuckle came back to me. **I thought you would.**

How would you know that?

Because she's a Witch, of sorts. And she's been followed by many Demons of late. I thought she might find a way to elude you too. After all, it's the only reason she's still alive.

You didn't think to warn me?

A soft laugh from my agent this time. **You? An almighty warrior of Heaven? Why would I need to warn you?**

A growl rolled through my throat and dragged my hand down my face. *Any suggestions for where she'd be?*

Go to her house tonight. I'm sure you'll be able to find her there.

Fine. Send me her address. The information clicked into my head like the inbox on a computer. *Thanks.*

Good luck, and please be more careful next time you have her. I have a strong premonition that this one could be the key for you, Gabriel.

A sigh rippled through my soul. The key for me? I wanted to

scoff but she'd probably find some way to reach across the distance between us and yank my ear like I was some kind of stubborn child.

It's been three hundred and fifty years, Tabitha. I'm starting to believe they'll never forgive me.

But even as I thought the words, my stomach tightened with anticipation. What if Kadie were the one? The final human who could put me back home.

Don't give up, Gabriel. Never give up. This one is important. You can feel it, can't you? That there is something special going on this time.

I began to ask why she was so important, when that familiar tingle up my spine made me twist around. My Target.

Red hair flew in a cloud down the street, having slipped out a side alley. I pulled invisibility around me, uncaring of who watched as I disappeared from the world.

I chased after her once again, my heart pounding in my chest. She darted to and fro like an experienced runner, around people and over the street. Just as I would reach out for her she whirled around and disappeared once again like a magician.

What the hell? What is this woman?

I stopped dead, reaching out for her with my senses and finding nothing.

Seriously. What is this? Was this disappearing stunt why the Demons were interested in her?

I turned in a full circle once more with my eyes wide open and saw no remnants of her.

I let out a heavy sigh. *Being able to elude me is no simple feat.*

There was only one thing to do, and that was to wait until nightfall.

Outside Kadie's house.

CHAPTER TWO

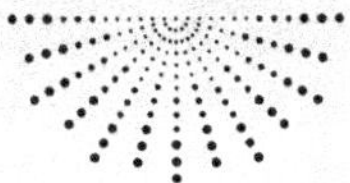

*D*arkness had fallen over the city—the worst time of day for anywhere in the world because it was the only time the Demons came out to prey. Demons didn't like the sun because the sun had the ability to reveal what they really were to the human eye. Not all humans would recognize them, of course. Humans loved living in their ignorance. However, there were a select few that had the ability to see Demons from what they really were. I had the feeling my Target was one of them.

In the dark, however…

I wasn't completely sure. I know Tabitha mentioned her having the ability to see them and run from them, but I wasn't sure if it was strictly during the day or if part of what made her so appealing was her ability to recognize them for what they were without being cloaked in darkness.

I sat on the ledge of an apartment building in a small street in the Bronx. Only two stories up this time, I wasn't risking losing her again although there was part of me that was impressed by her tenacity. I did like the chase. It was new, something I hadn't expected and wasn't quite used to. Part of me wondered what other tricks she had up her sleeve.

Movement to the right caught my eye and I watched my little disappearing witch sneak along the street, a dark scarf pulled tight over her abundant hair. But I could sense her, like a burning beacon in a dark sea. To me, it was obvious that her hair flamed for all to see and it was clever of her to hide it at night when the Demons were out. I wondered why she didn't just dye it to hide such an obvious part of her identity. I could understand wanting to hold onto something so innately her. Maybe the Demons could find her regardless, so why change in the first place?

I liked it. I'm glad she had it. It sure as hell made it easier for me to spot her, anyway.

I jumped off my perch and hit the cement, keeping my invisibility engaged like a shield so she couldn't see me. I didn't want her running off again.

Unfortunately, my plan didn't work as I'd anticipated. She looked straight at me and bolted for her front door, shoving the key in to the lock and attempting to get inside before I could get to her.

How can she see me?

If she achieved her aim, that wouldn't be great for me. All paranormals were restricted from crossing the threshold of a human house, unless personally invited in.

I flew faster across the road and reached out to her with outstretched fingers, desperate not to lose her once more. My hand closed around her thin shoulder and something completely unexpected happened. Desire poured through my belly like hot, molten honey.

Immediate, fast and intoxicating.

Damn. How long's it been since I felt that?

Kadie twisted around and attacked without warning, swinging her fist at me with practiced precision. I ducked and weaved her punch, my reflexes faster than any human, and held tight to the shoulder I'd grabbed.

I'm still invisible. How is this possible?

She cried out with rage as she swung again, this time with surprising accuracy and I had to catch her hand with mine. Tingles pulsed along my palm and my desire mixed with fear for her safety.

"I have three years of self-defense class under my belt, asshole. I could do much worse to you with my mouth."

Honestly, I wanted to see just what she could do to me with her mouth besides recite spells, but I couldn't let her or this overpowering sensation of desire for her distract me from what I came to do.

I glared at her with all my might. We needed to get inside, and quickly. "Stop fighting me. I'm here to help you."

She snarled up at me, her clear blue eyes throwing chips of ice like an Eskimo. "Yeah, right. Just like all the others."

She wasn't physically fighting me anymore, but I could still feel the anger pouring through her veins like fire. I wondered if it was her magic. It was time to cut to the chase with her. "Kadie, I'm a Guardian Angel. I'm here to help."

She glared at me and pulled her shoulder out of my grasp with a sharp twist. Obviously, like all the other Targets before her, she didn't believe me.

"I'll prove it to you," I offered, as I spread my black wings out to their full breadth and prepared myself to fly up into the air and prove to her that I was what I said.

It was a risk, of course. If she dashed inside, I wouldn't be able to speak to her until she came out again. But it was a risk I was willing to take for this Target to believe me.

Before I could launch up and into the air, her eyes grew to the size of the full moon. She shouldn't have been able to see my wings, or me, for that matter. My invisibility was still up around me, and even when it wasn't, my wings were an extension of my celestial self and were usually completely invisible to humans.

How is this possible? She can see them.

Kadie had once again broken the rules I believed were written in stone.

Her mouth opened and shut a few times, then she shook herself and asked. "Um… Why are your wings black? I always assumed they'd be white."

I cringed. I'd never had to tell my Targets the full story of why I was on Earth guarding them, because they'd never seen my wings.

But Kadie could, and I hated the answer that would have to come through my lips soon enough.

However, the fact that she was willing to engage in this dialogue rather than threaten me or run inside was promising.

"Because… I'm a Fallen Angel… working on Earth, earning my way back into Heaven."

I'd expected a negative reaction of sorts. More questions, a frown, a gasp, anything except what I got.

For some reason, Kadie's shoulders relaxed when I said those words and her mouth lifted up at the sides into a soft smile. She looked cute, and impishly cheeky.

What on Earth?

"You're trying to earn your way back into Heaven? What'd you do to get kicked out?"

That was not a question for her to ask, nor an answer for a human to know.

But I found myself telling the story, despite my misgivings. I liked to tell myself it was because I needed her to trust me. I needed her to believe me so we could both go inside and I could do my job. But deep down, it was more than that. "I was part of a love triangle that went wrong."

Simple enough.

I shook myself and clamped down hard on my jaw to stop myself from revealing it all. Tabitha had been right. This woman definitely had some Witch in her. That probably explained why she could see me beneath the invisibility shield. And compel me to tell her things I didn't feel particularly comfortable talking about in the first place.

"How long have you been down here?" she asked, crossing her arms over her chest, quirking her head to the side as though she were truly interested. The light in the porch archway flickered but she didn't even notice it. Her focus was solely on me.

Why am I the only one answering all the questions?

"Five hundred years."

She whistled. "Damn, that's a long time."

I blew my breath out of my nose in a puff. I'd met a lot of

unusual people in my time on Earth, but this strange little human took the cake.

I glanced to my left and right. I didn't like us being out in the open, especially in the darkness. I needed to get her to invite me in. She no longer looked afraid of me or the situation she was in. Instead, there was a curiosity and an offbeat sense of humor I wasn't sure I enjoyed.

"It is. A very long time. Now, can we go inside?" I gestured to her house and she narrowed her eyes at me, as though she was debating something. Probably on whether or not she should trust me. There was nothing more I could do, so I hoped what I had offered her was enough.

Finally, she shrugged.

"I'll let you in so that you can explain to me what's been going on with my world lately, but if you do anything to hurt me… you'll regret it."

Her spirit made me smile. "I know. And I won't betray your trust. I promise."

She opened the purple-painted front door and walked inside like she didn't have a care in the world. I was stuck to the mat like someone had glued my boots down.

I leaned forward to test the power of the force-field around her house and the strangest pain shimmied down my chest. Like the knife of God. I shuddered. No way could I push through that one. It would throw me out onto the road like a piece of garbage, even if I did manage to get a step or two inside.

"You know I can't come in, right?" I called out to her just as my awareness prickled with the feeling that Demons were on their way.

Heat teased my back like candle wax dripping down my spine. A sure-fire sign.

Kadie popped her head around the corner again, her beautiful red hair now framing her face. She must have taken her scarf off. "What do you mean?" she asked.

Ah, so she doesn't know.

"You have to invite me in, then I can pass over the threshold."

A pretty smile spread across her face. "Oh. Angel, come in."

The threat of pain fell away as though it had never been. I stepped through the entrance with ease and walked inside the small house. I had to duck my head to get beneath the door frame and she stared up at me with those beautiful blue eyes that reminded me of the crystal lakes back home.

I let myself become about six feet tall and reduced my breadth in proportion. I stood only a few inches taller than her now, and she smiled up at me with a wonder that I hadn't seen in too long to remember.

"You want a drink?" she asked as she slid her shoes off and grabbed a sweater from the couch to pull on over her bare arms.

Nighttime had arrived and with it, the chill of the dark. I felt the cold but it didn't affect me the way it affected humans and, apparently, witches.

"No, thank you." Angels didn't need to eat or drink.

I'd spent years on Earth jealous of human appetites, craving the taste of food.

Kadie bustled around the small kitchen and I stood by the worn sofa. What sort of Witch was she? She'd put up talisman to ward off evil spirits, but no unusual scents, no candles or herbs that dictated her potion strength. She didn't seem typical in any way.

She poured herself a steaming hot drink of some sort and came back into the living room. "Sit, Angel. Please. And tell me why you were following me."

She curled up on the couch like a cat, with her legs tucked beneath her. I made myself sit awkwardly in the recliner. I'd much prefer to stand, but there seemed to be an etiquette here and she would be more comfortable with me sitting, I knew.

In this early phase of guardianship I needed to develop a kinship, a trust with my Target. I needed them to entrust their safety, their life, unto me. And that took some work, more times than not.

I looked at her as I sat down and our gazes snapped together with that familiarity I was beginning to relax into. There wasn't an easy way to say this, so I may as well just get it out of the way. "You're in grave danger, Kadie."

She didn't falter, nor give me any indication that she understood.

Her hand lifted the cup to her lips and she took a sip as though I hadn't spoken. Perhaps she hadn't heard me?

"Don't you understand? Demons want you dead."

Well, it was worse than that, but she didn't need to know all the ins and outs of the underworld in our first meeting.

Our gazes clashed again as Kadie looked at me, and arousal snaked through my bloodstream like a slithery serpent, hot and lightning fast.

Damn it. Stop that.

I dug my fingers into my thighs and tried to focus on the meeting at hand, and not the adorable way she ran her tongue along her bottom lip.

She would taste soooo good.

Kadie settled back into the couch as though getting comfortable for a long chat. "I understand, but why? I'm a nobody."

My new Target appeared too calm and a shiver of nerves danced through me at her almost-unhuman demeanor.

"What are you?" I couldn't help but ask. Tabitha told me some, but I wanted answers. And, I thought, if she could question me incessantly about me being an Angel, certainly I could do the same to her.

Her eyes flashed a strange silver at me. She wasn't offended, exactly, but curious. "What do you mean?"

"Fairy, Witch, Warlock? A cross of some sort of Vampire, perhaps? There's some paranormal in you. You shouldn't have been able to see me at all when we were outside just now, let alone see my wings. They are invisible to all, except those from the Hell dimension."

Oh, hell no. She couldn't be.

She laughed loudly at that one. "Hell dimension? What are you talking about, Angel?"

This was beginning to feel like a set-up. She seemed too odd, too beautiful. The attraction between us too strong. I couldn't seem to dampen it down.

There was magic at work here.

"Why did you let me in here?" I asked, my eyes narrowing in

suspicion. Was this a test to see if I could avoid temptation? No matter what beautiful human they threw at me, I had always been able to resist. She would be no exception.

She slid her feet to the floor and iced me with her eyes once again. It was strange and fascinating to watch as her demeanor completely changed in merely an instant. "Me? You showed me your wings! Told me you were here to help me, and now you're questioning my motives? Get fucked."

Her language made me gape. Not the usual response I received when I came to help a human in need. I was more accustomed to blind adoration after I saved them from the Demons.

Such a strange little human.

I took a deep breath and forced my hands to relax. "I think we should start again. Kadie. I was told that your life is in danger, and I'm here to help."

She nodded, as though agreeing with me. "Well, it is. I'm pretty sure. I keep seeing these weird, black shadowy things following me, but they don't come into the house."

"They can't."

Thank the Gods, or all humans would be royally screwed.

She snorted in humor. "That's a comfort to know…now. I've lost a week's worth of sleep over that one."

I ignored the jibe. It wasn't my fault that Tabitha hadn't contacted me earlier. "Well, we need to work out why they want you. Which, to be honest, I don't understand yet."

She shrugged, a frown marring her beautiful face. "I have no idea. I mean…I have some abilities. I've always been able to foretell future events, and I can read people pretty well, but that's it."

The Demons generally track people who are integral to the continuation of the human species. Scientists, doctors, peace makers.

"Ha. That's not me at all. I'm a hairdresser."

I stared at her without saying a word. Had she just read my thoughts and answered them as though I'd spoken?

She was definitely *not* my normal Target.

"I own my own business, maybe one of my clients has a link to me…" She let her voice trail off, her eyes focused on the carpet as though searching in her mind for a reason behind these attacks.

"I doubt it. They obviously want you specifically." And with mind-reading abilities and being able to see me in Angel form, she had stronger powers than she realized.

"Then what's the plan?" she asked, her keen gaze slicing through my resistance once again.

She had beautiful skin… I could only imagine how pink her nipples were beneath her blouse. *Damn it! Concentrate!*

"The plan… I'll camp out and watch. Guard you day and night. At the moment we don't know if they're going to attack soon, or if they're only doing reconnaissance. They don't like to step out of the shadows for just anyone. They need to be certain that you're special. So, I'll watch for an attack, and if they attempt to grab you, I'll kill them."

A heavy silence hung in the room as she stared at me.

"Are you serious?" she asked, gaping at me as though I were crazy. Not an unusual reaction for a human. I'd had a lot worse through time.

"Of course." I gave a curt nod and shifted as the weight of the sword at my back made itself known. I'd been a warrior in Heaven, and I used my skills on Earth just as well.

Her gaze slid away. "Okay… what do you want me to do, then?"

Finally, some common sense and a question I was familiar with. "I want you to stay indoors at night and do exactly what I say, when I say it."

Her mouth twisted up and I knew I was in trouble. "No. That's not going to happen. I'm sorry. I volunteer at the soup kitchen at night and I can't give that up. I know that sounds trite and maybe even stupid, but these people are depending on me and I refuse to hide just because Demons might be out to get me."

I gave her my most serious stare, lowering my eyebrows and leaning forward on my chair. "This is your life, Kadie. This isn't a joke."

She shrugged nonchalantly. "I understand that, but surely this is a better idea than just hiding and waiting. If I draw them out, surely you can save me from them?"

"I can…" *Of course, but that isn't the point.* My job would be a lot easier if she would stay safe while I found those that hunted her. Although she may be right about drawing them out into the open… I'd never tried that deliberately before.

"Great," she said with a happy, dismissive tone. "Do you need a place to sleep, Angel? I have a spare bedroom. It's not huge, but…"

I cocked my head and stared at her, not impressed with her flippant attitude so far. "You trust too easily. That could be a fatal flaw."

She stood up with a fluid grace and looked down her nose at me. Damn, she was beautiful with her hair flowing around her like that.

"I read people, very well. If I'm honest… more than well. I know you're speaking the truth. Now, I'm going to make some dinner and head to bed. Are you staying, or are you going out to do whatever Angels do?"

I stood up and maintained my stunted height for her convenience. "I have a prior engagement, so I'll be leaving for a little while. Don't die before I get back."

Her lips quirked into an amused smile. "Lucky for you, it's my night off, Angel."

"It's Gabriel."

Kadie grinned. "Of course, it is. Goodnight, Gabriel."

She swept back into the kitchen and with my loins aching, I walked back out into the cold night air for some relief. I had to speak to Tabitha. She'd told me this woman was important and may earn me my place back into Heaven.

But how?

They're probably throwing my perfect sexual partner at me in a test to see if I can survive the temptation.

A smile tilted up my lips as I took to the sky. Tabitha may be right about this one, because it was not going to be easy keeping the beautiful, confident, Kadie alive.

Or me out of her bed.

CHAPTER THREE

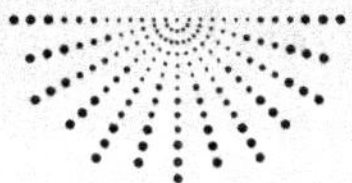

y frustration boiled over as I paced around Tabitha's kitchen. I didn't like being in situations where I didn't know what to expect. Surprises irked me. I didn't like feeling foolish, especially in front of a human. My Angel Agent had been less than helpful so far. This was supposed to be her job, wasn't it?

"Tabitha, I don't understand why you want me to protect this one. She's a hairdresser, for Holy sake!" Each step I took left small vibrations in my wake, now that I was back at my usual height.

And I'd like to slip my tongue inside her mouth and taste her flavors, which is crazy. It's been far too long since I've felt this way. I shouldn't feel this way about her. She was right — there was nothing special about her. And yet, there was a torment inside of me I couldn't quite deny. I needed her. I shouldn't need anyone.

Tabitha grinned at me over her cup of hot chocolate. I didn't need to eat or drink, nor did any other immortal person. But Tabitha seemed to be some sort of hybrid. She chose which human faults and frailties she adopted, and which ones she didn't.

Neither of us slept. Which came in handy for staying alive when Demons were sent to kill you on occasion.

"She's your Target, Gabriel. Why are you questioning me?

You've never done so before." There was an amused sparkle in her eyes. I didn't like being the butt of the joke. Especially when I didn't know what the joke was.

Her words rang true, but never before had I needed to question Tabitha's sanity. Nor the accuracy of the List.

"Why would the Demons want her?" I continued, throwing my arms out. I could feel my wings ruffle against my back. "Surely she can't be that important to the human race?"

Her powers were different, and certainly impressive, but if she didn't know what they were, surely the Demons couldn't either.

Tabitha shrugged and continued drinking from her mug. She didn't speak nor strive to continue the conversation. Frustration clawed at me. Why wouldn't my Agent speak to me?

"I'm dismissed, am I now?"

Tabitha sat bolt upright and cocked her head to the side as though listening to the voice of God himself. "Your Target is in trouble. Go. Now."

A shiver shot down my spine and I took off at a run. She wasn't far away. I could get to her in time. I hit the pavement at speed, extended my wings, and took to the sky. I could hear her screams inside my head as though she flew right beside me. Darkness had arrived. Evil loomed in the hidden corners and shelters, ready for action.

I flew through the city, following the sounds of her high-pitched shrieks until I came to an alleyway with large, abandoned buildings. Flashes of red and white filled one of the metal warehouses as if a fire blazed inside. *Kadie!*

I drew my sword from my back, invisible to all until it was unsheathed. The eerie red light from inside the building glinted off the silver blade, reminding me of all the blood this weapon had shed.

I raced inside the building, my heart pounding in my chest. The shadowy figures of flame were converging on Kadie and I was impressed to see that she wasn't meekly cowering in a corner, waiting to be rescued. She gave as much as she could. White magical light shot from her palms as she screamed in rage at them.

Movement caught my eye. I can't believe I hadn't noticed them before.

Demons. Two of them. In front of her. Each were trying to grab her, but neither were succeeding. I would have smirked if my heart hadn't lurched in my throat. I didn't like anyone near her, especially not Demons.

I ran forward, swinging my sword at the two Demons closest to her. They hissed in anger and spun at me to retaliate. I cut two of the flaming creatures in half with single blows and they burst into black flames and crumbled to the ground. Once they were out of the way, I jumped closer to my Target and we stood back to back. Three more came at us – I hadn't noticed them before, too consumed by my worry for Kadie - and I fought off two as Kadie took the third one down with her concentrated magic.

"About… time… you got here," she panted, her chest heaving with the stress of the fight.

"Let's go."

I sheathed my sword, picked her up in my arms, and took off, flying through the open door and up into the sky. She clung to my neck and buried her head deep into my shoulder as though she didn't want to see the building be consumed by lingering Demon flames. Her familiar scent tickled my nose and despite the danger, lust pounded in my body like molten lava.

"I need to get you safe."

"Take me to my house. You said no-one can get in without permission."

I frowned, unhappy with that being the only alternative. But I did not have a house myself, and at least her home could not be penetrated by the Demons.

"All right."

I dropped lower and headed for her house, surrounding us both in invisibility for the sake of the humans around us. I could see flickers of evil through the night, all over the city. On rooftops. In restaurants. In the streets. I would never be able to get them all, but at least I could keep my Target safe.

"Front door is easiest," she said, her voice hitching as she wriggled in my grasp.

The attraction between us flared higher still, the longer we remained in contact. It was a lot hotter than I had initially thought. I could smell her arousal, strong and sweet. If she, too, felt the tug of lust between us, it would be harder than I'd thought to stop myself from indulging in her.

I landed on the front stoop and placed her down carefully. She gasped as she stood on unstable legs and wobbled towards the entrance.

"That was some ride." She managed to get the door open and we both went inside, locking the door behind us. Not that the human lock would keep out anything except a human. Luckily, we had stronger magic than that on our side.

I shrunk down to a more comfortable size, feeling my own anger flare as I regarded her. It was starting to bother me at how indifferent she seemed to be by all of this.

"You didn't tell me you had powers like that," I said, unable to keep the accusation out of my voice. I'd been as honest with her as I could be, and she had deliberately kept a vital piece of information from me. "More than that, I told you to stay here."

"You told me to stay alive," she corrected, walking over to kick off her shoes once again. I noticed her hands shake and part of me felt better that it was possible to affect her in some way, even if she wanted to hide it. "I didn't know about my powers." She spun around to glare up at me. "That's never happened before."

I could see the honesty in her eyes, hear it in her tone. She was shaking more, from the stress, or anger, I wasn't sure.

"All right. Calm down. Sit." I nodded my head to the couch.

She fell onto her couch and I refrained from indulging in the desire to sit next to her, to wrap my hands around her body, to bury my nose in her hair. I had to do something with all the nervous energy racing through my body. I walked into the kitchen, took down a glass, and poured her some water without asking her.

My heart continued to pound. That had been close. Far too

close for comfort. They'd almost had her, and for once, it looked like they were trying to do more than simply torture Kadie.

Which was odd, in itself. More pieces to this puzzle that I simply didn't have any answers for.

Thank God Tabitha said something. I didn't know what would have happened if she hadn't spoken up at just that moment.

I walked back to my Target and handed her the water. She took it with trembling hands and I sat down in the recliner I'd occupied earlier this evening. I didn't trust myself to get too close to her.

Why hadn't she done as I'd asked?

"Now, tell me what happened. I thought you weren't going out tonight."

She cocked her head at me. "I didn't. That was yesterday."

Had it really been a day? I shook my head.

Damn. "Sorry. I don't have control over that. Tabitha's realm is untouched by normal human time."

I'd never understood why that happened, but I could lose days from a single visit that seemed like only hours. I'd asked Tabitha about it once and she'd never explained how her home worked in terms of human time. Her dimension was a mystery to everyone, including Tabitha, apparently.

"Who's Tabitha?" she asked, her voice hitching in a strange way.

Jealous, maybe? "My Angel Agent. She gave me your name and asked me to look after you."

Kadie took a sip of water. "That's weird."

I laughed, a strange, strained noise. *Me, weird? Coming from the human being hunted by Demons, who could vanquish them with white magic?*

"I suppose it is, to you. But that's how it works in my world. Tabitha learns who the Demons are after, and she directs me who to save. It's a simple but effective system."

"How many humans have you saved?" She looked up at me, her eyes still icy but there was a glimmer of desperation in them. Like she needed to hear the sound of my voice in order to calm her down.

I shrugged. *I'd like to say I don't keep count, but I do.*

"No, really, I want to know," she persisted.

"One thousand nine hundred and ninety humans," I answered, unable to deny her a simple fact.

"Whoa. That's…incredible." She continued to rub her palms on her thighs, trying to keep them from shaking.

Again, I shrugged.

Still not enough to get me back into Heaven.

"Well, that's just ridiculous. What's the magic number then? Two thousand? Five thousand?"

I stared at her. *Did she seriously answer a question I asked inside my own head?*

The answer came in the heated blush that spread up her beautiful cheeks.

"Are you reading my mind, Kadie?"

"Ah… I don't mean to." Her gaze dropped and the blush blossomed into a fiery red.

I felt myself drawn to her despite myself. I had to focus.

"But you are?" I asked again. I'd never met anyone who could do that. Not to me, anyway.

She stared at me with wide eyes. "Ah…maybe? I can't tell. They all sound like words to me."

I sighed and ran a hand through my hair. This got stranger by the minute.

"It's not that unusual, is it? Surely, I'm not that weird. Am I?" she asked, her voice half an octave above its normal pitch. She sounded worried. "I'm not… I can't be…"

And there was a good reason for that.

"Ah, yes. Yes, it is," I said. "It would be unusual if you could read a human's mind, but mine? That's just…unheard of. You may think you're not special, Kadie, but you are."

"I knew something was wrong with me," she muttered as she leaned forward and dropped her head into her hands.

I decided not to focus on that comment, as I knew there was nothing wrong with her. Instead, there were many, many things that were right.

Her erect nipples, for example.

Her head shot up and she suddenly crossed her arms over her chest.

Oh, damn.

"I'm sorry," I apologized, appalled that she could hear my lustful thoughts.

I really can't help it… you're way too beautiful.

"It's okay. I know how you feel. I can barely keep my eyes to myself either." The way she said it, she wasn't embarrassed. It was more like she didn't understand these feelings and was trying to. "I don't know why I'm feeling this way. I'm sure you don't either."

A strange warmth washed over me as she admitted to the attraction that I struggled with. Not that I'd ever had any problems finding sexual partners in Heaven, where love is shared freely. But down here, in limbo, I'd been alone for a very long time.

"Let's focus on your abilities, shall we?" I suggested. I cleared my throat. The last thing I wanted to do was talk about my desire for her. Or her desire for me. That was dangerous territory, one I didn't want to think about. "What were you doing to those Demons?"

She seemed to be able to kill them, which was impossible for a human, or so I'd been told.

"I…really don't know. I was so scared… and kind of angry, too. Then they came close, and I pushed out with all my fear, and white light shot out of my hands." She looked down at her palms in disbelief, as though she was trying to figure out if this was even real.

That sounded relatively simple. *Amazing, and spectacular. But simple.*

She continued on as though I'd spoken. "Well it wasn't simple, I can tell you. I had no idea what I was doing, and if I dropped concentration for a second, the light would go out and then they'd be at me again. I'm frickin' exhausted and can barely lift my arms."

I just stared at her until finally she realized what she'd done.

"Oh, I'm sorry! How do we stop me doing that?"

I have no bloody idea. "I'll try not to think too loudly, and I think you need to get to bed and rest."

I stared hard at her. *Or I will seduce you right now on this sofa and damn the consequences.*

"What consequences?" she asked. Her voice was low and caused a shiver to slide down my spine.

I wanted to laugh out loud, but it was more sad than funny. It would be so much easier for us both if I could hide my true feelings, and she'd never know what we'd missed. "We Fallen Angels aren't permitted to have sexual relations with humans, part of our penance."

A rule I'd originally thought was smart. It protected the humans and the Fallen Angels from years, or centuries, of heartbreak.

Now…I was beginning to see what the other Angels complained about. Because I wanted Kadie.

Whatever she was.

Would she count as a human, what with her powers? Did I want to take that risk and find out?

"How would they find out?" she whispered, the longing in her eyes tugging at me.

My cock stirred in my jeans.

"Oh, they'd find out." They had eyes and ears everywhere.

She frowned. "So, you haven't had sex in, like, forever?"

A groan rolled through my chest. "More than forever. Twenty times your lifetime."

"Whoa."

Yeah. Exactly.

"Now, usually I would retreat to a ledge somewhere and watch over your house all night. But seeing as you offered me a bed… I might take that space, if that's still all right with you?"

I wouldn't sleep of course. But a comfortable bed was a luxury I hadn't indulged myself in too many years to count. And while my Target was safe, I could relax a little, and I had many memories to keep me entertained for the night. Although, the temptation of being so close to her…

Maybe I was putting myself in an unnecessary situation.

"Yes, of course. Come this way." She reached out and took my hand to show me her guest room.

I gasped and froze at her touch, the feel of her skin against mine both pleasurable and painful. She was hot and sweet, and my lonely heart ached for more.

"Come on," she repeated, tugging my hand and dragging me into a small room with a double bed and a scent that made me groan.

Kadie's unique smell was one I would never forget, even if I lived another thousand years. She made me yearn for a home I've never had and that scent permeated everywhere.

Maybe I'd made a mistake accepting her invitation.

"Well… goodnight." Kadie went up on her toes and kissed me gently on the lips, the warmth of her spreading through my nerves like the sun defrosting the earth at sunrise.

I froze as she held herself there, barely touching me.

"And thank you for saving my life," she whispered against my mouth.

"You're welcome," I replied, breathing in the warmth of her.

God, how I wished I could pick her up, strip her down, and devour the beauty beneath the rags.

Kadie reached up and touched my wings, the lightest of touches that had my gut tightening, my breath quickening and my lustful cock going hard as stone.

She stepped away and gave me a soft, quivering smile. If she could read my mind, I was sure she knew the struggle I was under.

"Good night."

I nodded my head as she shut the door, anger and resentment pulsing through me like a brewing storm. This was so unfair. To her, and to me.

After so many saved Targets, and resisting every single woman who'd ever tried to seduce me, I'd finally found one I wanted to make love to.

Not just that, though. I wanted to fuck her too. I wanted to do it all to her over again. I wanted her to scratch my back so hard, her nails would leave red streaks down my back like a brand on my skin for the rest of my eternity. I wanted it soft and slow, rough and fast, in her kitchen, against the wall, on the floor.

I wanted her everywhere.

Surely, I deserved one night? After already serving such a lengthy sentence, how could they punish me for wanting to give Kadie the pleasure she deserved? It wasn't like I would be leading her on. She knew what I was and that a long-term relationship would be impossible.

I stripped off my clothes that clung to my hot skin and threw them on a nearby chest of drawers. Ancient jeans and a black hoodie I wore to blend in to the humans around me.

Naked finally, I lay back on the soft bed and let my mind wander. I was truly safe, for the first time as long as I could remember.

And also, for the first time in centuries, I spent the dark night hours fantasizing about a woman other than the one I'd left in Heaven all those centuries ago.

CHAPTER FOUR

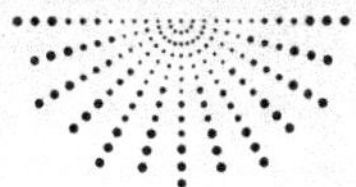

*M*y door opened some time before sunrise. I was surprised I survived the night. Not because Demons were after my Target, but because Kadie was so close to me and wanted me the same way I wanted her. I refrained from going to her, but my body felt like it was going to combust into flames. Darkness still clung to the city and the people around us were almost quiet.

"Gabriel?" Kadie's sweet voice filtered through the air around me. A siren call in the ocean of darkness around me.

"Yes?" I answered, not daring to move a muscle as I lay on the bed. I clenched my fingers into the sheets. I refused to go to her. I wouldn't even look at her. I didn't know what would happen if I did.

I was naked and I assumed she could see that. Yet, she walked further into the room and stood before me like a vision. The street lights shone in through the shuttered windows and shadows cast over her barely-clad body, making my blood burn.

Oh, hell. So much for not looking at her.

"Do you want me as much as I want you?" she whispered, her voice trembling. In fear? Or perhaps passion?

I sucked in a breath. I didn't know why she'd come to me, nor what she hoped to gain, other than the moment's pleasure. She knew I wasn't meant to indulge myself, and the lonely hours I'd suffered through the night so far had reminded me of that. I could get into big trouble. I didn't know the repercussions for humans – if there were any.

I had to be honest. There was no reason to lie. "You know I do, Kadie. But it is forbidden." They'd never told us why, but the rule was simple. I liked simple. It was easy to follow, easy to understand.

"But why? Why would they forbid us being together for just one night? What could they possibly do to you, or me? Aren't we being punished enough already? You saved me tonight. I could be dead right now, and I want to celebrate being alive—thanks to you." She stepped closer to the bed and my body tensed. Her mere voice shot lightning straight to my cock and my grip on her sheets only tightened.

Her words struck a chord within me and I kept my lips firmly pressed together as my iron will wavered. She was right, of course. She was on a Demon's hit list, and I was living in limbo, waiting for my sentence to be revoked. What more could they do to us? Make me save a thousand more souls?

Fine.

I would do it, just to feel her touch on my body. Just to feel what it was like inside of her, stretching her, feeling her slick heat wrap around me.

Then I saw her move, her hands gliding up her body in a seductive way I knew I wouldn't be able to fight against.

Oh, please don't. I don't have the strength to deny you this.

I didn't understand how she affecting me in such a way, how she had this sort of power over me. And yet, I liked it. Maybe I didn't want to admit it, especially to myself, but I loved how helpless she made me feel. I wanted more of it. I wanted more of *her*.

She hesitated for a moment, and I worried and yearned that she was going to change her mind. Then she lifted her hand and pushed one strap off her shoulder and let it fall down her arm, exposing one perfect breast to my gaze.

Lust slammed into me and I clenched my teeth in an effort not to groan. I could feel myself start to stir underneath the thin, soft sheet and I closed my eyes, trying to think of anything that might calm my responses.

Then she slid the other strap down and her twin mounds of wonder pouted up at my gaze. My mouth watered as I stared at her and I licked my lips.

The short nightgown she wore shimmied down to her indented waist, clung to her fleshy hips for a mere moment, then slid to the floor in a puddle of silk.

There she stood suddenly, completely naked. Like a statue of the Goddess of sexuality.

I didn't move. I couldn't move. What was a man supposed to do when a naked woman stood before him? A lump lodged itself in my throat and I swallowed hard.

I will just go a little further, then I'll stop… No, I should stop here. This is insane and illogical. So I'll give her pleasure… then I'll stop.

"Come here," I croaked out, unable to fight against her need for me.

She walked closer to me, her rounded breasts bobbing with her movement. My throat grew tight, my mouth ran dry.

It wasn't like I hadn't seen women more beautiful than she was, naked, who all wanted me. I wasn't some human unable to resist the beauty of a being. I was always in control and always managed my emotions. Especially when it came to things as primal as sex.

But somehow, for some inexplicable, frustrating reason, Kadie was different.

I shuffled over to the middle of the bed so there was room for her. I continued to lie completely still and watched what unfolded before me like a dream. She climbed onto the bed and instead of cuddling into my side as I expected, she slid a leg over my waist and slid her body over mine until she sat on top of me.

I groaned loudly and my eyes shut again on a wave of ecstasy unlike anything I'd ever experienced. She was the first drink of water I'd had in a thousand centuries of desert.

It was all too much for my starved senses. The heat of her.

I'd been alone so very long and here was a woman wanting me.

She began to rock her hips, rubbing her naked pussy along my aching shaft as she ran her hands over my chest. I shuddered in response to her touch. The love I could feel pouring out of her soul was inspiring. This woman had so much to give, it was as obvious as the moon in the sky. And she was giving that me. I didn't understand it. I didn't think I even deserved it. And yet, here she was, not hesitating, on top of me like I was something she could love for the rest of her short life.

They were right… Heaven deserved a soul like hers.

"You're very beautiful. Very…very…beautiful," she said, her admiration of my form clear as she stared down at my stomach.

I swallowed, unsure of how to respond to that. I understood that I was aesthetically pleasing in this form. It was one of the reasons I made sure to maintain it, because it was easy to get people to trust me this way. However, hearing the compliment come from her made me feel like I was special, not one out of a thousand angels, stronger and more beautiful than I was.

Her fingertips rubbed my nipples, eliciting an electric response inside my chest. My arms shook as I raised my own hands and cupped her breasts. I focused on the weight and heat of each one in my palms, her tight nipples between my fingers.

I am going to be punished so severely for this if I fail to stop in time…

She moved her legs back and around, then slid down so that she could lie on top of me. Her soft lips touched my nipples in a gentle caress and her breath slid over my skin as she slithered down.

"Oh. God."

I hope he didn't hear me as I broke whatever rule they laid upon us. The damned Angels.

She slid further down my body, taking my cock into the wet haven of her mouth.

"Oh, fuck." This wasn't the way it was supposed to go. I should have been pleasuring her, not the other way around. And yet, I couldn't find it in me to stop her.

She hummed and moaned as she tasted me. Her lips moved up and down my shaft. My cock throbbed and ached for her as she loved my body in a way no one had in so very long.

I clenched the blankets beneath me, grabbing hold of any sort of sanity left.

If only I… No…. maybe if I give her a little bit, then I'll stop.

Can she understand my every thought? My personalities clashing with each other.

I reached for her and grabbed her arms. I needed to stop this sweet torment, so I pulled her up my body, flipped us over, and slid my tongue into her mouth. She moaned and lifted her pelvis, wrapping her legs and arms around me like a limpet on a rock, enclosing me completely.

"Do we need to worry about… you know, pregnancy, or anything…" She asked on a gasp.

I shook my head. "I'm immortal. We don't carry diseases like humans, nor do we have offspring."

As I said the words, a twinge plucked me in the chest, which I promptly ignored.

"Great." She said, lifting her lips for another kiss.

I moved my hand between us and tweaked at her swollen clit, flicking that sensitive little nub until she was bucking at me to take her.

"Gabriel! Please." She bit into my shoulder and I shuddered again at the intensity of need coursing through me.

I let the head of my cock rest against her opening, making sure she wanted me. This one moment could set me back a decade from my goal, longer even. A century.

I had to master this temptation, regain control. Just as I had, so many times before.

But I'd longed for this feeling for too long, this intensity of affection and emotion that few people ever experienced. There was something so special about Kadie, the reasons to stay away from her were becoming fuzzier by the moment.

There was also a part of my conscience that argued that there was no way of knowing if I was ever getting back into Heaven. If abiding by some unknown law with vague restrictions without logical explanations would be worth it to me in the end. Perhaps it shouldn't matter. Humans believed in God without God Himself coming down and telling them He was, indeed, real. They had faith. Perhaps one of my lessons was to learn how to have faith in things I didn't know and didn't understand.

Tabitha had said this girl could be the key, but what did that mean? That I should fight my attraction to her—or not?

I have to find something to stop myself from sliding my aching cock inside that soft, wet pussy. Anything, anything to make her happy. Maybe that will settle the urge.

She cried out and grabbed at me as though she knew I was about to stop, which she would if she was listening to my thoughts.

But I untangled her from my limbs and slid down her body, pushing her soft thighs apart and thrusting my tongue inside her core. She screamed out as I tasted the sweetest honey. She grabbed my head as I lapped at her center, drinking the very nectar of her body.

Amazing.

This was not supposed to be pleasurable for me. But the adage of giving being as good as receiving rang true.

Her nails dug into my scalp and her panting began to peak, energy pouring out from Kadie's aura like an energized sun.

My cock wanted to feel her orgasm wrap around it so badly I could barely think about anything else.

I slid back up her gasping body and lined up my throbbing cock once again with her entrance. Kadie arched her back and our gazes connected in that eerie way that made my heart pound and my soul cry out for the connection.

Her lips separated in a soft gasp, her hand sliding up to cup my cheek. We needed to be joined in the deepest way possible. There was no other reason for us meeting like this.

Me *feeling* like this.

Somehow, deep in my heart, I knew this to be true. If I was supposed to learn faith, I was doing so. Because I had faith in *her*. I had faith in *us*.

The consequences were uncertain and yet, in this moment, they could be *damned*. Just as I had been.

I flexed my hips and sunk into her hot, waiting body. Kadie

lifted her hips up and met me half way. I forged all the way inside her and gripped the sheets beneath my hands.

She was so wet. And softly tight around my cock. The physical and chemical connection was perfect.

Damn, you feel incredible.

"So… do you" she panted, her eyes shimmering with the intensity of her feelings.

A laugh rose in my throat at her response to my thoughts.

I had not focused on the fact that she was probably registering every one of my crazy thoughts through all the lead up.

Yet she had ignored them and forged forward, regardless. She was obviously determined and was going to succeed in her seduction, despite any mental argument I made with myself.

My thoughts on whether I should feel complimented or impressed with her determination faded off because my cock was in a heaven on earth. And the mental pictures coming up on the screen inside my mind were something my subconscious had been dreaming of through all my time on earth.

My cock took over, my body automatically going through the movements to allow me to drive deeper into her. Then I slid right back to the top of her entrance, holding still until I was sure she wanted me back inside her again. As her pussy became more accustomed to my presence, I thrust stronger and deeper inside her.

How could I not do this? For all the battles, the wars, the momentous events in life, this was what I was made for—leaving her clenching body and then returning home to her in an ancient rhythm, as old as time and the Gods themselves.

Sweat gathered on her skin. Her face flushed with blood. She groaned and wrapped her legs around me tighter, taking me deeper. I held onto my sanity by the flimsiest of margins.

She gasped and grabbed onto me, biting hard into my shoulder as her pussy began to quiver around my cock, heralding her orgasm, and perhaps mine also.

It had been so long since I'd made love to anyone. Felt the tight clasp of the woman's pussy wrapped around me, I was never going to last as long as I wished. She was so perfect and fit me like a hand-made glove.

In a way, I was glad it had been so long. I was glad she had broken me out of my self-imposed celibacy. Because I didn't remember the others that came before her. They didn't matter. All that mattered was Kadie, this moment, this growing feeling between us that was so right and strong and pure.

It was destiny.

"Ah!" Kadie cried out, long and loud. White light surrounded us like the sun had risen in the bedroom.

I grabbed onto the bed head and fucked her hard and fast, riding through her orgasm until heat trickled down my legs and up my back.

I dipped my head and sunk my tongue inside her mouth just as I thrust to the hilt. She sucked on my tongue as my orgasm flowed over me in a heated wave.

My cock pulsed inside her spasming body, releasing my seed and bringing with it a choir of song inside my head.

"Ah…. Oh, fuck!" Kadie cried out as she began to come with me again.

Heated sparks flew around us and as I forced my eyes open, I realized it wasn't all inside my head. Kadie gave off a sparkling aura of fireworks when she came that made me hold her tighter and revel in the shuddering of her pussy around me.

We lay there until the energy around us calmed down and darkness settled in once again.

Whoa.

I rolled off her tiny body and pulled her with me as I moved. That had been utterly incredible. Soul altering. Life − or whatever this was - changing.

Kadie settled her head onto my chest, made a soft contented sigh, and instantly fell asleep.

I lay there through sunrise and beyond, stroking her hair. I'd found peace for the first time in nearly four hundred years.

And if it took me *another* four hundred years to get back into Heaven, then tonight had been well worth it for this moment alone.

AT SOME POINT, I did sleep. I was spent. I could fight a hundred demons and not be exhausted. One night with Kadie and I was exhausted. And yet, I woke refreshed, after feeling her stir and peel herself away from me.

She was probably getting herself sustenance.

"I'm going to the soup kitchen, Gabriel," she said from the kitchen. How she knew I was awake, I wasn't sure. "Want to come?"

I stepped out of my bedroom and gave her a stern look. This woman was as crazy as she was beautiful. "Are you serious? I've told you I need to keep you safe until all the Demons chasing you are either dead or they give up on you."

She grabbed a coat and slid her arms into the sleeves. "You've seen what I'm capable of. I'm sure they learned their lesson last night. Come on, please. I need to go. I'm late."

"Why?" I asked her for what felt like the hundredth time. I'd witnessed countless acts of cruelty in this world, and very few purely kind ones.

She smiled up at me. "Because helping people makes life worth living."

And there it was. The pure essence of who this truly unique woman was.

Who was I to stop her from bringing some light, and a warm meal, into those people's lives?

"All right. But I'm not leaving your side all night."

I was naively hoping that we'd killed all those Demons assigned to Kadie last night and they would now leave her alone. Deep down, I knew this couldn't be possible. However, I also knew that cowering until all Demons were destroyed – not something within the realm of possibility – was also not something feasible either. I didn't know much about Kadie, but I knew she wasn't one to hide. She also couldn't be kept away from the vitality of life. Part of her appeal was the fact that she connected with everyone, and keeping that important part of her life from her – through no fault of her own – seemed incredibly unjust.

She smiled at me. "Of course."

We headed into the city and a part of me enjoyed walking beside Kadie as we casually strolled along the street. Seemingly human, I must have looked just like everyone else. I allowed everyone to see me now.

Kadie squeezed my hand and glanced up at me. "Tell me more about why you were kicked out of Heaven."

"Pardon me?" I didn't think I'd told her any of the reasons, let alone *the* one.

"You told me you were in some sort of love triangle. What happened?"

Oh, I had told her some of it. That would be right. The one woman I don't want knowing about my past, I blurt out the real reason to.

I reached up to cup the back of my neck. I didn't want to talk about it, and yet, there was something about her that compelled me to do just that. I wanted to share more of myself with her, even the bad parts. The parts I didn't want to share with anyone. The parts I didn't even want to think about at all.

"Well, I was in love with a woman, a Goddess actually. But…" I paused, my chest tightening like an anaconda slithered around my ribs.

I hated telling this story.

"Someone else was in love with her too?" Kadie asked, seemingly un-phased by this new information.

We strolled together through the streets of New York, the sun glinting on the tall buildings, giving them a sleek shine. Birds flew overhead, looking for an unsuspecting person not paying attention to their food. Kadier naturally moved through this sea of people, as though she was going along with the tide rather than to fight against it.

I sighed, my mind drifting back to her question. Had there been people in love with her? There certainly had been. Many of us in fact. But there had only been one man entitled to do so. "Yes. Her husband."

This time she gasped and stared at me strangely. "You fell in love with a married woman? Shame on you." Kadie giggled and made a strange motion with her fingers.

I scowled at her. "Don't laugh. I was kicked out of Heaven for it." A punishment some said was worse than death. Only the enticement of Heaven once more kept the fallen alive.

It was something I wasn't sure I regretted or not. I understood I was not entitled to her. And yet, I couldn't help the way I felt. And if those feelings were natural, were they bad? Were they really bad enough to get me cast out of paradise?

We continued walking through the streets, weaving around the many people still bustling to and from work. Going to dinners, theatre, drinks.

Kadie poked me in the ribs. "I don't believe you. There's more to it than that."

Are you reading my thoughts again?

"Well… Teramea is a Goddess, one of the many daughters of the Supreme Being," I explained.

"Whoa, you mean God has other children as well?"

She seemed shocked and my mind pulled up the many Christian stories told of the Supreme Being.

"Yes, well…. It's hard to explain. There are actually many Gods and Goddesses in Heaven, but there is only one Supreme Being that created us all, yes. And she was his daughter."

"Was?"

Wrong way to phrase it.

"Well, still is. I just haven't seen her in several hundred years." And for many centuries I had yearned for the touch of her hand on mine once more.

But as I searched my heart for the pain usually present when discussing Teramea, it appeared my feelings had changed.

Kadie frowned, her thumb caressing the back of my hand. I don't think she even knew she was doing it. "Really? That's tough. She couldn't come down and visit or anything?"

This is where it gets tricky.

"Why is it tricky?" She glanced up at me with those penetrating blue eyes and my breath vanished. How could she have such a strange effect on me? How could she change who I thought I was with merely a glance, a touch? I didn't understand it.

I shook my head. *Why am I trying to keep things from someone who can read my mind?*

"Yes, why are you keeping secrets?"

I heaved out a sigh. There was no keeping anything from Kadie. "The truth is, I fought for the hand of the Goddess. And won."

"So, what was the problem?"

My chest heavy as I remembered that terrible day. I tightened my hold on Kadie's hand and she gave me a reassuring squeeze. "The problem was, we are forbidden to fight in Heaven amongst ourselves. That was my first mistake. And the other thing was that in winning the fight, I killed him… her husband. One of the most powerful of us all. And I was thrown out of Heaven for my sin."

We stopped in the middle of the sidewalk. Pedestrians got disgruntled by our inconsideration, pushing around us, grumbling under their breath. I was surprised someone didn't come right out and say anything.

She looked up at me with wide, disbelieving eyes. "And you want to go back?"

"Of course. It's my home. The final destination for all those who are good in this world."

Her gaze dropped away and a sadness crept over her face and posture.

"Hmmm… I'll take your word for it." She didn't continue, so we resumed our walk.

I looked around and decided to do some reconnaissance. "We're here so you go in and I'll be here waiting for you when you finish."

She kissed me softly on the lips and hurried inside the old building we stood in front of. I glanced up. By the looks of it, the place used to be an old church. Converted and gutted into a community building for all. She should be safe here. Should being the operative word. But I learned that holy spaces were not as revered on earth as they once were.

CHAPTER FIVE

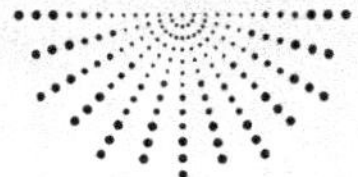

I was glad to get away from Kadie, just for the moment. When she was gone from me, I felt myself breathe again. Like I was myself and not someone else. I didn't like feeling weak and vulnerable, and telling her about my past definitely made me feel that way.

The sun cast its last rays of light over the landscape before sinking beneath the horizon. Dinnertime for most humans.

A bedraggled woman struggled along the foot path before me and stumbled inside the old church. One of the many lost souls on this planet. Someone Kadie wanted to help.

My lips tilted up at the thought. Humans were an interesting species. Some could be so incredibly selfish while others were kind and giving. I knew all sorts of humans who possessed all sorts of positive and negative traits. However, there was something about Kadie that transcended everyone I had met.

I stepped back. Worry knit my brow together and I frowned. Was I putting her on an impossible pedestal? She was still human, after all. She wasn't perfect by any means. Her nonchalance about everything grated on my nerves and her flippancy regarding the safety of her own life was frustrating to say the least. And these powers she had…

Magic wasn't regarded highly by those who interpreted the Supreme Creator's book. In fact, they thought such a thing came from the devil himself.

They were wrong about that, but all the intricacies of magic eluded me. I was still trying to figure out who she was and why I felt the way I felt around her.

Heat tingled on my neck and I saw a telling flicker of flame on the rooftops above me.

They were here. Again. Despite my presence. And despite the loss of their numbers from last night. Anger rippled in my gut, and also a sense of foreboding.

I was tasked with protecting her, and we had crossed some sort of line, I took the Demons and their desire for her personally.

I watched as a couple more flames appeared from the darkness. They must really want her. As Tabitha had foretold, Kadie was much more special than we'd originally thought. All the signs were pointing to it. Demons were usually only assigned to one person, and once I'd killed them off, there was no one else to hunt my Target. Thus I could move on and I knew they were safe.

It seemed that a second group of Demons had been assigned to Kadie. And I didn't think they'd stop sending Demons any time soon.

I pulled on my invisibility like a cloak, flexed my wings, and with a rush of adrenaline, flew up the building in front of me. I landed on the flat rooftop and growled at the Demon standing before me. They would not get through. I would not let them.

"You shouldn't be here." I said to the creature before me.

He spat fire back at me, the flames catching my hoodie. I smacked at them with my hand, burning my palm in the process.

Better my fingers than my wings.

I drew my sword from my back and raced forward, my heart pounding as I sliced at the flickering embodiment of Hell. Demons did not deserve to be on this plain, especially when their main function was to hunt those aiming for the Pearly gates.

They were wrong. Un-natural. Evil.

The Demon darted around the roof top and eluded my sword. They had no weapons except their ghoulish faces and heated bodies that seared anything they touched. My pulse quickened as the heat from the demon's body made my skin sweat.

It danced with me as I swung and parried. I was loathe to admit how much pain a Demon could elicit simply from touching my skin. I clenched my sword tighter in my grasp and growled at the in-human thing between my teeth. I did not want to think about them harming me in any way so that I couldn't protect Kadie.

If anything were to happen to her…

I swung again, but the Demon jumped out of the way.

Blasted thing.

I flexed forward and back, then another appeared. And then another.

Excitement zinged in my veins and the beginnings of a smile lifted my lips.

Now this was good. A proper challenge. It had been a while since they'd tested me. Attacked me with enough Demons to make the fight deadly for me. Pride wove through my heart as I thought of the little Witch below us.

Kadie really must be a prize to those in the hell dimension.

But she was mine.

I banished the possessive thought. I refused to reduce her to an object meant to bolster me or whoever won her affection.

And yet, I couldn't help that swell of pride in my chest. It made me want to fight all the more for her.

A loud scream cut into my mind like a knife and I faltered in my stance as I moved sideways.

No…. Kadie…

One of them swiped out at me, catching one of my wings and the feathers instantly burst into flames.

No. I dove to the concrete and rolled, putting out the flames. "Fu…uck!"

That part of my wing would never repair. I growled with menace as the realization hit me. They had deliberately separated us. I should have stayed down at ground level with her, rather than following the temptation of the Demons dancing above.

How could I let myself be distracted by my thoughts, by my tempting pride? With my focus on these things, some Demons snuck past me and managed to get to her.

I had failed – not only my mission, but Kadie herself.

I turned my back on the triple Demon flames still fighting me and took a running leap. I threw myself off the edge of the building, extended my wings and flew straight down to my Target.

My lover.

The Demons cries of rage rang in my ears as I flew down the building. Under normal circumstances, I would revel in the sound. However, I needed to refocus. The Demons had proved that they had no problem taking advantage of my cockiness.

My wings flapped strongly for a moment before I hit the ground, making the small shrubs that grew out of the pavement falter and lie down. I righted myself until my feet hit the cement, then I ran straight into the hall.

People were running about, screaming at the top of their lungs. Kadie was nowhere to be seen.

"Where is she? Where's Kadie?" I asked as I grabbed one of the men who ran by.

"The kitchen," he said, his voice quivering and his teeth chattering together.

They were here. Inside a church. Showing themselves to the world.

Fuck. Have I missed something? When did the rules change?

Demons were not allowed to be in sacred buildings nor were they allowed to reveal their true selves. This was unlike anything I had ever heard about in all my time on earth. If this was a possibility, why had Tabitha not warned me?

"Gabriel!"

I stopped completely. All questions vanished. Somehow, through the chaos, I recognized Kadie's voice. I had to get to her.

I ran straight through the door and saw Kadie standing on the kitchen counter, holding out her arms to three Demons who circled her. Her white light shined for all to see, like an angel's halo, only a thousand times brighter. The Demons turned black as her magic hit them as they failed to get close enough to hurt her.

I could tell she was losing steam, however. Using her power in excess when she never had to before was taking its toll on her. If I didn't do something, she would weaken and the Demons would take advantage of it. Right now, they seemed to be biding their time and waiting for such a moment, as though the death of their own would be worth it just as long as they could get their hands on her.

I wasn't going to let that happen.

I drew my sword and sliced one of their heads off, satisfaction rippling through me as it crumpled to the ground. The other two turned to me and I killed one, then the other, slicing their heads off their flaming bodies.

"Oh, my fucking… God!" Kadie exclaimed and I cringed at the blasphemy.

She jumped down from the wooden bench top, her whole body shaking. "What do they want?" She seemed more angry than afraid, which kept me calmer. I could work with anger. I was unfamiliar with tears. Tears – and overly emotive humans – made me uncomfortable.

"They want you. That's clear. But I've never seen them attack someone so openly before."

"They look like they want to kill me!" she panted, sweat dripping down her forehead and onto her cheeks. "You said they would try to torture me so I'd go to Hell. What's with this shit?"

She was right, and it raised an even more puzzling question. Demons didn't kill humans, they wanted their souls. And the only way their souls went to Hell was if they committed suicide.

Unless Kadie had already done something so abhorrent she was going to be sent to Hell no matter what? I shook my head, no. That didn't sound like Kadie.

Kadie represented everything that was good and pure in this world. She didn't cause harm and she didn't indulge…

I stopped. *No… it wasn't possible.*

If the Demon killed a human, the human would go straight to

Heaven normally, because the Demons only hunted those pure and special. So why were these Demons attacking, rather than torturing, Kadie?

Was it possible this form of torture was aimed at making her do something rash to get away from them? But it didn't look like it. They truly did look like they were trying to grab her, not just torture her, which would make death certain for Kadie.

"I agree." I took her hand in mine and tilted her head up with my palm. "It makes no sense. Which means we need to get you home. Now." I couldn't stop the way my voice came out, much rougher than anticipated. But thankfully, for once she didn't argue with me.

"Let's go out the back door," Kadie suggested as she pulled me into a small, dark courtyard. I wrapped her in my arms and flew us home.

What did the Demons want with her? And why would they want to lose her soul to kill her human body? Or was this the new way to torture talented Witches?

Or was their true target me? I didn't like to make assumptions or turn something that had nothing to do with me about something that might involve me. If I could stay out of garnering unwanted attention, I would. However, what if they were tired of me doing my job? What if this was their way to get their revenge? Maybe they were trying to provoke me into doing something I should not do because of the laws and nature of my being I was forced to follow.

Because I, for one, did not know what I'd do if they caught her now. She'd become far too important to me in such a short amount of time.

How did the Demons know this, though? I barely came to grips with it.

I didn't know the answers to all my questions. And that scared me, most of all. I did not like being unprepared. But I was. And I did not know how to fix it.

When we arrived back at her house, we let ourselves inside and I rushed to the shower to heal my wings. Water proved the salve for all.... even Demon burns. It purified even the blackest of souls.

Kadie stripped her clothes from her delicious body and joined me in the large shower. I adjusted the cold water to warm for her, and pulled my wings into my sides once again.

She grumbled to herself as she roughly washed her hair, white sudsy bubbles flowing down onto her shoulders. I stared at her, unable to help myself. She was so incredibly beautiful, the perfect distraction from my noisy, incessant thoughts. I loved everything about her. The rise of her cheekbone, the curve of her lip.

Apparently Kadie wasn't one to lie down and give up at the first sign of stress or pressure. Oh no, quite the opposite, in fact. I continued to watch her, and for some reason, I couldn't see any signs of her magical origins. In the past, I'd often believed that Witches had special markings upon their bodies so that they were easy to spot, but I could see nothing obvious on Kadie.

And speaking of which… I needed to address something with my little Witch.

"You're not going to continue with the lie now, are you? That you didn't know you had powers?" I didn't want to talk about this here, with both of us completely nude, but I needed to bring this up to her. After the last attack, I had my suspicions, but seeing her fight only moments before only confirmed them. She was in more control over herself than she wanted others – even me – to know. And if we were going to trust each other, she needed to be honest with me.

Kadie had tilted her head back as she rinsed the soap from her hair. At my question she dropped her chin and our gazes met. Finally, I could see the conflict in them. I crossed my arms over my chest and stared at her, waiting.

She looked away.

"You did know, Kadie. How could you not tell me?" I did not know why my heart tightened, like a bruise that had just been inadvertently touched. Being hurt by someone meant someone had attacked my physical body, not my emotions. Not my soul. This was an overwhelming feeling and I wished I could step back and not feel so damn much.

She turned off the water and grabbed a towel, quickly drying herself before wrapping a large white robe around her slender frame. "It's not as simple as that, Gabriel."

My first reaction was anger. I'd broken a major law for her, risked everything. And she hadn't been honest with me? But I slid the shower door open and waited for her to respond. Her eyes followed my collarbone down to my chest and then lower before she yanked her gaze back up to my face.

"Then explain it to me," I urged her, my voice gentle. I wanted to scream and yell and hitting the slick tile in the shower would definitely make me feel better for a second or two. But I knew she would not respond well to my anger, so I waited.

She ran her hands through her tangled hair, biting her lip as though deciding whether she'd confide in me or not.

Finally, she nodded and took my hand, leading me to her bedroom and sitting down on the mattress with me. "I'm a Witch, I think. I've known most of my life that I had these powers."

That didn't sound very certain. "What do you mean, *you think*?"

She started to pick at her robe. The soot from the fire was clinging to her clothes that were crumpled in the corner of her room, like a rejected lover. Her nostrils flared. "My mother died giving birth to me, and I never knew my father," she said.

Her eyes were still focused downward. I wanted to wrap my arm around her, I wanted to let her know that she was okay now and if she could listen to my past, I was more than happy to listen to hers without judgment. But I didn't want to touch her if that was something she wasn't interested in. I didn't know if physical comfort reassured her or if it irked her. I could only hope my presence was enough to remind her that I was here for her no matter what. "I was raised by the system…which means a whole lot of foster families. I was luckier than most and my foster parents weren't too bad. When I aged out at eighteen, I was able to get a job at a daycare center due to my experience with my foster brothers and sisters."

I frowned. What a horrible childhood to have. How had she come out so well balanced, so kind? My fingers tightened in the bedspread but I made sure not to say anything. Instead, I tilted my head to the side.

"All right," I murmured, "then that would explain your lack of knowledge, I suppose. But why didn't you try to find other Witches to teach you once you figured out you were special? I'm sure your powers weren't a secret."

She grimaced. "They weren't," she agreed. "In fact, they cropped up at the most inopportune moments. It was difficult for me to control them. So I did try to seek out help. When I was a teenager, I found that I could make that white light happen, especially when I was really scared. My foster mother was scared of me and kept her distance. She needed someone to watch the other foster kids for free, otherwise I'd have been gone." Wrinkles appeared in her forehead and I could feel the bitterness brimming off of her in slow waves. "After that, I learned to hide it. Then I moved to New York and thought I'd be able to find others like me, but there aren't any! I joined a coven, or so they said. But none of them had any real powers. They just liked to chant and carry on. I wanted to learn how to use my power, and I've been practicing how to control it for a long time. Mostly just to protect myself against people, men especially. I've had a few of them jump me in the evenings, on my way home."

I hope they're burning in hell somewhere.

This time, I moved my hand over hers, the one that picked at her robe. She stilled against my skin and finally looked up at me. Those ice-blue eyes paralyzed me. Everything about her was magic. "I bet they regretted that decision," I said.

She shrugged. "Yeah, a little. The light didn't work so well against men. It would push them back, but not really hurt them." I turned her over so I could start caressing her palm. It was surprisingly soft for the type of difficult life she had. I wondered if the warmth that thrummed from her skin was something innately her or was because of the powers that lived inside of her. "So, I didn't understand why I had it if I couldn't use it to protect myself. Until tonight, it's never really done any damage."

I set aside the fact that Kadie had been followed home by strange men and couldn't do much to protect herself. The thought unto itself caused my anger to flare but I curbed it down knowing she was safe now, knowing I was her beside her and had no intention of leaving anytime soon. Instead, I focused on what she said about her powers. Strange that they didn't protect her unless she was attacked by Demons. My brain began to whirl faster. This was special. "Your light could be a Demon specific fighting power but that's.... so rare. I've never even heard of anything like this myself, Kadie."

Not that I had infinite knowledge. I'd need to speak to Tabitha about this.

"Really?" Her eyebrows rose on her forehead. I couldn't tell if she was dreading what I meant or if it made her hopeful. I wanted it to be the latter, but humans had a knack for fearing their God-given talents, even if it was something odd like white light coming from her body.

"Really. And if those things ever come at you again, blast them back to Hell. You got it?' I leaned in close to her so our noses were brushing, grinning at her.

Her lips lifted into the first smile I'd seen in an hour. "Yes, Gabriel."

I reached over and opened her robe, exposing the creamy globes of her breasts and the pink tips that cried out for my lips. I pulled her closer and sent up prayers of forgiveness. I would love this woman tonight, and every moment I could, until the day they made me leave again. And I would regret absolutely nothing about it.

After all, what would be greater punishment than leaving her, now that I'd finally found some peace?

I SPENT the next six days following Kadie's every move, day and night. Watching her at work during the day, interacting with the children in her care, and holding her through the dark of night. I never took her time with me for granted, and continued to explore her body like it was new to me, like I was some kind of archeologist and she was some kind historical find that I didn't think I'd ever fully discover but would die trying. Those moments between us meant more to me than she knew, more to me than I had ever expected.

I didn't see a single sign of the Demons again. We'd set her up one night to see if we could draw them out. At first, she wasn't incredibly pleased by the prospect, but I asked her to trust me. If I knew what to expect, if I could see if Demons were still being assigned to her, I would be able to gage the best way to get rid of them without risking her. More than that, I would be able to see how they attacked her. Were they still trying to kill her outright? Or would they try some kind of torture tactic to ensure her soul went to Hell?

That night, she walked through the streets of New York, alone, her hair unbound and blowing in the breeze. If they didn't recognize her from that alone, the Demons were stupider than I gave them credit for. I kept a fair distance cloaked in my invisibility shield, trusting her to defend herself if necessary.

And nothing except for some homeless person who seemed more interested in her money than anything else.

When Tabitha called with another Target, I wasn't surprised to find out I had to move on. It meant that the Demons were no longer a threat to Kadie and I could focus on another human to protect. This should have been a good thing. And it was. But leaving her was the last thing I wanted to do.

It felt like I was falling from Heaven all over again. Losing the one I loved and being condemned to memories that would never match up to the short amount of time I had had with her.

"I shouldn't be disappointed to go, but I am," I confided to her the day I received the message from Tabitha.

I contemplated not saying anything to her, just to leave in the middle of the night when she was peacefully sleeping after a night of passionate love making. But I couldn't do that. Not to her. I'd found during the days with Kadie, there was no point in keeping anything from my little Witch. She could read my mind whenever she wanted to, and with her kind soul, there was no reason to hide anything. I also thought it was important for me to be honest with her without her having to go through my thoughts to find it. I wasn't exactly an open book, but what I could share, I would.

Kadie laughed with that full-bodied sound that I'd begun to love and ran her hands along my arms. "You mean, you're glad I'm no longer a Target?" she asked.

I should have expected her to always look on the bright side even though I could feel my chest clamp down, like someone was sitting on me, preventing me from catching my breath. It was surprisingly painful, and something I didn't particularly want to experience any longer.

However, she was correct. I was glad she was no longer a target. "Yes, very much so," I admitted. "But I don't wish to leave you. I've enjoyed our time together so much, I don't know how I'm going to go back to my old life now."

"Perhaps you could stay one more night?" she asked, her eyebrows lifting in a suggestive way. The way she bit her bottom lip after she said it made every muscle in my body tighten. I didn't understand how she could get me so hard without even touching me. Perhaps it was part of her magic. Either way, it made her dangerous – how she could render an angel such as myself completely and utterly helpless.

That look tugged at my heart strings, but I ruthlessly squashed such fanciful feelings. We'd already had more nights together than we should have had. I could feel the effect on me already, weakening the wall I had built up around my heart because I so desperately wanted to let her in.

And even if I did choose to stay, foregoing the task assigned to me, what would the outcome be? A human lifetime with my beautiful Witch, and then an eternity in damnation? Alone once again because Kadie would certainly go to Heaven unless her relationship with me had damned her soul to Hell. I couldn't risk such a thing for her soul. I would not allow the temptation of pleasure and happiness prevent her from seeking the glory she deserved in her afterlife. And me, walking this earth, saving souls, knowing I would probably never be given the same opportunity as I had been.

And that was if I was allowed to live after I'd turned my back on my Fallen Angel duties. That was never a certainty. The Supreme Creator and the laws He made were always changing. It was hard to predict what was acceptable and what was not depending on the circumstances.

"No, Kadie," I said. "We've already put ourselves in enough danger. I should go." I stood. I needed to put space between us lest she tempt me with that swollen lip, the way her eyes darkened when she wanted me.

Her lush bottom lip trembled. "Does that mean I'll never see you again?"

I shook my head. *Not a chance.* "I'll be back when I can. I'm always around New York."

This, at least, was the truth. I couldn't stay away from her, that much I knew, even though I probably should.

"Good. I couldn't stand not being able to see you again, Gabriel." She continued to touch me in that lazy, affectionate way she had, and I steeled myself against the warm, flowing energy.

This woman was far too addictive for my own good.

"You know I can't abandon my Targets to come to you whenever I would like, Kadie," I told her, my voice as tight as my body. Everything in me was tense, restraining myself from taking her against her bedroom wall and hearing her cry out in pleasure. My cock throbbed painfully. Who needed an eternity of damnation when resisting Kadie was more painful than anything else? "I'm on Earth for one purpose—to save those destined for Heaven from falling into Hell."

I tried to put some strength into my words, to give her something to cling to, as I had. A bigger purpose. Certainly, someone as good and as kind could respect that. I knew she would.

Her lips turned up into a perfect smile. "I know you do, Gabriel. Humans like me. I will never forget what you've done for me this week."

She went up on her tip-toes and kissed me, those perfect, sweet lips pressing against mine in the softest caress. Lust stirred in my loins even more as I broke away from the woman who had, in a very short time, become *home*. A word I never thought I'd keep in my vocabulary after what happened before.

"I have to go." I took a step back. I could already feel myself wanting to go to her, to take her in my hands and trace the curves of her body once more.

"I know," she groaned and let go of my hoodie where she'd gripped me and I hadn't noticed. Cold instantly swept my body the moment I lost her touch. The pain was remarkable and had me gasping for breath.

Kadie stared up at me with her clear blue eyes. "If I never see you again, Gabriel, I want you to know…I'm grateful for everything you've done for me."

I opened my mouth to refute her claim. Of course, we would see each other again! And soon. But I stopped myself from making a promise I couldn't keep. No one knew what the future held, not even me. I knew I'd fight the fires of hell itself and risk charred wings to make sure we would. If it killed me, so be it.

"Good bye for now, beautiful little Witch."

I touched her cheek with my fingertips one last time, memorizing the love I could see in her gaze. I didn't know if I would ever see it again. I didn't know if I wanted it in anyone else. If I could not have Kadie, being alone was preferable.

Then I stepped outside her purple front door and turned away from her, slipping into invisibility. The city held no allure for me today. I didn't want to walk among the people, as I once had.

Sadness crept along my soul, chilling me like the falling of snow. I recognized it in a way that you do an old friend you haven't seen in many years.

It had been centuries since I'd felt an emotion like it. My heart ached, tight and uncomfortable. But there was nothing for it, except to push past the feeling and get back to work.

You'll be back, I reminded myself. *You'll be back.*

I extended my wings and let them pull me up into the air and forwards, into my lonely journey here on Earth.

CHAPTER SIX

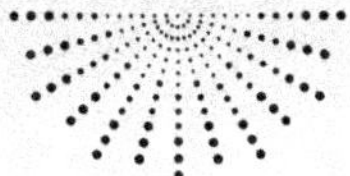

The minute I was in the sky, an address appeared in my head. I knew that was where I needed to go in order to find my next Target.

I'm on my way, Tabitha, thank you.

Good, this one is being stalked every night. He's terrified, so be wary.

I nodded, though she couldn't see me, and flew to the hospital where I'd been directed. I did have one advantage over these Demons. Being able to access my Targets during the day meant that I kept a lot more of them alive.

I felt good having something to do. Kadie was still in my thoughts more than I'd prefer, but at least this renewed my sense of purpose and reminded me why I was here. At the end of the day, I helped Kadie. I got to love her with my heart and my body. I would never forget what she had done for me. And I would try to see her again.

But protecting a Target was a good distraction from the heartbreak, from the way her scent still lingered on my skin and the way her lips touched my cheek.

I flew up to the rooftop of the tall building and there he stood, my Target. Standing on the ledge of a two-hundred foot building. About to jump.

No. Don't do it. Don't let them win.

He couldn't see me, and I kept it that way on purpose.

He must be in a lot of pain to feel so strongly about taking his own life. Many angels so this as proof of a human's weakness. To a degree, I agreed with this assessment until I spent time among them. Humans did not have easy lives. Those who still looked at each new day with a hopeful smile were strong, those like Kadie. To have Demons add to the despair made it impossible to resist the temptation of death. I no longer believed those who contemplated taking their own lives as weak, though those who overcame such thoughts were strong.

I flew up further into the sky and moved around to the space in front of him so I could catch him if he jumped. Not a preferred choice to interfere with the natural order like that, but with Demons in his head, the man could be forgiven for wanting to end his life.

He still couldn't see me, which was something I'd wanted to test. I'd thought that maybe my Targets would be able to see me in my invisibility since Kadie had, but once again, this situation simply proved her the exception. It just made the magic she possessed that much more intriguing. What else could she do, exactly?

But I could not think about Kadie now. I needed to focus on my target.

The man, Dr. Terence Winters, stared at the cement below as though it held all the answers to his life's problems. Which unfortunately, if he was being terrorized by Demons, would only be the start of his torment.

He leaned forward, his grey suit flapping in the breeze.

I could feel his fear. The palpitations of his heart inside his thin chest. The sweat on his palms. The tickle at the base of his spine.

No. Not today, Doctor.

I flew forward and picked him up by the arms. He shrieked and tried to fight me but I held tight and carried him to the center of the rooftop before setting him down and releasing my hold on my invisibility. He stared up at me and fell backwards onto his ass, scampering across the concrete like a frightened crab.

"What the hell are you?" He gaped at me and I flexed my wings, knowing he couldn't see them. Not like Kadie had.

I shook my head, trying to rid her of my thoughts. How could this be so impossible. I forced a chuckle at his frightened question, hoping it would help me refocus. An unusual response for me, but hey, my world was a little upside down at the moment. "The answer is much closer to Heaven than Hell, Dr. Winters. I am Gabriel, your Guardian Angel, and I'm here to save your life today."

He blinked several times and then stared at me. I watched his face pale and read the emotion in his eyes: awe, denial, doubt, reasoning, and then, finally, acceptance.

I smiled as gently as I could. "I'm real. I'm not going to disappear."

"I don't understand," he whispered, his heart still racing dangerously fast. I could hear the fluttering in my ears like a caged canary. He needed to calm down or he'd be in danger of a real heart attack.

I squatted down and tucked my wings in behind me so that I could look at him from where he still sat on the concrete. "I was called to save you from the Demons chasing you," I said. I made sure my voice was low and soothing. If he could get over his fear just to hear what I had to say, perhaps his body would start to calm down. "I know you've had some horrible nightmares and feel like the only way out is to plunge to your death off this roof."

The doctor's mouth opened and closed several times, like a fish. Finally, he said, "How did you know that?" He was still sitting on the concrete, looking up at me with a mixture of awe and fear. I could tell he was still deciding whether or not to trust me, whether or not I was part of his imagination or something out of his nightmares sent to haunt him even further. I did not know how to ease his trepidation, but I reminded myself that it was not my job to do so. He needed to find his faith and trust me if he was going to overcome the Demons.

"I know, because I'm the Guardian Angel sent here to save you," I said. "Believe me, you don't want to take your own life."

"Why not?" The poor man sounded defeated, hopeless, as though there was nothing else he could think to do besides this.

Most people asked me this question. About half the time, the answer was enough to make my Targets fight for their lives. "Because when you take your own life, the Demons that have been torturing you win. They get to drag you straight down to Hell. That's not where you're meant to go, Dr. Winters. If it was, I wouldn't be here."

Tears gathered in his grey eyes, making them appear glassy, like marble. "I've done some terrible things." He looked away and a tear crawled down his cheek. His lips trembled before he set them in a tight, white line, as though he was remembering.

His guilt for whatever trivial things he'd done in his fifty years or so was nothing compared to the weight of the world. Or the average person's sins, obviously.

"You may have, but you're still on the list for Heaven," I said. I was not going to deny his actions because that would be placating him and he did not need that from me. He needed honesty and something, a spark, to live for. "And you've been deemed important enough for the Demons to want to seduce to the darkness, so take it as a compliment. You have plenty of good work still to do in your lifetime."

The doctor swallowed awkwardly, pulling his eyes back to me. "What do I need to do, then?"

"You need to fight. The Demons will not kill you. They will only torture your mind so that you give up on life."

He nodded at me and dashed away the tears on his cheeks. "Well, they have certainly done a good job of that."

I met his gaze with my own. "Never, ever. Give up. It is not your time yet."

I stood up and walked over to where he still sat. I extended my hand out to him and pulled him to a stand.

"Now, we have a difficult road ahead, but I am here. With you. I won't leave you. Get up, and let's get you back to work."

I adjusted my height to only be an inch or so taller than him.

"I'm not dreaming?" he asked, his eyes wide and bright. I could hear the defeat in his voice, as though he thought this was his body's last-ditch effort to try and inspire him. His frame shook some, as though he were repressing the need to cry.

I chuckled again. "No, and I'm not leaving you. I will be by your side for the coming days. I will kill off any Demons that have been assigned to you, and hopefully by this time next week, you will be free of them forever."

A single tear dropped down his cheek and I saw the first smile from my Target. "That sounds…like Heaven."

I slapped him on the back and nodded. "Just hold onto your sanity, Doc, and you'll see it one day, you'll see that all I've told you is the truth. If you were not meant to be here, if you were not meant to grace Heaven with your presence, I would not be here."

"Is it beautiful?" he asked me. I knew immediately what he was referring to. It was a common question from a human.

We walked over to the stairwell and I answered as I always did, though my memories of late had begun to fade. Replacing them were hard pink nipples, pale white swells of heavy breasts aching for my hands to hold onto them. I internally shook my head of Kadie, especially those particular memories. It would not serve me well now. "More beautiful than you can even imagine."

Another week went by and I'd killed over a dozen Demons chasing down the doctor. I didn't know what he was working on or why he was so important. I didn't ask. It didn't matter. The Demons themselves were the only dictators of who they wanted and they, unfortunately, controlled my schedule.

I missed Kadie much more than I'd expected to. It was an odd and uncomfortable feeling, to desire a human's company so much. I hadn't expected to experience this much pain after leaving her to get on with her life. At night, when I allowed myself a few hours of rest just to recuperate my body, I thought of her, of us and our time together. I thought my feelings for her would begin to diminish, but the truth of the matter was, those feelings had only gotten stronger and more intense during our forced separation. It was something else that made no sense to me.

I'd been sure that a part of my heart would always love the woman I left behind in Heaven, therefore, not leaving any room for anyone else in my heart.

I may have been wrong about that. Because there was a single truth that I lived by at the moment, and that was that I missed Kadie. With every breath I wanted to feel that sensation of being home again.

I loosed a breath and stared up at the black sky. No wonder humans thought it had the capacity to answer all of life's questions — it was so grand, so vast, so open to every possibility. It was like a warm blanket, secure and reassuring. I wasn't alone, not completely. Not with Kadie looking at the same sky as I was.

The thought comforted me a bit.

Tabitha's voice suddenly came through my head, loud and clear., distracting me from my thoughts.

We have a problem.

Immediately, I sat up, my entire body on alert. *What's wrong? The doctor is safe.*

No. A beat. Like she was trying to figure out what to say. **It's Kadie.**

My heart stopped. *What do you mean? Have they killed her?*

My hands balled into fists. I should have sought her out sooner, just to ensure she was safe. I kept myself away because I thought I wouldn't be able to resist, but leaving her meant she was on her own, with no one to protect her.

No. Not yet. But they've got her.

What do you mean they've got her? I nearly growled in frustration. They had been trying to kill her before. Now they were taking here? It didn't make any sense. *Why would they take her? Are they going to torture her?*

I think I know why she was a Target to begin with.

I waited for more, but my Angel Agent was holding her breath. I knew she wasn't holding back to torture me. She was debating on whether or not she should say anything in the first place. *Tell me, Tabitha.*

A sigh came from her and I knew she resigned herself to answer. I felt anticipation bubbling up in my chest but I tried to quell it in order to focus on Tabitha.

There's a legend among us, about a woman destined to breed a new generation of Witches. Half-breed warriors who will make life for the Demons almost impossible on Earth. We've been waiting over a thousand years for such a woman and I'd begun to think it was just a myth.

I froze where I stood, my heart pounding like a war drum against my ribs. *I don't understand. I mean…please tell me you're wrong.* I looked to the left, where the sun was starting to rise. Beads of sweat dotted the back of my neck even though there was still a chill hanging in the air.

She's already pregnant, Gabriel.

I stumbled backwards and my spine crashed into a building. *Is it mine?*

This was a dumb question. Of course, it was mine. Whose else could it be? I knew Kadie was modern and I knew she was independent, but I could see the love she had for me in her eyes. I had no qualms about her moving on, I swear, I did not. I just did not think she would move on so quickly with a stranger after everything we had been through.

And yet, I couldn't be sure. It sounded impossible. She was human. I wasn't. We'd only made love a handful of times. A few weeks ago. I racked my brain. We did not use human contraception. I did not think I needed to. I never needed to in the past because I could not get a human pregnant due to the fact that I was not of this world.

Are Witches trule human, though?

My eyes widened at this sudden thought. Kadie looked like a human, laughed and ate and slept like one. And yet, there was more to her than a normal human. She had magical tendencies, things even I could not explain, and I had been alive much longer than any human could fathom. Regardless, even if she was pregnant – and I still was not entirely convinced she was - surely Tabitha couldn't know that already?

Yes.

I dropped to the concrete, dropping my face in my hands. I could not feel much of anything. I just heart the pounding of my heart, the sweat turning into streaks and gliding down my back. There was a weight heavy in my stomach that dragged me down. If the concrete wasn't there, I wouldn't have been surprised if I was pulled all the way into the flames of Hell itself.

Even if I was, I doubted I would feel a thing. I was too numb with shock to do anything, to speak, to even breathe.

Oh…fuck!

What have I done?

You need to find her and save her before they kill her. Your progeny is too important to this world, Gabriel. You must find her immediately.

My progeny?

I felt myself prickle with annoyance at Tabitha's lack of interest in saving Kadie to save Kadie. Instead, she seemed more focused on saving the fetus inside of her body.

Would they really do that? I asked, trying to take my personal emotions out of the conversation and failing to do so. *It would send her straight to Heaven.*

And perhaps one day I would meet her again. And our unborn child.

I still wasn't sure how I felt about the fact that I was suddenly in possession of a child. It was difficult to wrap my head around.

Yes. Which is why I believe they were trying to kill her originally, so she wouldn't bear your child. But now that she's pregnant, they will torture her instead. They want both of them for the Hell dimension. She is far more important than we first believed, Gabriel. Your child cannot die. They are both part of the cause now.

I wasn't sure how I felt about that, either. It wasn't Kadie's fault that I was a fallen angel and would be punished for my sins accordingly. But now our child would be thrown into the middle of this as well, simply because my loins produced it?

I could not react. Instead, I steepled my fingers over my nose and took in a deep breath. Right now, I needed to focus on finding Kadie and then saving her from the demons. After that, I could figure out how I felt about the news. *Where do I start?*

Here is her last location.

She sent the address to me. Out of state. I frowned. *Did they fly her?*

We don't know. The details are very unclear. This is all unprecedented and sudden. Even detecting her pregnancy came as a shock to me, but it's been confirmed. Which to be honest, I still can't believe either. How could you sleep with her knowing the consequences to you, Gabriel? You could be in more trouble than either of us can fathom.

I know… I know…

I still couldn't believe it myself some days.

But regardless of that… we can worry about it later. For now, I cannot express how important it is for you to find her quickly. I can only imagine what they'll do to her, Gabriel.

Tabitha was not one for emotions. She was helpful, certainly, and she did her duty to save those who needed saving, even though they were human. But to hear her voice shake in my head because she was scared over what could possibly happen to Kadie… it caused my blood to turn to ice.

I picked myself up and extended my wings. I took to the sky with the cold hand of fear gripping my heart and my sword burning into my feathers. I would kill many tonight, and if the Fates were kind and Heaven had my back, I would get out of there alive so I could kill even more. I would not rest until Kadie… and our unborn child were safe.

I LANDED on barren earth an hour later, my soul shivering with cold at the address I'd been sent to. I did not typically feel the cold and tilted my head to take in my surroundings. A castle reached up to the sky before me, situated on a hill in the middle of nowhere. Why had the Demons brought her here? What did they want from her?

More than that, did the cold affect Demons the same way it seemed to affect me? Demons, with their fire, could melt ice, but surely they did not like the frigid atmosphere. It could not be easy to maneuver in.

I turned my attention back to the castle. If they still had her, she had to be here. If they wanted her dead, there were quicker ways than the cold and a castle. If they wanted her tortured, surely, they could have done it better in New York so they wouldn't have to put in any extra effort to move her around?

None of this was making any sense.

Fear coursed along my spine at the possible other reasons they may have taken her. Perhaps this was a trap for me? Maybe they moved her here knowing the cold did something to me. They could isolate me, perhaps, put me in an environment I was not familiar with. Those from the Hell dimension had wanted my hide before, but they'd never quite gotten me. Let them try. I still had my sword. My wings may be black but they could still fly.

I took a step towards the castle, pondering the possibility of them knowing that I knew about my child. Maybe they made the assumption that if I knew they had a pregnant Kadie, I would come for her. They must know regardless of her pregnancy or not, I would not leave her with them. I would come.

Even if I was on my own.

I continued to pad up the hill, trying to keep myself as miniscule as possible. I tucked myself beneath my invisibility and adjusted my wings accordingly. It was daylight still, so I was hoping the Demons would have human lookouts. Humans, I could deal with easily. They would be susceptible to my invisibility. And my sword.

I ran through the overgrowth of large trees and reached the gates that were armed with barbed wire and an alarm. I chose to avoid those and extended my wings, flying over the top with ease.

So far, so good.

My boots squelched in the mud as I raced up to the side of the stone castle, my heart pounding and my fingers itching to grab my sword. I could sense Kadie nearby, her tender soul shining with that familiar warmth that I cherished.

She was definitely here. *Thank the Gods.*

I slowed as I neared the castle, tilting my head again to try and see if I could hear anything. This seemed almost too easily. The Demons knew my strengths and had found one weakness. Certainly they knew to expect me to fly. Certainly they knew to expect me to be invisible.

And yet, I had to keep going. Even if this was a trap, I needed to find Kadie. I needed to make sure she was okay.

That was the most difficult part – not knowing what were they doing to her. Panic crept into my heart and I steeled myself against it. I'd be no use to her if I froze from fear at a critical moment.

If you're scared, how do you think she's feeling?

The thought sent a flare into my bones and it caused me to move quickly.

I twisted and bolted up the stone steps, extended my wings, and then flew up onto the top floor. There were two human guards at roof level, holding machine guns. I almost laughed at the sight.

As if they're going to stop me.

I left the sword sheathed on my back and hit them with my fists instead. I was forbidden from killing humans, but injuring them was within my scope if it meant saving a Target. Part of me wondered if they were aware they were helping demons. Part of me didn't particularly care. My only focus was Kadie, and even if these humans were being manipulated, I still needed to get to her and they were in my way.

My shoulders tightened and bunched as I swung my fists at their jaws.

One fell, then the other.

They barely made a sound as they sunk to the stone floor like popped balloons.

The men hadn't been able to see me, which was a good sign that the rest of this rescue mission may be easier than I'd hoped. I just had to find Kadie and get her out before darkness, and the Demons, returned.

The door to the inside of the castle was locked. I was unperturbed. For my paranormal strength, this would be easy to overcome. I heaved my shoulder against the heavy steel and burst through the door. It clattered open with a massive bang.

Silence. I glanced left and right. There were too many hallways to choose from, and I had an unbelievably strong feeling pass over me.

I was going to die today.

The cold hand of death wrapped around my heart, warning me of what was to come. There would be no Heaven for me. Fallen Angels had nowhere to go after limbo.

There would be nothing. I would be gone forever.

No matter. Kadie was the only important thing.

When the thought floated across my mind like a cloud, I realized it bore the truth. I would be satisfied with my death, knowing Kadie would survive. It suddenly made sense; everything made sense. It was as though I fell to die for her, that my sole purpose of getting thrown out of paradise was so I could protect the one person in this entire expanse who filled my heart with the word home.

I cleared my mind of everything except my mission and crept along one of the halls. I drew my sword and held it at the ready. For one of the first times in my existence, I didn't know what to expect. It both scared and excited me, especially with the very real possibility of death just around the corner. It was a strange sensation: once I knew there was a chance that I would be nothing at any moment, I had never felt so free.

I moved further inside the darkened hallways and my muscles quivered. My legs grew heavy beneath me. Something was wrong in this part of the castle. My superior hearing heard a groan through the door ahead of me. I raced there, tried the steel handle and found it locked.

Something inside me shifted and I could feel Kadie as though she were pressed against me. I knew she was just there, behind this door. I breathed in and stilled my anxiety, trying to see if there was anything else I could pick up before going inside.

She was barely breathing, but alive. Inside this room. This cell. I threw my whole weight against the door and it split from its hinges, banging to the floor in a warped mess.

It was deathly dark inside the huge room that would have once been a banquet hall. Evil lurked inside, but so did my Witch. And I wasn't leaving her in there.

I crept inside, holding my sword out in front of me and using what little light spilled in from the doorway to see, while praying to God I didn't accidentally hurt Kadie. There were no windows, no way for me to actually see what lay before me. I would just have to trust in my abilities. I would have to have faith in the Supreme Creator that I would be okay.

Perhaps learning faith really was part of my penance.

I should be able to see through the gloom, but this wasn't a normal darkness. There was dark magic at play here.

I cleared my throat. The silence was too loud, gripping my skin, clawing at me like a feral cat. I whipped around to look behind me. I could feel Kadie here, but I saw and I heard nothing.

"Kadie?" I called out, my heart racing in my chest as adrenaline sizzled along my nerve endings.

More of that deathly silence that rattled my bones.

Come on, beautiful. I know you're in here. Perhaps if I could tease her thoughts, she might be able to respond in that way.

"Gabriel?"

I closed my eyes and tilted my head up, sending an appreciative gesture to my Creator. Whatever disagreements we may have had mattered little when Kadie was still alive.

Kadie's voice was weak, but she was here. *Thank the Lord.* I raced towards her voice and the door banged shut behind me, throwing us both into an unholy darkness. She whimpered and I drew closer, following my instincts. My eyes worked hard against the gloom and I could finally make out her shape.

A table. The lump of a body, in the middle of the room.

I stepped up next to her and ran my hands over her softness. I had to take her in my hands, my arms. I had to make sure she was okay. I could hear her, but I needed to feel her heart beating. I needed to be sure her voice wasn't some kind of wicked trick.

"You need to get out of here, Gabriel," she croaked. I pushed her hair from her face blindly. I tried to push her hair back from her face. I could feel cool sweat on her skin and wished I could reassure her that it would be okay. But the truth of the matter was, I didn't know. "Quickly. It's a trap." She sounded as though she hadn't had water in a long time.

Anger burned through me, but I had to temper it.

Not now.

"Not without you." *Never. Ever.*

She moved and I heard something clink. Suddenly, I realized what was happening with her. She was tied down. Bound by metal cuffs.

I gritted my teeth, muffling a growl.

"Are you all right?" I asked, though I knew it to be a ridiculous question. I was surprised I managed to get that much out. I wanted to rip her shackles and take her out of this castle, take her somewhere safe where no one could get to her ever again.

"Sort of," she replied with her characteristically dry sense of humor. I didn't understand how she was able to do that in such a dire circumstance. Most humans would complain – and for good reason. She was more concerned about me and making sure I was safe.

Suddenly the whole room lit up with light from an orange flame.

Holy shit.

"Run, Gabriel. Run!" Kadie screamed, and that's when I properly saw her. The Demons lit up the room like a summer's day and I could see every detail of my magical Witch.

Her stomach was impossibly swollen and large. Her arms still bled from puncture wounds. I realized she wasn't just shackled, but she was nailed to the table, as though they assumed there was a chance she might be able to escape if only one method of entrapment was employed. Her face was bruised and burned.

This time, I did not hold back my growl. It turned into something a wolf might howl at the moon, but much more ferocious.

Stabbing pain hit my gut as I swallowed the bile that rose in my throat as I screamed. This was all my fault. I should have been here for her. Damn the other Targets. There were more Fallen angels that could have protected them. Kadie was *my* Target, and I had failed her.

Why had I been called away from her when she'd still needed me?

"What have they done to you?" I grabbed hold of the clamps that held her down and used all my strength to open the metal bonds. I pulled and cried out as I wrenched at the metal. They fought against me, but as I put all of my strength into the challenge, they finally clanged open and broke apart. I threw them to the ground in disgust.

"This will hurt, little Witch," I told her, indicating the stakes that had been placed in her palms.

She nodded and looked away, like she didn't want to watch. I couldn't blame her.

I worked quickly. I didn't want to prolong the inevitable. My little Witch tried to keep her scream to herself but she could not. As I slid the first nail out, she let out a scream and then another as I did it to the second one. I needed to get her to a physician quickly. I could not risk her bleeding out. I could not risk this stress harming her – *our* – baby.

She sat up with my help, grabbing at her huge belly. Trickles of blood dropped down her palm and stained her shirt. She did not seem to notice. "Go. Quickly," she urged me, still trying to save me, beautiful woman that she was. Inside and out.

Leave you here to die? Never.

She turned her body, slowly throwing her legs over the table. She winced. I was certain everything in her was screaming in pain. Still, she tried to mask it with indifference, but her glassy eyes gave her away. As much as I appreciated her strength, I wished she knew she didn't have to be strong for me.

I took my sword from its sheath and turned to my opponents. I was surprised they allowed me to remove those shackles and stakes. I wondered if they were biding their time, if they were letting us do this because they knew we would not escape from here. A dozen Demons surrounded us, glowingly red and fiery bright. They were waiting for me to attack. I could feel my body lifting and changing, the warrior inside of me transforming for the fight.

My heart thumped harder and faster, a fate I hadn't known existed for me, opening up like the beginning of a waterfall.

"I am Gabriel, Defender of Heaven and Earth, and you… cannot have her!" I bellowed, my fingers tightening on my sword.

Don't give up on me, beautiful.

I did not turn to look at her as I stepped towards the Demons. Part of me wanted to get one last look at her, one last chance to say goodbye. But I did not. I needed to ensure her safety and I could not risk taking my eyes off these beasts.

I faced off against them and as they rushed me I could feel Kadie at my back, her white light streaming from her goodness. I wanted to scream at her to run. I wanted her to get help. Perhaps her magic was helping her heal. Regardless, I did not like her risking our child to save me. I was apt to do what I could, but everything would be in vain if I failed and she fell into their clutches once more.

I swung my sword as they ran at us, taking the head off one, slicing the arm off another. My shoulder burned as one touched me and I spun to take him out.

Kadie fell to the ground with a cry and I encircled her. My wings extended and folded backwards, attempting to surround her — a dangerous situation for us both as I would only be able to move in a circle around her. My body was repairable. My wings were not.

I swung and danced around her, taking out every Demon that came at us, unable to move far as I stayed to protect my woman and our child.

My hoodie was on fire, the heat burning at my neck and making sweat sting my eyes. I brushed it with my hands to put out the flames. A Demon slammed into my ribs and knocked me sideways, exposing Kadie from beneath me and causing pain to ricochet up my body.

Oh, fuck.

I grunted and fell. I was not expecting that amount of pain.

Kadie blasted them with her powers, the white glory giving me enough time to put out my flames, wrench off the hoodie and stand up. I could not deny that her presence, her magic, probably saved me from grave injury. As much as I wanted her to run to safety, I appreciated the risk she was willing to take to ensure I was all right.

My ribs were broken, my skin was burned, and there was still about eight of them. We needed to get out of here, and fast. With Kadie's own injuries, I did not think we would be able to take the rest of them out. I did not know if more were coming. I did not want to risk anything to find out.

But the only way out seemed to be the way we came in. I grabbed Kadie and hauled her to her feet, her legs wobbling uncertainly beneath her cumbersome body. She seemed fragile in that moment. I had never seen her appear that way before. I wanted nothing more than to cradle her against me, to feel her relax, but I knew we needed to leave as quickly as possible if we were going to survive. And as much as I ached to reassure her, survival had to be our first priority.

We need to get out, I explained to her, hoping the voice that floated in her head was gentle. *Run for the door to your left. I'll be right behind you.*

She nodded and turned, holding out her arms and staggering towards the exit. She blew white light at the Demons in our way and I sliced at them with all my might. I suppressed a grunt. The strain the movement left on my ribcage was enough to shake me. I had been injured before, but not to this extent. I did not think I had ever had this much to lose before.

Kadie made a hole in their defenses and kept going, staggering and moaning as she moved. She didn't give up. And she didn't stop. Tears clogged my throat, making speech impossible.

Keep going. Encouraging her was the only thing I could think to do. There were no other options. I could not let her give into the pain I was certain she was feeling.

I turned around and faced them, ignoring my own pain and injuries tugging at my soul. Both mine and Kadie's. The sensation of impending death was overwhelming, like a giant storm cloud rolling in and enfolding me with no chance of escape.

Three Demons rushed me at once and I thrust forward with my sword. I swung fast, dealt with the one in front of me, the other two diving for my wings like impossibly huge flames. They clung to the blackened feathers and made me scream out in pain. I could feel the sizzle against the softness. I knew my time had come. I did not think I would make it out of this one.

But Kadie could.

Keep going.

Daylight shone into the room as Kadie flung the door open.

"Gabriel!" she screamed, looking back at me.

She was safe. In the daylight. She still needed to get outside, but the Demons wouldn't be able to leave this room, I was certain.

Go, little Witch. Go!

All my strength left me as I swung around in a huge circle, turning the two Demons who clung to me into dust. I fell to my knees, the pain of my burning wings so intense I could barely breathe.

But it did not matter. Just knowing Kadie would survive, our unborn child would survive, was enough to ensure that I could die fighting. The pain I felt did not inhibit me, it inspired me. I knew with absolute certainty I would see my death today – and that was okay. It was a strange feeling – the same one I got when I first stepped inside the castle.

I would use it to my advantage.

I could hear Kadie's voice in the distance, screaming at me, my burning flesh reminding me I was still alive.

I couldn't give up now, though I wanted to.

I roared as I staggered to my feet and started swinging once again, hacking away at any Demons that dared get in my way. My sword, my trusted friend, had not let me down through any of my darkest times, and it continued to stay with me now. I backed up as fast as I could and made it to the door as the remaining solitary fiery creature let loose an evil howl in anger.

I wanted to laugh. Could Demons sense impending demise? Did it give them hope, as it gave me?

I thrust forward with my sword, stabbing one last Demon before I raced out into the daylight, the best defense against these evil spirits.

I collapsed against the stone wall, my breath coming in ragged gasps.

I was alive.

The daylight pricked at my eyelids and it took me a brief moment to adjust to the sun. But I tilted my face up towards it, like a sunflower. The Supreme Creator had not forsaken us. We were both alive.

But we could not stay here.

"We… need to go," I told Kadie, trying not to cringe as I raised my gaze and witnessed the state she was in. They'd really made a mess of her beautiful face, and I hoped to God Tabitha could help her.

She nodded, leaning back on her hands, stretching out her back. She was so pale I barely recognized the physical form of the woman I'd known only a week ago.

But she was my Kadie. There was no mistaking her heart, nor the strength that beat behind it. I wanted to cling to her, to tell her – to tell myself, really – that it was okay now.

I could not bring myself to do that. I did not know if it was okay. The only person who would know of such a thing was Tabitha. We needed to get to Tabitha, and quickly.

I carefully picked her up into my arms and ran as fast as my injured body could carry me, along the corridor, then I turned through the door that took us into the bright sunlight.

I blinked rapidly as the daylight bathed our faces. I stepped over the bodies of the guards I'd knocked out, and placed her down on her feet. I couldn't stop the groan that sounded through my throat as the pain burned down my arms.

"Can you fly?" she asked, her worried gaze running over my injured form.

I extended my singed wings and intense pain pulsed down my shoulders and around my ribs. More than half the feathers were burnt off, but I could fly. Or we'd die trying.

"I don't know until I try."

Her eyes went wide at my words and I couldn't hide the slight smile that tugged at my lips.

Noticing my grin, she quipped, "If I weren't so tired, I'd kill you."

"Yeah, yeah, get in line little witch." I tried to laugh as I gathered her battered body up into my arms once again and concentrated on the weight of her against me. Her warmth gave me strength.

I clenched my jaw, gripped her tight and pulled all my willpower to me and used it to lift us off the ground.

Pain shot through my back and along my wings. "Arghhh…" I couldn't stop a strangled scream from leaving my mouth as I lifted into the air. My grip on Kadie tightened, afraid I might drop her because it was too much for me to bear. I could not let her go, no matter what state I was in. She needed me. And I was not going to let her down.

I pushed forward. Each flap of my wings was like a stab and I was certain I would never catch the gentle breeze. It was too soft, too delicate, just like the woman here in my arms. But I did not falter. It took time and I grunted through clenched teeth, but I continued to push.

I kept flapping and got us higher, above the barriers of the castle and towards the clouds. Once there, I eased into my flight. It was much less difficult knowing the danger had decreased, if only slightly.

She clung to me, tightly. I glanced down at her mangled face. I could see she was trying to be strong, as she usually was. The thought that she was still my Kadie despite all of this made my heart swell with pride. I wish I had her strength. I knew, in that moment, I did not. But she did. I continued to focus on my woman, on how proud I was simply to be in the same space she was. My eyes dropped further down to the child growing inside of her.

My child.

The love I held for both of them push away the pain that tormented my mind.

I did not understand this sudden and unexpected love for something I did not plan nor did not think was possible. I supposed it did not matter about what I thought I knew. Things changed. Feelings changed.

The size of her belly confused me, and scared me, but I was hoping that Tabitha would have answers. She usually did.

CHAPTER SEVEN

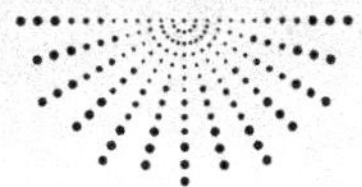

We flew over the castle and I kept going, following an instinct that would take me Tabitha. It was slow to come by – my flight – but as long as we were making some kind of progress, I did not mind the extra time. Kadie felt good and solid in my arms, her face pressed against my chest.

I didn't want Kadie to know just how difficult this was becoming for me.

I continued to push further.

Black spots swam in front of my eyes and I wanted to scream from the pain that pushed through every cell of my being. I collapsed outside a small house in Brooklyn. Not where I expected to be. I did not realize I had traveled so far. Focusing on Kadie, on my child, ensured that the time passed. Even though I could feel the pain, the person in my arms compelled me further. I wonder if her magic was at play here. I would not be surprised if it were – Kadie always had more than a few tricks up her sleeve. Nevertheless, we'd found my Agent. Why she changed houses so often, I'd never know. It was annoying, but as long as I was able to find her, that was all that mattered.

Kadie stood up from where we'd both dropped on the ground

and banged on the door. I tried to push myself up to stand with her, but I was overtaken by a strong, gripping pain, and faltered. "We need help," she cried and the door flew open.

"Tabitha," I croaked out from where I was.

Thank you, God. We made it.

And there she was. All five feet nothing of her.

"The… Angel Agent?" Kadie asked, breathless and leaning against the door frame as though she couldn't stand. Her hands went to the small of her back, arching up her torso and stretching out her muscles. Blood crusted on her hands from where she had been staked to the table, but it looked as though the injury had clotted.

She would be okay.

"Yes," Tabitha responded with a brusque nod. "Come inside, Kadie. I'll help Gabriel."

Tabitha came over to me and lifted me up like I weighed nothing. She tucked her shoulder under my arm, and with a strength I hadn't known she possessed, she practically carried me inside, into a room with two hospital beds.

She lay me down on one of them. I leaned back. Black, dancing birds clouded my vision. I shook my head, hard. Damn exhaustion.

I wanted to give into the darkness, to allow sleep to overcome me, but I also wanted to ensure Kadie was getting help as well.

"I thought you two were going to need care when you escaped so I moved into the human realm and stocked up on supplies," she explained, as my eyes slid shut and I relaxed into the cool sheets.

This was so much better than the castle's black room with the Demons. Even Tabitha's voice was like a balm on my injuries.

I knew this was temporary. I knew that there would be a time when we weren't safe. But at least I could finally relax. At least I wasn't constantly looking over my shoulder for now. At least Kadie was just as safe as I was, and I was with her to make sure she stayed safe.

"Kadie, lie here," Tabitha instructed. Her voice little room for argument. I heard her pat the bed near mine. "You need some fluids."

Tabitha continued to move about and I forced my eyes to open a slit. I trusted Tabitha completely with Kadie, but I still wanted to know what was going on. I watched as my Angel Agent put a drip into Kadie's forearm like an expert, and then washed her face with a cloth. Kadie leaned into the touch, needing the cool water to soak her injuries, to purify her being.

My beautiful, darling Witch was an utter mess.

Kadie opened her eyes and locked them with mine. She gave me a gentle smile as though she could read my mind. And I remembered, that she could.

"It's okay," she assured me, her voice still rough. "You should see the other guy," Once again, her hands strayed to her stomach. It could have only been a week, perhaps two, since we last consummated our relationship, and yet, she cradled her stomach with such tenderness and affection that it reminded me of how other humans who were forced to wait nine months until the birth of their child touched their bellies. Such a strong bond in such a short amount of time. It was a miracle.

Then again, the way I felt about Kadie was stronger than I had ever considered possible, and it was just as real. Miracles were more common than I understood.

"Is she all right, Tabitha?" I choked out around my swollen throat. My whole body felt like it was on fire, even against the cool sheets. My only reprieve, besides Kadie's safety, was that we were out of immediate danger so I did not have to worry about anything unexpected taking place. At least, not right now.

That said, my arms, my shoulders all cried out in despair. I glanced down and one of my ankles was black.

"I think so." Tabitha's sharp gaze fell on Kadie, her brow furrowed, her lips pressed into a thin line. Gently, she moved Kadie's arms and then legs before finally tilting Kadie's head from side to side, just to observe Kadie and truly make sure she was all right. Her eyes locked with Kadie's. "But what are these marks?" She gestured towards the marks on the crease of each arm.

"They injected me with strange things," Kadie murmured. "I don't know. Made me feel dizzy."

There was deathly silence in the room as Tabitha processed it all.

"Tabitha?" I asked when I could stand the silence no longer.

"Who did?" Tabitha asked, ignoring me. I bit my lip to push.

"Some men." Kadie shifted on the bed and I could tell the conversation had turned uncomfortable for her.

"The ones who took you?"

Kadie nodded. "Yeah," she said. Tabitha had her hand on Kadie's shoulder and sat on the edge of the bed. I wondered if Tabitha was trying to ease Kadie's discomfort with her touch. "I wasn't expecting humans to be on their side. They came into my house in the middle of the day. I thought I recognized them from the soup kitchen. I was going to let them know I'd be more than happy to help there, but they attacked me before I could get a word out." She clicked her tongue against the back of her teeth. "Stupid assholes. I hurt one or two of them in the fight, but they knocked me out." She sighed and laid back against the pillows, staring up at the ceiling. "I woke up in that dark room being smacked around and injected with shit. No idea what for."

Tabitha rubbed some salve on Kadie's wounds and her palms and then moved over to me. I did not like that she hadn't said anything in response to Kadie's story. I opened my mouth, ready to ask her what she thought, when she frowned and gave me a sharp shake of her head. The gesture alone was enough to silence me. "You need water. Now."

I closed my mouth and gave her a long gaze. I knew not to argue with her. At least, not right now.

"I know," I finally said. Perhaps agreeing with her would appease her and she'd be more than happy to tell me what was going on in her head once I acquiesced to her order. Water, the purest water you could find, was the best cure-all for an Angel. But it was the last thing I was looking for after I rescued Kadie.

Tabitha left the room, then came back with a bucket and a bottle of something green. I eyed the bucket suspiciously. Surely, she wasn't going to…

Tabitha lifted the bucket up, stepped forward, and tipped the cold water all over my head and chest.

I nearly jumped up even though my muscles were filled with the intoxicating contradiction of both pain and pleasure.

"Oh, fuck!" I could not help but cry out. I knew Tabitha did not like it when I used such language, but considering she just doused me with angel-created purified water, I was certain she would forgive me.

The pain was incredible, like stabbing needles that had been injected with the heat of hell and yet, there was a dull sense of relief that began to thrum through my bones. I bit my tongue to stop myself from crying out again. I was certain Kadie was watching me, and the last thing I wanted to do was add to her stress by causing her to worry about me. She needed to worry about getting better, about our child.

I tasted blood and swallowed as the pain began to back away. When my vision returned from the inky depths it had receded to, I realized Tabitha had gone away and she was back with more water, dousing my wings and legs with new buckets.

The pain intensified. I did not feel pleasure when the water hit my wings, but the pain let me know this purification was working. It burned, and made me scream against the agony, despite my attempt to keep my screaming to myself, then it disappeared like the tide receding, as my body began to heal.

"How did you fly with so much damage, Gabriel?" she asked, clucking her tongue. She dropped the bucket carelessly to the floor and placed her hands on her hips, giving me a raised eyebrow. I did not know how it was possible, but Tabitha had this ability to make me feel like I was some kind of naughty school child and she was contemplating whether or not she wanted to slap my knuckles with a ruler.

I coughed through the wave of pain, and then when it disappeared, I managed to sit up. The pain slowly began to fade. I could feel it slip off me, like a shirt that was glued to my body.

That is so much better. Oh, thank you, God.

"I don't know," I answered. "But I had to get Kadie to safety."

"Hmm." She said nothing more on the subject and turned to a

small nightstand I had not noticed before. "Now, drink this." She handed me the bottle of green. "I can't restore your wings, but this should heal most of your body and make flying easier for you."

I reached out and took the potion. "Thank you, Tabitha," I told her. I hoped she knew I meant it.

I lifted the green liquid to my lips, smelling of vile coal, and drank. It burned my nose and throat and I gasped for air after swallowing it all. What was she trying to do? Kill me faster?

But very soon after, I could feel a new warmth in my muscles, a deadening of the pain in my wings. It felt like relief.

"That's incredible." I collapsed back onto my pillow, my body sticky with cold sweat.

Kadie waved her hand as though to get our attention. Tabitha and I turned towards her.

She cleared her throat and I saw her shift due to the sudden attention. "So…um…can anyone explain this to me?" Kadie asked, her hands encircling her huge belly. "I know how to make a baby, mind you, but the last time I checked, it takes roughly eight to nine months for me to be carrying a child this size. Granted, I've never been pregnant before so I can't tell you one hundred percent from experience, but that's just based on what I remember from my high school health class."

I glanced towards Tabitha and then back to the woman carrying my child. A child that looked like it was going to be born much sooner than was normally humanly possible.

"Tabitha?" I invited my Agent to explain. Because the truth of the matter was, I did not know of this either.

The woman rolled her eyes at me and handed Kadie a bag of candy. Jelly beans, if I was correct.

"Eat," she instructed. "You need some sugar."

Kadie dug her hand into the bag, pulled some multi-colored candies out, and threw them in her mouth. She did not even hesitate. My lips lifted up at how easily she trusted Tabitha to the point where Kadie did not even question her.

Tabitha sat down on the end of Kadie's bed and put a hand on her leg. "I believe you're pregnant with Gabriel's baby," she explained. I could tell she took great care in saying such a thing, as though she wasn't quite sure how Kadie was going to respond.

It was Kadie's turn to roll her eyes. "Of course, I am," she said. I had to bite my bottom lip to contain a smile. I did not think I knew anyone who was so flippant with Tabitha before. It humored me more than I initially believed it would.

Kadie continued. "But how is that possible? And why am I like…full term in a week?"

"I agree. How is that possible, Tabitha?" I asked, surprised by how relaxed she seemed. I sat up in bed and winced at how the muscles strained against my body. I was not aware that she knew. I was not aware that knowing would compel her to be as calm as she was. She was handling it much better than I did.

Tabitha sighed, pinching the bridge of her nose. I was not sure she was as comfortable as I was listening to someone discuss their sex life. "There isn't much I can tell you, unfortunately, Kadie," she said, dropping her hand. "I'm the only other half-Witch, half-Angel creation that I know of, and I've never conceived a child myself."

Tabitha appeared human. She had long flowing blonde hair, pale blue eyes and wore glasses. Why, I wasn't sure exactly.

But now I knew that she was so much more than I'd thought! *Wow.* Perhaps if I'd asked her sooner, we could have avoided all of this. But how could I know? Perhaps that was why Tabitha was so insistent on me protecting Kadie. Because she felt some kind of kinship between them.

Kadie groaned in apparent frustration. "So, I'm half a witch now?" she asked, throwing her arms out. "This is so confusing. So being with an angel makes me half-Angel? I don't understand. Seriously, I wish my parents had stuck around long enough to explain some of this to me." Kadie pouted, then shoved another mouthful of candy past her lips, as though this was going to help her feel better about her current circumstances.

Tabitha smiled with real affection. "Well, you're something special, that's for sure." I hadn't seen Tabitha smile like that in a long time, and it made my own lips twitch. It was nice to see that Tabitha genuinely cared about Kadie the same way I did. Well, perhaps not the same way. But there was an affection between them that I appreciated.

Kadie nodded, her hands going back to her belly. I could not help but start thinking about her pregnancy and what this would mean for her. For me. Perhaps Tabitha could help us understand. At least maybe it would help prepare us for her impending birth.

"So, how long, Tabitha?" I asked gesturing to the baby in her rounded belly. I didn't know everything about human physiology, but from the people I'd observed, Kadie didn't look like she had more than a few weeks to go. And that was in human time. And that was if the baby went full-term. I knew that that did not always happen. I did not know much about babies but I knew that they dictated when they would come – most of the time. I hoped there was some way to know when this one would come.

"Oh. Damn, he moves a lot," Kadie said as she arched her back. Her face contorted into one of slight discomfort, but her hand continued to affectionately rub her belly. I glanced over and there was an obvious shift of flesh beneath her stretched t-shirt. It was so strange to see something like this. I knew it, of course, but seeing such a miracle on earth in person was stunning.

"He?" I croaked, suddenly letting her words sink in. I'd never thought of having a child, but a son would be…incredible.

"Well, I don't know what he is, technically," Kadie pointed out. "I haven't even seen a doctor. Besides the fact that it's only been a week, I wouldn't even know what I would even tell them. I had sex with an Angel a week ago, got pregnant, and I'm going to have a baby, like, now."

She gave me a tentative smile and hope fluttered in my chest. Perhaps eternal servitude in limbo was not my destiny? Could I have a real life on Earth? With a family and the love I'd always coveted?

My mind started swimming with possibility. I did not know what this would mean for us, but I wanted to explore all possibilities because, why not? Perhaps this was why I had been here for nearly five hundred years. Because I would eventually meet Kadie. Because we would be together and she would get pregnant. Because I would have the opportunity to be with a human… as a human.

I had never heard of something like this happening to an angel, of course. But I could not help but wonder if it was possible for me. If this was what I wanted. And the more I thought about it, the more I realized that it was.

"So, you mean...." Kadie froze suddenly and held her breath, grimacing.

"What's wrong?" I asked her, wanting to reach out and touch her, but still feeling the tremors of pain in every cell of my body. I could not hold onto her until I felt better myself. I hoped the vile drink Tabitha forced me to take would allow me to do so quickly.

Kadie dropped her head, inhaled slowly, and then exhaled just as slowly. Her breath was shaky.

Finally, she lifted her head and smiled. "Oh, that's better," she said. "If I didn't know better, I'd think I was in... Oh!" She bent right over again, wrapping her arms around her belly as she groaned in pain. This time, she wasn't simply breathing. She was letting out her pain.

"Tabitha," I said, ignoring the pain and standing up. I nearly stumbled over to her, needing to place my hand on her shoulder to let her know I was here, I would be here, in order to hopefully soothe her. "Is the baby coming?"

Tabitha jumped up as well. "Lay down, Kadie." Suddenly, any warmth and gentleness was gone. This was the Tabitha I knew – no nonsense and ready to go for anything that was about to happen. She was always reliable under pressure.

Kadie groaned and rolled to the side. Tabitha grabbed Kadie's old, bedraggled skirt in her hands and ripped it asunder. I heard the tear in my head. I don't think I would ever forget that sound.

"Look," she whispered as we both stared at Kadie's swollen belly, the obvious shift of the child beneath her skin as he moved into place.

He.

If her instincts were correct, my son was getting ready to come into this world.

"What do we do?" I asked Tabitha. I did not like feeling unprepared. I did not like feeling overwhelmed and ignorant and completely helpless. I was a warrior. I was trained to always be ready for battle. But now, I felt myself swept up in something I had never experienced in the centuries I had been confined to earth. I had watched the miracle that was childbirth a handful of times, but watching it and experiencing it were two very different things. There was no amount of watching, observing, or reading that could ever prepare you for this.

Panic rose in my throat, hot and painful. My hands started to sweat and I removed the hand from Kadie shoulder so I could wipe it on my shirt. I did not know what to do. I did not know what to do and that bothered me more than I cared to admit. If I could not help Kadie, what good was I for?

"Argh!" Kadie called out, her fingers reaching out for me.

I took both of her hands in mine and lowered my face to hers. "I'm so sorry, Kadie," I told her, unsure that I was saying the right thing. The words continued to spill out of me and I could not stop them even if I tried. "So sorry. I had no idea this could happen. I would never make you endure this by choice. You must know I would never want you to experience any kind of pain."

She arched her back up, her eyes closing tightly as sweat dotted her brow. When she relaxed again, her eyes opened and her lips kinked in a smile. "I know." Her voice shook, but it still sounded like my Kadie. "But I don't regret it. I've always wanted a child. And one with your face would be a wonder, I'm sure."

I felt my heart react to her comment, and warmth began to spread through me. It was very similar to the warmth one felt at learning they would be placed in Heaven for all eternity, but different. "As long as you don't mind the wings as well," I forced myself to say.

Her eyes flew open wide. "Wings?" she all but yelped. Her hand squeezed mine with a grip I did not realize was possible. "Are you serious? He can't possibly have…. Argh…."

She squeezed my hands even more and screamed as blood-stained water gushed between her thighs. I did not think it was possible for a human to have such strength. Then again, Kadie was not a typical human. If Tabitha was right, she was a half-Witch, half-Angel, after all. Perhaps that added to her strength.

I took a breath, trying to calm me as much as I wanted to calm Kadie. But how was I supposed to do that when I was just as nervous, if not more so, than she was. "I think the baby's coming, Kadie." I forced my voice to stay relaxed and calm. I did not think it worked. At least I was trying.

My mind started whirring with possible scenarios, scenarios that were not necessarily good. I should be more hopeful. I should be happy. But there were too many things we didn't know. I was an Angel. She was a some kind of supernatural being. Her pregnancy commenced a week ago and now she was going to give birth. So much could go wrong. What would we do if she couldn't birth him safely? A hospital was definitely the best place for her. They could save both of them if there were complications.

"No. No hospitals," Kadie cried. Another contraction seemed to be taking on her body. Her voice got strained with each word. I did not know how it was possible that she could talk through this, but she pushed herself to do so. "In case he's…not human. I do not want anything to happen to him."

"What could happen to him?" I asked. Perhaps I should know this but I didn't.

"I just…" She caught her breath as the contraction passed. "If they knew what he was, if they could somehow find out, they might take him from me and run experiments in the name of science. I just, I don't want that life for my child. I don't want to risk him."

Tabitha caught my gaze and nodded. The last thing she wanted was any questions about my babe, at best. But I couldn't have Kadie die either. I loved my child – I did not know how it was possible to love someone I didn't know, but I did – but I could not risk Kadie for my child.

I hoped I would never have to make a choice between the two of them.

"I'll be fine," she panted, responding to my panicked thoughts. "I'm strong, Gabriel. You know this. You know me. Get my panties off. Now!"

She screamed out against the pain and I ripped the material from her. Tabitha took her ankles in her hands and spread them apart to give my child better access at exiting Kadie's womb.

Kadie pushed herself up to a seated position, her hair slick and stuck to her forehead. I had never seen her look more beautiful than in that moment. "I think he's coming." She began to pant and Tabitha moved again to the place beside her bent thighs.

I stepped up closer to Kadie's face, staring into her eyes and squeezing her hands. Willing my strength into her. I knew she was right. I knew she was strong. But even the strongest could be taken down. It was all within the power of God. *Please, God, help her. Please. I beg of you. I will do whatever you ask of me, if only Kadie and my child would survive.*

"Please don't die on me," I couldn't help saying aloud. I pressed my lips together, wishing I could take the words back. I wanted to be strong for Kadie, but it would seem as though I was the weaker of us. I should not have been surprised by this. Kadie was much stronger than I was and always had been.

Kadie managed a strained laugh, her red face dotted with sweat, blood rushing to her face and making her look red and winded. Her lips pulled up into a strange grimace. "Not planning on it," she said. "Especially since you went to all the trouble to save me from… from… Gah!"

She broke off again and began bearing down, pushing and panting. Her face grew darker red and contorted as she willed her body into submission. I wanted to laugh but didn't. How did she have this power over me? How could she make me laugh when she was going through all of this pain? Who was this wonderful crea-ture? How had I been blessed to walk in the same space as she was? It made no sense to me. Perhaps it wasn't supposed to.

I glanced over at Tabitha, who was concentrating on the place between Kadie's legs. I still felt like I was doing nothing. I could not even say the right things in order to calm her down. Instead, I felt as though she was coddling me, wanting to make sure I was the one who would be okay instead of her. I felt like a fool.

What can I do? I asked Tabitha. I needed guidance. I had no idea what I was doing. I needed orders. Orders I could follow.

"Talk to me." Kadie yelled, her voice gravelly and deep. She was not even looking at me at this point.

Talk to her? That I could do.

"You were incredibly brave today, my beautiful girl," I said. I wasn't sure where to start but the words fell out of my mouth as though they were fighting amongst each other to get out. "I couldn't believe you were still alive when I arrived."

"I… Ah…" Kadie was past talking and strained to push.

Keep talking.

"You are such a wonderful woman." I began to rub her shoulder, hoping it was helping. From my limited knowledge, some women appreciated the comfort while others did not want to be touched by their partners. She had yet to yell at me about touching her, so I continued. "I can't believe after all this time alone, I found you. It feels like destiny, like this was meant to happen."

Kadie panted and looked up at me. "But what about… about…her?"

Her? Oh… Teramea.

How could Kadie remember her during this time? And yet, I could not blame her. I shared my past with Kadie, and I was honest about it. I told her how much that person from my past meant to me. She was the reason I was here on earth in the first place. In a strange way, she was the indirect reason I met Kadie. If I had not felt so strongly for her, I never would have met my little Witch.

I could never hate Teramea for that reason alone. But that did not mean I had any sort of feeling for her any longer. In fact, I had not thought of her in a long, long time.

"I don't dream of her anymore," I said honestly. "She's in the past, forever gone. Now it's only you. Please don't leave me, Kadie."

I wasn't supposed to say the last part out loud. Still, I could not help it. I have better self-control than this. And yet, I couldn't shake the feeling that Kadie would die giving birth to this child. I did not know why. It was simply a feeling I had. Sometimes, my feelings were accurate. Other time, they were not. I thought I would die in that castle saving Kadie, and I had not. Even so, I could not shake it. And although I wanted a child very much—more than I had ever thought—it was not worth the cost of my little Witch's life.

I let out a breath and closed my eyes. I continued to pray in my head. I did not mean to take anything away from this joyous moment, but prayer was important. It hadn't been before, but it was now.

As an Angel, the ability to reproduce was a foreign concept. A human thing. Something I had never acknowledged I was envious of.

But now…now I would know what being a parent was like. I would know what it's like to have something so precious, so fragile, that would bring me to my knees. My entire life was altered. My entire goal shifted to protection. I could not help but yearn for this experience.

"I can see the head," Tabitha announced.

From where I stood, I could only see Tabitha's shoulders hunched over the widespread sheet between Kadie's legs. However, I felt as though my heart had wings. This was a good sign. Granted, I had never heard of such a fast delivery. I refused to let myself get swept away in the negative possibilities of what this could possibly entail, what it might mean for Kadie, for our child. I would just have to remain steadfast in my faith that this was all meant to be. That this was a work of God, no matter how strange, and that this would work out in a positive light.

"Bear down a bit more," she continued. "Breathe, Kadie. Good girl. You're doing great."

Tabitha was saying all the right things and I didn't know what else to do. I let out a breath, my grip on Kadie tightening. When I realized my fingertips were digging into her skin – something she didn't even notice because of the pain she was currently enduring – I loosened my grip. I hope I didn't leave any bruises on her. I did not like to feel such nervousness but it could not be helped.

I pressed my lips to Kadie's feverish forehead and sent up a bargaining prayer to the Almighty.

I'll do another thousand years of penance, anything you want. Just please, don't take either of them from me.

I wanted a simple kiss to be enough. I wanted to convey my pride at her strength and her endurance, I wanted to be able to say all the right things to ensure that she knew how much I admired her for her conviction. Instead, I hoped my touch was enough to do that.

"Argh!" Kadie collapsed back against the pillows, spent. Sweat licked her forehead and her eyes were barely open. Her face was red from the amount of effort it took to push a living human out of her body. If anything, it looked like she was a marshmallow with no bones, her limbs limp. I looked around for a wash cloth to dab her sweat with, to cool her down, when a thin cry stopped me.

I turned around and there he was. My heart stopped beating. For the moment, there was nothing else that existed save for me and my son. I did not think this would be me. I did not think it was even possible for me to possess a child bearing my likeness, who could possibly inherit my legacy. And yet, here he was, real and solid and breathing. Glisteningly perfect. Covered in smears of blood and still connected to his mother. His little cries were like songs singing directly to my soul. I longed to reach out, to take him in my arms, but I faltered. I could stare down demons without a problem, but for some strange reason, looking at my son, holding such a fragile creature, scared me more than I ever thought was possible.

Tabitha snipped, then tied the cord off and wrapped him up in a towel she must have grabbed when Kadie initially went into labor. I must have been so preoccupied with Kadie that I did not notice.

"Take him," she said and turned back to Kadie.

Again, I hesitated. This was what I wanted. Every instinct inside of me wanted to reach out and take him in my arms and hold him tightly against my skin. But I was scared I might unknowingly harm him in some way. I did not know if I was going to be good at being a father. A warrior, I was certain of.

This?

I did not know. And I did not want to ruin my son in my ignorance.

"Oh, for goodness' sake," Tabitha snipped. "Take your son, Gabriel. You will not harm him. I must attend to Kadie."

I put out my arms, knowing Tabitha was right, and suddenly my child was here.

He was perfect. Human in appearance, I couldn't see any signs of his paranormal origins. A good thing. He was surprisingly warm and fit perfectly in the crook of my elbows. I felt stilted for a moment as I got used to his weight – so light, almost like he wasn't there. I wanted to hold him tight but I was afraid I might crush him.

He stared up at me with big, blue eyes, curious as to who I was. I did not see fear in his eyes, though. He was trying to figure out just who I was and what that meant for him. My lips quirked up at the sight. My son, an observer already.

"Come on, Kadie." Tabitha gently attempted coaxing Kadie out of her exhaustion. "Open your eyes. Meet your son." I could hear the worry in her tone. My heart skipped and I turned to look at my little, brave, strong Witch. I could see the effort there, attempting to open her eyes so she could do just that. I wanted to help in any way I could. I stepped closer to her and held up our son to his mother.

Kadie's face was an ashen white and her eyes were closed. Somehow her belly was now as flat as it had been a month ago. I knew that such a thing should not have been possible. Perhaps when it came to Angels, this was normal. But I did not know if it affected humans the same way, or if there was more of a risk. I did not like to think of Kadie risking everything for me so we could have a son together. As much as I was happy and joyous at the reality of the situation, looking at Kadie reminded me that we were not out of danger quite yet.

Worry curled around my heart like an icy hand. "What's wrong with her, Tabitha?" I dared to ask.

"I don't know," she answered, then began chanting in a language I did not understand. I brought my son closer to my chest, trying to protect him. From what, I was not sure. I just did I trusted Tabitha but I did not want him harmed or frightened even inadvertently. White light filtered from Tabitha's fingers and threaded into a glow around Kadie. In that moment, Kadie looked almost angelic, as though a holy white light weaved around her frame and bathed her in light.

"What *are* you?" I asked before I could stop myself, not blinking so I didn't miss a moment of the magic being woven.

"I am like your son," Tabitha said, her eyes focused on Tabitha. "My mother was half-human. She leaned forward and pressed her forehead to Kadie's.

My son began to cry and I held him tightly to my chest. I didn't want him to see this. I was not certain I wanted to see this.

I backed away from where Kadie was fading before my very eyes.

"What are you doing to her?" I demanded to know. I didn't know how to handle a crying baby. However, I began to bounce my knees and rock my arms slowly back and forth. I did not know if this was working, but it was something.

Tabitha eventually stopped chanting and stepped back. Her shoulders slumped, her face strained with an exhaustion I did not understand. I rocked our babe to soothe him, my heart heavy. I held my breath and waited. I was not sure what I was waiting for but I hoped to see some kind of life flicker in Kadie, perhaps a sign that revealed she was okay.

Tabitha turned to me. "You'll need to find a woman to feed him, Gabriel," she said. "Kadie's in a trance of some sort. A coma for humans."

"But...why?" I didn't understand any of this. "Will she be all right?"

"I don't know, exactly. I recognized a poison in her blood as soon as you brought her back here." Tabitha turned and began to rinse her hands in a bowl of water. Again, I had not even noticed it before. Trickles of water fell to the floor before she took a clean towel and dried off her hands. "I think that's what they injected into her. Their plan would have been to kill you, and then she would have slowly died also. And perhaps they would have taken your son? I really don't know. But the baby came early, thankfully, before the poison could take full effect." She paused to stare over at Kadie with wonder in her eyes. "And she is far more powerful than they realize."

"And now?" I asked.

"Now?"

"You said it was a good thing the baby came early," I said, shifting my weight as I continued to rock my son back and forth. "He came out before the poison could affect him. But Kadie? Has it started affecting her."

"I believe so," Tabitha said, her voice low.

I swallowed hard and steeled myself against the pain creeping in. "Will she wake up?" My voice cracked and I looked away. I did not like revealing my vulnerability, my worry, but it could not be helped. The thought of Kadie in a limbo without having met our son, the thought of her not waking up at all, was enough to still my soul.

"I've done everything I can," Tabitha said. The fact that she did not sound certain left me wanting. I looked down at my son, whose crying turned into a light gurgle. It was a brief break in my worry for his mother. A contradiction that was difficult to maneuver around. Going from joy to despair so quickly was not something I was particularly used to. Since it directly involved me and my emotions, it was worse than I could have imagined. "I gave her a potion when she arrived, and sugar to stabilize her. I've linked what magic I have with hers, so she has a grounding to come back to. But I don't know, Gabriel. She is the first of her kind that I've ever met. My own mother didn't survive my birth."

I clenched my teeth together. So giving birth to our son was enough to possibly kill her? How was I to know this? If I had known…

I do not know if I would have done anything differently. I could not regret my son. And yet, I wished that there was a different way for this to have happened. I did not like the feeling that I could not be truly happy. I had to let one thing go in order to possess the other. The thought of losing either Kadie or my son at this point was akin to losing a limb. Worse, even, because I could still fight without an arm or a leg.

How was I to fight without Kadie? Without our son?

His crying brought me out of my thoughts and reminded me I had a duty to him. I nodded to my agent. Tabitha had never steered me wrong before and I needed to trust her now. I knew she would do whatever she could for Kadie. I also knew there was nothing I could do in this moment for her. As such, I needed to step back. I needed to give myself a chance to have faith.

And what has He done for you and your family as of late? A bitter voice in my head pointed out. *Nearly killed the both of you? Gotten Kadie tortured. In a coma.*

Yes, I responded. *But Kadie is still alive. And that is important. If she is alive, there is always hope.*

The babe needed to be fed, and although there was always human means of feeding him- from a tin. But I was sure I could find a woman who would help me feed him naturally.

A Target I'd saved last year from the Demons had gotten pregnant with her husband soon after that. I'd go to her first. I did not like to put pressure on those I had saved because I did not want them thinking that saving them was part of any system of reciprocity. I saved them because I was instructed to, because they deserved to be saved, not because I expected anything from them. However, I did not know where else to start. If she could not, perhaps she could lead me in the right direction.

"I'll take him to be fed," I told Tabitha. "Will you stay with Kadie?"

"Of course." She gave me one of her curt, no-nonsense nods. "I can't leave her now. I'll watch over her until she regains consciousness… or she doesn't." A beat. "I do not want to worry you, Gabriel. You have already been through so much. But I will never lie to you. I will always keep you abreast of what is going on, whether you want to hear them or not."

I nodded at the woman who was fighting for my Kadie, the gratitude in my heart impossible to express. She was right, of course. As much as Tabitha knew, she was not God. She did not know what was going to happen. But I was grateful that she was here. She never lost her head to emotion, unlike me. I did not know if I would have handled things as well if Tabitha was not here. Actually, I did know. And it was not good. With a last lingering look at my beautiful, powerful and woman on the bed, I flew away.

My heart ached like it too had battled for its life today. It had. A Demon battle. The birth of a baby who shouldn't have been born, not because his existence was wrong but once thought impossible. Now, to know that Tabitha herself was like my son, to know that such things did happen, I needed to know how to fix this. How to make it right, so Kadie was not at risk and my son was always safe.

But, now, I needed to feed him. I could not think about our future without thinking about taking that first step towards caring for him.

I held the whimpering baby tightly against my chest and took my son to a home just outside Manhattan. I knocked on the door of a brownstone building and Jasmine opened it for me. She was a Target I had saved last year, spending months coaxing her from the brink of suicide to a stable place.

"Gabriel!" she exclaimed, her blue eyes light up at seeing me as she juggled a female child on her hip. Her eyes fell on my child nestled in my arms and her eyes picked back up to look in mine. "And who is this baby, Gabriel? He's beautiful."

"I need your help," I said. I wanted to thank her, to discuss the perplexities of child-rearing, but this was no social visit. "Are you feeding still?"

I opened my arms to indicate my barely born son, wiggling and mewling like a kitten. Jasmine gasped and nodded, drawing me inside her home. I knew I looked a mess. Still shirtless, covered in blood, but Jasmine didn't falter.

She'd seen me in similar states during the many battles I'd had with the Demons hunting her.

She put her daughter down in a crib of some sort and took my child from me. "Whose baby is this?" she asked as she sat down on her sofa, opened her blouse and put him to her breast. It seemed so easy for her to do, so natural and simple. I was awed by this. I thought it would be more complex. I thought she might resist giving away natural nutrients in her body specifically made for her daughter in order to give them to my babe. But she did not question me. I was grateful for that. I was not sure I could bring myself to explain anything further than what I already had.

Instead, I focused on my child at her breast, relief flooding my body, knowing he would not be hungry any longer – at least right now. His dark-haired head bobbed around for a moment before settling to feed with noisy hunger. My lips cracked upwards on their own and I felt tears prickle my eyes. This day had been too long and I was hit with a plague of exhaustion to the point where I could not keep a handle of my emotions, it would seem.

"Gabriel?" Jasmine's voice shook my out of my thoughts. "The baby? Whose is it?"

I cleared my throat, my hands on my knees. "Mine," I said. "His mother is in a coma, and I didn't know what else to do…" A sob broke through my throat and I closed my eyes, trying to pull myself together.

"Oh, Gabriel…"

I shook my head to stop her from approaching me, which I knew she would. And focused on what needed to be done. My son needed me. I could break down later. "I… ah knew he needed to be fed, and you were the first person I thought of who could help me."

I stood from the couch and began to pace the living room, full of restless energy. For the first time, I let the tendrils of anger lift up and grow inside my gut. I was angry that it was not Kadie feeding our son. I was grateful for Jasmine, I was, but this should have been his mother getting to bond with our babe, and not a near-stranger. Kadie should be awake. She should not have had to endure the pain she had because of me. I was glad she was strong, but that did not make her okay.

"I owe you my life, Gabriel," Jasmine said, her voice gentle. I stopped pacing so I could look at her but her eyes were on the child. "If you need someone to look after him until she wakes up, I can do it. You wouldn't have to worry."

"I don't want to leave him here, Jasmine. But I think it may be the only way, until Kadie wakes up." My heart squeezed at the mere mention of leaving my precious child behind, but I had a world to save, and a woman to avenge.

"It's fine, Gabriel. Truly." Jasmine smiled down at my son and I ran through a final check list on whether this was the right decision.

Jasmine was a truly beautiful soul, and I trusted her with my son. But…

"What about your husband?" I understood the human tendency to be possessive over certain circumstances. If it were my child, I would prioritize my child above all else. But I hoped that regardless of any Darwinian tendencies, compassion still won out, even if I was not as privy to it as others.

It did not help I'd only met him once and to say he was shocked by my presence, would be an understatement.

"Don't worry about Charles." She looked down at my babe with a gentle smile, ruffling his hair as he continued to suckle her breast, "Plus I've got everything the baby needs here. Clothes, diapers, milk. I will take good care of him, Gabriel. You can trust me."

I ran a hand through my hair. I hadn't even thought about any of that. It was such a different feeling, being human. Thinking as though I actually was one. Diapers were not something at the fore-thought of my mind. Safety was. Kadie was. Nourishment and sustenance, certainly. But something as innocuous as diapers was not something that I had even thought of.

I wish Kadie were here. She would have thought of diapers and blankets and clothes and whatever else babies required. She would teach me the things I needed to know about raising a child. I would teach her about his angelic legacy. We would be partners.

But I did not have her just yet.

Which was why I was here.

"If you could…just for a few days." I stood from the couch, my eyes on my child. He would be safe here with her, I reminded myself. And his safety was now the most important thing in my life.

Jasmine nodded and looked down on the child at her breast once again. The look on her face was something I could only describe as maternal. A prickle of anger at Demons, at Hell, at everything that was wrong with this, I took in a deep breath and released it. This was not Jasmine's fault. I was lucky to have her.

"What's his name, Gabriel?" Her voice broke through my thoughts and I shifted my eyes once again to Jasmine.

"We… haven't decided yet." And I wouldn't decided until his

beautiful mother was awake long enough to choose something with me.

If I could trust that my child remained safe, I could leave him to hunt down those responsible for kidnapping Kadie. And I planned to. If Jasmine didn't help me, then I couldn't do my job. I couldn't protect Kadie. I couldn't protect my child.

A strange tingle moved up my spine and I sat down on the couch once again next to my old Target. My knees bounced up and down, my hands dangling between my knees. I did not like to think about what would happen if I could not complete my task.

"I must get back to her," I told Jasmine. I did not like waiting. I did not like leaving my child. But I knew I had no other option. If I wanted to ensure his safety, Kadie's safety, I needed to extradite the Demons and make sure earth was safe once again. "I will return tonight. Are you sure you can keep him safe, Jasmine?"

I didn't want to appear ungrateful for her help, but I now had something much more precious to lose than my place in Heaven. If Jasmine did not want the responsibility, I would not hold it against her. I would understand. I did not want her to place herself at risk – especially since she had her own child and husband to care for – unless she knew she could handle it.

"Yes." There was absolute certainty in her voice. "And I will call for you if I see anything out of the ordinary."

She'd gone through Hell herself, fighting off the torture of the Demons chasing her last year, and she knew every trick in their repertoire.

"All right. Thank you." I stood up and turned to leave, but the invisible strings of love tugged me back. I dropped my head and pressed a kiss to my child's soft hair. "I will be back, my son."

I gave Jasmine a smile and locked the front door behind me.

My destiny had changed in one night.

I no longer cared if I ever found my way back to Heaven. I wanted Kadie alive and well, and my son safe.

The hunt had changed and so had I.

ASCENDING ANGEL

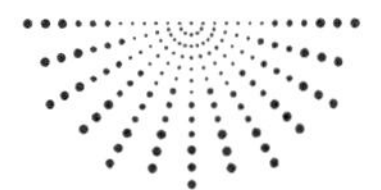

CHAPTER ONE

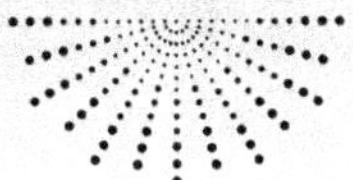

My instincts screamed with the scent of death and I curled my fingers into tight fists.

My wings twitched, wanting to shoot out and take flight.

Everything inside me wanted to hunt the Demons who caused my love, the mother of my newborn child, to be placed into a coma in order to save her life.

I wanted to shred the skin of those monsters who forced me to leave my newborn son with an old Target of mine who had milk in her breasts to nourish him.

I stepped out the front door into the cool, late afternoon. For a moment I swayed on the spot, standing on the doorstep of Jasmine's brownstone.

Fear, an unknown emotion to me up until today, shivered along my spine like ice. Cold, strong and unwanted.

I released a shaky breath. I'd just made the biggest decision of my life. Leaving behind someone who was arguably the most important thing to me was like ripping off my sword arm. Trusting another to guard him as I would was near-impossible, but Jasmine was the closest person I could think of who would do just that. *My son…* I still couldn't wrap my head around the very concept of him.

This was not supposed to happen – a half-human, half-angel progeny. But apparently, this was not the first time this had occurred. I just did not think it would happen with me. I still had a penance to pay for falling from Heaven, and while I did not know when that penance would be repaid, I had been unwavering when it came to my duty. Saving humans Demons wanted to destroy was easy and satisfying, but I had longed for home.

Until Kadie.

"They can all get fucked. I have a new home now."

A light breeze ruffled my hair. It was difficult for me to get cold because of my angelic tendencies but my skin pinched all the same.

Kadie was different in every way. She was a Witch. She was genuine and beautiful and kind. She was the woman I loved and the mother of my child. She was the person I intended to save, even though I had technically already fulfilled my duty in regards to her.

My duty was only to her, to my son. Everything else fell to the wayside.

I had two options: I could stay and protect my child, in Jasmine's home while she tended to him. But that would not bring his mother back to me, nor to him. And if she died because of this poison infesting her body – where her only chance of survival was to place her in a coma - how would I explain it to my child in the years to come? How could I look him in the eye and tell him I had done absolutely everything to save her? What kind of father – what kind of man – would I be?

I needed to do everything in my power to get his mother back— for him, and for me. And to do that I must solve the puzzle before me. Why was Kadie so important to the Demons?

I stretched to my full height beneath my shield of invisibility and extended my blackened wings. They screamed in relief. I glanced at the singed ends, the battle I had fought – was it only a day or two ago? – flashing in my mind. Demonfire was deadly to an angel. I could heal myself against almost anything, but I could not regrow my wings if they were burned off with Demonfire. However, they still worked and I intended to use them to the best of my ability. But first, I needed clothes and a plan.

Kadie's home was where I needed go. A place I could be alone to think without fear of being attacked. Despite my invisibility, the Demons were able to track me if they needed to. I needed some time to slow down and wrap my head around everything that had happened. Everything had happened so incredibly fast and my brain was struggling to catch up with my new reality. As much as I wanted to rush in and fight, I knew that was not the most intelligent decision. Not if I was going to do this the right way.

I leaned forward, cleared Jasmine's stoop, flapped my wings and catapulted myself into the sky. I flew higher and higher, until the clouds were at my elbows and Earth was far beneath me.

I glanced up at the never-ending expanse of blue above me. I hadn't ever stopped to ask "why." I'd been taught it wasn't my place to question my fate, nor the overall "plan." But here I was, still a Fallen Angel, and a new father to a son who Tabitha, my Angel Agent, said could be the beginning of a race of super-soldiers.

Why was the question I should be asking. Why had this happened? Why me? Why Kadie? Why?

How had Kadie and I achieved such a thing? And why was I still an Angel if I was able to father a child? Shouldn't I be demoted to a human, at the very least? Taking away my immortality seemed like the perfect punishment.

Although, if I could grow old and die after a life spent with Kadie, it wouldn't be a punishment at all. Quite the opposite, in fact. I'd finally found someone to exist for, to love. And because of that love, everything had changed.

I'd changed. I wasn't trying to get back into Heaven anymore. I wanted to stay on Earth, stay with the mortals I'd protected for so long.

But there was so much more to think about than my impending mortality.

Did Hell's Demons want my unborn child?

I wasn't entirely sure if my son was who they were after, or if it was Kadie, or if was me. They had been trying to get their revenge on me for a while, and I thought that attacking Kadie was their way of doing that.

But what of my son. Certainly, they knew he existed. But did they want him as well?

No answers came to me.

In desperation I closed my eyes, extended out my arms and thought of my lover, the goddess *Teramea*. The reason I'd been thrown out of Heaven. The woman I'd loved for millennia.

The air surrounded me and my wings flexed out, stretching as best as they could. I flew as high as I could go and there was a whisper in my ear. The faintest of words.

Go now, Gabriel. Quickly.

My eyes snapped open and I dove back to Earth. I wasn't going to ignore Tabitha's warning.

I rode the currents of air over the city and landed with a loud thump on the concrete outside Kadie's house.

It was moments before sundown. I glanced to my left, then to my right.

A heated tingle of warning stroked my spine. The Hell Demons were rising. I would soon need to hunt them down, killing them before they reached their Target.

I'd never tried to capture a Demon before, nor question them. My goal had always been to exterminate them on sight, their very existence on this plain a crime. But I needed information from them now, and that would require a different dance.

I sneered as I shifted my weight, turning my eyes once again to Kadie's purple door. I did not like admitting that I needed them at all. I did not like depending on Demons to assist me with anything, let alone something of grave importance. I would not put it past them to use tricks and deceit in order to attempt to keep me from reaching my goal while interrogating them.

If it was even possible to interrogate them, because if it was, I'd be willing to do anything to find out some answers.

I walked up to Kadie's door and adjusted my height to suit her small house.

Unbidden, a small smile rose to my lips as my gorgeous Witch filled my mind. Her red hair spread over her pillow as she cuddled me and laughed with happiness. As though she had nothing to worry about.

We'd been blessed with beautiful time together, although too short. I prayed to the Gods above that we'd have more, especially now with the birth of our son.

Coldness crept inside my gut once again, and I pushed it away. Kadie was not gone, nor was she dead. I needed to stop mourning her life. I needed to stop thinking we would never get more time or that she would never get time with our son.

I scooped up the potted plant by her front door and pulled the spare key from its hiding place beneath the bottom soil.

I needed clothes and somewhere to think, and this was the place to do it.

I opened the door, not bothering to let go of my invisibility until I was inside, with the door shut and locked securely behind me. There was a calming affect this place had on me. I felt home here. However, there was an obvious emptiness that permeated through it due to the fact that Kadie was not here.

Perhaps I would feel better if I knew how she was.

Was Kadie still unconscious? I sent out a message to my Angel Agent.

How's my little Witch doing, Tabitha?

An exhausted laugh sounded in my head.

Me? Or Kadie?

I stumbled for a moment. I needed to remember that Tabitha was part Witch too. And she wasn't doing well either, since helping me with Kadie. Apparently, magic used a lot of energy and that energy could be both depleted or restored. Using too much in a short span of time made it difficult to recover for witches. They needed peace in order to build the magic back up. Unfortunately, we did not have that sort of time.

Both of you, of course.

Kadie's still alive, although her energy is low. I have her tethered to me, so I won't be able to help you much with your search. She is consuming a lot of my power.

I could hear the exhaustion in her voice, though she tried to hide it. I could not help but feel a swell of gratefulness for having her in my life. I did not know how I would be able to do this without her.

Thank you, Tabitha. I don't know how to tell you how grateful I am for what you're doing.

I walked to the couch and finally let myself drop into it. A heavy sigh escaped my mouth. My entire body crumbled like a sturdy mountain during a trembling earthquake. I did not realize just how exhausted I had become during this process and it felt good to just sit for a moment. Now that I knew Kadie was okay, I was able to do just that.

For just a moment.

I'm doing this for all of us, Gabriel. Kadie is more important than we know, I'm sure of it. The Demons want her desperately, and there has to be a reason for it. If we win this hand, it may turn the tide for Heaven.

And that was all I'd ever wanted. My side to win. The good team. Those who fought for the best of humanity on Earth. Not the worst.

Do we know why *they want her?* Perhaps now was not the best time to inquire about such a thing, but I could not help but question it. If I was able to figure out why Kadie was so important, it might make it easier to protect her or it might reveal a beneficial strategy on how to defeat the Demons. Any new information I could get, I would take.

Unfortunately, no. We just know they want her. And if they want her this much, something must be special about her, more so than we could have predicted.

I nodded my head and then remembered that she could not see me.

Please let me know if there is anything I can do from here.

There was a brief pause, but something told me that Tabitha was not finished.

Is your son safe?

The mention of my son caused me to pick my head up. I let out a breath. I wish I could hold him now. How something so fragile could be so powerful. I was contented to know he was in good hands, however, and a flicker of a smile lit up my face.

Yes. Jasmine has him.

That's good. There was an approving tone in Tabitha's voice. It reassured me that I had made the right decision leaving him with her, even though it was the most difficult thing for me to do. More so than fighting Demons. More so than falling from Heaven. ***Now, don't worry about us. You need to focus on hunting down those responsible for this, and finding an antidote to the poison, if you can.***

I blinked. How could I have so easily forgotten? I needed to find an antidote to the poison coursing through Kadie's body. I dropped my head into my hands, trying not to stress too much about all I needed to do. I had done more. I had fought more.

But now, I had so much more to lose than ever before.

Yes. I will. Thank you, Tabitha.

I let go of the connection to my Agent, her dimmed energy filtering through our connection and leaving me cold and lonely. I leaned back against the couch and stared up at the ceiling, as though there might be some chance I would find my answers up there, written in the cracks.

I'd gotten used to a solitary existence, but never felt this clueless or helpless. I couldn't look after my son properly, only Jasmine could do that. I couldn't keep Kadie alive, unlike Tabitha. What good was I for then? Besides endangering the few that I loved?

Today marked the day I learned that I could rely on others, and trust them to do the right thing by me and my loved ones. Trust was not something I easily acquired. Trust had done more harm than good for me. I stopped trusting people long ago.

And Kadie changed everything, as she was apt to do.

I pushed up onto my feet and headed down the hallway. I ignored pictures of Kadie on the wall, my heart squeezing painfully together.

I stepped into Kadie's bathroom and flicked on the water in the shower. My clothes were little better than rags after the fight, and I was covered with the blood of my woman and child.

My family.

I shook my head as I shrugged out of my tattered garments. I could only imagine what Jasmine thought when she saw me in front of her home, as though I was touched by Hell itself. I was glad Kadie hadn't seen me. I was glad my child couldn't register what my appearance truly meant. Angels didn't have families. We had our Gods. We had our legions of warriors. And the Fallen had Angel Agents, to guide them on their path back to righteousness. We had friends, sort of… But never a real blood and flesh family.

What was I now? Part human?

I stood beneath the spray of hot, clean water and washed away the decay of the day. The dirt of the Earth, the blood of the battle. One unlike any war I had ever fought.

I did not feel any different. If I had been reduced to part human, it did not register on my person. However, I could not deny there was that possibility. I was not quite sure what to male of that fact. I don't think I could wrap my head around that possibility if I tried.

I tilted my head back and let my body relax, willing my mind to re-construct the puzzle before me. I did not want to think of myself or my place in this. Rather, I wanted to focus on what actually mattered: Kadie. My son. What all of this meant.

Kadie was a powerful, but untrained Witch. The Hell Demons had originally wanted to torture her to the point that she'd commit suicide, or so I'd believed when I'd first been put on her protection duty.

But maybe I'd been wrong. Perhaps it had been their plan all along to capture her. After all, they'd shown themselves in plain sight of other humans, and openly attacked her. That was something they never did, no matter who they were going after. Even when Kadie fought back, they kept coming. They were not perturbed by her power. If anything, it seemed to make their desire for her intensify. They were willing to take unnecessary risks to ensure she fell in with them.

But why? That, I did not know.

Was I also part of the plan? Our child too, perhaps?

Probably not. They'd been following Kadie long before I'd begun protecting her, so how could they know that I'd be assigned to her? That couldn't. Demons were clever at times, but they were not smart. They could not reason outside their emotion. There was no way they could have predicted that I'd impregnate her. If they'd foreseen that, then the Demons of Hell had more power than we gave them credit for.

I did not believe it, and I don't think anything could convince me otherwise unless God Himself told me such a thing.

The child, *my* child, would have been a bonus for them for certain, but he was not the main reason for kidnapping her, I was sure of it. I did not even know what he was capable of, or what his existence meant for Angels and Demons and humans. He was important, certainly, and now that the Demons were aware that he existed, there was a good chance that they would go after him. But to say he was the reason for their attack on Kadie was not something I believed.

Kadie was the true key, and I had to work out why the Demons wanted her so badly.

The steam softened my facial muscles and, for a moment, I let my head hang and basked in the hot water running down my body.

I picked up Kadie's flowery smelling homemade soap and scrubbed at my body until my skin ached, then turned the water off.

Her towels smelled like Kadie. That sweet, slightly earthy scent that always reminded me of how real and genuine she was. How close to nature she was. How she marvelled at the earth the way I seemed to marvel about her.

I groaned aloud in the small bathroom.

This is crap.

My eyes snapped open. I had to pull myself together. I was no use to anyone when I was weakened with sentiment. As much as I loved Kadie, I could not allow her to be a hindrance. She already caused my heart to sag heavily, like an anchor deep in the sea. I could not allow her to do the same for my rationale.

I pushed aside any struggling emotions with ruthless efficiency and dried myself quickly. It wouldn't serve Kadie for me to fall apart now. Nor my son.

Or the Gods for whom I'd always fought.

CHAPTER TWO

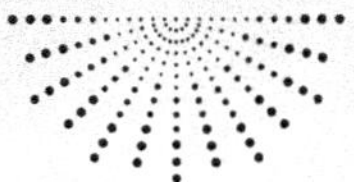

I needed to re-trace my steps. Perhaps go back to the castle where they'd held her?

I shifted my weight, hands on my hips. I was well-aware how naked I was, standing so openly in her home, so vulnerable, but somehow, this vulnerability gave me strength. Focus. Perception.

The castle was a good starting off point. I could see if the Demons left any sort of evidence behind. Demons weren't exactly careless, but they were arrogant enough to assume others wouldn't recognize importance when they were confronted with it. I hoped to take advantage of that, at least.

Yes. That was the plan.

If I was lucky, I would find a way to the truth, and if that meant following those Demons into a dimension not fit for my kind, then so be it. I'd been burned by them before. I would be able to handle whatever they wanted to throw at me. I had something to fight for, and they didn't quite know just what that meant.

I strode into Kadie's purple-painted bedroom and opened her closet.

There, hanging next to all her bohemian style long skirts were a fresh pair of jeans and long sleeved shirts for me. Why she'd bought me clothes when I told her I didn't need them, I hadn't understood at the time. I had been forthcoming with her during our short time together. I always told her that I would have to move on to another Target, as that was my duty, and as much as I loved her, I could not neglect my duty. However, my stubborn little Witch did not seem to care for what I said and insisted she buy me clothes anyway – just in case. Now I was intensely grateful for her kind gesture. It was obvious she wanted me to be a part of her life, and the feeling was entirely mutual. Part of me was looking forward to telling her she was right, even if it would bruise my pride.

I tugged the clothes off their hangers too hard. They twanged from the pole to the floor and I left them there, not wanting to bend over and disturb another thing. If she ever returned home and I wasn't there, I hoped she would understand that I used the clothes she had for me. The disturbance was my little way of showing her that we were still connected, even if we weren't with each other physically.

My mind was strangely shut down and I realized that I didn't want to analyze what I'd lost or remind myself that there was a good chance this might not end well for us. Our son was cared for and that was important, but I could not say the same about Kadie and myself.

As I pulled on my shirt, I began to reflect on my time with Kadie. For a few short weeks I'd had a very normal existence. A human life. It was strange and marvellous. I could not put it into other words. My mind did not know the correct words to use in order to describe it.

Kadie had made me feel good, just for being me. There was nothing she expected of me in return. She did not demand information about my past, but I was compelled enough to give it to her anyway. And when I did, she did not judge me like my fellow angels, like God Himself. I wasn't used to that genuine acceptance for who I was – not who she wanted me to be - and I knew that I could become very comfortable with her loving me. It made me think about myself in a totally different way. A way that was very "un-angel" like, more human-like.

I'd adored her for the peace she'd given me. I was meant to bring people peace. Not the other way around. It was just another way Kadie was so special.

I reached for the light switch, and flicked it on so I could see in the room. Night had fallen, once again. The last thing I wanted to do was go back to the castle ruins now. But still, I pulled my jeans up my thighs, did up my shirt buttons and tugged on my ancient black boots. At least these mundane tasks gave me a reason to focus on something else. I did not like to think about it, and yet, it was an inner war I could not win. Because I had to think of Kadie. She was everywhere. Thinking about her made me feel good, and I wanted to hold onto that feeling for as long as I could. It was the perfect motivation to fight for her – or die trying.

I stood when I was ready, steeling my thoughts not on my lover, but on my new destination.

The Demons had an advantage at the castle that I'd never seen anywhere else. There was something strange about the air, as though the very atmosphere was impregnated with evil. It was probably why they were so arrogant as to let me walk through the doors and to Kadie directly. My first time there, I barely encountered any opposition until I found Kadie. Their arrogance would be their downfall. It would lead me to a weakness I could penetrate.

It had to.

When I'd rescued Kadie, the Demons had seemed supercharged. Able to break the rules on where and how they could exist. It had been hard enough getting Kadie out of there during the day. I couldn't even imagine doing it at night.

My eyes flickered to the window. Darkness settled around New York. I knew I had no other choice but to leave now, to figure this out now. I could not tarry any longer. I could not waste time.

I stepped out the front door once again, carefully locking it behind me. No paranormal creature could step foot in Kadie's house uninvited. Somehow, her home was protected as long as she stayed inside it – at least from the paranormal. However, she'd told Tabitha and I that she'd been kidnapped by human men, so there were enemies everywhere now and they had no problem getting into her home despite the protection.

I jumped down the front steps and flexed the muscles in my chest and back. Better than before. That God-awful tonic Tabitha had forced me to drink had done its job. It was more than I could hope for, after my last encounter with the Demons.

There were Demons nearby. And despite the fact I had no current Target to protect, I had another mission. I was more determined to solve this than anything else I had ever done. With the Demons near, perhaps I would be able to reach my goal more quickly than I anticipated. These Hell creatures would either tell me what was going on or die an extremely painful death. I would make sure they suffered a particular type of pain before they perished. In fact, I yearned for the opportunity.

I stepped out onto the grey pavement, and slipped into invisibility. I cracked my knuckles, tilting my head to see if I could pick up a scent, a hint, of where they might be lingering. There was a loud gasp to my left as a human witnessed my disappearing trick, but I didn't stop to worry about that now. Humans had the uncanny talent to rationalize supernatural forces, even when they had come to witness them directly. The majority of the time, they did not believe their own eyes because they had become so indoctrinated by science regarding what was possible and what was not.

The human would chalk it up to his eyes playing tricks on him, I was certain. His conscious brain wouldn't believe in the fantastical. So few did. It was something I did not take advantage of if I could help it, but under current circumstances, I appreciated it.

I spread my black wings wide and opened my senses to the evil lurking nearby. It took a moment. Then, another. They were being careful. Not careful enough. Despite the fact that they were trying to mask themselves from me and my reach, they failed.

I sensed them. In the block behind Kadie's house.

Why?

I shook my head. There was no time to think about that now. I needed to act, not to think.

My back muscles contracted hard as I flapped my damaged

wings and took to the sky above the old stone buildings of the Bronx, searching out the fiery Demons I'd come to truly hate.

I hadn't thought Angels *could* hate, until I'd come face-to-face with those aiming to destroy the mother of my child. That was the moment I'd learned what emotions I was truly capable of. To be honest, these emotions were new and unsettling. I did not like to be ruled by something so intangible. However, I was starting to get acquainted with them. I did not mind their presence because they bonded me to Kadie in a way I did not think was possible for someone like me.

There was a flicker of orange flame in the backyard of a small house below me. A woman's agonized screams pierced my ears.

That's my cue.

I might have smirked if an innocent human's life wasn't in peril. I felt anticipation run up and down my spine. I curled my fingers into fists and pushed forward.

I descended on a gust of cold air like the vengeful Angel I was. I pulled my sword from my holster and landed in front of the cowering woman. Why they were attacking this woman, I wasn't sure. I didn't know if she was a tool used to draw me out or if they actually wanted her for some reason. I thought it was too coincidental that they were so close to Kadie's home.

They were still after her.

"Surrender or you will die." My voice boomed across the few feet between us. I waited to see if my words would have any effect on the two flaming Demons before me.

The black holes where their eyes should be didn't even flicker with change or recognition. I furrowed my brow. That was strange. I didn't know what I'd expected, but it wasn't nothingness. Where was the burning hatred? The anger and fear?

Where was the understanding of what and who I was? The recognition? I did not care one way or the other personally for my pride's sake. However, the fact that they seemed wholly indifferent to who and what I was was both unexpected and unnerving. I gripped my sword tighter and waited a beat.

They charged at me and I heaved a sigh. I should not have been thrown off. Of course, they would attack me. That was their sole goal for creation. Why had I thought I could speak to these things? It had been a moment of dumb hope, obviously. They were little more than wild animals. This was where my new human-like tendencies were more of a detriment than a benefit. Humans had this surprising tendency that they believed they had the power to ignite change on an individual basis, whether it was through relations or on a grander scope, such as politics or the environment. The reality was that change happened, but not because of humans. Because it was God's will. I used to find their beliefs amusing; now, I had nearly succumbed to the same thing.

I clenched my jaw. I would not allow that to happen again.

I spun in an arc, slicing at one Demon with my silver sword, then I ducked and swung at the other.

The Demons lost limbs to my blade, if that's what they were. Their hollow screams echoed in the small space as I continued to dance around them, chopping off parts of their red and yellow glowing bodies until there was nothing left but a pile of black ash on the grass before me. I felt a sense of satisfaction course through my body as I ripped each limb from their body.

I stood still finally, my heart beating too hard. Too fast. My head, a whirling mess of confusion. I turned towards the back of the fence and waited for the next wave of attacks. But nothing came.

It was still. There was a gentle breeze – a caress of the oncoming autumn season. New York was never still.

A woman squeaked and I twisted around to face the beautiful little house where the Demons' victim still cowered.

"Please don't kill me," the woman said, and once again I was shocked into speechlessness.

Wasn't I under my invisibility? I checked my energy, and yes, I still was.

How was this possible?

"You can see me?" I asked her, and slid my sword onto my back once again. Kadie seemed to be the only person who was able to see me like this. But I was wrong. There was more of her kind. I was not sure how I felt about that. Perhaps Kadie was not as special as I once assumed – at least when it came to what the Demons wanted.

She would always be special to me, however.

The woman nodded frantically, her eyes wide and fearful.

This was not good. Why wasn't my magic working?

Unless it wasn't this woman at all.

What if I truly was becoming human? What if I was losing touch of my angelic side and succumbing to this new role of being human?

"Don't be afraid of me," I told her. I needed her to be calm more than I needed to understand what was going on. I held out my hands, hoping to placate her rather than intimidate her. "My name is Gabriel. I came here to kill the Demons who were sent here to torture you. Now that my job is complete, I intend to leave. I will not harm you."

I would have liked to say I was there to protect her, but she wasn't my official Target.

"Demons?" she repeated, slowly rising to her feet. I leaned forward to offer her my hand but she pulled away quickly. I could see the hesitation in her eyes; she did not want to touch me at all, unsure if she could trust me. I could not blame her for that and I stepped back, not wanting to intimidate her further.

She was older than I'd first thought, perhaps forty-five or fifty years old. She trembled like an amber leaf in a fall breeze, but there was the same magic about her that I had sensed in Kadie. Now that I was not fighting Demons, now that I was not reveling in their deaths, my senses picked it up almost immediately.

Another Witch, perhaps?

I addressed her question. "Yes." I nodded once. "Warriors of Hell. They were here to frighten you."

"Not kill me?" she asked, wrapping her arms around her body. She looked down the empty street, blinking once, twice, as though she wished she could unsee what she just experienced.

"Ah… no. I don't think so."

Though, what did I know about the strange world this place had become? For centuries, I had believed the Demons I killed had a solitary mission, which was to torture people into committing suicide so they could take their souls. But these new attacks were completely different and didn't fit the original pattern. The first was Kadie. But this woman? Now, it was becoming a pattern, a strange one that I could not yet predict or rely on. It left me feeling unguarded and hesitant. I did not like it whatsoever.

"Has this happened before?" I asked her, shifting my weight and giving her my full attention.

She nodded. She was still trying to catch her breath, and refused to look at me. I wished she would trust me, if only a bit.

Damn… why wasn't someone in charge of protecting her?

It made no sense that she wouldn't be assigned a Guardian.

"I didn't get your name," I said. Maybe if I learned more about her, I would be able to figure out why she didn't have protection.

"M…Margaret." She twisted one of the silver rings on her index finger, which drew my attention down to her jewelery.

I recognized the sign of a Witch in one of the many bands adorning her hands.

"Margaret, do you practice Witchcraft?" I made sure to keep my voice neutral. I did not want her to think I judged her for her chosen spiritual path; I needed her to be comfortable with me to be honest.

Her gaze flew to mine and her eyes showed a depth of intelligence I hadn't expected.

"Why do you ask me that?" she demanded, her tone changed. Now stronger and more defiant. I almost smiled. She reminded me of Kadie in that moment. Fierceness must be a requirement for a Witch.

"Because I think someone is specifically hunting Witches in New York," I replied honestly, ignoring the pang in my heart at the reminder that Kadie was still incapacitated, "My last charge was taken and tortured, poisoned. And I'm trying to find out why."

"Poisoned? What do you mean?" she asked, taking a step closer to me. Her eyes were filled with worry. I tilted my head, curious if she knew more about what was going on than even I did. Considering she had been attacked, I would not be surprised.

Her eyes were bright and interested now, and her trembling seemed to have vanished.

I narrowed my eyes at the woman who now seemed to have been faking her previous terror. "What do you know about this?" I asked. Again, I tried to control my voice as best as I could. I did not want her to stop talking, but I could not help but feel she knew more about what was going on than she initially made me believe.

There was a path in front of me now that there wasn't before.

Kadie was obviously not the first Witch, and perhaps not the last, who had been pursued and conquered by this enemy.

The Demons had a new mission, and it had something to do with the Witches of New York.

CHAPTER THREE

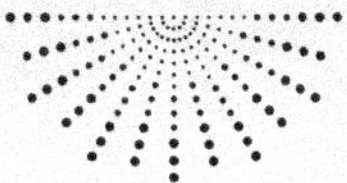

argaret crossed her arms over her chest, a strength in her stance that hadn't been here before. Had she been feigning her fear earlier to get my attention? I did not know. Surely not. At least, I hoped not. I did not like to think humans – even those with powers such as Witches – had the ability to render me so easily fooled.

"I know very little, Gabriel," she said, her voice soft-spoken but firm. There was no quiver in her voice, no indication of fear. "The question is, who are you? And what brought *you* here today?"

I took a breath and weighed my options. I ignored the flare of annoyance that sprung up when she questioned me about who I was and why I was here. We weren't supposed to divulge our identities to anyone except our Targets. And yet, her voice held a commanding tone that I didn't appreciate.

However… if I wanted to help Kadie, I could not let my pride dictate how I felt and how I acted. This was more than just about me. I huffed a sigh, my eyes drawn to the faded concrete beneath my feet. I was technically without a job. I didn't have a current Target, and my former Target, Kadie, was back on my agenda. And if I needed to protect a former Target by talking to someone who technically wasn't a Target, it was within my duty to do so.

At least, that was how I rationalized it.

I bit the bullet, so to speak, and prepared myself mentally to tell her the truth.

"No. Don't tell me. It doesn't matter," Margaret said, waving a hand at me. She shook her head and crossed her arms over her chest, looking down a nearby alleyway. I was surprised how quiet things were for New York, even at night. Usually, there were people bustling about, regardless of the time. "You killed those Demons for me, and I should trust you." She took a slow breath then looked me straight in the eye. "Shall we go inside?"

That was probably a good idea.

I nodded and she waved me towards the direction of her house. I was surprised to find it close to where Kadie lived and I couldn't help but wonder if Witches were innately drawn to each other or if they knew each other. Maybe there was some kind of connection between witches the same way there was between Angels. We walked down the block and she led me into her home. I noticed that her hands shook as she slid the key in lock before opening the sliding back door. "Please, come in and sit."

We walked into a small, cool room full of healing crystals and colorful lights. I immediately felt a strong energy in this room, one that soothed as it empowered. It made me feel like everything was going to be all right.

"A few months ago, Witches in the New York covens began to report strange happenings," Margaret began as I took a seat on the small couch. "Would you like some herbal tea, something to drink?" After I shook my head, she scooped up some of the crystals on her coffee table and began to gently shake them in her hand like they were dice. Instead of sitting, she continued to walk around her room. I wondered if the idle gestures were enough to soothe her nerves. Her hands were not shaking any longer. "Shortly after the reports started to come in, the disappearances started."

"Disappearances?" I asked. Margaret nodded once. "How many?"

"About twenty in total, that I know of." She stopped pacing and opened her hand, looking down at the crystals. "I've tried to keep track of any clue that might indicate where they are, who might have taken them, but I am only one Witch."

"That's a lot of women," I agreed.

How was this the first time I'd heard of such things happening? I wondered if Tabitha knew about this. Would she have told me if she did? Or was she required to keep quiet?

I chewed my bottom lip. I didn't want to think Tabitha would keep things for me. Then again, she was what my son was – part Angel, part Witch, and she had only told me about it within the last twenty-four hours even though we knew each other for centuries. Then again, was it my business what she was? Did I have a right to know?

I shook my head. I kept going back and forth. Part of me was angry for being kept in the dark. The other part understood why Witches kept things to themselves the way, as a Guardian, I was supposed to do the same thing.

Still.

I didn't like being left in the dark, especially when I had been assigned a Target who was more than just a regular Target. Now that I knew there were disappearances associated with what Kadie was, I couldn't help but wonder what else was being kept from me, what else I needed to know, what else I was allowed to know.

Twenty women, powerful Witches? All disappearing at once and I hadn't been told to protect any of them?

"Were they all Elders of your coven?" I asked, assuming the abducted Witches would need to be quite powerful for the Demons to want them. I did not know much about Witches, but I knew Elders were the most experienced, the ones who had the most power and knew how to use their power with expertise.

"No," she said and shook her head. She looked up from the crystals and began to shake them in her hand again. "That was the weird thing. They were often strangers to us, or recently joined. New Witches, with very little cultivated powers. It took us until last week to work out the connection between our covens, because no one really missed the women. As in, they weren't officially part of any coven. We all assumed when they no longer continued coming to our meetings, they just decided no longer participate."

"And that's common for such a thing to happen in your community?" I asked, not quite sure if I believed it.

"Think about how many people shun God every day," Margaret pointed out, her voice gentle rather than defensive. "We allow them to come, we allow them to leave. It's all part of free will. We cannot force anyone to stay if they do not want to. We wish them well in whatever they endeavour. It's just…" She stopped once again. "the amount that we were losing them…"

"They were looking for Kadie," I muttered to myself, as though it suddenly clicked into place.

Or someone like her. New. With untapped power. Power that could be manipulated and controlled due to lack of experience.

"Who?" Margaret asked, sitting down on a stool near the table. Her hands folded in her lap, her thumb running over the stones pressed tightly in her palm.

I pushed up into a standing position, my energy buzzing with the heat of undiscovered Demons slinking through the night out there. There were many out hunting tonight. I could feel it.

I looked at the woman opposite me asking questions. Margaret. I wasn't sure if I should tell her the truth about Kadie. As much as I wanted to trust her, I didn't think it was my place to reveal so much about someone so dear to me, especially to a stranger. It didn't matter that she was a Witch. It didn't matter that maybe she and Kadie knew each other – though I doubted that because when I brought up Kadie's name, she did not seem to recognize the name.

What I needed to figure out – and figure out quickly – was whether Margaret would be a worthy alliance, or an adversary? As a New York Witch, and someone who was obviously on the Demon's hit list, she *may* be someone I could confide in. However, I also knew this could be an elaborate trap. Margaret herself could have set it up in order to get information on disappearing Witches, or she could be working for the Demons, trying to get information on the whereabouts of where Kadie went. I did not like the fact that I could not tell one way or the other. I did not like this confusion that seemed to be taking hold of me and making me doubt myself.

At the end of everything, though, I wasn't sure I had much of a choice, considering the path I was now on. If I was going to find Kadie, I needed people in my corner. I could not do it without them. Which meant I had to force myself to trust them, whether I wanted to or not.

"You said the Demons had only been taking the young, untrained Witches," I said. Margaret now had her palm open, attention on the variety of crystals in her hand. Each rock looked smooth, but they varied in both shape and color. "Why would they attack you? I beg no offense, but you seem to be more knowledgeable."

She shrugged her shoulders. "I don't know." She began to replace the crystals on her coffee table where she found them, but not before giving each crystal and caress. "Maybe something has changed. I'm one of the elders of my coven, but I had no idea how to stop their attack."

So, she was an elder. This information did not surprise me. What did surprise me was that she did not know how to stop them. And yet Kadie had been able to kill them on sight. Her instincts were far superior to that of any Witch I'd ever known.

"You've never seen anything like them before?" I asked, although I already knew the answer.

"No." She shook her head, her eyes still focused on the crystals.

This wasn't making any sense. "Why would the Demons hunt down inexperienced Witches, only to go for an Elder now?" I asked. I turned, thrusting my hands behind my back and tilting my head up to look at her ceiling.

"Who's Kadie?" Margaret asked again, ignoring my question and looking at me with a searching expression.

I clenched my jaw. My eagerness at ensuring Kadie's safety was compelling me to make rash decisions. I needed to be more careful until I was certain I could trust someone. As much as I wanted to trust Margaret, I did not know if I could just yet.

"She's a woman I'm … in a relationship with," I stumbled to

find the right words. That seemed to be a good way to describe what I had with Kadie without giving too much away. It was honest without the detail. I did not think she needed to know more than that. However, my eyes narrowed slightly as I watched her take in this information. I was curious to see how she might react to it.

"A relationship" was perhaps not the best way to explain it, but the Target/Guardian Angel thing was a bit far-fetched for most to understand.

"What does she have to do with us?" Margaret asked, her eyebrows narrowing in suspicion. My body tensed. I did not like the way she was responding to Kadie even though it was by no fault of her own. She was suspicious because she did not know Kadie, and perhaps she was worried about the disappearing Witches. However, my defences stood erect at anyone suspicious of my lover and I could not help but bristle.

"Nothing, directly. I don't think." I forced the words out, turning and resuming my pacing so she would not see how flustered I was. Me. Flustered. Over an appropriate question. I did not like to think about what I had been reduced to. I refused to think more on it and continued. "The Demons were tormenting her. I chased them away and killed most of them, but when I wasn't looking…"

I clenched down hard on my jaw. Why had Tabitha called me off Kadie's case when she'd still been in imminent danger? The question only now popped into my mind, but I realized it was something that was still bothering me, even now. Her actions didn't make sense. "The Demons enlisted human men to kidnap her and take her to a castle to torture her."

Margaret's eyes went suddenly very wide. "Are you serious?" Her voice was deadly quiet.

"Yes." I nodded once. I wasn't sure if she was shocked at the prospect in general, or if there was more to her surprise. As in, maybe she had heard about this before. "I don't know why."

"Where is she now?" Margaret asked, shifting on her stool and moving forward as though very interested in my answer. She tucked her skirt under her legs and crossed them at the ankles. There was something about her posture that reminded me of a very disciplined teacher. She was in control of her body and how she presented it to others, cognizant of who was watching her.

"She is with a friend of mine," I said. Again, the words came out slowly, like my tongue was lathered in molasses. Again, I knew I should trust her, but part of me was reserved, like I didn't want to share Kadie and what she was going through with anyone else. "She is very unwell. Poisoned, close to death. I'm in pursuit of her kidnappers. And I need your help."

Well, that was the short version anyway. It was the version I could live with sharing.

"What was in the poison?" Margaret's fascination with all of this perplexed me. I still could not figure out if she was genuinely interested or if she knew more than what she was saying. I shifted. Once her tone settled in, I realized there was something about it that alerted me to the fact that she may know more than I did.

"I don't know." More honesty. "Why do you ask?"

"This Kadie… she is an untrained Witch?"

I furrowed my brow and nodded slowly. I told her this already. Kadie had said she'd tried to join a Witches' coven in the Bronx, only to be disenchanted by their lack of skills.

"Yes."

Margaret was nodding, her eyes darting around as her fast brain processed my words. Her hands reached for more crystals but she stopped before pulling them out. I was missing something here. "What aren't you telling me, Margaret?" I demanded to know, my voice still soft. I positioned my body so it faced her, stopping movement all together. I needed to focus on her and I needed her to realize I was in no mood for word play and other deceitful tricks. I needed the truth. Now.

Her gaze snapped back to me, and there was a light in her eyes that hadn't been there before.

"There's so much…" She jumped to her feet and began to move. At first, she tried to have her hands behind her back, but as she spoke, they moved with her words so disjointedly, I was afraid she was going to hurt herself. "First, an untrained Witch can often be the most powerful. They are very primitive, and use their emotions to harness their magic. It can be very volatile if they are strong."

I nodded. That fitted Kadie's description perfectly.

"And once they begin to learn and expand their skills, that power sometimes fades a little because they learn to control it more," Margaret explained. She looked at me over her shoulder before turning around and facing the wall. She adjusted a painting against the wall, one I hadn't noticed before.

"Why would it do that?" I asked, watching as the black night painting was straightened. The full moon hung low in the painting against the sparkling stars.

I pressed my lips together, slowly sitting on the edge of the couch, steepling my fingers and resting my elbows on my knees. It seemed wrong to have a skill that once harnessed would be less prominent.

"Because it is under their control," Margaret repeated. "It is much harder to steal or take advantage of once harnessed. It is a good thing for everyone. Both for the Witch, and those around her. If we could figure out how to keep the raw strength *and* make it safe for everyone as well, that would be better, but we haven't yet." She tsked at herself, shaking her head in obvious annoyance. She stepped away from the painting to look at it for a moment before nodding once to herself.

So Kadie had maintained her powers because she hadn't been taught how to be a "proper Witch." And she left covens because she assumed those Witches weren't powerful at all. How ironic.

"Does that have something to do with the Witches who were taken?" I asked. "The fact that they were untrained?"

She shrugged again, her gaze dropping away as though she were hiding something. "Could be, and that would make sense." She walked back to her coffee table and grabbed a dark blue stone, her thumb already caressing the smooth rock. "An untrained witch doesn't know how to guard her energy, and her magic can be easily stolen. Some very young and possibly powerful Witches have gone missing."

I knew there was more to what she was saying. However, I would deal with that half-honest answer later. I needed to find out more about the poison that was affecting Kadie.

"What could possibly keep Kadie so sedated and weak, but not kill her?" I asked. "Near-death, but not actual death." I hoped I was making some kind of sense. My knee started bouncing and I folded my hands in my lap.

My theory was that the Demons, or their human counterparts, had wanted to keep her alive until the baby was born. And then she could die. But I was more than likely wrong.

"Ah…" With her free hand, she began to scratch the back of her head. Not because there was anything wrong with her hair. It seemed like a nervous tic. "There are many things that could make her very sick, but Witches are very sensitive to specific substances that other humans are not."

Margaret was being cagey and I rolled my eyes with frustration.

"I don't need your secrets, Witch." I relaxed my fists and tried to be more patient. I wouldn't get anywhere with her if I scared her off, and she didn't seem like she would respond well if I demanded answers from her. Intimidation wasn't something I took advantage of and I didn't plan to start now. "I need an antidote."

If Tabitha, my only friend for over three centuries, was risking her life by connecting into Kadie's fading energy, then I needed to find help. Not only was Kadie at risk, but Tabitha was as well. Besides my son, those were the two most important people in my life, and I didn't want to risk them anymore than they already were. Their lives were in danger and I couldn't lose one of them, let alone both. I had to act quickly. I had to act *now*. But I could do nothing without information.

"I'd need to see her before I prescribed anything." Margaret said softly, turning around to look at me.

"Not a chance," I said, meeting her gaze squarely. I shook my head before she even finished her sentence.

"I can't help your Kadie if you won't let me." Her voice had more bite in it than I expected it to for her and I leaned my head back so I could get a better look at this Witch. Who was she, exactly?

"It is much more complicated than you can imagine, Witch," I tried to explain.

She lowered her brow and glared at me. "Listen, Angel. If you're not going to help me solve this puzzle, you can leave," she said. For one thing, she was apt at hiding her strength. For someone who had seemed so frail when I first encountered her, she had a resilience I wasn't expecting. "I need more information about this enemy, but no matter what, I'll help you. Because this has more to do with just your Witch. It involves all of us, but I need a favour too."

I stopped bouncing my legs and let her words sink in. A deal was being made and I wasn't used to that. I was a soldier, a very good one. I followed orders dictated by those more intelligent than I. But now, I had the opportunity to bargain. I could gain something without fighting. If I was willing to share information with her, she would be willing to share information with me.

"And how can I help you?" I asked, suspicion etched into my tone. I still wasn't sure I could trust her. I didn't know if I wanted to. Then again, I didn't have much of a choice. I had to keep reminding myself of that.

Margaret's gaze slid sideways and she called out softly. "Simone, come out sweetheart and meet our visitor."

I stood up and steeled myself for an invasion, my muscles bunching in my shoulders and back.

There was someone else here?

My body was tense, ready to pull the sword from my back, ready to attack. If I was being honest, I craved it. I wanted something to do with all of this excess energy. And a fight was something I knew how to do without thinking. It didn't require talking or thinking or cunning.

A young girl, about sixteen or seventeen years old, stepped out from behind a closed door. She had long brown hair and a pretty face, but was otherwise totally unremarkable.

I stared at her for a long moment. I should have done a better sweep of this place before letting my guard down. I clenched my teeth together and looked from the girl to Margaret to the door.

What's going on here?

CHAPTER FOUR

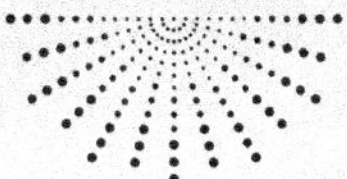

"This is my niece." Margaret said, drawing the girl closer with her outstretched hand. "You look like you're going to attack her. Does she look threatening to you?"

I did not let her words sway me. My body stayed taut, and I waited. I could tell there was more to this scenario than Margaret was letting me in on.

She sighed when she realized her words had little effect on me. "The Demons weren't here for me," she finally said in a low voice. The dark blue crystal had been replaced on the coffee table. Now, Margaret's hands were on her niece, almost as though she was protecting her. "They were looking for her. Her name is Simone."

I nodded slowly, her words making more of the puzzle pieces fit together. That made more sense. Margaret did not seem to fall into the same category as the missing Witches.

"She is a young, untrained Witch?" I asked for clarification, my eyes focused on the girl.

Simone's eyes widened visibly as though she couldn't believe I'd said the word.

"Yes," Margaret said simply, though Simone's breath whooshed quickly in a gasp.

"Then they were trying to take her, not you." I ignored the young Witch's reaction and shifted my eyes to Margaret. "So the pattern still fits." It was unnecessary to share this out loud but I felt as though doing so helped my jumbled thoughts begin to focus on putting the pieces of this intricate puzzle together.

Now, the real question was, "What are we going to do about it?"

No matter what the Demons wanted these women for, it wasn't anything good. It couldn't be. What that was, I didn't know. Right now, I wasn't sure if it was important. All I cared about was preventing them from getting Kadie. But this was getting bigger than just Kadie. Would solving the problem on a grand scale help Kadie or would it take precious time away from my little Witch? I did not know. I needed information.

Although, as they weren't my Targets, they were not my responsibility. *Technically.*

I made a mental note to ask Tabitha why they weren't being protected by another Angel. It was obviously a giant loophole the Demons were jumping through. What made Kadie special and Simone not? Why was Kadie granted a Guardian but Simone did not? It made no sense.

"Looks like my date with Heaven is off," I muttered aloud. My days of being a dutiful soldier were done. The idea, although shocking, sat on my shoulders rather easily. If anything, it was a relief. Like I didn't have to fight for something I didn't truly believe in, not when my focus was on other things.

I was going rogue.

"Pardon me?" Margaret said, standing up and staring at me as though I had two heads.

I shook myself, hard. The path before me, clear as a crystal lake.

I looked up. I completely forgot she was there. "Nothing," I said. "Do you have a plan?"

I didn't know where to start, but if I had an idea, I might be able to formulate something.

Margaret surveyed me with her eagle eye, her grip on her niece tightening. "We don't have any plan other than trying to protect our young, and keep them alive until we can figure this all out," she said slowly. She sounded genuine. "Do you have any idea of where these… Demons could be?"

I did. And when the dawn came, I would be visiting that wreckage of a castle once again. I wasn't sure if that was the best place to start, but it was something.

"Yes." I slowly relaxed my body. I did not think anyone would attack me, even if this girl was a powerful Witch. "But I need to wait until first light to travel there. In the meantime, I need you to help Kadie."

She nodded. "Can you bring her here? I can set up a care station for her."

I relaxed a little with her request. If she was willing to let Kadie come into her home, for me to bring a sick woman here, then perhaps I could trust her.

"No, I will take you to Kadie, it will be much simpler as I do not know if she is safe to move. In return for your help, I vow to do everything in my power to keep your niece safe and to destroy whatever forces are coming after your family."

A bargain. I wasn't used to doing these. I did not know if I was doing it right. But it was all I could think of, and it seemed as though both involved parties were getting what they wanted.

Margaret nodded. "That sounds fair," she allowed. "Although I don't know what I can do for Kadie until I see her. Depending on the poison being used on her, I can't make any promises, unfortunately."

I was out of options. I'd take what I could get at this point in time. I did appreciate her honesty and I could understand it, even if I wanted something more concrete for Kadie.

"Okay," I said.

I turned from them, deciding to reach out to my Angel Agent so I could let her know what was going on.

Tabitha. Can you hear me?

No answer.

Shit!

Tabitha? I tried again.

Regardless of what Tabitha was doing, I knew, without a doubt, if she heard me reach out to her, she would respond no matter what.

Tabitha?! I did not keep the urgency from my call this time.

Still, there was nothing and my heart began to pound in my chest as true worry set in. Tabitha had never, ever, not answered me before. We had direct communication. An angelic link.

Something was wrong. Whether Tabitha had been attacked or her energy was depleted from giving hers to Kadie, I could not be sure. But I was almost out of time and wanted her guidance.

My gut twisted as my hands began to shake.

I forced myself to calm down. I needed to act, not freak out.

"I'll take you there now," I decided, turning back to Margaret. I wished I could have given Tabitha a warning – she might have told me if this was a good idea in the first place – but since I could not reach her, I would have to do what I must for Kadie. And now, maybe for Tabitha as well. "Can we leave your niece somewhere safe?"

"She'll come with me," Margaret said, and judging by the way she spoke, there was no room for argument.

"That would be tricky." I glanced behind me, as though I could see my currently folded-up wings. They had been irrevocably damaged in the last attack and I wasn't sure how I'd go carrying two Witches to Tabitha's house.

Margaret persisted. "Simone is a born healer," she pointed out. "She can help, and there is no one on Earth I trust with her safety against those things." Her eyebrows raised to her hairline, crinkling her forehead. Her tone had returned to that no-nonsense, no-argument one she had used with me earlier.

I shifted my weight and my eyes went to the painting Margaret had originally been straightening. I did not know what I should do. Again, I hated the uncertainty I felt. It seemed like it was constant. I needed guidance.

I closed my eyes. Perhaps reaching out to Tabitha would get me an answer this time. She was the only one I could think to ask my questions to.

Tabitha. Please. Answer me.

When nothing came, I gave up hope of getting guidance from my Angel Agent. We were either too late already, or she was putting all of her energy into keeping Kadie alive and couldn't respond. I would be forced to make decisions on my own, without her assistance. I liked to be certain about everything. I hated that I was not. I hated that I had to make decisions I wasn't sure about, especially decisions that involved Kadie.

"All right," I finally said. If Margaret was telling the truth, Simone's services would be appreciated. She might be needed for more than just Kadie as well. If Tabitha needed help, having a Witch there who could heal might be a good idea. Regardless, that didn't mean they were allowed to dictate my decisions from here on out. Just because I was uncertain of things did not mean I wanted their guidance. I would discuss things with Tabitha when she was not indisposed. "But a warning. If I see anything that worries me, I won't hesitate to kill you both. And it will happen much quicker than you can anticipate. I am much worse than those Demons could ever hope to be."

Simone squeaked and Margaret pulled her niece into her side even further. I did not feel guilty for what I said. They needed to understand I was not the sort to waste time. Even so, being so forward with probably innocent humans would set me back centuries in my quest to get back into Heaven, but at this point it didn't matter. I was desperate. And I refused to allow anyone to threaten those I cared about.

When Margaret nodded curtly in agreement, I waved a hand at them. "Good. Get what you need, and we leave quickly. Remember, pack light. With both of you, it will already be difficult to fly. Do not bring things you do not actually need."

"Can you be more specific with our travel arrangements, Angel?" Margaret asked as Simone disappeared down the hall. "You said something about flying. Why do I have the feeling you don't mean on a plane?"

"I'll carry you both," I said.

Not an easy task considering my damaged wings, but it could be done. I would make sure of it.

Margaret narrowed her eyes at me. "And what assurances do I have of our safety? No offence Angel, but this screams 'trap' to me."

I cocked my head at her. "You're right. And I'm not sure how to reassure you other than to swear on my life, that I would never do you any harm."

Margaret stared at me for long moments, her gaze assessing.

Then she turned away, as if she'd made up her mind.

She called out to her niece. "Simone, make sure to pack lightly," she reiterated. With one last glance at me, she said, "We'll only be a few minutes."

"Thank you, Margaret." I said, as gratitude washed over me.

I nodded my understanding before Margaret turned and left the room, hopefully in search of the magical ingredients that would bring Kadie and Tabitha back to me. I began to pace, hoping they would only take a few minutes, as they stated they would. I did not like to sit idly by when I could be doing something productive. The problem was, I did not know what I could do. I wanted to go back to the castle and search for clues, but if Simone could heal Kadie, that was more of a priority.

I decided to walk outside before I put a dent in Margaret's carpet. The minute I stepped on the concrete, closing the front door softly behind me, I immediately sensed the distant heat of Demons in the air. I lifted my head up, eyes narrowing. There were none left in this area now. Would more come to capture Simone? I didn't know, but I would be on guard if they did. I wasn't exactly her Guardian, but I would protect her as though I was. If she was willing to help Kadie, I would do anything.

I drew my sword and extended my wings, ready to fight. My body was tense. My eyes were sharp. I was ready for anything.

"You're a fallen Angel." Simone's gentle voice whispered behind me.

I turned around to stare at the young woman. At least I was not startled enough to jump. "You can see my wings?" I asked, tilting my head to the side. My grip on my sword did not waver.

She nodded.

How was that possible? Perhaps Kadie had changed me? Maybe

these women were of Kadie's bloodline and they were all the exception to the rule?

In the end, it did not matter. It was something to concern myself with later. If Kadie had changed me in some way, I would need to know about it. But I could do nothing right now.

"Are you taking us somewhere off-world?" she asked, taking a few hesitant steps forward. I could not tell if she was scared or curious or a mixture of both. There was bravery in her eyes, a genuine thirst for knowledge there, but besides that, she was cautious, probably because of everything that had been happening to her and her aunt. I could not blame her for her feelings. Part of me wanted to protect her even though she was not my Target and she was nowhere near as important as Kadie.

"Not exactly," I responded. "Tabitha, my Angel Agent, lives in a sort of hidden realm. Still on Earth, but untouched by mortals. That's where we will be going first."

"Angel Agent?" She cocked her head to the side and that curiosity made itself known more prominently. She took another step towards me, wanting to know the answer to her question more than she wanted to keep her distance.

Hard to explain to a human. "She's my friend who guides me to my Targets and advises me on certain matters. She's half Witch."

"Okay." The young Witch didn't ask any more questions, simply slid her backpack onto her shoulders and stepped forward so we were side by side. If that meant she trusted me, I would take it. If she really could heal the way her aunt claimed she could, I needed her to be on my side. I needed her to do everything she possibly could for Kadie.

I extended to my full height of over seven feet, and reached down for the young girl with one arm. "You'll need to hold on tightly, and breathe slowly," I instructed her. I made sure my firm voice was also gentle, but I did not want to have to repeat myself or warn her again. Flying was no game; there were risks, especially when transporting humans. Since I would be carrying two − something I hadn't done before − I needed her to realize the risks and how serious this was. "I have been told that Tabitha's realm is not the same as the one you live in so please prepare yourself for a change in atmosphere."

Simone nodded again, tucking hair behind her ear. She did not seem to talk much, which I appreciated. She stepped forward and I closed my arm around her, securing her lithe body in my grip. She was not as heavy as I thought she would be, even with her willowy frame. I hoped that meant this would be an easier journey than I anticipated.

Margaret walked into the backyard, tucking herbs and bottles into a side bag.

"You're going to carry me too, Angel?" the older Witch asked with a small smirk to her lips. She already knew the answer to this question. She was simply goading me into a reaction. Perhaps I might have cracked a smile if things were different, if the situation wasn't dire, but it was. And we had to go. I had already waited long enough.

I grabbed her up in my other arm and held them both tightly against my chest. I wanted to ensure I was used to their weight in my arms before I took off. I had carried humans who weighed more than they did combined, and yet having both of my arms occupied was not something I felt comfortable with.

"Put your arms around my neck and hold on to me," I said.

My wings extended to their full breadth and the tingle of celestial magic wove around us. Both women did as I said without question, which I appreciated. I needed to concentrate right now. I beat down and my feet left the ground. Simone swallowed a shriek as she buried her head into my neck. I would not be surprised if she preferred the ground to the air. I gripped her even tighter to let her know I was here and I supported her.

I enveloped us all in invisibility as we moved through the air. It was a difficult task and took a lot out of me to do so. Making myself invisible was one thing, but two extra people when I was already carrying their weight and flying with broken wings took more out of me than I could handle. We went up, higher and higher, until I found the door to Tabitha's world. It was easier to find than I remembered. Maybe it was because with two grown women in my arms, I was desperate to go through so carrying them wouldn't last longer than what was absolutely necessary.

We flew through and I knew immediately that something was wrong, different. There was a chill in the air, not one that usually brought me a refreshing sense of peace and stillness. More like a shudder ripped down my spine, causing every muscle in me to tense up, preparing for a battle with an unknown assailant. There was a darkness of the sun as well, which seemed strange and impossible but it was the only way I could really explain it. Shadows lived here where there once was vibrant life. I looked around and was suddenly hit with the thought: this place was touched by death. And not just anyone's death. Tabitha's.

Tabitha was dying. And Kadie along with her.

I did not know how I knew this, and yet the minute the thought crossed my mind, I knew it was the truth.

Oh, God no. Please no.

"We're almost there," I reassured the Witches as we flew over the endless clouds to Tabitha's house and landed on the grass outside. I did not want to worry them. Part of me wondered with their powers if they had the ability to feel the offness of this place the way I had. Certainly they were touched by magic, but they hadn't been here before and did not know what it felt like to be here prior to now. I ignored the tightness in my chest and the ache that seemed to run uncontrolled through my body, like someone had clamped a vise around my ribs.

I'd like to pretend it was from the exertion of flying with two humans, but I knew it wasn't.

I swallowed. My mouth had gone dry. I forced my eyes up and glanced at the front door, fear filling my arms and legs, making it impossible to move forward. I didn't want to step inside that house if it meant I lost both of the women I loved. And yet, I knew I could not stay where I was. The Witches would know, if they did not already.

"There is sickness everywhere," Simone said. She stepped out of my grasp and moved towards Tabitha's small flower garden that lined the pathway up to her home. The Witch ran a hand over some wilting garden flowers, a deep sadness in her eyes, as though she understood more than she should have for being as ignorant as she was.

"Yes." I nodded once. There was no point in lying when she could clearly feel what I did. "She is gravely ill. They both are. Come."

I pulled on the armor of battle and pushed away the fear threatening to overwhelm me. I had to take these Witches inside the house, regardless of everything in me screaming to stay outside, to stay naïve. Once I set foot in this place and saw what was truly happening, there was no going back.

I took a deep breath and opened the door. The pungent reek of death assailed my nose, acidic and rotting. I faltered. It was as though my legs stopped working. I could not stop, though. Not now. Instead, I forced myself to walk through the doorway, to immerse myself in this place. However, the musky smell was overwhelming. It nearly brought me to my knees. It could not be possible, and yet, how could I argue with this? How could I fight something that might have already occurred?

"No." *Not that. Not yet. Please.*

I did not know who I was speaking to. I did not know if I was calling out for Kadie or Tabitha or God Himself. But whoever could hear me, I needed my girls to be okay.

I rushed through the small house and turned into the room where I'd left Kadie and Tabitha, only to come to a grinding halt in the doorway.

"About time you got here," Tabitha panted from her place on the ground next to Kadie's bed.

She kneeled on the carpet as though in prayer, her face obscured by her long hair.

I nearly smiled with relief when I heard her usual dry voice. The quip rolled off my shoulders like water from a cleansing shower. Tears filled my eyes but I would not let them fall.

I walked into the room slowly, my gaze on Kadie's still, pale form. She looked like death had already claimed her and yet I knew Tabitha would not still be here if Kadie had died.

"You're both still alive," I whispered, unable to believe my eyes.

Relief swept through my heart like a tsunami, taking my strength with it.

I stumbled and clung to a nearby chair, my knees dropping to the floor. I could cry. Judging by the moisture on my cheeks, I was crying.

"Yes. Barely," Tabitha answered, the thread of her voice as thin as I'd ever heard it. It was odd to hear her speak this way when she typically was so strong and so certain. Now, it seemed as though she could barely get the words out.

No wonder she couldn't answer me when I'd called to her. She barely looked strong enough to speak at all.

I clung to the back of the chair and pulled myself over to the head of the bed. Kadie looked so peaceful, like one recently claimed by death. I reached out to touch her but hesitated. My heart ached at the sight and my throat burned from swallowing the tears that rose. I wanted to feel her, to reassure myself that she was still here, that she was still alive, but I could not bring myself to do that just yet. I was afraid. I was afraid that I might be deluding myself and that Kadie was really dead.

"Gabriel?"

I turned to the doorway where both Margaret and Simone popped their heads in. They both were reluctant to come in, and I assumed it was because they did not wish to intrude. I appreciated their thoughtfulness. In truth, I had nearly forgotten they were present. Now that I was reminded, something might be able to be done about this.

Tabitha lifted her head, her skin the color of a stormy sky. Grey, with black edges. Her eyes narrowed at the doorway, as though she could not sense whether she could trust these women or not.

"You brought help?" she asked, her tone brighter than when I'd arrived. She must have sensed something in them that compelled her to trust them. Which meant I was right to trust them as well.

Suddenly, realization hit me. My beautiful, immortal friend had thought she was going to die trying to save Kadie, and I loved her all the more for it. Gratitude caused my heart to swell and it almost hurt as it knocked against my chest in a slow, rhythmic pace. I did not deserve Tabitha.

"You are not going to die, Tabitha, and neither is Kadie," I promised. I did not know how such a promise was possible to make, but I believed it with every fiber of my being.

I reached up and took hold of Tabitha's arm. I wanted to disentangle Tabitha's form from Kadie's, but I paused when I felt the coldness beneath her skin. I wasn't sure if that would kill one of them. Or both.

"Don't disengage them." Margaret came up behind me, peering over my shoulder. I could feel stray strands of her hair caress my shoulder. I did not have to see her to know her eyes were narrowed, deep in thought. "They are too tightly bound together." She pulled away, only to look over her shoulder. "Simone, can you work out exactly what they've been poisoned with?"

Simone came closer and gently touched Tabitha and Kadie, inspecting them as a doctor would. Experience filled her youthful eyes. For someone as young as she was, it was clear she knew what she was doing within the realm of her powers and her capabilities. No longer was she the shy, meek girl I had seen at her aunt's home. Given a task she was comfortable with, she was bold and certain. It reassured me greatly.

CHAPTER FIVE

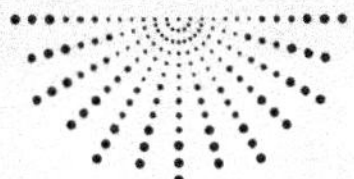

I stepped further away and decided to explain the past events that had brought us here, to help the Witches understand. Perhaps it would help them deduce what had happened to both Kadie and Tabitha. Plus, it gave me the sense that I was doing *something* instead of standing around, watching, feeling completely useless.

"I found Kadie with the Demons a day ago," I said. Even as I told her, it was difficult for me to believe that this had only been about a day ago. It felt as though eternity had passed. More than that, I was torn up internally at the prospect that so much could happen in a span of twenty-four hours, that Kadie could go from living, vivacious, and carefree to nearly dead. Quite honestly, it scared me, how much something could change in so little time. I had never really cared before because, to an immortal like me, time seemed meaningless. But now… so, so much had changed.

I cleared my throat. Simone continued to look at me, and I realized she was waiting for me to go on. "She had been beaten badly, so I brought her here for Tabitha to help her." I wrung my fingers together. I did not realize how difficult simply talking about the events that transpired would be. "But she succumbed to whatever poison they had fed her and Tabitha connected herself to Kadie to keep her alive, but…" I let me voice trail off. I did not know how to continue. Instead, I gestured to the mess of fragility before me. What else could I say?

"I think it's a mix of water hemlock and deadly nightshade," Simone said after a minute. I had no idea where she had come up with that information. I did not know if she could sense things I couldn't, or if she could simply look at Tabitha and Kadie and just *know*. However, it did fill me with hope that if Simone had an idea of what it was, there was an idea of how to treat it.

"Why would someone do that?" Margaret asked, her eyes narrowed with anger. She crossed her arms over her chest tightly, as though she took what had happened to Kadie personally. Whatever this mixture was, it must be bad.

I only had one question. "Can you help them?"

I didn't have any knowledge of poisons, let alone ones specifically designed for Witches. As much as I could understand their discomfort at the fact that something like this existed – which was clearly a threat to their kind – all I cared about was how to help Kadie and Tabitha.

Simone and Margaret exchanged glances that would have gutted a lesser being.

"Tell me," I demanded. I curled my fingers into fists, trying to control my frustration. I wanted to know. I had a right to know. It was the only reason I brought them here in the first place, for this type of information. False hope was not hope, and I knew the difference.

"We can try," Margaret said quietly. However, there was little, if any, hope in her voice. If anything, it almost felt as though she were humouring me. "But it always depends on the strength of the Witch in cases like this… whether she can come back. They're both very weak."

"They're both very strong," I corrected her. I did not mean to snap. My fingernails pierced my palms but I did not feel the pain. "Do whatever you need to do and I'm sure they'll rise to the challenge."

Simone and Margaret exchanged another glance and Margaret nodded her head once. I did not understand the look that transpired between them, but when they both began to move, the tension eased out of my body and my fists unclenched slightly.

Margaret grabbed for her bag and Simone hurried from the room, coming back with bowls of water. How she knew where bowls were, I didn't know. I was just glad she didn't ask. She was capable enough to figure things out on her own. I appreciated that, especially in times of high stress.

"We need to make a tonic, try to cleanse their insides of the poison, then perhaps, a bath?" Margaret said, looking at Simone for guidance. It was strange that the older was looking to the younger for assistance.

"Not yet." Simone shook her head sharply once, her hair following her abrupt motion. She focused on placing the bowls of water on a nearby nightstand. "They're too weak to be separated. But a poultice over any wounds may help."

There was something in Simone's voice that seemed more reassuring than Margaret's. For that, I was grateful.

"I'll make the poultice, you do the serum." Margaret grabbed for her bag and pulled out a plethora of herbs and small glass vials.

"What can I do?" I asked, hating the feeling of being so helpless. My fingers had completely relaxed by this point and I started shifting my weight from one foot to the other. I had all of this energy inside of me and nowhere to direct it. Even now, my wings tingled with the urge to fly around the small room because at least it was something.

Perhaps I should check on Jasmine and my son. See if she needed anything.

"I need clean rags," Margaret said, placing a variety of vials and containers next to the water bowls. She did not even look up at me, too focused on what she was doing.

I could do that. I left the room and moved through the house. I tried searching for clean rags, but the only ones on hand were soiled.

I'd never been inside Tabitha's bedroom, but in it I found a wardrobe full of clean clothes. I tore some white dresses from the racks and took them back to Margaret. If this saved Tabitha's life, I hoped she would forgive me. If not, I was more than willing to purchase a new wardrobe for her, if need be.

"Her rags are soiled," I informed Margaret when her face looked confused. "This was all she had that could be of use."

"All right," the older woman said, surveying the clothes, before ripping one of them into several pieces. I almost envied Margaret, tearing and ripping up the dresses. My hands needed something to do and creating fists and releasing them was getting tiring.

Simone mixed and ground several things together, the smell, one of Earth and ash permeating the room. It smelled of peace but also of grounding, as though a capable head was all one needed to restore peace and life.

Please let this work.

Simone spread her green and black mixture over three of the rags Margaret held out to her. "Help me put them in her most damaged areas," Simone instructed. "There, there, and there." She gestured toward each body part but I was unable to keep up with how quickly the young Witch maneuvered. It still fascinated me how commanding her voice was, even to her aunt.

"May I?" I asked.

I did not feel as though I should ask for permission. However, something about Simone compelled me to do so. She looked at me, curious, but nodded her head.

"Aunt Margaret can hold the covers back," she said. "You can place the sheets on the wounds."

That seemed reasonable. I could do that. I picked up two of the plasters and moved over to Kadie's body. Margaret peeled back the sheet and I gasped at the horror before me.

"She was fine only a few hours ago," I said. My voice barely registered. If I was being honest, I could not say for sure if I had actually spoken out loud, or if those were the thoughts rolling in my head over and over again. *She was fine, she was fine, she was fine.* Though her body had been bloody and bruised, she had been otherwise untouched. There was still hope that she could be saved, that she could be healed, that she would be my Kadie again.

"Here and here," Margaret said, pointing to flesh wounds in Kadie's neck and arms, reiterating what Simone had already instructed me to do.

I blinked, shaking my head. Even though Kadie looked bad – and that was an understatement – I still had a job to do. If Simone thought there was still a chance, certainly I could hope for the same thing, could I not? At least, for Kadie's sake, I would fight for her until she drew her last breath.

I clenched my jaw. I did not even want to think of that.

"Gabriel." I glanced up, surprised to find Simone was the one who had spoken. She did not seem to be the type who was brusque with her comments, but it almost seemed when she was so focused, she did not realize what she was saying and how she was saying it. "I know the sight looks hopeless. But you must be more positive. Do you understand?"

I nodded my head, feeling properly chagrined. I pressed my lips together and placed the poultice on each area. Margaret began smoothing the mixture over Kadie's skin, into every little wound, bruise or injury.

Within minutes, she looked like a mud wrestler.

Tabitha let out a strange sigh. My eyes shot to her. The tension from her facial features seemed to relax, if only slightly. That had to be a good sign, right?

I dropped to my knees and cupped her cheeks to draw her head up. When she was looking at me with pained eyes, I asked, "Are you okay?" It was a stupid question. Instead, I quickly amended my original question. "Are you feeling better?"

She gave me a wobbly smile as though she knew I knew it was a stupid question, her eyes glinting in the same way it usually did when she was amused by something I did or said. "You owe me for this, you know that, right?" she said, growling in that teasing way of hers.

I nodded fervently. "Of course. Anything."

"Don't tempt me, Gabriel," she mustered. "You know I have no fear in asking it of you."

I'd do another millennium of service and not complain once, if it meant they both survived this.

Tabitha groaned, her eyes falling shut once again. "Good, good," she mumbled. Whether it was directed to me or in general, I did not know. I was just glad she had the ability to talk still. I would sit attentively and listen to her read the phone book, knowing she was okay. "Now, keep going. I can feel a change in her already."

Simone seemed to be throwing everything she'd brought into her concoction. It was bubbling and churning, as though alive.

"What are you making?" I asked, hoping my voice conveyed just how much I appreciated it. I was intercepted by her aunt, however, who shook her head and drew me away.

Simone's eyes were glowing with a white power and as she began to chant. She probably had not even heard my question in the first place. Instantly, I could feel the change in the air. Thank the Gods.

Simone reached for two cups, dipped them into the swirling mess of purple and orange, and pulled them out. She handed them to me, her eyes still white.

"Quickly," she instructed. "They must drink."

Margaret took one of the cups from me and took it to Tabitha, who downed it instantly with the older Witch's help.

When she finished, Margaret removed the cup from Tabitha and stepped back to give my Angel Agent some space. Tabitha gasped and groaned and shook like she'd been poisoned herself. I tensed.

I stared down at the still-moving mixture. Was this really the right thing to do? To Kadie? The mother of my child? Was it a risk I should take?

"Angel!" Simone called, her voice harsh. "Now!"

There was no mistaking the authority in Simone's words and I gathered Kadie into my arms. Her head lolled back until it hit my shoulder. With my free hand, I tilted her chin down so her lips would part and then and tipped the cup to get the drink down her throat. Her lips were loose and half of it spilled down her chest, but I kept pouring, hoping some of it made it into her stomach. From my angle, I could see her throat bobbing up and down. I knew she was drinking it. I knew some of it was getting into her system. But would it be enough?

When it was all gone, and Kadie's beautiful body was covered in even more of the Witch's magic than before, I lay her down against the pillows once again.

Tabitha groaned and pushed herself to her feet, gagging on the liquid still moving through her system. As she stood up, she withdrew her hand from Kadie's arm and panic flashed through me.

"What are you doing?" I demanded to know. From my peripheral, I saw Margaret flinch at the sound of my voice, as though she wasn't expecting such anger from me. I was not expecting it myself, but I did not take it back. I did not understand what Tabitha was doing, when releasing Kadie could mean her death. "Why are you letting go of her?"

Tabitha waved a hand at me as she reeled back and sat on the opposite bed. She did not seem perturbed in the slightest by my aggressive tone. Instead, she brought a hand to her mouth and coughed and spluttered some more.

"I'm not letting go of her," she snipped, though her voice was still weak and filled with exhaustion. "Don't worry, Gabriel. She's on her way back to us. I can feel her. She's gaining strength, and will soon be back with you thanks to the concoction your Witch friend made. Whoa…" Tabitha swayed a little and gripped the blankets on either side of her.

"I'm sorry," I said, though I wrung my hands together, not entirely sure how to put what I wanted to convey into words.

She waved my apology off. "Don't choke on your words, boy," she said. "I know how difficult it is for you to admit when you've made a mistake."

I smiled despite myself. "I should not have spoken to you that way," I said.

"No," she agreed. "You shouldn't have. But I do understand why you did."

"Thank you, Tabitha," I whispered as I turned my attention to my woman. I sat on the bed and stroked Kadie's forehead. Her hair was damp with cold sweat but her breathing was steady.

"Come back to me, beautiful girl," I whispered to her. "Our son needs you."

Kadie didn't wake up, but I could see the changes beginning in her body. Her muscles began to repair. The streaks of red that indicated blood poisoning across her skin regressed and retreated. Color came back to her pale face. Her lips weren't cracked or dry. Instead of looking as though she was on the brink of death, she appeared like she was just napping.

I picked up my eyes and shifted them to the Witch who was responsible for Kadie's health. "How long?" I asked her.

Simone moved from where she had first made the concoction and was now checking Kadie's vitals. She placed a finger against the inside of Kadie's wrist, checking her pulse before cracking open Kadie's eyes and checking out the dilation of her pupils.

"I don't know," she said, running a hand over Kadie's throat. She inspected some bruising that lingered there before dropping her hand to her side. "She does seem to be responding, which is good. I just don't know how long this will take." She let out a sigh. "We aren't out of the woods yet. Not quite."

I lifted my gaze and met the young Witch's. "You've saved her," I said. There was awe in my voice, something I had not heard since I spoke with Kadie. I hoped this Witch knew how much what she had done meant to me. "I don't know how I can repay such a debt."

She met my look head on. "You can find out those hunting us, and kill them all." Her words were direct, so pointed, that I blinked in surprise. I did not expect such violence from someone so seemingly innocent. Then, I reminded myself that she and her aunt were enduring much suffering when it came to the disappearance of young Witches. Maybe some were her friends. She was forced to hide out with her aunt until her aunt deemed it safe. That was no way to live, especially for a young Witch with so much power and potential.

I stood up and shook the last of my weakness from my bones.

There would be no mercy in my quest for vengeance. For Kadie. For Tabitha. For Margaret. For Simone. And for the others.

"It would be my pleasure." There was sincerity in my voice. She recognized it too because for a moment, her eyes turned to steal and she nodded her head once, hair fluttering over her shoulder. Then she turned back to Kadie.

"We should know more in the next twenty-four hours," she said, "if not sooner."

I nodded but I knew she did not see me. Sooner was what I hoped for, but I would stay by Kadie's side for as long as it took.

CHAPTER SIX

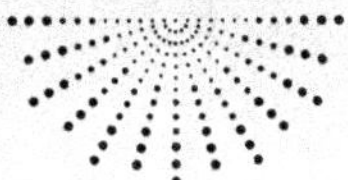

Despite my desire to kill more Demons, I stayed at Tabitha's house until sunrise. There was still no difference in Kadie despite the physical reaction to what we did. It was better than I could hope for, but I wished more had happened. I wanted to know the recovery process was working in a way where Kadie would be healed as soon as possible.

Through the night, Margaret and Simone slept on and off, coming into the room often to check on Kadie's progress.

She had yet to come back to consciousness, but Kadie's physical form was improving. I forced myself to remember that that was enough – for now. My impatience was overwhelming. I suddenly understood the human phrase about taking an inch and expecting a mile. Instead of focusing on what had not happened, I turned my attention to the little improvements that had occurred throughout the night. Her skin had a new glow to it. Her heartbeat was strong, and her body was healing all over. The bruises were fading. The cuts were scabbing. This was good. She looked more like Kadie.

The sun began to creep through the curtains, teasing the shadows before causing them to vanish completely. It had to be sunrise now. We still hadn't hit the twenty-four hour period just yet, but with every passing minute without Kadie waking up, I started getting tense again. I tried not to, but I had the urge to fix everything now and I hated that I could not.

"You're pacing like a teenage girl waiting for a boy to call you," a grouchy voice said from somewhere behind me. "What's the matter with you?"

My lips curled up in relief, hearing Tabitha berate me. I could close my eyes and imagine it was old times where she hadn't been at risk to die. I stopped my pacing and turned away from Kadie so I could regard my Angel Agent.

"How much longer, do you think?" I asked Tabitha.

She snorted. "Your patience has always been an issue for you, hasn't it?" she asked. She started to cough and I waited for her to finish. I hated the sound of it but because she was conscious, because she was speaking coherently, I knew that she would be okay.

"I want to know what to expect so I can finish this," I told her. I wanted to stay by Kadie's side. I wanted to make sure she was healed. And yet, I started to get restless. I needed to do something more than just dab Kadie with strips of cloth and pace around the room. I wanted to punish. I wanted an outlet to release my violent emotions I had been holding back. I wanted to fly back to Earth and find who had done this. And then wipe them from the face of the planet. I just didn't want to miss the moment Kadie woke up.

Tabitha sighed, pinching the bridge of her nose with her dainty fingers. "I don't know, Gabriel." Her voice was suddenly tired. "She's almost healed physically, but that doesn't mean she's just going to wake up."

"I know," I said, but I wanted her to. *Now.* "She has twenty-four hours."

"That's just an estimation, remember." Tabitha's sharp eyes sculpted my face. "Do not lose your faith, boy, no matter what happens." I opened my mouth, wanting to know what she meant by that, but she shifted in her seat and cut me off before I got my chance. "Where's the baby?"

I decided to not push her. Instead, I felt my shoulders roll back.

"With Jasmine." I began to crack my knuckles. The pop each knuckle let out gave me a sick sense of satisfaction. "He's safe."

Tabitha's shoulders visibly relaxed. "Good."

"What baby?" Margaret's voice sounded behind me. I hadn't even heard her come into the room. I whirled around, trying to contain my surprise. I pressed my lips together, unsure of how to proceed. I hadn't told her of Kadie birthing my child before as I wasn't sure I could trust her. But now, as Tabitha stood slowly before me healed from her fight with the poison, and Kadie finding her way back to me, it seemed I could trust the Witch.

I cleared my throat. "Kadie conceived my child less than two months ago, and then, yesterday, birthed him," I explained. I did not know if there was a better way to say it.

Margaret's eyes grew wide. "You must get him," she said. I was expecting her to ask more questions, so her initial reaction threw me off-guard. "If he is taken by the Demons, then we're all done for."

I turned to face the Witch. "What are you talking about?" My words came out slow and sluggish. I did not like her insistent urgency. It started to make me feel worried, and I didn't like that I was starting to get worried when I had been under the impression that everything was going to be all right.

Simone and Margaret shared one of their speaking looks and I slammed my fist into the table. I did not have time for this. When it came to my son, I was furious that there was something I should know that was being kept from me. I would not tolerate that, not after I trusted them. Not after I chose to let them in and help.

"If you have been keeping something from me…" My fingers curled back into fists and I narrowed my eyes. I did not even bother finishing the sentence. I did not have to. Certainly they were intelligent enough to decipher the intended threat – a threat I would make good on if I thought they were conniving against me. I did not care that they were female or Witches. If any harm came to my son because of them, because they withheld something important from me, I would make them pay and I would have no regrets about it.

Simone waved her hands. "It isn't like that," she insisted, waving off my concern as though it was nothing. As though I was overreacting. "We didn't realize that she had your child. You didn't tell us."

I held onto my temper by the barest of margins. "Talk," was all I could manage. She might think I had no cause to be upset, but I disagreed. And until I heard something to convince me otherwise, I would not allow myself to be manipulated.

Simone stepped forward. Instead of dismissing my anger, she held up her hands, as though she were trying to be more gentle, more placating, regarding this delicate issue. "There have been tales of half-Angel babies since the dawn of time," she said, her voice soothing. It had little effect on me, though IK was more open to hearing what she had to say rather than her aunt.

"Yes…" I said, acknowledging that statement with a nod.

"But within our covens, there is also a legend," she continued. I stiffened. A legend? "Of a man who will save all of humanity. A half-Witch, half-Angel child, who will be stronger than both."

I looked at Tabitha and she nodded slowly. She'd mentioned something like that to me yesterday and I had struggled to comprehend it then. But now that I heard it from Simone…

I clenched my jaw together and tried to breathe but it did not do much good. Instead, my eyes fell to the ground and I brought up my arms to cross over my chest. I was not sure what to do with this information. Before, I could place it within a realm of possibility. Now, though, it had been confirmed. And if it was confirmed… what could I do?

"So, you're telling me that you think this is why the Demons wanted Kadie? And old… wives tale?" I said slowly, trying to work out the logic in my head. I picked up my eyes to look at Simone. Besides Tabitha, her word was the one I trusted. I just didn't feel as though Margaret knew things the way her niece did, and I did not wish to waste more time. "For our baby? But they were chasing her well before I met her."

Margaret nodded. "Yes," she said, capturing my attention despite the fact that I did not want to hear from her. "But if a good person is terrorized, are you not called in to help? Which happens first, I wonder? Were they trying to find the baby, or were they trying to destroy all the women who may conceive such a child?"

Margaret had an interesting point. I did not like to admit such a thing, but it could not be helped. Nothing was certain in this topsy turvy world—quite the opposite. But I could see how a person who was as strong as Kadie, could bring havoc to all those who inhabited the Hell dimension, which was why they wanted her. And perhaps not just her. Perhaps a slew of strong women who could potentially give birth to this legend.

Losing this war was not on their agenda, and my child may be the key to stopping them all. It was an overwhelming thought. I dropped my hands to my sides again and decided I needed to sit down again. I dropped to the edge of the couch, careful to keep my own space so no one would touch me. My wrists dangled between my thighs. My eyes went to the wall in front of me. I felt as though I had been punched in the gut.

"So, how can we stop them?" I finally asked. "Why are they still hunting women like Simone if they know that my child has been conceived?"

"I don't know." She shrugged. "Perhaps they believed the baby to be poisoned also? Could he be dying and you not know?" She looked at me as though I had the answer to everything when the truth of the matter was, I knew nothing. I was more ignorant than Tabitha, and Tabitha wasn't directly involved in any of this. Once again, I felt helpless.

Fear slithered through my heart like a rattlesnake. "I have to go," I said, pushing to my feet. "Will you both stay here until Kadie wakes?"

"Of course," Margaret said.

I headed to the door, my mission clear. I had to check on my son and ensure he was safe. I thought leaving him with Jasmine would protect him. Now, I worried he was in greater danger without me. I had to get to him. I had to make sure he was all right. Kadie would never forgive me if something happened to him. *I* would never forgive *myself* if anything happened to him.

"Thank you," I said when I opened the door. I turned to regard them over my shoulder. "All of you."

I ran outside before any of them could respond and took to the sky, flying back through the portal. I did not look back.

The sun had risen and its warmth on my skin reminded me that there was still an Earth to fight for.

It was a new day.

More than that, I *knew* my son was still alive. And Kadie would be okay. She was healing. I had more than most. I had people I cared about, people I loved, worth fighting for. And I was ready to do just that. To fight with everything I had, no matter what the cost.

I flew straight to Jasmine's home, where my child should be. When I landed, the heat on my spine was like a blow torch. Demons had been here through the night. Some still lurked in the shadows. I paused, trying to gage whether or not some still lingered. I wanted to break down the door and guarantee it, but I withheld my fear and anger. Revealing myself might be worse. I had to wait. I had to be sure they were gone.

I banged on the front door with my fist and waited. There was movement on the other side of the door before a tentative pause. I imagined Jasmine or her balding husband peeking through the hole to see who was on the other side of the door. I appreciated the fact that they were being cautious. After another moment, the door swung open and Jasmine's husband revealed himself, an angry expression was one I expected. "About time you came back."

As much as I wanted to be polite, I did not have time to waste. I pushed past him and moved into the lounge. "Where is he? Is he all right?"

"Of course, he is," Jasmine answered calmly as she walked into the room, holding a tightly wrapped bundle in a blue blanket.

I turned to face her, relief draining the tension in my muscles, but only slightly. If Demons had been here before, there was a chance they would come back. I always had to be ready – just in case.

Jasmine handed my son to me and I stared down at his sleeping face. It had only been a day or so, and yet, I felt as though this baby was a different child than the one I left Jasmine with. He already seemed older, his face fuller having gained back the baby weight he lost right after Kadie birthed him. More than that, there was no distress on his face, as though he was content here with Jasmine. My heart swelled with unconditional love and I placed a kiss on his forehead.

"I told you," Jasmine said. Her voice was not one that held defense; rather, she was teasing and gentle. Her aura was so calm that it began to relax my fears, but I asked my questions anyway.

"You haven't seen any signs of discoloration, or poison?" I asked her as I unwrapped him and stared down at his perfect hands and little blue outfit. I mentally counted his fingers and removed his socks so I could do the same with his toes.

"No of course not, why?" She crossed her arms over her chest and peered up at me, her expression perplexed. "Gabriel, is everything okay?"

"What did you bring into our house, devil?" her husband shouted at me. My son stirred in his sleep, his light eyebrows pushing together before settling down once again and emitting a contented sigh. I turned to glare at him. He'd always been an asshole. I had no idea why Jasmine married him. I was glad she took my child without having to ask him first. I knew he would say no immediately.

"Jasmine, I suggest you ask your husband to leave the room before I do something we will all regret," I said. I did not want to threaten him since Jasmine did care for him and she had done me a favour, but I could not contain my frustration at his hostility with me, but most of all, with my son.

Although, I could not help but ponder my odds at what would happen if I did do something to keep him in line. I was already serving an eternity. What was a few more years for permanently maiming her husband, especially when he deserved it?

Jasmine went straight to her purple-faced husband. "James, please." Her voice left no room for argument. "Can you take Zhara to her room and change her? I won't be long."

Her husband glared at me with all the venom in his tiny heart and stomped from the room. I was surprised he actually listened to her.

Jasmine came back to me, unzipped the baby's outfit, and checked his pale skin. There did not seem to be anything of consequence on him, not even a birth mark. There was no discoloration. No rash or bumps or anything troubling. He looked… fine.

"He looks fine, Gabriel," she pointed out, reiterating my thoughts. "Why? What's happened?" She looked up from the babe, her eyes filled with confusion.

I shifted under her vulnerable stare. She was yet another person I had not discussed things openly with. I asked her for a favour and she agreed without questioning me as to why I asked for it in the first place. It was then that I realized just how much I did not trust those, even the ones I claimed to care about. I did this to protect myself, to protect my son, but now I was forced to waste time, explaining things that I should not have to explain. However, Jasmine deserved to know what she had gotten herself into and I wanted to try to be more trusting of those who deserved it.

"His mother was poisoned before she gave birth, and I was afraid it might have gotten into him," I explained.

I should have thought of it earlier. I did not know why such a thing had not occurred to me. I'd had so many things to focus on when he'd been born. Feeding him seemed like the main priority, and I was already going to track down whomever was responsible for what happened with Kadie. It slipped my mind that my son could be affected by this poison as well. I was glad to rectify that mistake and make sure he was all right, however.

I stared down at his round tummy and assessed him again. "Has he grown a lot since yesterday?" I asked.

Jasmine laughed softly. "Definitely," she said. Her eyes dropped to the baby, her gaze filled with warmth and love. I did not understand how someone who did not birth the baby could look at him in such a familiar way, but I was glad. Jasmine was the correct selection to feed him. "I don't know how, but he's grown dramatically in only one night. I'd like to think it was my milk, but my daughter is undersized for her age and I seem to be feeding her more than I'm feeding him."

With his gestation being less than a few months, I wasn't surprised he was continuing to grow at such a rapid rate. I was not certain if this was the norm or if this should trouble me. I wish Kadie was here – and by here, I meant cognizant. Even if she was not able to give me a definitive answer, at the very least I would not have had to bear this burden alone.

"How is his mother now?" Jasmine asked, cutting me out of my thoughts. She picked up her eyes to look at me, though her fingers continued to caress my son's hair.

"Doing much better, although still unconscious." *So still unable to feed him, and he needs human milk to grow strong…*I let out another breath. "Are you able to keep him safe for another day, Jasmine? I know it's asking a lot, especially with your husband -."

She waved a dismissive hand. "Don't worry about him," she said. "He's protective of our daughter and thinking any milk given to another child is less for her. He doesn't quite understand how breast milk works." She began re-dressing the sleeping baby. "Of course, I can. It was hard last night, though. I have to tell you. They're everywhere. In our backyard. At our windows. We're lucky we live in a house like this one. We all slept in the nanny's quarters last night. There are no windows in the cellar."

I looked away, guilt seeping through my body. "Oh, Jasmine, I'm so sorry."

The fear and panic they must have gone through. All for me. All for my son. Perhaps her husband had a reason for his hostility. I'm sure I would be the same way if some stranger put me and my newborn child in danger.

I should never have asked this of Jasmine and her family.

"No." She shook her head, tugging at the zipper. "No, it's fine. It reminded me just how lucky I am to have survived what I did. And that's all because of you. You forget how much you've done for me, Gabriel. For my family. So, don't worry, I won't let them have him. I won't leave the house. None of us will, until you come to take him back."

"That's definitely the smartest move." I did not know what else to say to that. She was willing to do so much for me, for my son. I did not know how I would ever be able to repay them. Jasmine seemed to imply I already had, but saving her from Demons was my calling. It did not seem like it was enough.

Not when they were all vulnerable to attack. My son the most of all.

I really had brought my son to the best person. Jasmine could not only feed him, but was fiercely protective, and equipped to deal with this unique challenge. She might be afraid, but she would not cower. She would stay strong, no matter the cost. No matter what. Was there a reason she had been my Target in the first place? Was this fate, as though God knew I would need her for this purpose and helped me forge a relationship with her to ensure she would be ready to take care of my son when the situation called for it? The more information I knew, the less informed I was.

"Hopefully I will be able to get him later today, or early tomorrow," I said. "As soon as Kadie is well enough, I'll be back. I promise."

I did not know if I was telling her this to be informative, or if hearing it out loud was enough to be reassuring to me. Kadie *had* to get well so she could look after him. There was no other option.

I lifted my son up to my face and pressed a kiss to his soft forehead. He smelled of good health and happiness. Like flowers in the rain. Everything I wanted in this world for him. He smiled in his sleep and my heart melted.

I was so lucky.

I handed the baby back to Jasmine, who promptly swaddled him back up again and tucked him into her arms. She was skilled. When all of this was over, I would have to ask her for a few pointers.

"What is he, exactly, Gabriel?" she asked in a low voice. Her gaze was still on the babe, making sure he was still comfortable wrapped up so tightly in the blanket. "I can't help feeling that he is someone very special."

I lingered. Seeing Jasmine hold him made me want to stay and hold him as well. However, I knew if I did not leave, I wouldn't be able to. As much as I wanted to be selfish, I could not. Not when I still had to take care of the threats imposed on my loved ones, on those innocent Witches.

"He is going to become very important," I agreed. "I just have to keep him alive long enough for him to grow into the man he's meant to be." I did not know how to explain further than that so I made no attempt to do so.

Jasmine held the baby tighter within the cradle of her arms, her face set with determination. I was glad my answer appeased her. Jasmine wasn't the sort to push when I explained something. I was grateful for that.

"I'll see you tomorrow then, Gabriel." Jasmine said, her voice soft and fragile.

I smiled, unable to do anything else. "Thank you, Jasmine."

I left her brownstone building, my heart lighter than it had been only moments before. My lips tugged into a smile. It had been incredible to see my son again. The sunshine in the storm we were currently wrapped inside.

My son is healthy and growing. I could not help but cast to Tabitha. I felt my cheeks heat as I cloaked myself in invisibility before spreading my wings. I reminded myself of one of those humans who constantly shared photos of their children whether others cared or not.

Thank the Lord for that. Her voice was stronger than when I left. A sense of relief flooded my body.

Kadie? I cleared my throat, shaking my head. *Any change?*

No. I'll let you know when there is.

Tabitha's tone sounded ominous and despair began to fill me. She made no effort to mince her words or lie to me. It was something I appreciated about my Angel Agent, but every now and then, there were moments – like this one – where I wished she would just let me hope. Before I could feel the pain such a loss would cause me, I switched off our conversation and took to the skies once again. I didn't want to dwell. It would distract me, and that was the last thing I needed right now: a distraction from my mission.

It was daylight. The sun warmed my skin but couldn't seem to break through to my insides. I felt cold, despondent. My lips pulled into a tight line, brow furrowed over my eyes. It was a beautiful day, the sky painted a beautiful blue that instantly reminded me of the color of my son's eyes. My heart panged. I longed to hold him again. I longed to press his tiny body against my chest and hope that some small measure of enveloping him in my arms would make him feel safe against me.

Don't.

I couldn't let myself think about things that made me sad. Sadness made me weak, and I could not be weak right now. Not when it was time to search out the Demons who'd kidnapped and tortured Kadie.

I flew over the city of New York and headed in the direction my instincts had taken me last time. To the overgrown hedges and barren earth of the Demon castle. I had been waiting for the perfect opportunity to return, knowing this was where I needed to be to finish everything.

I landed where I had last time I was here. The stilted air was cold, despite the warmth of the sun on my back. My entire body was tense, filled with a knowing that things would end soon. What bothered me was the fact that I did not know what that ending would entiail. Before, I used to revel in such an uncertainty. I did not need to know specific things and I appreciated the fact that I did not have to be responsible for everything. Now, I needed to know every-thing or else I somehow felt unprepared, as though I could not suffi-ciently do my job. I wished I knew more. I wished I knew that being here was right. I wished I knew that Kadie and my son and even Tabitha would be okay after this was all over.

But I knew nothing other than the fact that I needed to be here.

I slipped beneath my invisibility knowing my magic wouldn't work on any Demons in the area, but it would conceal me from their daytime human watchers. The human watchers were more surprising than the Demons. I hadn't expected them the last time I was here but I would not make that mistake again.

I crept up to the castle this time, not rushing as I had when I was here to rescue Kadie. There was no urgency the way there was last time. I needed to take it all in. See what I had missed before. My insides bristled at such a thought, but I reigned in my patience. This was important. This was what needed to be done in order to sufficiently complete my task – the right way.

I searched the exterior building and saw nothing of real note. Crumbling blue stone and rock kept the huge building afloat. Each tower was peaked with a flag of black. There was no modern security I could see.

Good.

I moved around to the huge double-door entry and extended to my full height as I pulled my sword from my back scabbard. The feel of it in my hand eased my tension albeit slightly. However, it reassured me and at least gave me a tool I could work with if I needed it.

I hated killing humans. It was part of our code that we never harmed a mortal.. But those who were working for the Demons, here in this evil place, would not be completely innocent. I need not bear the burden of guilt if I had to take one of them down. That was for God to decide. Whether they were corrupted and still had a sliver of hope for redemption or whether they would be sent straight to Hell for their wicked crimes was not up to me.

I knew, in that moment, I would not hesitate to do what I needed to do in order to ensure the safety of myself and my loved ones. Even if it meant killing humans.

I reached for the large metal door handle and pulled hard, expecting resistance. It gave way easily and swung open. A loud creak ripped through the silence. I froze and waited. Had I revealed my location?

I tilted my head to the side and waited, hoping to catch any sound of scuffling feet or low murmurs. Anything I could do to see if I could pinpoint their location.

I looked back at the door I just opened once I determined no one made a noise. Something was strange to me but I could not put my finger on it. The breeze ruffled my hair and another squeak – this one smaller – touched the daylight. Suddenly, I was slapped in the face with how obvious it all was. Why wasn't this place locked up? Shouldn't it be heavily guarded by Demons or, at least, human watchers? Shouldn't it be difficult to enter? I shouldn't be able to walk in without repercussions.

I stepped back and held up my weapon, waiting for the attack to come. Silence filled the air. I hated it. It was worse than any kind of threatening noise. I knew how to handle a threat. I was less certain about silence. Gripping the hilt of my sword, I stepped inside and swung the blade in a wide arc. Perhaps I should have thought before acting, but I did not want to take any chances.

Nothing.

There was nobody here except the standing ancient armor of knights who served their king, decorating the halls as though it were 1155 BC.

CHAPTER SEVEN

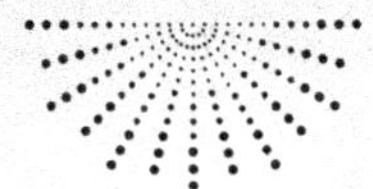

 nside, every part of me screamed, this is a trap. But I took
another step forward.

A chill shivered along my arms, making the hairs stand on end.
There was pure evil in this castle. Part of me couldn't believe that
my beautiful Kadie had made it out of this place in one piece. The
other part couldn't believe I had not realized just how deadly and
dangerous this place was beforehand. Without thinking, I crossed
myself – a silent show of appreciation that we made it out alive the
first time.

I wasn't so sure I would be able to say the same for this time.

I took a cautious step forward, expecting a trap to fall from the
ceiling. I looked up, then around me. Nothing happened. No one
revealed themselves. There was nothing to see, nothing to hear.

Coldness chilled the air. Instead of being filled with the promise
of restoration and growth, it was empty and hollow, the sort of
feeling that came with death and decay. The sort of feeling that one
got when the situation was utterly and completely hopeless.

I continued to move forward when no attack came, through the
huge double-height entrance and around the ground floor. I took
the time to search every room, always mindful of where the

windows were in case I needed a hasty escape. I also kept my eyes out for any information I might need, any clue on what was happening and how to solve the conundrum I was in.

I saw nothing of consequence. Felt nothing unusual besides that feeling of pure evil. Not even the tingle of heat that should be here if a Demon was nearby. Disappointing, to say the least. Not to mention confusing as hell.

I was certain I should be here. And yet, there was nothing for me here. Nothing I could work with, anyway.

As I moved back into the foyer and took my first steps up the large, winding staircase, I began to re-think my conclusions about this place. Perhaps the Demons had abandoned it now that they'd found Kadie. Had they retrieved what they'd needed from her when they'd brought her to this place? If that were true, why did it still feel as though a heaviness permeated the place? Why did I feel such a strong sense of evil here? Was I imagining things? Was I making it worse than it really was because I could not come to a place like this and not feel angry because of all that transpired?

And if they had left, if they had taken what they wanted from Kadie and did not need anything more, why were they still attacking young Witches like Simone? Why were Witches disappearing? None of it was making any sense.

I crept up the stairs, holding my sword erect and ready to use. Despite the fact that it seemed empty, I could not ignore that something was off about this place. I could not let my guard down for even one second. I shifted my eyes back and forth, straining to sense anything that looked out of place or foreign.

I finished my climb and finally reached the first floor, where the stained carpets caught my attention. Were they splattered with blood as the patterns indicated? If it was blood, was the blood fresh or ancient? Or simply a horrible choice in décor? I got closer to the stains, but unfortunately, couldn't be sure.

I continued to move along the hallway, spotting the familiar doors I'd witnessed last time. Kadie had been held on this floor. My mouth went dry. I tightened my grip on my sword.

I glanced down a hallway to my right, where the human guards had been last time. There was nothing there now. Nobody to be seen at all, no demons, no humans. The only thing in the space was silence.

This isn't good.

Anger swirled in my gut like the beginnings of a storm. I did not like this emptiness. I did not like the uncertainty. I did not like the confusion. Most of all, I did not like this puzzle I'd been presented with and could not seem to solve.

I wanted an enemy to fight. A resolution found. I wanted a constructive outlet for releasing my pent-up aggression. I wanted something to do besides wait around and see if Kadie and Tabitha got better, to see if a Demon would attack, to see if another Witch disappeared. I wanted to *do* something.

I marched faster along the hallway and opened the first heavy door. It was dark and I could barely see a thing in the gloom. But there was a smell I could not deny. The reek of fear. A woman's blood, sweat, and tears ran in this room. Or they had, not so long ago.

I took a breath and surged into the inky blackness, looking for a sliver of light. When it called to me, I raced forward, grabbed hold of the old curtains and wrenched them open.

I twisted back around and vomit rose in my mouth at the sight of the girl on the table in front of me. I was nearly brought to my knees.

Oh, God.

Please let this girl be in Heaven where she is meant to be.

She couldn't have been more than sixteen as her face still held the fullness of youth. She was held in chains, and cut up like a piece of meat on a butcher's table. The putrid scent of her remains buried itself in my nostrils. I did not think I would forget the smell as long as I lived, and I expected to be alive for a very, very long time. I looked down at my hands, suddenly worried that blood was stained on my fingers the same way blood seemed to stain each room in this castle. Nothing. And yet, I had this sudden urge to wash myself, this sudden urge to cleanse myself. It was as if this evil had found a way inside of me and no matter how hard I scrubbed, it wouldn't matter.

Faded crimson would forever be under my fingernails, on my finger-prints. It would show up in everything I touched.

My shoulders heaved forward but I held back my guttural response. I would not desecrate this room more than it already had been.

I took a deep breath. I needed to control myself. I was a Guardian, a warrior angel for goodness' sake. One body – no matter how badly savaged – could not unhinge me. I could not possibly be that weak.

I forced myself to look at the body once again, trying to get a hold of my coherent thoughts. It would do me no good to allow myself to get caught up in my own weakness – a weakness I did not realize I possessed. A weakness that filled me with shame.

Focus, Gabriel. The voice in my head sounded like Kadie. It helped me push forward. It helped me overcome the helplessness I felt in the pit of my stomach.

My eyes went over the injuries inflicted on this human. I tried to pick up any tell that would help explain what I was looking at. More than that, I could not help but wonder what the demons were looking for within this beautiful girl? Why did they need to torture her in such a way that caused her blood to run over the table and drip down the sides and into the carpet like a fountain of blood overflowing.

I walked forward and tried to assess her for information to take back. Anything I could use to help my woman. The scent nearly had me reeling back. I stopped, bent over, and tried to breathe in fresh air. I pushed out a sigh and straightened. Anger surged through my body. I could not be this vulnerable. I could not be this *weak*.

The scene from Kadie's torture tore through my mind. The poison had been her main instrument of agony, and yet this room was very different. There were no drips, no needles nearby. Had they simply tortured her to death by the human instruments of pain? Or had they taken something more useful from her? Were they looking for information? Or did she possess something they desired, something they deemed as absolutely necessary to take?

I looked closer and saw that her belly had been almost entirely removed. Bone and gut spilled out around the gaping hole. The blood already clotted, a dark, disturbingly blackened color that did not resemble human blood in the slightest.

Had they been looking for a babe? Or perhaps a power that could not be found in mere flesh?

This could have been Kadie, a voice told me.

Knowing that, I was going to be sick. The thought of Kadie enduring such torture, such pain, more than she had already faced, was enough to bring me to my knees.

And yet, it was not, another voice reminded me. *Do not martyr your memory simply to force yourself to feel things. You do a disservice to Kadie and to this poor soul.*

I pressed my lips together. The voice in my head was correct. What-if scenarios were not going to help me right now. If anything, they would only make things worse. I needed to get back on track.

My stomach churned once again, my gaze drawn to the twisted grimace of pain upon her face. I didn't want to leave her here, but I needed to find more answers to the new questions that popped up. There was no choice.

I picked up a blanket from the old bed in the room and draped it over her. It was all I could think to do to keep her warm in this evil place. It was ridiculous, more sentimental than logical, but I did not care. Just because it seemed a moot point did not mean the gesture was unimportant. If I was being honest with myself, it felt wrong to leave her exposed to the elements. It felt wrong to leave her out in the open where anyone could stumble upon her. It was what little respect I could offer her. It might not be much, but I hoped it was enough.

I stepped back and shook my head of compassion. Instead, I had to start deciphering what I was looking at and what it could all mean. My first assumption was that the victim had to be a Witc. Demons did not seem to focus such awful attention on mere humans, especially since it was much easier to inflict pain and terror on humans than on Witches.

If she was a witch, where was she from? Was she like Simone? Was she important or just an innocent person in all of this? Did she have powers that threatened Demons, or were they making their own assumptions about her?

I wondered if Simone and Margaret knew her. If this was one of the missing Witches, where were the others? Would the Demons be coming back to clean up their mess or was this body left behind on purpose? Kadie had been here almost two weeks ago and this girl had not been present. When was she taken? And why hadn't Tabitha known about all these disappearances?

Then it hit me, like an ice shovel in the face. The Law of Targets. As Guardians, we are only assigned to those who will make a huge difference in the world. Pure souls of great importance and intelligence. The Demons had used our own rules to get under our guard. It had to be. It was so clear now that I recognized it.

These Witches were so young, barely old enough to appear on the elders' radar. And even if they were old enough, they obviously weren't going to change the future of the planet. Not enough to warrant being on The List that us Fallen Angels were destined to protect. Which meant they escaped our notice. These disappearances didn't register with us because why would they? We weren't watching them. We didn't even know about them in the first place.

Until Kadie.

I thought back to my first observations of her. That she was ordinary. Un-remarkable in the huge scheme of things. I'd questioned why I'd been sent to protect one like her in the first place. At the time, I thought it was some kind of mistake. I didn't understand how someone who appeared so ordinary could make a difference in the grand scheme of things. It just showed how little I knew about the grand scheme of things.

I didn't realize why she was important until after it had happened;.she had been destined to birth my son - a man it was prophesized could rid the Earth of the Demons seeking to destroy it. The very threat to their existence.

I looked at the girl lying on the table and regret pulled through my heart. I hated leaving her here. Once we knew more, and I knew this place was safe, I would bring Margaret and the others here to bury the Witches they knew that had gone missing. Assuming there were more than just this one on the grounds and we found the bodies. Assuming they still had bodies to bury.

I'm so sorry. I promise, with every fiber of my being, to make this right. Your death will not be in vain.

I stepped into the hallway once more and took a deep breath of clean air. I couldn't breathe properly in a room with the dead. Death always made the air cloying and heavy, especially when that death was terribly brutal.

I continued to walk through the castle to see if there was something I could work with. I did not want to leave empty-handed.

The next room was empty, save for tubs of grease and lard. I assumed they were left over from a time when this castle was a functional home. It was difficult to picture since it reeked of nothing more than death currently. I clenched my jaw and continued onward.

The third room held only pools of dried blood and nothing more. No body, no skin, no innards. Nothing. Perhaps that was a good thing. I did not react well to the body from before. I was not sure how I would react if I saw another one.

How many women had they brought here? And had any except Kadie survived?

I clenched my free hand into a tight fist, my nails digging into my palm. I would not allow any more to suffer at the hands of Demons. If I had known, if I had been more aware of what was going on, perhaps this tragedy would not have happened. Perhaps the number of missing Witches would have decreased. Perhaps –

"Stop it." I said aloud to myself.

I could not continue to head down a path of hopelessness. It would not do me any good.

I released my fists and my skin tingled with a hot anger I could barely control. I clenched my teeth, holding back a snarl. I'd seen a lot of death in my time. Senseless war and suffering. But I'd always been distanced from it. Never taking personally the ridiculousness of man.

But this *was* personal. And I knew it was going to get a hell of a lot *more* personal before this was over.

The final room at the end of the hall was the one Kadie had been held in. I hesitated. I did not want to go in here. I did not want to relive the moment when I saw Kadie, when I saw how much pain she was in, when I thought I might lose her completely. But I knew I had to. I had to press on or else there was no point to this. I could not let my fears from the past take over my present. I took a deep breath and released it before I put my fingers on the door handle. Heat seared up my spine in a warning.

Demons.

I froze. They were here. In this room before me, when they weren't in the rest of the house. More than that, they did not seem to sense my presence. Unless this was some sort of elaborate trap and I was in the process of falling into it. Perhaps the other torture rooms were run by humans.

What a sickening thought.

There was something uniquely terrible about this end room that I remembered from last time. There had been the presence of Hell itself. A feeling of magic and evil, darkness and power and hopelessness.

This was where I would find the answers to my questions. This was also where I might end. If I faltered, if I made one misstep, I could die. And if I died…

I refused to entertain that thought.

I pushed open the door and held my sword in front of me as I stepped inside. There was no sound. There was no movement. Nothing.

Was I mistaken? Were the Demons gone? Was this room truly empty?

The blackness was unnatural, and as I looked around for even a glimmer of light, I found none.

I flung the door open wider and pushed it against the wall, using what little light the open door afforded to cast my eyes around the room.

I needed fire, and a torch. There had to be something in this castle I could work with.

When I turned to leave, the eerie blackness of the evil room, a flicker of light caught my eye. It glowed from inside the room and I grinned.

Good. They're back.

They must be returning from wherever they had been now. It was the only explanation as to why I was able to feel them and why they had not attacked me when I stepped into the room.

A single Demon grew right in front of me from the tiniest flicker of flame, to a huge, glowing beast that lit up the room. My lips started to quirk up in anticipation. My grip on my sword tightened. Adrenaline shot through my body like a bullet. This was what I had been waiting for.

Once the Demon was as big as a full-grown man, I addressed it.

"I have a few questions for you," I shouted at the monster, who seemed surprised to see me. I tilted my head to the side as I took in the quizzical brow. I did not think it was possible for a Demon to be surprised about anything.

He didn't move, didn't speak. Instead, he just stood still, glowing in the darkened room. Giving me the much needed light that I required. This was strange. I did not understand me. I felt unnerved, uncertain. He was not attacking me. Everything inside of me screamed to end him, and yet, I did not move. I waited.

My gaze skittered around the space, looking for clues or information I could take home with me. Looking for a reason why this Demon was doing nothing but lighting my way.

The room seemed to be in the same state as it had been when I'd taken Kadie, which was good news. Hopefully they hadn't taken any more girls hostage.

I continued to keep my sword pointed at the Demon all the while trying to take advantage of its light. From where I stood, I saw a black bag opened up with needles and clear, plastic bags of fluid pouring out of it. I moved my head and saw tools and other instruments inside, caked with rusted blood.

The bags themselves were dark. I stilled. Was that blood? Was it Kadie's blood? Blood they'd taken out of her? Poison they'd put into her? I didn't know.

I tilted my sword so it pointed at the Demon's chest and surged forward, the heaviness of the air making me want to choke on my own tongue.

The Demon began to glow a fiery red, and as I lifted my blade higher to slice at his head, he disappeared into thin air.

Like he'd never been here in the first place.

The room went pitch-black once more, enveloping me in heavy darkness. I stopped in mid-thrust, my inertia nearly causing me to topple forward.

I spun around, sweat coating my skin as I waited for the attack.

Nothing came and I was left waiting, my arms aching with readiness and my heart thundering in my chest.

What was going on here? It didn't make any sense.

I turned again, lunging in the darkness, hoping to catch some part of its flesh.

Nothing.

I let out a breath and tried to calm myself down. I let my eyes look over the room, even in the darkness.

This was where I'd almost died.

I stalked back towards the door, then thought better of leaving with nothing. I grabbed one of the dark bags of fluid from the medical table and a used syringe. I did not know if this would tell me anything. I did not know if these were just leftovers from another Witch or if this was used on Kadie specifically.

But it was something.

Better for Margaret or Tabitha to look at these and tell me what was going on here if they were able to.

I scanned the room with eyes that struggled to see anything in the gloominess one last time, then marched back to the open door. Disappointed I hadn't found more, nor the fight I'd been craving, I stalked outside.

Walking back through the empty, eerily quiet castle reminded me of a battlefield the day after the soldiers had left. When the dead lay quiet and the living had taken themselves home. It caused a shiver to creep down my spine, like a leaky faucet that dripped out water slowly yet deliberately. I felt like I was missing something. I felt like I was leaving something behind but I could not put a finger on what that was. It irked my very core but there was nothing I could do about it.

I moved along the terrace where I'd taken Kadie when we'd been running away from the Demons. It seemed so long ago, and yet it was only two days day since I'd picked her up in my arms, my wings barely able to carry us home.

I glanced down at my wings, battered and burned, but healed thanks to Tabitha's ministrations. They'd still carry me, but they'd never look the same. Not that I particularly cared. If anything, it reminded me not to take things for granted. That even angels had the capacity to fall.

With the blood bag and the syringe in my hand I took flight, flying higher while the sun danced on my skin.

I had to return to Tabitha's and hopefully when I got there, Kadie would be awake, and able to tell us what happened to her.

CHAPTER EIGHT

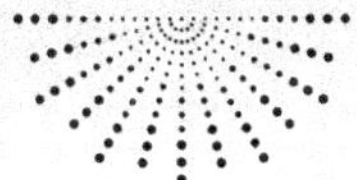

When I walked into Tabitha's place, it was too quiet for a house with four women. I started running until I found one of them. Margaret. In the kitchen, sitting by herself. She looked dazed. I did not think it was a happy look. However, it was not one of defeat, either.

"What's happening around here?" I asked, worry squeezing at my chest like a vise. I glanced around, hoping for any clue as to where the others were. I found nothing.

"Nice to see you too, Angel," she replied dryly, sitting up straighter, but otherwise not changing her tone or facial expression.

She was exhausted, that was obvious by her slouching shoulders, her limp legs. I could not remember if the bags around her eyes were new or not.

"Where is everyone?" I asked.

"Simone's with Kadie, and Tabitha had to go off to some meeting, or something," she said, waving her hand dismissively before using it to cover her mouth while she yawned.

Well that didn't seem too alarming, and at least she wasn't reporting something drastically bad had happened since I'd left. I tried to relax but couldn't. Not completely.

"Thank you, Margaret." I nodded my head once at her.

I strode into the room where Kadie was, and was confronted by the sight of her still-unconscious form. My sleeping beauty. I nearly dropped the bag and syringe where I stood. I had been hoping… But alas, that was not the case. She was not better. Then again, she did not appear worse.

Simone stood over Kadie's still form, wash cloth in hand. It almost appeared as though she was wiping something off Kadie, perhaps a cool compress against hot skin.

"Is she doing any better?" I asked into the quiet room.

Simone jumped up from her position over Kadie, nearly dropping the wash cloth, and placed her hand over her heart. "You scared me."

"I'm sorry." I stepped further into the room. Unlike the castle, it was easier to see through this darkness. Shadows criss-crossed against the natural light that was seeping in through cracks against the window. Instead of the room being pitch-black and feeling like all hope was lost, this room was grey. That didn't necessarily mean survival, but there was hope here. Love. Warmth.

I took in Simone, the bags under her eyes, the pale color of her skin. She was exhausted, but there was a determined glint in her eye that spoke about resilience, about never giving up. I knew she wanted to end the threat of Demons, not just for herself but for all Witches. I was glad she was here. I was glad I trusted her enough to take care of Kadie. I didn't think anyone else could do a good job the way Simone was already doing.

My eyes dropped to the cloth in her hand. I frowned when I saw it was muddied with green and black smudges.

"I've just been cleaning her," Simone explained through a yawn. "Her body is doing so much better since the cleansing."

"Good," I said, and meant it.

Simone went back to rubbing the poultice grime off Kadie's skin and I walked around to her other side, trying not to get in the way. For a moment, I watched Simone. The young Witch was gentle as she rubbed the cloth on Kadie's skin. Kadie's face seemed much more relaxed now, even in her unconscious state. It was not as pinched as it had been before. I wondered if Kadie somehow knew what was going on. I was sure she would be glad to get rid of the grime occupying her body.

Gratitude for Simone caused my heart to swell in that moment, but I pressed my lips together. I didn't like feeling beholden to someone, even if they deserved it. Simone would have my undying thanks for the rest of my long life. I would never be able to repay her, but I made a silent vow to myself to do everything I could to at least try.

I turned back to Kadie and pushed stray strands of errant red hair from her skin and curled them behind her ears. I took a breath and bent down, pressing a kiss to her forehead. The scent of her wasn't right yet. It definitely wasn't Kadie's.

I snapped up and turned to Simone, suddenly on my guard.

"Why does she smell so different?" I asked the young Witch who seemed to have vastly stronger powers than her much older aunt.

Simone sighed heavily and shifted. My heart dropped. Something had happened. That was why Simone was hesitating to respond. It was why she could not even look at me.

"Simone," I pushed.

"Her soul is not as it was," she finally said.

I narrowed my eyes at the young girl. What a thing to say!

"Did you know her before?" I asked through gritted teeth. How could a soul change? It was the essence of a person. Unless that person changed, how could a soul?

Simone shook her head. "No. I've never met another Witch before, other than my aunt, Margaret. She's kept me pretty much in the dark and away from her coven. I hadn't realized why until recently."

"So how do you know?" I asked again. I gripped the sheets by Kadie, trying not to let my frustration show. I didn't want to hear that Kadie's soul was different now. I couldn't stand that. Our son needed to know the true beauty of his mother.

Simone didn't answer, she simply pulled the blanket down and continued to wash Kadie's body, which was looking so much healthier and stronger now. I thought that was a good thing, a sign of her waking up soon. And yet, Simone seemed to hint that even if she did wake up, she might not be the same woman I fell in love with.

The sores were healed, her skin was a normal color. She even had a soft glow in her cheeks. And yet, she was different. She smelled different.

"Then how do you know something is wrong with her soul?" I repeated.

Pain was burning in my gut from my attempt to stay calm. I didn't want to know that Kadie had changed. That she may wake up different. That her soul had been changed in some way. Or worse, that she had become soul-less.

Had the Demons really changed her that much? And was it all my fault?

Simone shrugged. There was regret in her eyes. I could tell she didn't like being the one to tell me this news. I did appreciate her candor even though it hurt me, even though I didn't want to hear it. "I shouldn't have said anything," she muttered more to herself than to me.

"No, you shouldn't have," came the admonishment from the door.

I ignored Margaret, my eyes burning into Simone's profile.

"Yes, Simone, you should say something if you two know anything that I don't," I insisted. I released the sheets and stood up. I longed to hit my full height, to intimidate both of them into revealing any more secrets they might be purposefully keeping from me, but I reigned that instinct in. Intimidation would not help things here. "And speaking of which, these are for you to analyze."

I pulled the dark fluid bag and the syringe from my shirt and placed them on the empty table next to Kadie. I had nearly forgotten about them after seeing Kadie, smelling her. After Simone revealed yet another secret I was not aware of.

"What do you have there?" Margaret asked, walking forward to examine them.

"I took them from the room inside the castle where they held

Kadie," I explained. I shifted my weight, crossing my arms over my chest.

Margaret picked up the bag of blood from the foot of the bed and weighed it in her hands. Simone paused what she was doing to look it over as well.

"This isn't blood," she finally said. "This is the poison they infected her with." She moved out of the room and returned with a huge bowl and a knife.

When she picked up the knife, I stepped forward. "You aren't going to open that, are you?"

If it was, indeed, the poison that had been killing Kadie, I did not understand how opening a bag of it would help anything.

I didn't want that stuff anywhere near Kadie again. I didn't want there to be a chance that she could get infected again – or anyone else, for that matter.

"Only one way to find out what she was actually poisoned with." Margaret's tone was obvious as though I should have thought about it before I opened my mouth and asked the question. I didn't want to admit it, but she might have been right.

Margaret sliced open the bag with a quick flick of the knife along the plastic, and black gunk oozed into the bowl like a vomiting swamp. I sneered as I watched it. A heavy, metallic scent clawed its way out of the bag and hung out in my nostrils. I wasn't sure I would be able to rid myself of it for a long, long time. I held my breath while the two Witches gagged.

"Take it outside!" Simone screamed as she fell to the ground in a fit of retching. Her shoulders bobbed up and down in spasms she couldn't control. Her voice was garbled, like speaking was difficult for her to do.

Margaret grabbed the bowl and hurried out the open window. I heard it crash to the street below, the bowl shattering into in pieces.

I followed her and watched as she spilled it onto the grass in the backyard. The green grass hissed and burned, slowly dying before my very eyes, as though it had been hit with acid. Smoke or steam – I could not tell which – rose from where the poison touched the grass.

"What the hell was in that?" I asked.

"Cyanide and hemlock, among other things," the Witch panted, staggering back to bed. Simone seemed to have a better grip on herself and was able to stand at her full height now that the poison wasn't tainting this room.

I put an arm around her waist and helped Margaret to a sitting position in the chair Simone had been resting in before she started wiping Kadie's body. Simone left the room, muttering something about opening the front door and all the windows in the house to rid the house of the evil.

"I hope that was worth it." I said, glancing at the women who looked deathly pale and quite distressed.

Margaret should never have opened that inside, but no point in laying blame now.

"Now that we know for sure what is poisoning her, I'm afraid we're going to need more than a few herbs to bring her back," Simone said, her mouth drawing into a painful grimace. She could not look at me. Instead, her eyes dropped to her hands, to the wash-cloth. She paused wiping down Kadie, almost as though there was no point in doing so. Not anymore, anyway.

"What do you mean?" I asked, frowning at the young Witch. My mouth went dry at Simone's words and it took everything in me to refrain from demanding answers. I needed to be patient if I wanted them to keep talking to me, to keep helping me.

Simone coughed a few times and then drew in a few deep breaths near an open window. She dropped the cloth to the floor, discarding it as though it was a mere piece of trash and nothing more.

"I mean, that concoction is more clever than I first realized," she said. "It is designed to seep slowly into a victim, inflict pain and torture, ripping out the insides of a Witch. Then, after that, it, kills its victim. And ensure she can never come back."

"What do you mean, never come back?" My heart stopped. My mouth pressed into a thin line once I said the words. There was so much more I wanted to say, so much more I needed clarification on. And yet, I waited. I did not want to make any assumptions. I did not want to think about things if they were not true. I wanted them to tell me – I *needed* them to tell me what was going on with Kadie and what we could do to save her.

We *had* to save her.

Still, Simone's words confused me. What did she mean about Kadie never coming back. I always thought death was always finite. Since when could Witches come back from the dead?

Margaret stepped forward and sat down on the chair next to the empty bed, her skin still the color of ash.

"Simone doesn't mean in the flesh," the older Witch explained, her voice low. "Not technically, anyway. But we have some special religious nights throughout the year when our communication abilities with our elders and relatives who have passed on are enhanced. This poison they've mixed up would make sure that Kadie could never return for any of that. She would be cut off from this world once she left it. And all of her magic with it. And if that happened, she would be lost to us forever. There's no coming back from it."

I struggled to comprehend the information the Witches were giving me. So, they were telling me that this poison was designed to not only kill the Witch who took it, but destroy her very soul as well? Was that what Simone meant when she said that Kadie's soul had changed? Had she already reached a point where she could not come back?

"Do you think this poison has been used on all those other girls?" I swallowed hard as I remembered the girl they'd left to rot on the table. Guilt gnawed at my gut for leaving her but I knew I could not bring her back. I could not risk exposing Tabitha, Simone, Margaret, and Kadie to more poison if the dead Witch had been poisoned. I was not sure how the poison worked but I did not want to exploit my ignorance.

I should tell Margaret and Simone about the Witch – perhaps they knew her - but later. Once Kadie was better I would take them there myself so they could see her. If she was still there, of course.

"What do you mean?" they asked me at the same time.

"I don't know," I admitted, "but based on what you've both told me, it almost seems as though the Demons are trying to steal these

Witches' power. Their magic. I don't know why or how. I don't know how they target certain Witches. But it's the only thing that makes sense right now."

Margaret nodded slowly, her eyebrows drawing down into a thoughtful frown. "I'm afraid so, but for what purpose?"

A hardness fell over my body as the anger set in. My mind raced with possibilities. I thought about what I knew about Demons. I thought about what I knew about Witches. "There's only ever one purpose for beings of evil," I said. "Power. Witches must have a magic not even Demons are privy to. Perhaps they are threatened by it. Perhaps it is something that can cause actual harm. But I would not be surprised if they are eliminating threats and stealing the magic for themselves so they can grow more powerful themselves. So they can be unmatched, even against angels."

I needed to stop them before they worked out how to harness these girls' magic. Especially Kadie's. She seemed to be unusually powerful. I wondered if the demons knew that. I wondered if she had been targeted for that specific reason or if it had just been a coincidence, if they knew Kadie was as powerful as she was or if they only knew she was a Witch.

"What are you going to do about it, Angel?" Margaret asked me suddenly, her eyes glittering with an anger I also felt. I knew she wasn't taking her anger out on me. I knew she did not like any Witch threatened by Demons, threatened by anyone.

I understood. That raw anger was burning inside of me as well.

"I'm going to find whoever it is that is doing this, and stop them," I promised. "And if that means tearing a hole in the fabric of space and time, and diving into Hell, I will."

I meant every word I said even if it sounded dramatic. I intended to get to the source, before they found a way to us.

The younger Witch stepped closer to me, reaching a hand out as though seeking a connection. I allowed her to take it, offering what she needed.

I needed it as well.

"You need to be careful, Gabriel," she said, her voice gentle but also filled with a warning. "Your son is very important, and he will need you." There was something off with her tone, something that did not sound like how she normally did. I glanced over at her, ripping my eyes away from Kadie and looking at Simone. Her eyes glowed with that strange silver essence they had sometimes. I realized her voice was monotone, as though she was in some sort of trance.

"What are you?" I asked and she dropped her gaze from mine as though embarrassed. She shook her head, snapping out of whatever trance she had been in, her cheeks turning pink.

"She's a Witch who hasn't even come into her powers yet," Margaret said, though it didn't really answer my question.

It was no matter. Mage, magician, powerful Witch or fortune-teller. As long as Simone fought on our side, her true calling was not my concern. She was powerful. She was knowledgeable. And my gut told me she was loyal. We would be lucky to have her on our side. We *needed* her to fight for our side. But I could not make her if she did not want to. I could not make either of them stay if they wanted to retreat.

"Shall I take either of you back to your homes now?" I asked as my restlessness began to shiver through me once again.

There was a war coming and I needed to be prepared for it. I needed to know who would cower and who would fight.

"I'm staying with Kadie," Simone declared, grabbing for the blanket that covered Kadie's body as though I would tear her away from her patient. Her eyes were fierce, daring me to argue with her, daring me to tell her that she must leave.

I had been bred to read humans well, and Simone had no ill intent towards Kadie. Quite the opposite. She was fiercely protective of the fallen Witch, even though she barely knew her. I appreciated that fierceness, that unwavering loyalty. There were not many people in this world who possessed such traits.

I turned towards Margaret, who nodded her head.

"I will come with you," she said, agreeing with her niece.

She was firm in her conviction, and while there wasn't the same passion her niece had, it relieved me all the same.

"I need to make more medicines for Kadie if she has any hope of returning to us."

There was one more question that had been tickling the back of my mind and I had to ask it, despite my fear of the answer.

"Will my son be all right?" I forced out. I had purposefully attempted not to think about him while I was here. It would not help being torn down the middle with one part of me with Kadie and the other with my son. I needed to be completely present if I was going to succeed at my mission. I could not let anyone or anything distract me. And yet, this was important. I needed to know about the safety of my son. Because if my son wasn't safe, what was the point of all of this besides saving Kadie? "After all, he was inside his mother when she was poisoned."

Margaret chewed on her lips in worry for a moment.

"I believe so, although I have not seen him," Margaret said. She refused to give me false hope, which I appreciated. "Your child is half-immortal, which will give him a strength we do not possess. And as a human woman, Kadie's body was designed to protect her babes while taking the brunt of any abuse herself. He got the best of both worlds, I would hope."

The babe had looked well when I'd seen him with Jasmine, so for the moment, I needed to focus on that. I couldn't let myself focus on negative possibilities. It would eat me alive and drive me insane. I had to remind myself my son was safe. It was the only way I'd be able to think of how to defeat the Demons and get rid of any threat against us.

"All right." That made me feel better. Slightly. "I will drop you back home, and gather whatever information you think I need. Because the next step, I'm afraid, is to go back to the room where Kadie was held and force my way into their dimension."

I wasn't sure but my gut feeling told me that they were jumping from Hell to the castle, like the castle was a portal. It was the only thing that made sense. My mind kept replaying the Demon from before, how he manifested from nothing and suddenly arrived with no warning at all.

Margaret's shocked gasp filled the room. "You won't survive

that, Gabriel," she stated. I did not know why she made that assumption or how she could know about Angels and our abilities. But I wasn't going to let her certainty deter me.

"Maybe," I acknowledged with a nod. "But I can't think of any other way. And something must be done or nothing will change."

"You rushing into danger won't save Kadie," Margaret said, her voice stoic, her eyes narrowed at me at though she was angry at me and my decision.

"Perhaps not. But maybe it will help other potential victims, including the Witches who are getting stolen. I can't say for sure why the Demons want the Witches, but I think it has to do with them seeking power. And if I can stop them, even if it means going to their dimension to do it, it will all have been worth it. I do not want Kadie's suffering to be in vain."

And it was true. I needed to confront whatever force was trying to steal the Witches power. Or already had.

I tried not to think about the possibility of them being successful. In truth, I had no idea what I was getting into. I did not understand the risks. I worried that they would be more powerful than I could ever be, but I could not continue to stand by and do nothing.

Margaret waved her hands at me. "I will call a council meeting," she announced. "I'm sure we can find others who will fight with you. Help you. It can't possibly end this way. And you shouldn't have to do this alone."

I slowed down my thinking, taking in what the Witches around me were saying. I wasn't into suicide missions, but I was very willing to give my life for the protection of this world and for the people in it. However, I wanted to know my sacrifice would make a difference to those I loved. I did not want to do this if it would be in vain, if it wasn't going to matter at the end of the day.

"Perhaps I could continue to fight Demons as I have been?" I said, tilting my head to the side. I was open to hearing what they had to say. "Kill as many as I can. Protect my son and let him grow."

To be the warrior we have been waiting for.

Tabitha's voice sounded in my head and I turned to watch her rush into the room. Rush as must as she could, at least. I stepped towards her, ready to help her if need be, but she shot me a look that told me not to even think about assisting her when she was fully capable of handling things on her own. Tabitha's pride was nearly as bad as my own.

Before I could speak with her, however, I noticed the tension in her lips and forehead. Something was wrong.

"What is happening, Tabitha?" I asked. My body tensed, as though it was preparing for war.

I could not shake a wave of happiness as it crashed over me, despite the anxiety I felt coursing through Tabitha, despite the own rigidness my body was experiencing. She looked so much better than she had earlier in the day. This gave me hope – not only for my Agent but for Kadie as well. If Tabitha was getting better, surely that meant Kadie had the potential to as well.

"Gabriel!" Tabitha exclaimed, cutting me out of my thoughts. "You need to get to your son. I sense Demons closing in on him."

She didn't need to tell me twice.

I took off at a run and blasted through the front door and into the sky. I should have grabbed him the second time I went to visit Jasmine. My instincts told me to take him with me, but I refrained. I did not want to bring him into this war. I thought if he was with me, he would distract me.

And now, I was told I was wrong.

Tabitha always had an annoying way of sharing bad news with a smile on her face. Then again, the fact that she had this information was extremely helpful. I did not want to think about what could have happened if Tabitha hadn't been able to say anything in the first place.

I flew through the air, heat tingling in my spine even at this height above the Earth. *Damn it.* I pushed harder and wove through the sky over New York City and down to Jasmine's street. I did not think I had ever made it to her home so quickly. My wings – already ruined due to my last encounter with Demons – were strained. It felt like they wanted to collapse off of my back, I pushed them so hard. Still, I was here.

My feet hit the pavement and an eerie quiet descended on me. It was still early evening, darkness had not yet fallen, yet I could feel the Demons in the darkness. Waiting for the opportune moment to strike. It would be any time. I needed to act quickly.

I ran to the front door and banged on the wood. I did not care if I broke the door down – though a small logical part of my mind told me that if I did do that to the door, it would take away a layer of protection from Jasmine and her family. Still, I could not remove the urgency in my knocking. I needed to see my son. Now.

Nobody came. I banged again.

Dammit.

My spine tingled with a Demon's approach. I turned, ready to take my anger out on the bastard only to find nobody there.

I growled.

Fuck this.

I slammed my body against the door and cracked it right down the middle. I needed to get to my son and I'd always been welcome in this home. Maybe Jasmine's husband wasn't my biggest fan, but I was positive he at least understood that I had saved his wife's life.

"Jasmine!" I yelled out as I raced through each of the rooms of her house. She'd said she wouldn't leave and yet the entire house was empty. Where were they? Panic infiltrated my bloodstream and prevented any coherent thoughts from entering my mind. It was as though I was acting on instinct because there was absolutely no way I had the capability of rationalizing what was going on.

When I reached the kitchen, there was food sitting on the table, uneaten. Toys scattered across the floor, as though children had been playing only recently. I faltered. What happened here? Where was my son? Where was Jasmine and her family?

Then there was a woman's terrified scream from below.

"No!"

I didn't think, I just reacted. I immediately headed for the front room where there was a staircase that led to their cellar. They had to be there. That was the only place I hadn't checked. God, I needed them to be there, unharmed..

I flew down the steps to the concrete floor and before me was a horrible sight. My baby was surrounded by fiery Demons. How were they here when darkness had not touched the city yet? More than that, why had they not attacked him, or at least, reached out and taken him?

It didn't matter. I needed to act before they had the opportunity to do either of those things. Before it was too late.

"No!" I screamed again as I charged forward, drawing my sword and swinging it in sharp arcs, mowing down the Demons closest to me.

Jasmine clung to my baby and her own daughter, tears streaming down her face as she faced off against the fires of Hell. I had no idea where her husband was. I didn't particularly care.

I sliced straight into the infernal circle and shoved Jasmine behind me. Then I turned and pushed her back to the now open stairs as I faced off against the remaining Demons. I needed her and my son out. I did not want her there to distract me. If I knew she wasn't in immediate danger, I could fight much better, without worry.

"Run. Go!" I yelled at Jasmine, and she took off. Her ragged breathing and her fast footsteps up the stairs echoed in the room.

I turned to the Demons, my face contorted into a scowl.

"You will never touch him!" I yelled at the remaining Demons, swinging my sword as they converged together. "You will never have him. I will never let you touch him. Do you hear me?"

I ran forward and they all disappeared into thin air, like they'd never been here at all.

Just like at the castle.

I let out a roar of frustration.

"Fuck!"

I ran up the stairs after Jasmine, still gripping my sword hard. Had they followed Jasmine? Had they reached my son?

"Where are they?" I shouted, looking around for any sign the Demons had followed Jasmine above. "Are they here?"

But Jasmine was mute, clinging to her screaming daughter and my son as though she'd never let them go. Her whole body shook like a leaf, her face white. I did not think I would get any sort of response from her right now. She wasn't in the right frame of mind.

My heart was pounding so hard it sounded like I had the rush of an ocean in my ears. I whirled around once, twice, looking for any hint of where they were.

Nothing.

I took several breaths and consciously told my hands to relax from their death-grip on my sword. I was losing it. I needed to focus. I would be no help to anyone if I didn't relax. I would not be able to fight the way I knew I was able to if I didn't get a grip on myself.

"Everything's okay now, Jasmine," I forced myself to say. I realized I was probably scaring her the way I was scaring myself. And if I was scared, she would have a hard time helping me. I needed her to be level-headed, especially now. "I'm so sorry. I'm so sorry."

Jasmine trembled as she stepped closer to me. "Take him. Please." Guilt pooled in her eyes but her voice – even though it shook – was firm. There was no way she wanted to risk any other losses for my child. I could not blame her.

I took my son, who was now crying softly. My heart went out to him. My heart went out to Jasmine and her daughter as well.

This entire situation was not fair. Everyone involved – besides the Demons – had suffered through pain, a loss, or fear at what they expected to come. Lives were lost, missing, and at risk. I had an idea as to why, but I wasn't sure. I hated this. I hated that I could not fix it with a snap of my fingers. I hated that if I was in this position again, risking Jasmine and her family, I would make the same choice because it would protect my son.

Jasmine began rocking her daughter with both arms wrapped around her, shushing her in that way that all mothers did. I reached out my arm, wanting to place my hand on her shoulder and offer her a reassuring moment after all she had been through, but I stopped myself. I did not know if I was the person she needed this from. I did not want to upset her even more than she already was. Since I did not know if my presence would help her, I decided not to risk it.

I sighed silently and looked down at my son. He was still crying, on and off, his head turning, his eyes closed. It almost seemed like he was looking for comfort, perhaps a nipple to suckle on. It was time to take my son back to his mother.

However, I had to ask a few questions first. I needed to get as much information as I could while it was still fresh in Jasmine's mind. This way, I could leave without needing to intrude on her again.

"Jasmine," I said. Her eyes opened, though she continued to cradle her child protectively against her. "What happened? How could they come into your house? During the day?"

She wiped at the tears still streaming down her face. I'd always admired Jasmine's ability to stay calm, even in the most adverse situations.

"I don't know." She shook her head, blinking her eyes rapidly in a way to try and get rid of the remaining tears. She wiped the back of her hand against her nose using her sleeve before replacing the hand on her daughter's body and providing the reassurance her daughter sought. "My husband refused to stay home today despite what I told him you said. He had someone come... work on the furnace downstairs..." She let her voice trail off and looked away. Her eyes found the shattered door to the cellar. "Do you think he let them in somehow?"

I thought about it for a moment. That was not out of the realm of possibility. However, there had to be more to the story.

"Humans helped kidnap Kadie," I said, talking more to myself than to Jasmine. An idea tickled the very outside of my mind. I grabbed onto it, not sure where it would lead me. I just knew I had to follow it no matter where it led me. "They took her to the Demons. Perhaps the Demons have hired more humans to do their dirty work now? I know they work with humans. They've used humans as guards, as watchers." I straightened my shoulders. It made sense. Jasmine's husband inadvertently hired a human to repair their furnace, not knowing this human was working for the Demons. Which meant, essentially, he led the Demons straight to Jasmine. Straight to my son. I clenched my hands together, trying to contain my anger. As much as her husband did not like me, I knew he had no malintent towards my son. He might send Demons my way without a care in the world, but I knew he would not risk my son. "I'm going to check it out."

I slid the baby into my shirt, keeping him safe against my chest This seemed to be the comfort he needed – skin to skin. In less than a moment, his mouth hung open and his eyes closed. Judging by his steady breathing, he was already deeply asleep.

Now that my son was content, I shifted my thoughts on these humans and the Demons they worked for. There had to be a way that these Hellish creatures were venturing into the day. A portal or key, perhaps? Did it have to do with the type of humans they hired, or did the humans not matter in the grand scheme of things, besides being able to move around during the day? But if the Demons could now do just that, why continue to use humans in the first place.

Unless they weren't using humans anymore.

Unless they were somehow able to disguise themselves as humans now.

I needed to leave. Now.

"The light switch is at the top of the stairs," Jasmine called out as I moved through the door to investigate. I flicked it on.

The fluorescent globes barely lit the room below, but there was enough light to see the ash I'd reduced one of the Demons to. There didn't seem to be anything else around that indicated it had a link to Hell. No portals. No objects out of the ordinary.

I'd have to get Jasmine down here to see if there was anything she could point out that shouldn't be there. She'd know much better than I.

But not today.

I took the steps back up to the landing three at a time. This place needed to be cleansed. Burned down, if necessary.

"We need to get you somewhere safe, Jasmine," I told her. I did not feel comfortable leaving the cellar without Jasmine looking at it. Unfortunately, I did not think she was in any sort of shape to help me. Tears had started gliding down her cheeks in a gentle manner. I did not think I could stop her tears even if I wanted to. Perhaps she needed to ensure them. Perhaps it would help cleanse her fears and any guilt she might harbor putting her family at risk because of me.

"And where is that?" she asked, looking at me through red rimmed eyes. I could not blame her for her derivative tone. If it wasn't for me, she would not be involved in this mess.

"The Hotel."

The Angel Agency had a hotel in central Manhattan where we took people who needed the ultimate protection, when a Guardian could not provide everything that was offered because they needed to investigate Demons or because they needed to protect a new target.

I should have sent Kadie there after I'd helped her. If only I had the foresight to know this would happen, that this was even a possibility... I stopped myself from thinking further thoughts. I made my choices and now I must live with the repercussions those choices produced. I did the best I could with the information I had at the time.

Regardless of the truth of that, it did not make me feel any better.

If I remembered the Hotel, if I hadn't been so consumed with my feelings for Kadie and my fear at keeping her safe, this would never have happened.

"The Hotel?" Jasmine asked, unsure. "I'll have to take my daughter. And my husband will have to meet us there."

"I will make sure they take all of you," I promised.

I'd very rarely used the Hotel as a refuge for anyone I was protecting, as Demons tended to only have one Target. And once I'd killed all the Demons that had been assigned to my Target, the threat ceased and the Hotel was not needed.

But that didn't seem to be the case now, and Jasmine and her family needed around-the-clock protection.

Because of me, a tiny niggling voice said in my mind, but I ruthlessly shoved it aside. I'd allow myself to feel guilty later.

"What about... everything?" she asked, glancing around her beautiful home. Her grip was still tight on her daughter, and I knew that that baby was the only thing that truly mattered to her.

However, leaving her home she built with her family was akin to giving up, running away, all because she agreed to be involved in something that didn't involve her,

Guilt, again, threatened to invade me body and distract me from my goal, but I pushed past it. The longer I was with Jasmine, the more I realized just what she had to give up because of me, the easier it was for the unfamiliar emotion to trickle through.

"Don't worry about the house," I said. "You and your family are the only important things to protect. Just pack what you need and I'll take you there now."

She nodded, still breathing as though she'd just run a marathon. Her eyes were focused on a picture on a stand next to her couch. I hadn't noticed it before. I hadn't really looked around. To Jasmine, besides her child, that seemed to be her entire focus. I wasn't quite sure what to make of it. Despite being immersed in the human world for centuries, it was still difficult for me to understand their emotions.

"Jasmine," I said, trying to keep my voice gentle. Her eyes snapped into mine. "We must leave. Now."

She nodded, shaking herself out of her stupor. Clutching her daughter to her chest, she headed up the stairs to where their bedrooms were.

I'd put Jasmine, her husband, and their beautiful baby girl in the Hotel for months if necessary. It had around-the-clock surveillance and no dark corners for Demons to hide in. I would have sent her there with my son, but I assumed Demons could not get to them during the day.

If I had access to Tabitha, if she was healthy, I was certain she would have nagged me about it. But I was so focused on getting nourishment and a safe shelter for my son, for getting Kadie and Tabitha better, for figuring out what was going on and why, I had forgotten, and as a result, Jasmine and her child nearly died.

I clenched my teeth together and buried my head in my son's essence. There was something sweet about a newborn scent. I wouldn't say it was intoxicating, but it was as though I recognized myself in it. I did not think I would be as soothed if I was holding any other child but my own.

Never again, I promised myself I would not forget such pertinent details because of my own selfish desires. I would not risk an innocent for myself.

The only exception, of course, was my son. I would do anything to protect him, no matter what that was.

I brought my son out into the light and stared down at his perfect face. He slept now, the drama of the day finally gone. His Cupid's bow upper lip trembled with each breath and little cries came from him. Those cries reminded me of aftershocks of an earthquakes and I smiled to myself. I understood humans hated the sound of a newborn baby crying. To me, however, it told me my son was still alive. The cries reassured me that he still had the capacity to breathe. He still had the capacity to shout and scream and yell. And that gave me hope.

A tear slid down my cheek without warning and I wiped it away.

What magic was this? This tightness around my chest? This need to grip my baby to my heart and never let him go?

I did not understand it, and yet I would not trade it for anything in the world or Heaven. Nothing and no one, not even God Himself could tempt me from possessing my child. I did not understand how parents could give up their children. Logically, perhaps the choice was best, perhaps the choice was difficult to make, but I still could not fathom doing the same thing. I could not give up my child or allow any harm to come to him.

Anger pulsed in my blood out of nowhere and as I closed my eyes and let the feelings fill me up, boiling my blood, tightening my muscles in my body. I had to ignore the urge to punch through walls and take down buildings. Kill anything that stood in my way.

All because this baby existed. A perfect miracle.

I kissed his nose and made an oath to my Gods.

I will keep him safe, no matter the price. Whether I get back into Heaven, or you send me down to Hell itself to fight, no one will have him. No one will have him except those I choose for him. No harm will come to him as long as breath circulates through my body and keeps me alive.

My thoughts were interrupted by footsteps on the stairs. Jasmine returned with two bags and the baby in a carrier. She went over to where she stared at the picture, hesitating. I was not sure why she simply didn't take the picture and put it in her purse. Then again, the confliction of human emotions was lost to me, save for the emotions I had already experienced for myself. Finally, she set the picture down and headed back to where she set her bags down. Her baby cooed happily, completely oblivious to everything going around her. How I wish I could be that ignorant.

"Okay, Gabriel, we're ready," Jasmine said. "I'll call James when we get there. I can't wait to be somewhere safe for a few days."

I didn't tell her it may be more than a few days. I didn't tell her I was planning on keeping her there for months if I had to. I knew it would be a complete upheaval from her life. I was also aware that she never asked for this. But her safety, her family's safety – even her husband's – was the priority. I could not risk them any further, especially after everything she had risked for me.

We walked out of the house. The sun was still up. I hoped that would keep the Demons away. I hailed a taxi and we piled inside. I gave the driver instructions and driver sped off, taking us into the city. Traffic was prevalent and the sidewalks were filled with tourists. The ride was silent. I kept my eyes on the sun, watching it slowly descend. This was taking too long.

Finally, we pulled up to the Hotel. I helped her with her bags while Jasmine grabbed her baby carrier. When we stepped in, I checked her family in, insisting they stay in Tabitha's suite. After verifying my identity, they agreed. Luckily, Jasmine was focused on feeding her child and did not hear when I said her family would be staying there indefinitely. I did not want to worry her. I did not want to upset her. Eventually, I would tell her the truth if I had the opportunity. For now, I wanted to give her a sense of safety. It was the least I could do.

I owed her my son's life. And in a way, mine as well.

Deep down, I knew it was a debt I could never repay.

CHAPTER NINE

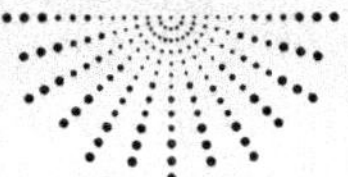

Once settled into their new rooms, Jasmine thoughtfully changed my son and gave me two bottles of milk for him.

"If you need me to feed him still, you can leave him with me," Jasmine offered as she stroked his head. "I hope it did not come across that I didn't want him still. I just…" She let her voice trail off as her lips trembled. Despite the fact that I was aware just how much Jasmine had endured, it still struck me as strange to see the trauma written so easily on her face. It reminded me that even though she had immeasurable strength, she was still human. "I just wanted to comfort my daughter."

I nodded my head. "I understand," I said. "Our progeny are our priority. I would never fault you for that."

She smiled. "He makes the cutest grunting noises," she told me.

The fondness she felt for my son was painfully obvious, despite the fact that he had put her own daughter's life in jeopardy. I knew she felt conflicted. I knew she was guilty. I was not sure if I would have done the same thing had our positions been reversed.

I would always admire her for her courage. It was courage I did not think even I possessed.

"Thank you for the offer, Jasmine," I said, my words sincere. "But I'm hoping his mother will be awake by the time I get back."

Kadie had to be awake. If she wasn't… I didn't know what that meant but I knew it couldn't be good. Tabitha was in pain but she was up. She was moving. She was conscious. Kadie, on the other hand…

I did not like to picture the way she was. I shook it from my mind and focused on my son. With reluctance, I tucked him into the carrier Jasmine had given me to wear while I flew. It would be handy if I needed to fight with him in my arms. That was not something I wanted to entertain because it would put him at risk. However, I could not predict what would happen with these Demons who seemed to disappear from one place to the next, who could somehow come out during the day.

I swallowed hard as I prepared to make my apologies.

"I don't know how to thank you enough, or apologize fully for the danger I placed you in, Jasmine," I said. My voice was scratchy and I swallowed, hoping to alleviate myself of the annoyance. It did not work, however. "I should have brought you to the Hotel earlier. But I honestly had no idea the Demons could get to you inside your home."

The truth of the matter was I had completely forgotten about the Hotel in the first place. But I would not tell her that because I was a coward, at least, in this respect.

I ran a shaky hand through my hair and Jasmine gave me a soft smile of understanding. I'd never used Tabitha's hotel before to save a Target. Never. I fought hard and long against the Demons, and they never returned once I'd vanquished them.

But something had changed.

Dramatically changed.

What was worse was that I was putting people in danger, people who otherwise would have no quarrel with these Demons. People who could be living a life of safety.

"It's all right, Gabriel," she said. "As I said before. I owe you my life. Nothing is too much for you to ask of me."

Jasmine stepped closer and put her arms around me, squeezing tight while I kissed the top of her head.

So much affection.

Such a strange year I was having after so long without human touch.

I tried to step away, but she held me tight.

Part of me wished she would lash out. Part of me wished she would tell me to go to Hell or blame me for how topsy-turvy her life had become. I wanted her to lash out, to hit, to slap me across my face. It was what I deserved.

But she didn't do any of that.

Instead, she held onto me tightly and I could feel her love coursing through her and to me. She was trying to reassure me. In essence, she was doing my job. I was the one who was supposed to reassure her. I was supposed to make her feel safe and cared for. I was supposed to be doing the protecting.

Instead, she was doing that for me. She wasn't broken. I was.

I kissed the top of her head again, trying to regain my capabilities once again. I could not be weak any longer. I needed to make myself strong.

"I need to go," I said, straightening. She tilted her head up to look at me. "You know what to do. There are Angels and well-trained humans everywhere in this Hotel. If you see even a glimmer of fire, you scream your head off. Got it?"

Jasmine finally pulled away and wiped away a tear that had slid down her cheek.

"You know I'm kinda jealous," she said. Her voice had gotten softer, as though she was not quite sure she wanted to admit this, even to me. "Of Kadie and you."

A ripple of unease ran through my chest. "What do you mean?" I asked.

My hand reached through the carrier strapped to my chest to feel the rise and fall of my son's stomach. I could not explain it, but it was important to me to ensure he was still breathing.

She wiped at the air with her hand as though to dismiss what she'd said. Her face was red, with shame or embarrassment, I did not know. Her eyes would not meet mine. Instead, she focused them on her daughter. They softened when they saw her.

"Oh, I know I'm happy now, and I have my baby girl," she said. "She's honestly the best thing that ever happened to me in this life. But I had such a crush on you when you first saved my life. I wanted you to need me as I needed you." She sighed. "But it didn't happen. And that's okay. I just… I don't even know why I'm telling you this in the first place, to be honest. The words are coming and I can't seem to stop them."

I shifted with discomfort. I wasn't quite sure what to say to that. I wanted to be honest, but I also felt compelled to reassure her the way she had been so reassuring to me.

"We aren't allowed to have relationships with our Targets," I said. I recited words I'd said a thousand times before. It wasn't reassuring exactly, but it was honest.

She raised one eyebrow and glanced down at the baby in my arms, seeming to indicate that rules could be broken if participants were willing to take the risk.

Heat raced up my cheeks like a fiery flood. I didn't know what to say. How could I tell the beautiful human in front of me that Kadie had been the first woman to tempt me in three hundred and fifty years without coming across like a hypocrite? I knew humans well enough to know that Jasmine might take my choice of Kadie as a rejection of her, and that was not the case at all. Kadie was different. That was it. However, it was difficult to put that into words and make Jasmine understand.

"Kadie is part Witch," I said. It was the only explanation I could think of that might persuade her. "I don't think I had much of a choice."

I hated that this was a lie. I hated that I blamed Kadie for my feelings when I knew, deep down, they were organic and came from within. I painted Kadie as a temptress willing to use spells to compel me to have feelings for her when I knew Kadie would never use such manipulation on anyone.

Jasmine frowned. "Part Witch?" she said slowly, tasting the explanation on her lips. "Is that how she managed to conceive your baby? I would have thought it to be practically impossible, since you're immortal."

She sat down on the couch. I knew I needed to leave. My son was still sleeping and he felt comfortable against my chest. It was time to reunite him with his mother. And yet, I stopped myself from leaving just yet. I wanted to speak to her, to make sure we were okay. More than that, she might have a point of view that I hadn't considered before when it came to Kadie herself and why the Demons wanted her and our son.

"We know it is possible now. But it came as a complete surprise to me. I had always assumed I couldn't procreate." I nodded, tickling my son's foot. It was covered by the fuzziness of his onsie and he did not stir from his slumber, but touching him, feeling him against me, calmed my soul. "What are your thoughts?"

Jasmine was extremely clever, empathetic, and slightly clairvoyant. She was not a Witch, per se, but she was intuitive. These were many of the reasons she'd been a Target of the Demons and how she managed to survive them.

She rocked in her seat for a little while and I went to the door to double check that it was locked. I also glanced through the peephole to see if there were any suspicious people lingering about. I knew we were safe in the Hotel, but if the Demons were still using humans, I could not be sure of anything. I turned from the door when I was satisfied and waited for her to say something.

"I knew something was different about him," Jasmine murmured, her eyes dropping to my son. Clarity touched her irises and her lips were turned up into a gentle smile. "Not just the Angel-Dad thing, but I could feel that there was this magic about him. It was hard for me to explain. But he possess a fate that will not be denied."

"I know." I looked down at my son and cradled the top of his head. He had so much hair for just being born. I tilted my head down and inhaled deeply. I was addicted to his scent. It brought me such peace, such warmth, even in trying times such as this one. "Is there anything you can tell me to help me in this quest, Jasmine?"

She turned her head to look at me, her eyes focusing on my face in a strange way. I wasn't sure what to make of it. I hoped it wasn't bad.

"You can't go to them, Gabriel," she said, her voice soft. It almost sounded as though she was worried someone might overhear, which seemed silly, considering we were safe. Then again, I was paranoid the Demons were still using specifically chosen humans to infiltrate buildings like these ones. "You'll die. You have to get them to come to you. Take them all on, with the woman by your side. You need to kill the uprising."

"The uprising?" I had not heard that word used before in relation to the Demons. There were so many questions I had. Every time I received an answer, even more inquiries invaded my mind. What did uprising mean? What was going to happen? How did this involve Kadie and my son? Why could I not go to them and how could I get them to me?

My son started making a noise – it was a cross between a purr and a whimper. I looked down and found him to still be sleeping. I bent my knees and bounced slightly, hoping to help rock him back to a deep slumber, one he could not easily wake from.

Jasmine's gaze fell away and she moaned a little, as though in pain. Her hand reached up to clutch her head.

"Are you all right?" I asked, stepping forward, offering my hand. I had no idea what she could use it for, but it was there in case she needed it.

"I have a headache," she said, her eyes pinched closed. She tried to stand up and nearly bumped into her daughter's carrier.

"Lie down, then." I gestured to the couch she sat upon and she slowly lay down. I bent down, awkward with my son strapped to me, and removed her daughter from the car seat. I did not want her in any unnecessary danger, even if it was danger we might have inadvertently placed her in. I picked her up and she let out a small cry. I froze. What if I had waken her up? What if her cries caused my son to cry? However, after a moment, she settled back down. I turned. There had to be somewhere I could place her for the time being. When I stepped into the bedroom, my eyes rested on a cot tucked into the corner. It was perfect for her.

I set her down and made sure she could not roll off or otherwise hurt herself. When I finished, I went back to the living room. Jasmine was resting her head on the arm of the couch, her body curled tightly into the fetal position.

Despite her insight into what was coming, I knew that was the end of Jasmine's strength.

I sighed, trying to keep my frustration to myself. Her insights were helpful but vague. I did not know if I could even prepare for this uprising if I did not know what it entailed. The only thing I could do was follow her advice: instead of going to the Demons, I had to wait for them to come to me.

More waiting.

Great.

"I'll go now, Jasmine," I told her, padding to the door, "but will check in on you tomorrow."

Jasmine's hand snaked out and grabbed me as I crossed her path. I was surprised by how tight her grip was, despite the exhaustion she was enduring

"Be careful, Gabriel," she said. Her eyelids descended slowly and her words came out slowly. "You and your son are the only things standing in their way."

Her eyes slid shut once again and I placed her hand back on her stomach so she could rest peacefully. I stepped back and headed for the door. This time, I did not stop for anyone or anything.

So, there was an attack coming? Of course, there was.

I opened the door and stepped out. When I placed my hand on my son's stomach once again and found myself filled with reassurance with the steady rise and fall of his breathing.

When I stepped into the elevator, I couldn't help but think of destiny and whether or not it existed. Humans liked to think they had freewill, that they got to determine their path. Perhaps that was true. Humans were treated much differently than Angels and Angels were treated differently than Guardians. But I knew that was not the case for me. My path had been determined from the moment I was born.

I pressed the button that would lead to the first floor and stretched out the tendons in my neck.

I needed to stop them. I needed to stop the Demons if I had any hope of watching my son grow up in a world where his life wasn't at risk. I had assumed this was the case, but hadn't really put it all down to one final battle. Until now. Until Jasmine's words.

Did that mean I could call on the other Fallen Angels? If I did, was that putting them at risk? And if I failed at this mission, did that mean the war was over and the Demons won? And if so, what did that mean for the world? For humans and Witches? For Angels and Guardians? Would all hope be lost?

I damn sure hoped not. We hadn't battled it out for millenniums for the good side to lose while I was still standing, ready and willing and *needing* to fight.

I stepped out of the elevator and headed outside. The crisp, fresh air caused a spark to flare through my body and give me life. I looked around. There was a glimmer of silver in the black clouds surrounding me now. Jasmine had said that Kadie would be there, fighting by my side. If I took everything else she said as true, this had to be true as well. I would not let myself think otherwise.

I cloaked myself in invisibility and kissed the crown of my son's head once more. I inhaled his scent and felt my lips turn up slightly. I did not know why I was smiling when everything seemed dire and hopeless. However, I did not push away the feeling. I revelled in it. I let warmth fill me up. I let myself hope that we could get through this. That we could figure this out and stop this uprising – whatever it was – before it even begun.

I flew to Tabitha's dimension with my arms wrapped around my sleeping son. The moment we landed, he woke up, his bright blue eyes far too alert for an infant as he tried to look around. I nearly chuckled at the faces he was making as he attempted to make sense of his surroundings. He seemed so serious yet so intent on familiarizing himself with this new world.

I took him out of the carrier and held him up to my face where he reached out a hand and stroked my cheek. His look softened. I could not be certain, but it seemed as though he recognized who I was. He knew me. Perhaps he did not know who I was to him, but he understood I was someone he could trust. Love blossomed inside my heart like the desert flowers under the moon. My throat closed up and tears tingled at the back of my eyes. How was it even possible to love someone so much after such a short amount of time?

"Gabriel."

I turned towards the familiar voice. Tabitha was waiting for me on the porch, arms crossed over her chest. She did not appear to be happy, but then again, Tabitha was not known for her joy.

"How's Kadie?" I asked, though I could see the answer in my Angel Agent's face.

Some of the hardness in her eyes softened and she nodded her head once. "She's alive and doing well, though not yet conscious." Her eyes dropped to my hands and widened. "Oh, is this him?" Her voice sounded strange. I wanted to say it was affectionate, but it was difficult to place affection in the same sentence. She reached out her arms, stepping towards me. "Let me hold the baby who has been foretold to save us all."

I chuckled at Tabitha's tone as she reached into my arms and gently took the baby from me.

She stared down at him the way that Jasmine had, with total adoration. But there was more to her gaze than just that. There was familiarity.

And then I remembered: Tabitha and my son were the same type of angel. A hybrid. Something rare and thought to be impossible.

If that wasn't a miracle, I didn't know what was.

"Don't put the world on his shoulders just yet, Tabitha," I told her. "It seems like much time has passed, but he was only born yesterday."

She lifted him up and down for a moment and unwrapped his blanket to look at him properly. Her eyes scanned the top of his head and turned downwards. Her fingers softly took a look at his hands – at each individual finger – and did the same for his feet and for his toes. She turned him around, tracing his spine with a delicate fingertip, before turning him around once again.

My son stared openly at Tabitha. He did not cry, being in someone else's arms, but he did not smile and gurgle happily the way he had with Jasmine. Judging from the look on his face, I would say he was studying my Angel Agent, trying to get a read on her, before he decided he approved of her or not.

I bit back a smile. That, indeed, was my child, and my heart soared with unmatched pride.

"He's grown a lot in only a few days," she commented more to herself than to me.

"Yes." I nodded once, though her focus was solely on the child. "His growth is quite accelerated, if Jasmine is to be believed."

Tabitha nodded, her mouth twisted with thought.

"I wonder if…" She let her voice trail off. I knew she was not speaking to me, not with her hushed tone and intense focus on my son. "Maybe, I'm not sure it would make a difference, though perhaps…" She lifted her head, keeping her eyes on my son. Her eyes crinkled as she smiled – I was surprised to see her smile in the first place – and said, "Let's take you to see your mother, shall we, handsome?"

It was such a strange sight, I could swear I was dreaming. Tabitha was not one to mince words, even when she was being nice and helpful. To hear her coo at the baby was something I did not think was possible. I wanted to record it so I had the memory and could come back to it later as proof that this had happened and was not a figment of my sleep-rattled mind.

My son reached out for Tabitha's long hair. It would seem he approved of her, and now wanted to get to know her through touch rather than sight.

"What are you going to call him, Gabriel?" she asked, as we walked into her house.

It was as though she could read my mind.

I kept my mouth closed as I thought about my answer. We crossed the living room and turned down the hall. My son managed to grab a strand of Tabitha's hair and pulled. Tabitha gave no hint that his tugging affected her in any way, and I realized she was much more patient than I realized.

When we reached Kadie's room, I walked over to the side of the bed and took a seat. Kadie still slept peacefully, something I was grateful for. It was not ideal that she was still unconscious, but at least she did not appear to be in any pain.

I ran my hand along Kadie's arm, needing to touch her in some way, needing to know she was still tangible and not some figment of my imagination. She was warm, and felt strong. I let out a breath of relief. But she didn't move, she didn't make a noise as I touched her.

I tried to ignore the twinge of disappointment that ran through me and brought my hand to my lap. It was silly of me to think being connected through our bodies suddenly meant I was her saviour and could wake her with a touch or a kiss. Fairytales were for the young and foolish. Reality was not so simple.

I released a sigh and moved hair from her face. So badly I wanted her to wake up. I wanted her to be well. I wanted her to be coherent. I wanted everything for her. And yet, a selfish part of me needed her to recognize me on top of everything else. I could not bear it if she had forgotten me so completely.

Despite my initial reaction to fairytales, the sleeping beauty tale was weaving through my head. My touch did not seem to have any effect on her, but maybe something else would. Maybe if I kissed her…

But no.

And yet, even as I tried to focus on something else, I couldn't get the idea of kissing Kadie out of my mind.

I was a fool, then. A broken-hearted, hopeless fool.

"He doesn't have a name yet?" she asked again, breaking me out of my thoughts.

I looked from Kadie's face and up to Tabitha once again.

"I think his mother should have a chance to name him," I told her. "At least, we should discuss it is together. It's one of the most important things a person can do, naming a child, don't you think, Tabitha?"

She nodded quietly. She walked to the other side of Kadie and pulled down the blanket to expose her breasts. I had forgotten she was naked underneath them, only to be reminded that Margaret and Simone had cleansed her body before administering her with medicine. Apparently they never dressed her again.

"What are you —"

I cut myself off when I watched her place our son on a breast.

"What are you doing?" I tried again, slightly alarmed. Wouldn't he roll off?

"Just watch," she said, taking a respectful step back

CHAPTER TEN

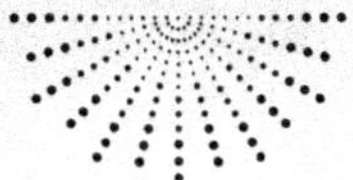

The baby began to softly cry, his head coming up and bobbing around as though looking for something. I reached out for the babe, hoping to offer him comfort. Tabitha reached across the bed and swatted at my arm, shooting me a look. I felt chagrined and dropped my arms, focusing my attention on my child. Kadie didn't stir, but the baby kept searching for her breast. His head came right up and he seemed to be looking at her face, before continuing to bob around with his mouth open. He moved sideways, his mouth on her skin as he licked her. Tasting her.

I wanted to support his head and neck. It was clear that while he exhibited surprising strength for a babe born only a few days ago, he was not able to lift his head up on his own just yet. I shifted my eyes to Tabitha, trying to decipher if she would swat me away again. However, she seemed focused on the babe, on whether he would be able to do accomplish his task.

He came closer to my side of the bed. I refused to let him continue bobbing around. His cries had taken hold of me. I did not want him to endure anymore frustration when all he wanted to do was feed himself. It must have been his feeding time. I placed one hand on his back and then offered Kadie's breast to him.

He dove on the nipple like a starving man and made grunting noises as he suckled. I kept his head in place as he fed himself.

A noise interrupted my thoughts.

"He's feeding," I said with awe, to no one in particular.

"Kadie's coming back to us," Tabitha said. "She must be. Breast milk gives life. She could not give life if she was teetering towards death. It would not be possible."

My heart soared at her words. Tabitha was not the sort to lie to make someone feel good. Which meant this was true. Kadie was coming back.

I hoped that meant she was coming back soon.

I put my hand on my son's back to make sure he didn't roll off, and bent my head to kiss Kadie's lips.

I was under no illusion that this would not wake up Kadie. But I could not stop myself, even if I wanted to. I had to touch her. I had to taste her.

Her breath caressed my mouth as I pressed my lips to her warmth. I almost melted into the kiss. God, I wanted her to be awake. I wanted her to kiss me like she meant it, the way she used to.

But like all good things, this had to come to an end. I pulled away, my eyes remaining on her the entire time. I was sure I was filled with an unmatched longing. I didn't care that Tabitha saw me. I didn't care that she was no doubt judging me. At that moment, Kadie's eyelids fluttered.

I blinked. Surely, I'd imagined it.

"Kadie?" Tabitha asked, grabbing for her arm.

Obviously, it wasn't just me who'd seen the movement. My breath hitched in my throat. I wanted to lean over Kadie and kiss her again and again. If my kiss would wake her up, I would kiss her a thousand times, and then a thousand times more.

At that moment, Simone came rushing into the room with a mug of steaming hot water that smelled like the bottom of a sewage pond. I hadn't realized the Witches were there. Silly of me to have made that assumption. I had been too wrapped up in myself, in my thoughts, to remember that we weren't alone. We had help that wanted us to succeed, that wanted Kadie awake.

"Are you certain you should be giving her that?" I asked, wrinkling my nose and eyeing the cup. "It smells awful."

Simone nodded her head and gave me an intense look. "Trust me, she's going to need this," she murmured, stepping around Tabitha and sitting carefully on the edge of the bed. She steadied the mug, ensuring nothing spilled over. "Get the baby off her and get ready for the fight."

Without a question, I grabbed for the mewling baby and placed him safely in a basket on the floor. My body thrummed with eager anticipation. I might have once demanded an explanation. I did not want to have hope when there was none. I did not like the fall from being so high and having such a long drop when hope was snatched away from me.

However, I could not help but wonder what she meant by getting my son ready for the battle. Was he supposed to be present? Or did Simone mean he should be prepared to be somewhere safe while we faced the battle? If either, I was stuck. For one, I wanted my son nowhere near the battlefield where he could get taken or worse. I refused to put him in a situation where he could be used against me, to manipulate me and get me to do whatever they wanted me to do. Where he could be injured or even killed.

And if I was supposed to get him to safety, I was not sure where to begin. I did not want to take him back to Jasmine so soon. She was the only person I trusted to take care of my son except Tabitha and Kadie. Tabitha would no doubt be on the battlefield beside me.

And Kadie?

I did not want to speculate. She, too, was powerful, but if she did wake up – and that was a big if – then I could not be certain she would be able to fight let alone care for our son.

I released a breath and shifted my eyes over to Simone. What did she know?

At that moment, Kadie sat bolt upright and began swinging her fists at me, screaming in a vicious tongue I didn't recognize.

My heart leapt into my throat. I didn't even react. I could not. I was overjoyed to have her awake but I did not wish for her to accidentally clip our son. I turned to Tabitha and placed the dozing babe in her arms so I could turn to Kadie with my full attention.

"Hold her down," Simone instructed. "She needs to drink this!" She maneuvered around Tabitha, who carefully stepped back, cradling my son with a tenderness I had never seen from her before. She carefully reached forward with the awful-smelling drink, a look of grim determination in the lines of her young face.

"Get away from me!" Kadie screamed, her face turning red. Her eyebrows hung over her eyes and her lips were curled into a snarl. I had never seen her so angry before. I did not understand this reaction at all. "You all deserve to be thrown into hell! You do! Oh, you fucking do!" She grunted and laughed as she scratched at my arms with her sharp nails.

I grabbed her wrists and held on tight, pulling her arms above her head and tugging her backwards so she was lying down again. I was careful not to grip her too tightly. I did not want to harm her even if she saw me as her enemy and was attacking because of it.

She writhed and screamed at me. I tried to peer into her eyes, tried to see a flicker of recognition in her eyes. I found nothing. Taking advantage of my careful study of her, she spat at me. Her saliva slowly slid down my cheek, but I did not relent.

"Do whatever you're going to do, or I'm going to have to knock her out," I told Simone, my heart cracking as Kadie fought me. I wanted nothing more than to wrap her in my arms, to hold her, to murmur things to her about how she was safe and that our son had her eyes. I wanted to tell her everything that had transpired when she had been unconscious. I wanted to run away with her and leave everyone and everything behind.

I could see none of my beautiful Kadie left in the woman who now fought me like the Demons that had tortured her and I could not risk having my son anywhere near her until she was herself again.

I would not let myself consider that that might never be a possibility.

Simone came forward and Kadie kicked at her. She held onto

the cup, though a couple of drops of the concoction fell onto the bedspread.

"Tabitha!" Simone said. "Get her legs."

Tabitha nodded and disappeared from the room momentarily. When she returned, my son was gone. For that, I was grateful. I understood that babies at this age could not remember what happened. Regardless, I did not want him to see his mother, to be around her, when she was like this. Perhaps Margaret was holding him now. Perhaps he was lying in the other room, tucked safely on a bed, positioned between two pillows that prevented him from rolling off the bed. I was not sure if he was able to roll off the bed just yet, but I hoped Tabitha protected him in that way.

When she returned, Tabitha wasted no time positioning her body across Kadie's thighs, using her body weight to hold Kadie down. I kept my grip on Kadie's upper body. I knew she would receive bruises from the way I held them even though I made sure it wasn't rough. But the way she was thrashing and pulling, she was inflicting damage to her own delicate skin.

Even so, I was impressed by her strength. She had been unconscious for a while and she woke up with an unmatched fire inside of her.

Simone walked forward once more, clinging to the mug she held for grim death. There was a determined glint in her eye that seemed to say she would get this drink down Kadie no matter what she had to do.

Margaret came up from behind me and gripped Kadie's tormented face. If she was here, I assumed my son was in a room, safely away from all of this. Margaret pried open Kadie's mouth by pulling down her chin and Simone was finally able to dump the black muck down her nostrils. I frowned. What an odd way to deliver the concoction. However, it was not as though Kadie was complying. Her teeth were clenched together so tightly I was surprised the vein in her forehead did not pop. This seemed to be the only way to get this to her.

It went up her nose and into her mouth. Kadie screamed in outrage, damning everyone in the room to a Hell most horrible.

All I could do was hold her tight and cling to the hope that the woman I knew was strong enough to claw her way back to us.

"More," Margaret instructed, her voice firm. She sounded sure, strong, but when I looked over at her, I could easily see the mixture of fear and hopelessness in her eyes.

I realized then that this was our last hope. If this didn't work, nothing would. If this didn't work, Kadie would be lost to us forever.

Simone threw more of the liquid into Kadie's screaming mouth until the mug was empty and the room was filled with a pond-like stench. She coughed up some of it, trying to spit it out, but Simone forced her hand over Kadie's mouth, preventing her from doing so. She had to be careful – Kadie did not seem to have any qualms trying to bite Simone.

After a long moment, Kadie's screams began to slow and then she was no longer fighting us.

Simone slowly released her hold on Kadie's mouth and took a step back. She continued to watch Kadie with expectant eyes, waiting to see if the concoction did its job.

Then the sweetest words came into the room, on a wave of hope after disaster.

"Tabitha?" Kadie's voice sounded raw, scratchy, as though she hadn't spoken for a year. And yet, it was as sweet as a bird's song early in the morning. "Gabriel? What's going on here?" Kadie's eyes were now clear and she looked at me with utter confusion. She remembered me. More than that, she was looking to me for answers.

"Oh, thank you, God," I declared to the sky and let go of Kadie's arms.

Tabitha came forward with a towel and offered it to Kadie, who sat up and wiped at her mouth. I realized that all her thrashing and fighting caused Kadie's blanket to slip, revealing her nakedness to the room. Despite the fact that besides myself, the room was filled with women, I pulled at the blanket over her body so she could retain her modesty and keep warm.

I relaxed once again on the side of the bed and pulled her into my arms, holding on as tight as I dared. All my prayers had been answered. Relief swept over me like a gentle wave hitting the shore. I buried my face in her hair. I did not care that I would have to pay the piper for bringing home my girl. I would do whatever I needed to. Kadie had come back to me, and that was all that mattered.

"You came back," I whispered out loud, unable to hold it back. My heart knitted together stronger and brighter than before. I could not stop smiling if I tried.

Kadie softened in my arms and pulled away so she could look up at me. "You came for me," she murmured. I did not know why she was relieved. It was as though there was part of her that believed I would not. Before I could tell her I would always be there for her, she picked her head up from my chest and furrowed her brow. "Where's my baby?"

I smiled down at her and touched her face with my fingertips for a moment in reverent prayer. She knew our son. She remembered him.

"He's here."

I had not realized Margaret had left the room, but upon her return, she stepped in with our son tucked in her arms, wrapped in a blanket to keep him warm. Small cries of frustration at having been ripped away from her breast filled the room.

Margaret handed our babe to Kadie and he threw himself back in a horizontal position, expecting to be fed.

"He's still hungry," I said at her confused smile and she dropped the blanket to offer the baby her breast.

"Here you go," Tabitha said, arranging a pile of pillows behind Kadie so she could rest back a bit.

The baby attached hungrily once again and Kadie gasped at the pressure. I had not realized breast feeding could be a painful exchange. Perhaps there was some way to relieve Kadie's pain, a balm that could be applied to the nipples that would not harm the baby in any way.

"What happened?" Kadie asked, absently stroking our son's head. Every now and then, her face would contort in pain, but she refused to move our son from her. I was certain it did not help that this was the first time she was feeding him, so her breasts were hard with a heavy supply. "And what on earth is that smell?"

I looked towards Simone and Margaret, who both stepped forward. They were looking at Kadie with a strange awe-like wonder, which I wasn't sure I entirely understood. I knew they knew Kadie was also a Witch, but it seemed to be more than that.

"I'm Margaret, and this is my niece, Simone," Margaret said, gesturing at both herself and Simone. "Gabriel found us and asked us to come here and help you pull through."

"Was I badly hurt?" Kadie asked, her gaze shifting to me, a lack of understanding clear in her gaze. She did not know all she endured. For a moment, I did not want to tell her. I did not think it was privy for her to know. And yet, she deserved the truth. Perhaps there was a way to tell her without unnecessary detail. I did not think she was ready for everything just yet. Not until she recovered more thoroughly.

"Your wounds healed well," I told her, choosing my words carefully. "It was more the poison they'd fed you via a drip."

Kadie gasped and turned back to the women. "You're both Witches?" she asked.

"Yes," Margaret said, nodding once. "Simone is a new, untrained Witch, like you. Yet, she has great power and a natural ability for potions. She brewed the remedy that you can smell, and probably still taste. Unfortunately, we cannot make it smell any better without tainting the potion's healing capabilities."

Kadie chuckled. "I thought there was something strange going on with my stomach, but as I am intensely grateful to be alive, I wasn't going to ask about the flavor in my mouth." She patted our son's tush a couple of times and he sighed contentedly as he continued to suck at her breast.

Tabitha handed her a cup of tea. "This will be really sweet, but your body needs the sugar," she said. Kadie used her free hand to grasp the cup carefully. She did not want to drop any of the hot liquid onto our son. "Drink up."

"Thank you, Tabitha," Kadie said.

"Can I take him?" Tabitha asked. At Kadie's nod, my Angel

Agent proceeded to pick up the sleeping baby and tap his back, trying to burp him.

"So, what have I missed?" Kadie asked, hugging the blankets to herself and gripping the sugary tea like she needed it for an anchor. "Besides the fact that I was poisoned by Demons, had a child, and was saved by two strangers who happen to be Witches."

I stepped up. If I wanted Kadie not to know everything, I needed to be the one to tell her. I explained what had happened at the castle that night and almost everything since. I told her how Jasmine took care of our son and even her premonition. Perhaps I shouldn't have done that. Perhaps the premonition was too much.

"So, our son is two days old and people are already seeing visions of him saving the world?" Kadie shook her head and laughed. "I know some parents have unrealistic expectations of their children, but that's a bit much."

Tabitha brought our son closer again and spoke to Kadie softly.

"Your son's conception and birth is a true miracle, Kadie," she murmured. "One that we have foretold for centuries. He will be immortal, like his father, like me. I am also the child of a Fallen Angel and Witch conception. But I was not the saviour they had all predicted, even though they thought I was."

Tabitha swallowed hard, and for the first time since I knew her, I sensed the pain inside her. The disappointment at being born the wrong sex. At the wrong time.

I reached out for Tabitha and lay a hand on her shoulder. "You have been my saviour for over three centuries, Tabitha," I said. I knew my words were stilted, probably something she did not want to hear. But I could not imagine my life without Tabitha. I needed her more than I realized, more than I was willing to admit to myself.

"Thank you, Gabriel," she said. She cleared her throat and clapped her hands together. "But we are going to lose this war if we aren't careful."

"What war?" Simone asked, looking at Tabitha with a furrowed brow.

I sighed. This was not a discussion for humans even ones with magical abilities.

"There has always been a war between good and evil," Tabitha said, giving them a modified truth. "The Demons fight on the side of evil, and with their growth of power, comes a blow to our side. This has been going on for centuries but I believe it's finally reached its climax with the born of the saviour. We can't let the Demons win the war, because we have no idea what they'll do if they succeed in overcoming us all."

Kadie shifted as she sat up straight. "Not to be selfish in any way, but what about me?" she asked. "Am I to die like a normal human?"

Kadie looked to me and I looked to Tabitha for the answer. I didn't know.

Tabitha pulled herself up straighter just as my son burped, and I knew the answer wouldn't be good. "My mother died at a normal age for a human of her era," she stated. It wasn't exactly an answer but it was enough to know what that meant.

"Which was when, exactly?" I asked.

"1310," Tabitha replied, a slight twitch at her shoulder belying the pain she'd gone through in seeing her mother die so soon and living without her for so long.

Kadie slumped in her chair, pain rippling over her face. "And your father?" she asked.

Tabitha turned away as she began to rock our child. "Gone also," she admitted. "At the hands of a Demon. Very soon after my mother died."

A shiver coursed up my spine at the images those words invoked in me.

We rarely lost a Fallen Angel to a Demon unless there was a group attack, or the Angel was compromised in some way. Heartsick at the loss of Tabitha's mother, perhaps? Was such a thing even possible?

"Tabitha?" I managed to ask, though the question I wanted to know couldn't be voiced.

She stared straight at me for long moments, as though she was able to read my mind. "You know that Angels love with all their hearts Gabriel," she said.

Tears threatened my eyes as I looked away.

I did know that, and I'd once thought my love for Teramea would be my undoing. But as I looked at my son in Tabitha's arms and Kadie resting, alive and smiling, I now knew what true love was.

Kadie caught my eye and she pulled herself up. "I need a shower and some food, and we need a plan," she said, ever practical in times of doubt. "I don't know about you, but I'm not really interested in sending my newborn son off to war at all, let alone without me."

Fire burned in my gut as my blood began to pump around my body with renewed heat.

I did not know what was going to happen. I did not know if we were going to win. All I knew was we would fight – even if it came to our death.

Kadie put a hand on my arm and I turned around to her.

"What do you think about the name, Nathaniel?"

Love blossomed in my chest and I let a smile spread across my face. Hope was not dead.

"I think it is just… perfect."

WARRIOR ANGEL

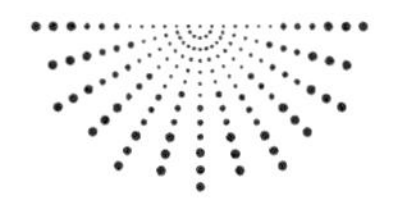

CHAPTER ONE

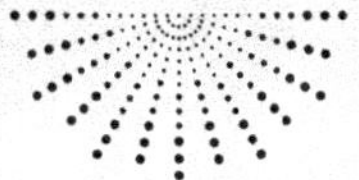

We decided to name our son Nathaniel. It was both accurate and fitting for him. He truly was a gift from God. Surprisingly, Tabitha was the one who suggested it. When Kadie agreed, I couldn't argue. Not that I wanted to.

Nathaniel.

Perfect, just as he was.

Nathaniel grew every minute of every day. His smile was as infectious as his laugh, and all who saw him fell in love with him instantly. This was what we were fighting for. This was what we were fighting to protect. Life, in all of its innocence, hope and faith. Even those who were lost. We wanted to protect them all, and my son constantly reminded me of that every day.

My pride in being his father grew as fast as he did. Everything my son did amazed me and if I could shout it to the world, I would.

But even as my child became stronger, a black cloud darkened our view of the horizon. Every time Kadie and I would share a look, the tilt of her mouth and the slight pinch to her eyes belayed the calm front she put on. She grew more worried with each day that passed and I couldn't ignore it any longer, even if part of me wanted to.

It had been a month since Nathaniel's birth and he was the size of a nine-month-old child. I understood that some babies were just big for their age, but this was more than that. I knew it. Tabitha knew it. Kadie knew it. There did not seem to be any sign of this rapid growth to slow. At first, this seemed like a good thing. Being small and fragile was not something I wanted for my son, even as an infant. But how long would that growth rate continue?

Tabitha didn't remember how long it took her to become fully grown, or she didn't want to say for fear of scaring us. It was moments like this one I wished I knew how to read my Angel Agent. I didn't think Tabitha would keep anything from me, especially not to protect my feelings.

She had always been fierce and blunt, two traits I appreciated. However, a child changed everything. A child was an innocent life, barely fleshed out, and ripe for the picking. If she was lying to us, I understood her hesitation even if I didn't agree with it. At the rate Nathaniel was growing, within a few years we'd have ourselves an adult son. And that was only if we could keep him alive until then. There were no guarantees anymore, and that shake of confidence was not something that sat well with me.

The attacks on Witches had increased. There were dozens of Demons assaulting powerful young women every night and there weren't enough Guardians to protect them. Neither the Witches, nor Tabitha could determine why they were continuing to grow in number and strength and we couldn't say for sure what they were after, which made it difficult to determine who to protect.

I had my theory, of course. They continued their onslaught because they still hadn't gotten what they needed. But what was it they needed? Truly? A powerful witch? My son? And what would they do with them, once they had them?

Every night as darkness fell, I left Kadie and my son in Tabitha's realm and went back to New York City to hunt and kill the Demons attacking the Witches. I did not think I could make a difference, but it kept me in practice and it made me feel useful. Margaret and the elders of the covens tried to unravel the mystery of what the Hell-creatures wanted but still came up with nothing.

I had so many questions that were nowhere near being explained and that bothered me more than I cared to admit.

What was the poison that Kadie had been injected with? And if they took something from her during her torture they could use, what could it mean for all of us?

Jasmine had moved back home with her husband and daughter after two weeks at the Hotel. I sent Margaret over to her to do a cleansing and put a protection spell on her house. I wasn't sure if that would actually work, but at least it was something.

Happily, Jasmine hadn't seen a Demon since she'd stopped nursing my son, and I was grateful.

I was still trying to assuage some of the guilt I felt about putting her in such a dangerous situation. Not only had she been at risk, but so had her husband and her own child. Her husband did not like me very much. Despite knowing who I was and what I did for his wife, he still treated me with disdain he didn't hide from me. If I was being honest, I couldn't blame him. The only reason I had come back was to put them at risk again.

If anyone came to Kadie, putting our son and her at risk, I'd probably feel the same way.

I was at a loss for what else to do about the storm coming our way. Perhaps it was time to return to the castle once more. Maybe I'd missed something that last time?

I hated the thought of returning there. So many unpleasant memories. Memories I would never be able to cast away. Memories of Kadie in pain. Memories of demons torturing her. The scent of blood. The void of darkness.

I was not scared to return. The place itself was unpleasant, and I had not come up with much to go on.

Still, it was a start. I had been so focused on Kadie's health that there was a good chance I had missed something. I did not like to think of myself as careless, but Kadie had always been my weakness, ever since I met her, and caused me to do things I normally wouldn't do.

"Do you think I should come with you?" Kadie asked from the doorway, reading my thoughts accurately. Her eyes wary with her own memories. The fact that she was even offering to do this showed me just how much courage she had. If I had been kept and tortured someplace, I highly doubted I would ever want to return to it.

The only thing that made me think it was possible that she could come with me, was her magic, which had returned. Tabitha and her had been working together on building her strength every day.

I turned to greet her as she walked towards me. I heard Nathaniel giggling from his playpen and headed over to him.

"How'd he sleep?" I asked, putting my arms out for my child. He practically jumped to get to me. I purposefully avoided her question. I was not sure if she should come. I wasn't sure if it would help or hurt us. If I knew how she would react after dealing with such trauma, maybe. I also had to consider our son as well.

"Like an angel," Kadie answered with a huge grin on her face.

I shot her an amused smile. This wasn't the first time I had heard this joke.

I bounced my beautiful, chubby boy on my knee. He had bright blue eyes and long dark lashes. He smelled sweet, like a perfect baby should, but also something similar to Kadie's scent that made him seem like home to me.

I grinned as he grabbed hold of my hands and pulled himself up to a wobbly stand.

"So strong already," I said, admiring the determination in his face and the look of sheer joy once he'd succeeded in his task. I wasn't familiar with human babes, but I was aware their development was not as quick as Nathaniel. It tickled my pride that my child had accomplished so much in such a short amount of time.

"He is." Kadie sighed and I could hear the pain behind her proud words. She was more concerned about Nathaniel's development than I was, though I did understand her worry.

Not only did we not know what to expect from Nathaniel's rapid growth transformation, Kadie was sad that Nathaniel would outlive her by centuries.

According to Tabitha, it was the natural course of things, but I didn't want to believe it. I couldn't. Why should my son become an orphan?

If Kadie died as any normal human did, then what would become of our son? Would I be able to be a parent if I was bound to be a Fallen Angel and therefore a slave to the powers above? Tabitha only knew so much, and I did not understand the rules – if there were rules at all.

I didn't know how I was going to change Kadie's mortality, but I would speak to the Witches after this was all done and work on a plan to fix it somehow. At the very least, I wanted to ensure that she got to be with our son as much as she could.

But first, we needed to save the world from the impending invasion.

"Do you think that would be wise?" I finally asked Kadie, addressing her original question about coming with me. I continued to hold Nathaniel and he gurgled and cooed happily. "You were tortured in that place."

And after everything she'd already been through, the last thing I wanted Kadie to feel was more pain.

"That's exactly why I should go," she argued. The way her eyes scanned mine, I knew she was not going to give this up so quickly. She was stubborn. It was a trait I loved about her. It was also a trait that frustrated me. I did not comprehend how I could feel two different ways about one thing.

Then again, Kadie had a knack for bringing out the conflict in me. Always teaching me. Always keeping me on my toes, so to speak.

Kadie's brows furrowed, her tones firm and unmoveable. "I might remember something that's useful. Because, you know… nothing else is working at the moment. The Demons are getting more and more numerous, and the Witches are doing nothing helpful. Not for lack of trying but because, at this point, what can they possibly do? At this rate, they'll be lucky to have any Witches left in New York."

I sighed, looking away. That was true. There had been more and more young Witches taken and there was no way for us to stop it.

We could not predict who would be taken and, so far, I did not know of any Fallen Angels who had been assigned to this.

Which meant, since I knew more about this situation than most, the responsibility fell on my shoulders.

Some of the Witches had even been killed in the process of the kidnapping. Which meant there was blood on my hands since I had yet to figure it out.

There must be something I could do. Anything that would help. An idea lit up my mind. One that hadn't occurred to be before now.

I turned my attention back to Kadie.

"Maybe they're not really kidnapping them for a purpose," I said. My words tumbled out of my mouth quickly. I was trying to keep up with them, my thoughts racing. I had never felt this way before, where speaking my thoughts out loud helped me figure out what made sense and what didn't. "Maybe they're removing them from the fight before it begins. If they take away all the powerful Witches from the state, they can bring forth their armies with no resistance. The humans can't fight them, after all."

Kadie bit her lip and chewed on it for a moment in thought. For the moment, I seem to have distracted her. "Yes," she allowed, nodding her head. "That makes sense, except…" She let her voice trail off.

"Except what?" I asked. I wasn't bothered by her critique. I needed to know why my idea was wrong so I could edit it until it made sense. I was after answers, not accolades to my pride.

"Except, why bother?" she pointed out, gesturing with her hands the way she did when she was passionate about something. "It's not like the New York Witches are a united force. Or well trained in the art of killing Demons." She shook her head as she began to pace in front of me. "No… I think it's more subtle, more insidious than that. They have a larger goal."

I frowned, allowing her rationality to seep into me. "I think you may be right," I said. I shook my head, chewing on my bottom lip. It was the only thing that made sense. I did not understand. If they weren't removing the Witches, what was their real plan, then? "Did they take anything from you that night that had you? Blood? Energy? Magic… even?"

I knew I was doing what humans referred to as throwing spaghetti against a wall and seeing what would stick. I had left all rationality at the door at this point and was trying to figure out what else it could be. I did not know if it would get us anywhere. I did not know if I was only going to confuse us or distract us from what was really going on. But it was something to try.

She looked at me strangely and then began to grin. "You're seriously asking me that?" she said, cocking her head to the side. She stopped pacing and her face softened as she regarded me. I knew, in that moment, how much she cared for me. The look of love did exist and Kadie had it for me. "I have no idea what they took from me. Especially in terms of magic. I can't even boil water, or summon anything to eat."

This much was true, and perhaps she was right when she hinted that it was a silly question in the first place. Tabitha had been working with Kadie since she'd healed from her poisoning, and Kadie's skills were not returning as everyone had expected. In fact, she barely had any magic at all, if Margaret and Tabitha were to be believed.

Which of course, I did not. I had a lot more faith in her than that. Not to take away anything from her ordeal or to downplay what she must have experienced. I just thought if anyone could properly recover – with speed – it was Kadie.

"I'm not sure about that, Kadie," I said, placing my fingers under her chin and tilting her head up so she could catch my gaze. I wanted her to know I was being serious. "I've seen you do some pretty incredible things."

Even when half-dead and heavily pregnant, she had fought off Demons with nothing more than the power that shot out from her palms. How could that possibly be someone who had no magic? She was a miracle. Everything about her was a miracle.

It was hard to remember a time when she had not been in my life. Strange, since I had been alive for five hundred years, regulated to Guardian as punishment for my behaviour. I continued to do good deeds, to protect, to do my duty, as God intended me to, hoping it would serve my penance faster and I would be able to return to Heaven.

But then I met Kadie, and Heaven did not seem so special any longer.

My penance was not a curse, but a blessing. And every minute spent with Kadie was another affirmation that God was real, that God had a way of taking the darkest nights and shedding light on them.

We might not see the answer now, but we would find it. Somehow, we would figure this out.

Kadie lifted her arms and stared down at her hands in disappointment. Her lips tugged into a frown and I was tempted to kiss her until she smiled again. I dropped my hand from her chin and she tucked it to her chest, looking at her hands.

Instead, I waited. I knew moments like these were for her to think, and I did not wish to distract her. When she was ready to speak to me, she would.

"Maybe I gave it all to Nathaniel?" she said, her voice hopeful. She looked at her palms, as if she might find the answers there. "And when he grows up he'll be super-powerful." She turned her hands down so her palms were hidden from view. "Or maybe it's all gone now? Not that I had any control over it in the first place." She shook her head.

I reached for her waist this time and pulled her onto my lap to comfort her. My arms encircled her, pulling her closer to me so our body heat could mingle. Kadie's arms went around my neck and clung tightly. She shouldn't be feeling so defeated when I was so grateful to have her alive. She always seemed to take the burden and rest it on her shoulders when there was no reason for her to carry so much weight. She could share the load if she wanted to. I was here, as was Tabitha. She had us to help her.

She sighed heavily, dropping her head onto my shoulder. What could I say to make her feel better? I still had difficulty with such things. Being an angel for so long made it difficult to remember, and not understanding how to be human made me feel as though I would never be able to connect with her.

But I refused to give up due to a lack of knowledge. I would seek out words and, hopefully, the right words would find me.

"Kadie, I know that when it comes time to fight, you'll be right there by my side, protecting the world and our child from whatever evil things come our way," I told her. "They wanted you gone so you wouldn't have Nathaniel. And once you'd conceived him, they wanted to do… God knows what to you. To him." I clenched my teeth together. I did not realize how difficult it was for me to say words I thought would help her. Instead, I nearly choked on them, trying to get them out. I did not want to even think about what could have happened. And saying the words, bringing them into existence, was unpleasant.

Perhaps I should have been more considerate before saying anything at all.

I still shuddered to think what they would have done with my two loves if Kadie had given birth in the castle. It was a weakness, something I did not like to indulge in.

She popped her head up. "Why are you so certain that I'll be there by your side?" she asked. I could tell by her tone that she was trying to understand my unwavering faith. "Why do you have so much faith in me?"

She bit her bottom lip, eyes looking up at me wide.

I knew this answer meant a lot to her. I could not downplay it by giving her gentle words and empty compliments. She would know I was trying to make her feel better rather than be honest with her.

However, my words could do both. Because my answer was easy. Anytime it had to do with Kadie and my faith in her was easy for me to speak of.

"Because I know you." I was not sure if that would satisfy her, but it was the only one I could offer her. It was the truth, *my* truth. "Your heart is pure and your soul has the strength of a warrior. I told you what Jasmine said to me about you being there?"

She nodded, biting her bottom lip again. I wish she would not do such things in front of me. I was trying to concentrate, and when she bit her lip, it distracted me more than I cared to admit.

"Well, I wasn't surprised she said it, not at all." I shook my head once, twice, to emphasise my point, and I have her hands a gentle squeeze. "I knew that if you pulled through from the poisoning, you'd be back by my side, fighting with me. If you could survive something like that, you'd be able to survive anything. I have every faith in you, and I know that together, we can work out what's coming and we can fight. We are both strong on our own, but united? We're unstoppable."

Her eyes lit up with a joy I hadn't seen in months, and behind it sat her grim determination. My heart skipped at the sight. This woman was the love of my life, my mate, my soul. And she was as beautiful as any person who had ever lived.

Human couples tended to refer to themselves as teammates. Being on the same team. That sort of thing. I did not particularly understand the meaning behind the phrase because, as Guardians, we were often on our own, independent and extremely individual. However, I realized that being on the same team as Kadie, working together towards something we both wanted, was a crucial part of our relationship.

I had my flaws. She had hers. But when she was down, I would do everything to revitalize her. It wasn't just that I had faith in her. I wanted her to stand on her own two feet. I wanted her to have faith in herself. And I knew, without a doubt, that she wanted the same for me. I could count on her.

I had never had that before with anyone. I was lucky to have it with someone like her.

"Then you need to take me back to the castle, Gabriel," she said. "Let's ask Tabitha if she'll watch Nathaniel and we'll go now. Together."

My Angel Agent walked into the room at that moment and scooped our son off the ground where he was sitting and playing. It was almost as though Tabitha had been listening in on our conversation. In fact, I was sure she had.

"Of course, I'll watch our beautiful boy," Tabitha cooed,

holding Nathaniel tightly and kissing him on his chubby cheek. I smothered a laugh. Tabitha had been eavesdropping and didn't care in the slightest that she was revealing that to us. It was not as though we could do anything about it either.

I watched as she cooed at Nathaniel. She'd practically adopted Nathaniel the moment he was born and I was grateful to have such a knowledgeable and powerful force standing behind my son.

"We're going back to the castle," Kadie announced, jumping off my lap. She straightened her clothing even though we had done nothing untoward during our time together. When she stood upright, she curled a stray strand of hair behind her ear.

Tabitha's gaze slid over to mine, a warning clear in the blue depths. "Be careful, both of you," she said, her words clipped. "Please. That place is the center of evil and the last thing I want is for Nathaniel to lose both of his parents."

She wasn't wrong. Evil had pervaded my soul every time I'd gone there. If I didn't feel like we *had* to go back, I would happily avoid it for the rest of my existence.

"That's why we need to return," Kadie countered, grabbing her sweater that lay across the back of the chair. "It is the center of all evil and if we don't do something about it, it will continue to be the center of all evil." She glanced at the clock hanging in the room over the doorway. "We only have a few hours until sundown, Gabriel, so let's go. Please." She turned her gaze over to me and lifted her brows.

I weighed up my options. I did not immediately want to reject her words but I also did not want to rush into things either. Instead, I looked at the pros and cons, and unfortunately, I came to the same conclusion. Kadie had to come with me. Not only did she have power that seemed to be effective against the Demons, she may be the only one who could see something in the castle that I couldn't. She'd been there as an unwilling captive and would hopefully know if something was important to the Demons, or out of place now. I had to have her with me, or me going by myself could be a suicide mission.

Everything inside of me screamed to not let her do this. I did not want to risk my son losing both of his parents. But if we wanted to fix this, if we wanted to prevent more evil and deaths, and disappearances, we needed to do this together.

"All right." I nodded once. "But we're going to need some powerful flashlights to take with us. The room you were kept in has no lighting and the castle is dark and dingy. I can see through almost anything and I had difficulty discerning my surroundings."

Not to mention the fact that it appeared to be a portal of evil to the underworld with a magical darkness that allowed Demons to exist in the daylight. But that wasn't something I really wanted to say aloud. I would prepare Kadie when the time called for it, but I did not want to shake her confidence. Not until I had to.

"Right. I have something like that." Tabitha said and disappeared with the baby.

Of course she did. Tabitha always seemed to be prepared for anything in ways even I couldn't prepare for. Once again, I was confronted with the fact that I was lucky she had been assigned to me. I didn't know what I would do without her.

Kadie threw on her sweater, tugging at the hem so it fitted past her waist. I tilted my head to the side, wanting to reach for her again, but deciding not to.

"Are you sure you want to do this?" I asked Kadie one more time, pushing my brows up.

She rolled her eyes, pulling her hair out of her sweater. Clearly, she was annoyed with my concern. "Of course, I do," she said as though it was obvious. "You're the one dragging your feet."

She raised a single eyebrow at me and I couldn't help but laugh at her confidence. We could both die and she was making jokes. Of course, she was.

CHAPTER TWO

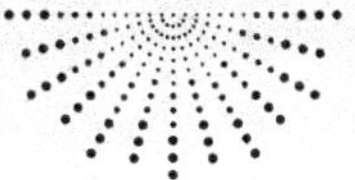

Tabitha entered the room once again and handed me two huge flashlights while still juggling Nathaniel on her hip. She didn't put him down unless we made her, which wasn't often, preferring to keep him securely in her arms.

"We'll be back in a few hours," I told her.

My Angel Agent nodded as though she knew this was the decision we were going to make. "Just be careful," she said. She knew she didn't have to tell us such a thing, but it seemed to relieve her to say it. She turned her attention to Nathaniel and kissed the tip of his nose. He beamed at her and my heart swelled.

How I hated leaving him. Even if I knew it was for the best, a part of me broke leaving him behind.

Kadie stared at Nathaniel with longing. I knew she wanted to pull him from Tabitha's arms and hug him tightly to rain his face with butterfly kisses. But she hesitated.

It was probably for the same reason I, too, hesitated. It would distract us from our mission, and if we were going to leave, we needed to do it now.

I picked Kadie up into my arms and walked outside, into the

warm air. I loved the feel of her against me. Light and strong at the same time.

When I touched her, everything seemed right. Like she was meant to be there. Like my arms were meant to hold her. Always.

I grimaced at my failed attempt to switch my mind into warrior mode. I shook my head. First, Nathaniel distracted me, and now Kadie.

I had moments of regret sometimes, for the softness Kadie had caused inside me. I no longer wanted to ravage the planet and fight every war. I no longer saw earth as a place I was visiting temporarily, but my home.

I no longer saw humans as something *other*. To be ridiculed for their weakness and emotions when now I looked upon them to learn about the new emotions I, myself, started to feel for Kadie.

Instead of running from her, I craved her closeness. I never thought I could love anyone as much as I loved my son but I did, more and more every day. I was content with this new view on the world. I was at peace.

I needed the fierce competitor, the warrior that would slaughter a threat without hesitation, without concern. I needed to be emotionless. I needed to be able to act without thinking. Especially now. This truly was the calm before the storm. The shiver of an earthquake before the life-ending tsunami. I needed to call on my old strength, and I didn't know how to do that when Kadie made me soft.

"All right. Let's go." I clung to my beautiful little human and we flew away. Away from the safety of Tabitha's realm, and towards the cold air that surrounded the Demon castle.

For the moment, I indulged in one last moment where I tried to memorize Kadie, what she felt like in my arms, the temperature of her skin as it touched mine. But it was gone too soon, and I was confronted with the fact that I might not ever get a moment like this with Kadie again.

Don't think such things. Not when you're so close.

My spine tingled with heat as we landed on the solid earth. Demons were here.

"Fuck!" It had to be the day I brought Kadie with me.

"What's wrong?" Kadie asked, turning her startled gaze to me. I set her down but she stayed close to my side.

"We're not alone." I didn't look at her as I spoke. My eyes were fixed firmly in front of me, scanning the area, waiting for something. Anything, to come out of the shadows.

Kadie's eyes sparkled with excitement and she curled her fingers into a fist. "Let's go kick some Demon ass."

I drew my sword from my back and gripped the handle tightly.

I glanced at Kadie. Everything in me wanted me to tell her to stay, to wait, until I got a lay of the land. However, I knew that convincing Kadie to stay here, safely outside the castle while I explored the property, was a waste of breath.

"Don't get caught, no matter what you need to do." I said. "Blast the shit out of them."

Part of me was terrified that she would be so scared she would freeze, or even worse, run. I couldn't stand the idea of her being attacked while she ran for her life. She'd be tortured, or burned at the very least. I didn't – wouldn't – let myself think about it.

But if she faced the demons, she would kill them with her magic. I knew she could. And I had to have faith, that under pressure, she could do it again. She might not know how the magic worked, but that didn't matter. She had access to it and I knew she was capable of doing anything. Perhaps, even, more than I could.

"Will do," she said, surprising me. I expected a fight, perhaps a quip about me telling her what to do. Instead, her brow furrowed and her lips pressed together in a grim line.

I took a step towards the castle, then looked back over my shoulder at my red-haired beauty in her flowing long skirt and cardigan. She looked straight out of a masterpiece, a period piece, something that brought to mind peace and tranquillity and days when arranged marriages and dowries were prevalent.

Not the picture of a warrior I'd ever seen going into battle before.

I nearly laughed at the contradiction. Laughter would prevent me from crying.

"Our son needs you, Kadie," I said, pulling my eyes away so I could refocus them away of me. "No matter what, you find a way out of there."

I didn't know how she'd get back to Tabitha's realm from here without me, but I'm sure she'd find a way if she needed to. I had every bit of confidence in her. For our son, she would move mountains.

Kadie glared at me. "He needs you more, Angel," she said, her voice rough with frustration. "You're the immortal one, not me."

"But…" I stopped. She probably needed to know. I stepped closer to her and grabbed her shoulders, craving the physical connection to her as I told her this. I tried not to get swept away in her scent, her her warmth. "I won't survive without you, Kadie. Didn't you understand what Tabitha said about Angels? We love with all our hearts. If you die, as her mother did so long ago… I won't be able to exist without you."

Kadie's eyes went wide with surprise, her mouth falling open. "I thought her father…" She let her voice trail off, unable to complete her thought.

I shook my head. "No Fallen Angel would die at the hands of a Demon unless he was severely compromised," I explained. "Or it was a huge, group attack. To me, and to Tabitha, it's obvious. He didn't want to be on this Earth without her."

Tears swelled and began falling down Kadie's cheeks. "But… you can't do that, Gabriel!" she explained as a silent sob racked through her body. "N-Nathaniel's a baby! Please, you need to promise me that you'll never leave him. Please!" Her eyes narrowed. "No matter what happens to me, you have to stay with him. You have to make sure he's okay."

I dropped the sword and grabbed her by the arms once again, hauling Kadie close to me and pressing her mouth to mine. It was such an emotional response, I did not realize what I was doing until it was too late. My mouth searched hers, needing clarity, needing something to reassure me that we would both be right. Needing a distraction from any other possibility that might occur. She responded in kind, groaning and pushing her body into mine as though she wanted to become part of me. Her arms locked around my neck and her fingers tangled themselves in my hair. Kissing her was like breathing in life after suffocating for so long.

We'd been unable to enjoy much lovemaking over the past month, as her body continued to heal from her labor and the poison. I'd missed this more than I'd admitted. I wanted more. I wanted to lay her down and take her right here, to forget about the threat and everything else we had going on.

She pressed her pelvis into my hardening cock and thrust her tongue between my lips, the passion between us flaring to life like an out of control brush fire.

The heat on my spine intensified, and unfortunately I knew it wasn't due to the arousal flooding my system.

We had to survive. Just so we could take up what we'd been forced to leave.

I regretfully pulled away from her embrace and twisted around to grab my sword from where it lay on the dirt at my feet. In hindsight, I probably should not have so carelessly dropped it. While it had not affected us, it could have. It was decisions like that that reiterated to me that Kadie was a weakness. It reminded me that having her here with me might not be the best idea. Around her, I made stupid decisions that could potentially cost us our lives, and that was not something I wanted to do.

Focus, I reminded myself.

I held up my trusted blade in front of me, expecting an enemy to appear out of nowhere. If they were going to take advantage of my vulnerability, now would have been the perfect moment.

There was nothing there.

I took a step forward, every muscle in my body locked and prepared for a fight. I heard Kadie following me, light on her feet. She was not as prepared as I was, but from my peripheral, I could see her trying to make out something in the darkness. She reached behind her and pulled out a flashlight in order to help light our way.

It wasn't a good idea to alert the demons that we were coming, but regardless, her hold on the tool was steady and made it easier to see what was ahead of me.

My heart pounded like a hammer against an anvil. I knew danger was not far away.

"What is it?" Kadie said in a low voice from behind me. I was grateful I did not have to push her back and protect her. She was already behind me and even something as simple as moving her where it was safe was a move we might not have time for.

I glared at the front door of the castle, now hanging open. I tried to remember if it had been shut when we arrived, if I was perhaps envisioning things due to my fear. "They're here," I stated simply.

I looked over at my lover, who stared back with determination in her eyes. She flared her nostrils and gave me a subtle nod. I would have denied she had moved at all if I hadn't caught it quickly.

"We come out alive, no matter what," I declared.

"Both of us," she agreed.

I gripped my sword and Kadie swooped tightened her grip on the flashlights. Together, we moved towards the front door. Whatever was in there, we would discover together. No matter what.

CHAPTER THREE

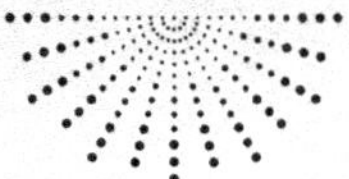

e took careful, measured steps towards the looming castle. One of my biggest fears was that we would not only be battling Demons inside, but humans as well. I wasn't sure how I would handle that if that did happen. It was against the code to kill humans.

Now, if they were working on the behest of Demons, that was where things took a murky tone. I did not think angels ever expected the Demons to work with humans.

Demons, like angels, saw humans as beneath them.

That seemed to have changed though, as Jasmine had told me. It had been humans who had altered her home and allowed the Demons to enter. Obviously the Demons had realized they could use humans as tools, to do things they did not have the power to do themselves, such as move around during daylight. Was that because the humans actually wanted to work with the demons, or was it because the Demons were manipulating the humans?

We progressed further. Instead of staying behind me, as I hoped she would, I saw Kadie creep up to my side. I wanted to tell myself it was because she was holding a flashlight and wanted to ensure we took the best path, but I knew it was so she was not cowering behind me like a damsel.

Stubborn woman.

We reached the top of the steps and I took a deep breath. This was it. Once we crossed the threshold, there would be no going back. I looked at her. This was her last chance to stay out of this.

Kadie looked back at me with hard eyes. It was as though she knew what I was waiting for and she wasn't going to give me that satisfaction. Her eyebrows knit together, as though saying, *'What are we waiting for?'*

I nodded once with finality, finally accepting that she was here with me. That she would not be turning back.

It was deathly silent as we stepped inside the stone building. There was a chill nipping at my neck. Did Kadie feel the same thing?

From my peripheral, I glanced at Kadie and didn't notice a change in her expression. I couldn't sense any Demons in the foyer, but I didn't trust my instincts in this place. There was something about this castle that distorted reality.

I held my sword at the ready and stepped through the front door, swinging the blade around in the empty room just in case there were any lingering bodies, poised to attack.

The blade swished empty air.

Nothing.

I motioned to Kadie to come in. "Safe, so far," I said, each word clipped.

She nodded and her gaze turned unerringly towards the hall that would lead us to the rooms where she had been held. Though it was dark, I could see that her face paled at the sight of it. I was suddenly filled with the instinct to wrap her up in my arms and tell her everything was going to be okay.

"Do you remember this place?" I asked her, though I knew she did, even if it was on a subconscious level.

She frowned, her forehead dotted with sweat. "I don't know… maybe," she said. "My body does. I can feel myself resist. I know I don't want to go down there." She inclined her head to the hallway. "I don't know why but that hallway looks familiar."

We moved stealthily along the hallway, Kadie a foot behind me at all times. She would protect me fiercely in the same way I would protect her.

My ears pricked for any sense of movement, any hint of human activity. I stretched out all of my paranormal, heightened senses to feel for any danger. But there was nothing.

This felt off to me. Just as before when I came here. The entire time I had been left waiting, for an attack that never came.

We stepped over the rotten carpet and moved along the corridor until we came to the door of the room where I'd found Kadie. I swallowed, squaring my shoulders. Even I could not step into that room without hesitating. I still dreamed of that night, terrible dreams that kept me awake.

I looked down at my lover. There was no pretense of terror, but she did seem wary. Her jaw was locked, her eyes narrowed. Though we were not touching, I could somehow feel how tense her body was.

"This is it, isn't it?" she asked, her voice catching in anxiety. It was low, as though she did not wish to disturb anything that might be lingering around.

"This is where I found you, yes." I nodded once, though she did not look at me. Her eyes were focused ahead of her. "Shall we see what's inside?"

She didn't answer, but her eyes shifted so they could meet mine.

I put my hand upon the wooden door and concentrated on it. I couldn't tell what was inside the room, and that made fear skitter along my spine. What I was able to distinguish was a terribleness about this room. I could not find the right words to explain it. But it was wrong. There was dark magic at work here, cloaking its inhabitants. Making my senses dull.

I dropped my hand and stepped back.

"Can you feel anything, Kadie?" I asked, wishing I'd brought Margaret with us now. Or even Simone. I should have used the Witches better. They would probably be able to tell me what was going on. They would be able to see things more clearly than I or Kadie would have.

But we couldn't go back now, not yet. There was an urgency about today that pushed me forward. I needed to know what was going on.

"Nothing." She shook her head and my fear transitioned into disappointment that this visit may also be a waste of our time.

"Well, let's go in and see if you can remember anything," I said, nodding my head at the door.

I slid my sword onto my back and took one of the flashlights from her. I gave her one last look. I wanted to make sure she was ready. I didn't want to force her because I knew things could go poorly.

She offered me a gentle smile and a nod, hair falling in her face. *Beautiful.*

I placed my hand back on the wood and pushed open the door. The inky blackness that permeated the room made me blink in the same way staring at the sun would. This room was definitely laden with an unnatural gloom.

I sensed no movement and saw no light in the darkness. Nothing to indicate there was anyone inside the large room. I took a breath and walked inside, holding the light up high. I appreciated the feeling of the cool metal of my sword pressed against my back, reminding me that I had a weapon and could defend myself and Kadie if needed.

The bright beam of the torch I held barely penetrated a foot in front of me.

Impossible.

"Come in," I called to Kadie over my shoulder, though my eyes stayed fixed firmly on the emptiness in front of me. "But we're not going to be able to see anything."

I gestured for her to move closer, my senses telling me that we were safe for the moment. I did not like it, however. This place dulled senses. Could it manipulate them as well?

I did not know.

Kadie hesitantly stepped into the room with me but as soon as she was within arms-reach of me, the door slammed shut with an almighty bang. Kadie had been too close to me to be the culprit. Something had done it. *Someone* had locked us in here.

Flames burned all around us and Kadie screamed as two men emerged from the shadows and grabbed her by the arms, pulling her backwards. I could see some of her magic shimmer around her, white and bright, but it had no effect on the humans.

"No!" I yelled, dropping the light and pulling my sword from its sheath. I tightened my grip on the handle and took several steps forward, the light from the flaming Demons helping me to navigate. At least it was not black the way it had been before. At least I could make out what was happening.

"Ow! Let me go!" Kadie cried out. I couldn't see what they were doing to her but I could hear her struggling. She was resisting as ferociously as she could.

Fear gripped my heart with an icy hand and I threw caution out the window. I would not allow for anyone to place their hands on her, no matter who they were.

"Release her!" I charged forward, ready to fight and die this time if it meant ensuring her safety.

Then Kadie staggered towards me, clutching her neck with her hands. "Are you okay?" I whispered urgently at her, grabbing her and holding her tightly against my body.

I couldn't see any blood running past her hand, but that didn't meant they hadn't done any damage.

"Yeah… I think so." She managed to say, although she sounded dazed.

She got free and that's all that mattered now. My heart filled with relief, but now was not the time to let down my guard. Not when they could attack at any moment. I held my sword out in front of us and pointed it at the Demons in the room.

They flared a brighter orange and moved forward as one. I stepped backwards to try to locate the door behind us.

"Can you find the handle? We need to get out of here!" I urged Kadie, my heart beating like a drum in my tight chest. As much as I wanted to fight, I knew I would not be able to stop them. Not by myself. They moved too fast where they were able to grab Kadie from me without me even realizing what was happening. I did not want to admit that I was in over my head, but I could not fight to the death on purpose, if it would mean nothing.

Suddenly, someone turned on the sun. I blinked rapidly, struggling to see in the brightness. Kadie and I both faltered, trying to collect our bearings.

The room lit up with a stark white light and that was when I saw two men standing at the end of the room near what could only be described as a crack in the air.

A crack that was more than two yards tall and a yard wide.

A crack where I could see the whirling blackness of Hell and the Demons that marched on the damned souls.

Oh, Heaven, help us.

"You've lost, Angel," a Demon said. His voice was hard to discern, monstrous and venomous, like white noise. "We have her blood. The last missing ingredient. Our Demons are going to destroy Earth and no one can save you now."

I watched in horror as the men threw a syringe of blood into the crack and a blistering fire began to blaze in the Hell beyond. That was why they grabbed Kadie. They needed her blood.

"Oh no, oh no." I could feel Kadie shaking her head more than I could see it due to how bright it was in here. "Gabriel, we have to go. Now!" Kadie was yelling at me hysterically, pulling at my shirt, yanking at my arms.

The Demons around me weren't moving. They were frozen. Watching. I was not sure if that was a good thing or a bad thing.

"But…" *I can't just leave! Not when I was so close to finishing this.*

The door flew open behind me and the Demons didn't flinch at the sunlight as it streamed inside the room.

Oh, no…

If the sun did not strike them powerless….

The crack that had begun as merely the size of a large man, expanded. Bigger and bigger it grew, until it swallowed the floor beneath it.

A flaming Demon the size of a large man stepped out of the

opening. He was so bright it was hard to look at him. Then another stepped out and fear froze my chest, their fiery presence flushing heat against my face.

The room exploded like a sunset of orange and yellow, reigning fire over us all.

"Gabriel!" Kadie yelled, clawing at me to retreat.

The Demons laughed through their black holes of mouths.

I gripped my sword and stared them down. I wanted to fight.

I *needed* to fight!

If this was the portal through which they were entering our dimension, then this was where we needed to stop them.

I was a fool to think we should have retreated. Why would I ever run from a fight? Kadie could leave – she should. Nathaniel needed one of us. She was his best option, only because I was able to do something to these Demons before they got out of hand.

I had to fight. It was the only way this would work.

I slashed at a Demon that closed in on us. Then another. Sweat rolled down my back and my arms bunched with strength and anger.

Three more rushed toward us and I sliced up two of them with a single swing. But another snuck up beside me and caught hold of one of my wings in their fiery grasp.

Pain blistered my side and I cried out as my feathers burned.

I opened my mouth, ready to tell Kadie to run, to flee this place while she was still able to, when a white light blasted the Demon who held me in its burning grasp, into black ash.

I nearly sagged in relief now that he was not gripping my wing any further.

I turned my head to see Kadie shooting magic from her fingertips. There was a wrinkle between her brow as though she was frustrated.

She glared at me. "Gabriel, we need to go!" she snapped. "Now!"

"No!" I snapped back. Her eyes widened. Not because she was afraid of me, but because she was surprised I would talk to her in such a way. I kept that in mind as I continued. "We need to stay and fight. Keep them all here so they have no chance to leave and go somewhere else. So they have no chance to harm anyone else."

If we could keep them contained, we could find a way to seal the entrance to Hell and stop them from destroying the Earth. If we did that, we could eradicate Demons from coming here altogether.

"They're not all here!" she screamed at me, her fear a palpable thing. I was not sure how she knew it, but she believed her own words. Judging by how serious, how worried, she appeared, I could not help but believe her as well.

I just did not understand why she thought such a thing.

That was when Tabitha's voice came through my head.

Gabriel, are you there?

Yes, I replied.

Thank God. The Demons, they're out in force in New York City. In daylight. You need to meet the others in Central park. Save the people or else the streets are going to run red.. Quickly, before it's too late.

"Fuck!" I put all of my frustrations into the word. It made me feel better, but only slightly.

The huge crack in the room was now the size of a mini-van. More and more Demons were coming through. Too many for Kadie and me to fight. Logically, I knew we needed to leave. We needed to get out of here and head back to New York. We needed time. And reinforcements because there was no way Kadie and I would be able to rid the world of them without it. However, I hesitated. Despite knowing this, a part of me wanted to stay and destroy them all. And I was angry I was not able to do just that.

I took in a deep breath. The room brightened with each new Demon as they charged out a swirling vortex of bright fire and light.

The scent of fire and brimstone tugged at my senses, reminding me that I could not delay. We needed to act. Whether that was resuming our fight or retreating, something had to be done, and quickly.

There was no easy way out of this. I had to trust my Angel Agent and the woman behind me when they told me I had to leave this Hell hole.

"Damn it!" I cursed and backed towards the door.

Much to my chagrin, I turned and bolted. I scooped up Kadie and ran all the way to the front door of the castle. I was amazed that she still clutched the flashlights even though I was sure her hands were clammy with perspiration from the heat and perhaps her own fear.

I secured Kadie around me, making sure she wouldn't fall off, then launched up from the concrete and flew as fast as I could to New York. I did not stop beating my wings until the foggy skyline came into view. Because the Demons had singed my wings, I was forced to work harder, to fly harder. Feathers burned off, making my wings look pathetic, but the usage of their tarnished forms was much worse.

At least I was still able to use them. At least they got me back to New York with Kadie even though I did not want to leave in the first place.

What the hell had happened back there?

I looked down to see Kadie alive and seemingly well, but holding her wounded neck tightly. I had forgotten she had been injured. I had forgotten they had taken her blood.

How could I have forgotten such an important thing?

We landed outside her house, the only place I thought to go since Tabitha hadn't given me any instructions on where I was flying. I was just told to return as quickly as I could, and that was what I did.

CHAPTER FOUR

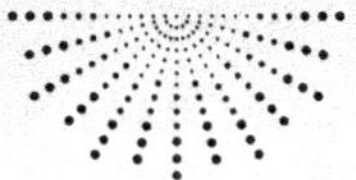

hen I released Kadie, I turned my body to get a good look at my lover. Gently, I placed my hands on her shoulders. She held her wound at an odd angle, blood trickling between her fingers. Her eyes were at half mast, and I realized that she was going to faint if I did not do something.

I brought her inside her home and locked the door behind us.

"You need medical aid," I said, though that much was obvious. I felt better saying it, however.

I pulled Kadie's hand down and gaped at the huge gash they'd made in her neck. I nearly staggered back in horror, but I could not let myself react so openly, not when she was looking to me for assurance. I focused my eyes on the wound, my body controlled tightly to not reveal my emotions. Before Kadie, I was an expert at masking them – if I felt anything at all. Now, there were times I had more difficulty.

Blood flowed freely when I took the pressure off and she placed her hand back on the wound to stop the flow. The gesture was weak, however, as though she was already starting to feel the effects of such blood loss.

"It can wait," she said as I eased her onto her couch. "We need to get to the epi-center of the chaos." She went to stand back up and the breath hissed from my teeth as blood ran down her neck.

"No." I couldn't have her bleeding to death when I needed her so much. She would become a liability if she fought. I needed her here, to recover.

Kadie stared at me, reading my thoughts as she always did. Then she rolled her eyes, and stood up once more. This time, she was quick enough to elude my arms, and she disappeared around the corner.

I sighed. I would not go after her. I would wait for her if I must. Sometimes, she surprised me with her pride. I wondered if I was as annoying as she was being.

Since I had the time, I sent a message back to Tabitha. *Is the baby all right?*

Yes, he's fine. Are you near Central Park? That's where I'm sending everyone.

Everyone? It's the middle of the day, Tabitha. We can't be seen! The Demons can't even be out at this time.

She groaned loudly.

Gabriel, they are coming to destroy New York, and all of the inhabitants. There will be widespread mayhem and chaos. There already is. This is the war to end all wars, we can't worry about being seen! The Demons sure as hell don't care anymore now that they're able to walk freely during the day. I don't know how they have managed to break into our world, but they have. They're coming in from everywhere, in the daylight, no less.

I could feel her exasperation and fear that the rules we believed were infinite, were in fact, very malleable. Something had to be done. We could not sit and wait.

They took some of Kadie's blood and it seems to have opened a portal, I told her. *Back at the castle. Once the portal opened, Demons began to emerge, too many for us to stop. The portal kept getting bigger. I did not know how to destroy it.*

Oh, Jesus, Mary and Joseph. Then she's the key, Gabriel.

Please don't tell me that means she has to die, Tabitha. I wasted time by vocalizing my concern to my Agent, but I did not care. Kadie was too important to me to risk, and if that was what was going to happen, I needed to step in and plan accordingly. As much as protecting the inhabitants of this world was my priority, Kadie and Nathaniel always came first. No matter what. *Because you know I won't survive that.*

Silence.

I tilted my head. *Tabitha,* I tried again. When she still would not answer, I screamed her name in my mind. I needed some kind of response.

Something.

And yet, her silence was telling enough.

Oh, fuck… no. I will not − I couldn't even finish the sentence. *I won't.*

Do what you can to save her, Gabriel, but know that your son is safe and I will be here for you all, at the end of this.

Her voice was not hopeful. If anything, it was resigned, as though she knew Kadie was not coming out of this alive and had accepted such a fate.

I, on the other hand, was not going to accept it. I would save the world, certainly, but I was going to save Kadie in the process as well.

At that moment, Kadie came running back from the hallway, her neck covered in white bandages she'd found in her bathroom.

"I'm patched up," she announced. She seemed stronger than she had been, more steady on her feet. "Let's go."

I opened my mouth, ready to tell her no. She glared at me. I did not know why I bothered. Kadie was too stubborn to understand. She did not even require my assistance with her bandage even though I was right here, willing to do anything to ensure she was safe.

I wished she cared about herself the way I cared about her.

Ignoring the intense feelings of pain threatening me, I wound us in invisibility. Kadie clung to my neck as I launched off. There was no point in arguing with her. It would be a waste of time for all of us.

I flew high into the air, the terrified screams of people around us ringing in my ears. The Demons had already touched New York City, but it was unnerving that they had the power to be out during the day.

Just follow the flames to the park.

I looked down and instantly felt like I'd been kicked by a horse in the stomach. I blinked, then blinked again. I couldn't be awake. This couldn't be reality.

And yet… it was.

It was my worst nightmare come true. New York was on *fire*. The windows in the large buildings showed flickering flames and cracked glass. The people in the streets were screaming with terror.

Horns honked from below as people abandoned their cars, blocking the streets. Women clasped their babies and children too them, their fear permeating the air making every hair on my body stand on end.

There was chaos and terror everywhere.

No. Perhaps this wasn't my worst nightmare. Nathaniel was with my Angel Agent, which meant both were safe. Kadie was also alive and her normal self. It could be worse, but that was not saying much.

Regardless, the place was filled with terror. The people were running for their lives, screaming as though they believed they would die and did not have hope that they would somehow come out of this alive.

I could hear the flames snap and cackle around me. It was daylight and yet heavy grey smoke filled the sky, like a beacon pointing the way to where the danger was.

I could see Central Park up ahead of us. It appeared, so far, to be untouched. Which was un-nerving, considering the destruction around us.

But why was the park untouched when chaos reigned every-where else? Why was this patch of land left unscathed? Was magic woven into the trees to keep it safe? And, if that were true, were the weavers of this magic friend or foe?

They had to be planning something. Central Park was a big expanse of land immersed in a concrete jungle. It would have been one of the first places struck, simply due to the number of people who frequented the park, especially in the middle of the day.

What was going on over there?

I shook my head to clear the worries and flew lower. Tabitha had never steered me wrong before. And I was not going to stop trusting her now, simply because I did not understand what was happening.

I landed on the lush green grass of Central Park, Kadie still in my arms, and glanced around. I did not want to put her down unless I absolutely had to. At least in my arms, I knew where she was and what she was doing. She was not lost to me.

"Why are we here?" Kadie asked, her confusion a feeling I shared. She scanned the tops of the trees, as though she was looking for someone. As though she was not quite sure what to expect. The frown that curved her lips and jutted out her bottom lip told me she did not understand and did not like this.

"Tabitha told me to come here," I explained. "She said she was sending everyone over here. She said we needed to get here immediately due to the importance of what was going on."

And by everyone, I assumed she meant the other Fallen Angels in America. All five of us.

Five did not seem to be a big enough number.

We're done for.

"Don't say that!" Kadie admonished, glaring at me. Her grip on my neck tightened.

I gently set her down, but she did not untangle herself from me. In truth, I had forgotten she could read my mind.

"I'm serious, Gabriel," she said. She cupped both of my cheeks and turned my head down to ensure I was looking into her eyes. There was something about her insistent stare, something that indicated she was not kidding around. But there was more to it than that. I did not know why, but it almost seemed as though she was personally offended by what I told her. "I can't have you giving up before we even begin. You can't charge into a place, thinking you're going to die. That's a suicide mission."

"I do not intend to die, my little Witch, but I also can see that we are not exactly in any way prepared to win, either," I said. "I can hope. I can have faith. But I will not lie to myself to make me feel better. I would rather be morose than a fool."

"You think I'm foolish for believing we can win?" Kadie asked, dropping her hands to her sides.

"Of course not," I said. "The power of belief is crucial to survival in the first place. If you believe it, truly believe it, that is your reality. But do not go into this assuming that we will win. We may have God's favour, but that will not win us battles. It will not win us wars. Do you understand, Kadie?"

Kadie's eyes were wide with disbelief when she said, "So you're okay with thinking we'll perish?"

"Not *we*," I said, the very idea of her dying filling my body up with cold dread. "I'm okay with my death if I do die, knowing Nathaniel is safe, knowing that you are alive. If I can stop this terror and I die doing so, I will have lived a full complete life. But I am also aware that it might not be possible. We might be too late." I curled an errant strand behind her ear, letting my fingertips linger on her skin. "It would behove you to do the same."

An intensity burned through my blood. I had to do something more than just speak to Kadie, remain safe while others were currently being slaughtered in the streets. I could not continue to talk when the time for talking had passed.

Now, we needed to act.

I grabbed her hand and began running through the park.

I wanted to be in the streets, fighting. However, I did know there had to be a reason that Tabitha had sent us here of all places.

Up ahead of us I saw movement, flashes of color that bled into one another that gave me the stark understanding of how Van Gough saw the world. People running.

We made it into a clearing and stopped. There were more people assembled than I could count.

"Who are all these people?" Kadie asked, her eyes scanning ahead of her, brow furrowed.

As though a siren had gone off around us, the huge group all turned to look at us. Whispering, smiling. They looked happy to see us, though I could not say why.

Titan, another Fallen Angel, walked up to us. His large blackened wings tucked were into his side and his blond hair was slicked back from his face. To humans, he might have resembled a Viking from old lore.

To me, he was like a brother who cared only of being the best at everything, including doing his job. He was a pain in the ass, but an asset to have in the field, during a fight.

"Gabriel," he said. "I'm glad you're here." He clapped his hand on my shoulder and tilted his head down, as though he wanted me to know that he meant what he said.

Titan and I had never gotten along in Heaven, nor here on Earth. But in this moment, I was intensely glad to see him. He was on our side.

"So am I," I returned, meaning each word. "Who are all these people?"

"Witches, mostly," he said. "And, of course…" Titan moved aside and spread out his arm to indicate something hidden.

Behind him was a legion of Angels, their white wings glistening in the sunlight like regal magic. My heart lurched in my throat at the sight of them and a smile spread across my face. I was so happy, tears sprung into my eyes. I would not let them fall, but I was grateful that they were here to help.

My warrior brothers. Two dozen of them, at least.

"They're here to fight with us?" I asked, baffled as much as I was happy.

Angels of Heaven were forbidden to step onto the Earth's surface. It was part of the original agreement between Heaven and Hell.

Titan grinned. "Yeah, since they're breaking every rule in the book, we figured we could too," he said. "I mean, is it really playing dirty if the other side starts it first?"

I wasn't sure how the Gods could justify such a thing, but I didn't care. If this meant we could turn the tide and save the humans destined for a Hellish existence, then I was all for it. Perhaps Kadie was right. I shouldn't immediately assume things were bad, not when I could not see the whole picture. I needed to have faith, not only in myself, but in God and what He could do for us. To remind myself that God would never leave us alone when we needed Him the most.

"This must be Kadie," Titan said, stepping closer to my woman.

I lifted my arm to create a wall between them, stopping his trajectory. Just because we were on the same team did not mean I trusted him with Kadie.

"Yes. Kadie, this is Titan," I said, turning my attention to my little Witch. "It seems that we have an army to fight with us."

Titan gave me a surprised look, then fell back as he began to understand how important she was to me.

"There have been whispers of a champion stepping forward to win the war for us, but I didn't think it would be a woman," Titan murmured. I could not say if he was telling me or if he was simply muttering to himself under his breath.

Kadie and I exchanged a look. We hadn't thought so either.

"I've heard predictions from Witches, that our son will be the warrior to win this war for us," Kadie said to me. She chewed on her bottom lip, as though she was trying to make sense of what had been predicted in the first place. "Even so, he is still very young. Perhaps they were mistaken."

Titan's eye brows rose up his forehead as the shock of that statement struck him.

"So, it is true…" He now looked at Kadie with a renewed respect. He tilted his head so his chin brushed his chest as a way to show that respect in a small bow. I did not think it was possible to see Titan bow to anyone save for God Himself.

But Kadie was no ordinary woman.

Regardless, I'd had enough of this chatter. We needed to move, not dillydally. Once this was over, once the Demons were sent back to Hell, we had all the time in the world for discussions. Now was not that time.

"Titan, we need to fight," I said. "People are dying in the streets. The Demons have taken too much power. We need to show them that they cannot keep what they have."

I could feel the pain and fear from the humans and perhaps even from the Witches as though it were my own. Like a raging, screaming bull in the back of my mind.

It was taking all my strength to block it out. My throat was dry and my arms already ached like they'd fought a month-long battle. Exhaustion teased my senses, tempting me to withdraw from the fight and collapse onto my bed and sleep for as long as slumber would have me.

Titan nodded, distracting me from my thoughts. "Then we need a plan," he pointed out. "We don't know how these Demons are getting onto our plain, or why they're attacking in daylight, but this is bad. We need to stop them, I just do not know how to go about doing it."

"It is worse than bad," I said, glancing at my Witch from the corner of my eye. "I've been told that Kadie is the key, but we don't know how to use her to fix this. We saw a fissure in our dimension at the castle where Kadie was held hostage, and there are Demons entering through it. My thought is she knows how to send them back, but she doesn't know how to access that part of her."

"Should we go there and shut it down?" Titan asked, rolling his shoulders back. His body tensed, as though he was ready to take off at any moment.

"We may need to send people there, but I don't believe it's the cause of all this." I gestured to the chaos going on in New York.

The legion of Angels shifted their focus and suddenly walked over to us, marching in time.

My throat tightened as I stared at them moving as a single unit. I recognized all of them. Warriors I had fought with, for nearly four hundred years.

Only a little while ago my only goal was to become one of them again. And now, I was glad I was not. I was glad I was a Guardian, with Kadie and a child of my own. I was not sure if I was sad about the loss, though I hadn't really acquired that goal yet so it was not mine to lose.

Kadie pressed against my side and the feelings of regret faded away like morning dew beneath the hot sun. Warmth spread across my body, lifting me up and giving me my strength.

I was where I was meant to be.

The head of the guard walked closer and spoke. "We're going to start the first round of defense," he said. "Beginning from the outskirts of the park and moving through New York, until they're all extinguished." Michael's arrogant tone carried over the whole group.

He wouldn't look at me, and I wanted to roll my eyes for all the shit they believed about me. That I was unworthy of their company. That I'd broken an unbreakable rule, and they'd never accept me back. I was lower than dirt as far as they were concerned, but for once I didn't care what they thought. They were here to fight. Our personal feelings did not matter. We had a job to do, and we would not allow petty differences to come between us and our mission.

I addressed Titan. "Do what you have to do," I said. "Kadie and I will fight alongside the Witches and figure out how to stop them from continuing to enter this plain."

I gave Michael my dirtiest look, concentrating on lowering my eyebrows and flaring my nostrils. He glanced away. I did not know if he regretted his treatment of me now that he knew we were in this together. I suppose it did not matter.

Good.

CHAPTER FIVE

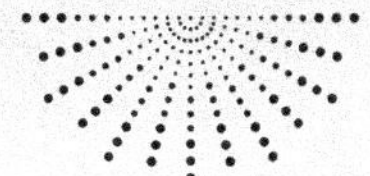

adie grabbed my arm and tugged me towards a large group of Witches, leading me away from the angels I knew, the angels I used to want to be. I was glad to be away from them. As the cool air pricked my skin, it reminded me that I was so much more than an angel.

Margaret rushed forward, her face looking stressed and troubled when she saw Kadie. "Gabriel," she said, turning her eyes to me. "Thank God, you're here. What are we going to do?"

"We need to find out where they're coming from," I said. I knew Margaret would listen to me, even if Michael would not. "Originally, I thought the portal was inside the castle where Kadie was being held, but we were there when they stormed New York, so there has to be another somewhere nearby."

Margaret nodded, a look of excitement in her eyes. "One of our young Witches was attacked and we tracked down the men responsible to a place near Queens," she explained in a rush, one word toppling over another. "We didn't report them, instead we followed them to an old, abandoned warehouse. The magic coming out of that place is toxic. It was smothering, as though I could not breathe."

I looked to Kadie and she nodded.

"Sounds like the place to start," I said. "Excellent job, Margaret."

I was surprised she beamed back at me. I looked over at Kadie and was surprised to see her face pale.

She bit her lip. "Yes, it probably is, but we need to help here too," she said. "We can't just leave all the fighting to everyone else. We need to do our part."

I flared my nostrils, nodding once. "You're right."

"Kadie, take these. I thought you might want to participate yourself." Margaret said, handing Kadie a black bag.

I pulled my sword from my back as Kadie opened the bag Margaret had given her and dragged out two long knives. Her eyes widened, but her lips curled up into a smile. She held the weapon in her hand as though she wanted to test it out for herself, to make sure she felt comfortable with it before using it herself.

Kadie turned to Margaret with a smile. "Thank you," she said.

She looked at me and I gripped my sword tightly. "You ready?" I asked, though I need not have said anything. I could see the look in her eyes.

She nodded. "Let's go."

We decided to make our way on foot. My wings were still recovering from the burns the Demons had given them recently. I did not know how they would fare after all of this was over. I suppose it was not something for me to think about until I knew I would survive.

We ran through the park, looking all around. Waiting for the appearance of our enemy. So far, there was nothing. The smell of freshly cut grass and hot dogs filled my senses. From my peripheral vision, I could see colourful balloons lifting into the sky as though they had been cut at the string and set free.

We kept running.

As soon as we emerged through the trees we saw them.

Dozens of Demons everywhere, their flaming fury lighting up the New York sidewalks, leaving destruction in their wake. I could smell the sulfur, the scent finding its way back to my nostrils. I nearly had to stop running and gag because of it. But I kept going, forcing the bile back down my throat. I would not allow myself to be weak, not when we were so close to ending this.

"Stay close to me, Kadie," I instructed my Witch without looking at her. I could not risk even a moment in case the Demons took advantage of that and attacked when we did not expect them to.

I held up my sword and ran forward, slicing the first Demon in half and then the next. The way my sword cut through them was like cutting through butter. It delighted me to know that despite this new power the Demons seemed to have found for themselves, I was able to get through them just as easy as I had before.

Though I promised myself I wouldn't, I kept an eye on Kadie as she attacked the Demons coming at her. I could not help but want to ensure her safety. If she needed me, I needed to be there for her. Killing Demons with a sword was much different than with magic. A weapon did not mean one was automatically protected. One had to wield the sword with strength and conviction. To be successful, they also needed confidence and, if possible, experience. Kadie had the former two qualities but not the latter. There was a chance she might need my assistance and I wanted to be ready for her.

She cried out as one of them managed to touch her and I leaped sideways, cutting the Demon's head off his shoulders.

I rushed towards her when I was certain I had a path to her. Somehow in the battle space separated us.

"Are you okay?" I asked, assessing her for damage. I tried to do it quickly, knowing there would be more Demons soon.

She dropped the knives onto the ground.

"Yes," she said, looking at her forehead. "But I don't think these are my weapons of choice."

I whirled around and sliced at two more fiery Demons coming at us, the heat of their flames on my face.

"No." I agreed. I didn't get a chance to watch her use her knives, but even I knew what she needed to use. "Your weapon is your magic, Kadie. Use it."

She nodded and lifted her hands up. It was almost as though she needed my permission, like she didn't want to use her power for some reason.

"Are you afraid?" I asked, frowning. I glanced to my left and could see a couple of Demons. I tightened my grip on my blades but I made no move to head over to them. I wanted Kadie to feel comfortable. Confident. I did not like the fact that she seemed unsure of herself. Now was not the time to doubt her abilities.

"I just," she began. Shifting her wait. "I'm afraid that I won't be able to control it, Gabriel. More than anything I want to help, and there's part of me that's scared I won't be able to."

The two Demons from before got within range and I quickly stabbed one in the gut. I pulled my sword out, cut the second Demon's head off before angling my body and doing the same thing to the first Demon.

I turned my attention back to Kadie. I could smell the fear on her and it made me weak. I didn't want her to get hurt, I did not want her to stall because she was worried about her own insufficiency, and anger pulsed through my blood.

I couldn't feel like this and function as a warrior. I needed to focus on the Demons. Once they were taken care of, I could help Kadie. I wished I had more time to help her now, but unfortunately, I did not. Demons were a pressing issue and I could not move forward with Kadie without first addressing them.

"Don't worry about me!" Kadie yelled as though she could read my mind.

I opened my mouth, telling her of course I worried about her, of course I wanted nothing more than to ensure she was all right, when she spun around from me. I wanted to call out to her, to demand she stay put, to at least ask where she was going, but I did not. I was not her keeper. I had no control over her choices.

But I did worry about her.

For her to command me otherwise was humorous.

Yeah, right.

I lifted my sword and slashed through the Demon running at me, the flames of his body folding into black dust at my feet.

Heat ran down my spine like candle wax and I twirled around to fight the Demon behind me, cutting his head off and then looking around for Kadie.

She was nearby, fleeing a Demon chasing her.

I practically dropped my sword.

"No!" I ran towards her and the Demon turned on me, rushing at me with arms wide spread. As long as it was not after Kadie, I did not care where he turned his attention. I just wanted Kadie to be safe, to be out of harm's way.

That was when I heard Kadie's angry cry and she threw back her head and exploded with white light.

Three Demons nearby burst into black ash, and an Angel standing close to Kadie stared at her, his mouth hanging open.

When she curled her fingers, her light disappeared. Her mouth hung open, though it wasn't exactly because she was surprised by her power. More, she was breathing hard and trying to catch her breath. She looked down at her hands, as though in awe. As though she could not quite believe that she was successful using her powers. Finally, she turned her face up and closed her mouth. It reminded me of a human searching for a sign of God somewhere in the sky. Perhaps Kadie was doing the same thing.

Either way, she needed to keep moving. She could not allow herself to be so easily distracted.

"Great job, keep it up!" I yelled out. Relief pulsed through me that she was all right, but the last thing I wanted to do was let down my defences. There were still Demons around. The threat had not yet been vanquished.

Damn she's powerful.

She didn't have control over her magic the way she wanted to. And yet, the sight of a Demon going after me seemed to inspire the right amount of emotion to push her power out.

Maybe if I kept getting myself into a fight nearby, she'd explode in an attempt to protect me. Maybe that was how Kadie could fight them, with the thought that they would do significant harm to me if she did not.

We fought side-by-side through the streets of Manhattan, but they just kept coming. I had no idea where they came from and I was loathe to admit it, but my body was starting to tire. I noticed sweat drench Kadie's face and cause her hair to frizz. Her face was read from sheer exhaustion.

Several Angel warriors, including Michael, found us on the street moments later. For the time being, we could congregate without any Demons threatening us. I knew they were still out there, but this space was empty.

For now.

"They aren't thinning out. No matter how many we kill, they just keep multiplying," one of the Angels said. He could barely speak, he was breathing so hard.

Though I was winded myself, it amazed me to see such a thing. Angels were notorious warriors. To see one before affected by his battle was not common.

Then again, Demons during the day without an end in sight also wasn't common.

"We need to stop them at the source," I said, deciding to put my two cents in. "One of the elder Witches told me that they think it's all coming from a place a few blocks away on the outskirts of the city. We need to go there and see if she's right. Perhaps if we take out where they're coming from, they will not have the ability to continue to multiply the way they seem to."

I looked around at the people fighting—Witches and Angels alike. Dare we leave them to handle this on their own? I was not sure they could handle it.

"Yes!" Kadie said, spinning her head to me. "We must go. Come on, Gabriel."

I acknowledged her with a nod but I did nothing except stare at Michael. I would not ask him for permission, but I also would not leave unless he allowed it. Despite our differences, he was still my superior and I would respect that.

He nodded once. "Yes, we will go with you," he said. "Let's fly."

I picked up Kadie and spread my wings. They twinged, still touched by damage from my last encounter with the Demons.

Three of his nearby Angels took to the sky and I followed them,

Kadie light in my arms. The heat of the evil in the air lit up my whole body, making it tingle and burn. My wings were still strong, however damaged, though it took longer than it normally would have to reach our destination.

As I flew, I looked down, just to gage what sort of work we had before us. I couldn't believe how many Demons there were. We'd killed so many, and yet they were still growing in numbers. It was exhausting just looking at them all.

"Over there." Kadie pointed to a significant part of the city shrouded with shadow. "I can feel it," Kadie had to yell over the wind in my ears.

I looked towards the area where she pointed and saw the building the Witches had been talking about. It did indeed have an evil, black energy about it. But was this the place we were looking for? How did Kadie know?

I did not have time to question her. I would not. I needed to trust what she said.

The white winged Angels around me flew down, all gasping and spluttering as we landed.

"Sulphur," Kadie said, hacking and coughing on the fumes that surrounded us. She was most affected by the smell than we were only because as angels, we had a resistance to things such a scent. And yet, even we were overwhelmed with it.

This was definitely the place.

As though answering my conclusion, Demons ran towards us, pouring out of the warehouse like escaping bursts of fire.

The Angels and I pulled out our swords and mowed them down, one fiery Demon at a time. Even Kadie was able to access her powers and burn the Demons on sight. I hoped that meant she was able to control her abilities better because they would help significantly in this war.

Sweat rolled down my back and my chest heaved with exertion, but, God, I felt alive. This was what I was created to do. Killing Demons felt so natural, so right. I flared my nostrils, sucking in a deep breath. The sulphur burned my nostrils but I didn't care. Not when I was killing Demons. Not when I heard their anguished screams.

"We need to get inside," Kadie called out, bolting down the sidewalk, towards the structure, getting away from me. I understood her urgency, but I could not help but wish she would stay put. I had too much on my plate right now, with the Demons continuing to pop up, that I needed her somewhere close by where I could still keep an eye on her. I slashed at the final Demon who stood in my way, and while it was still disintegrating into ash at my feet, I ran after her.

"Kadie! Come back!" I yelled, following in the wake of her white energy. I wished she understood that she was putting herself in unnecessary danger by running from me.

I moved my legs faster and pumped my arms as hard as they would go. Kadie was still too far in front of me. I pushed harder, the building looming in front of me. Exhaustion caused my muscles to burn. I let out a frustrated grunt. My wings pinched from the pain they were still in.

I reached out and managed to grab Kadie's shoulders just before she opened a side door to the warehouse.

"Hold on," I said, not bothering to hide the frustration in my tone. "You don't know what's in there." I dragged her away from the door so she wouldn't be able to get to it as easily as she tried to.

"I know it's not good," she replied, trying to get around me. "You need to let me go."

Her words sounded so final, as though she'd already made the decision to sacrifice herself for the greater good.

"No... I do not." I glared at her. Anger now burned through me. "Kadie, you're not allowed to go into a building in order to sacrifice yourself."

She pulled away from me and gave me an intense stare. "Gabriel, you know that I may need to do something in there you won't like," she said through clenched teeth. "But you're going to have to let me do it."

No…. please…

"You're being selfish," I cried. "Why do you get to decide what to do for the greater good without considering what it would do to me? To our son?"

"I'm selfish?" she asked through a scoff. "I'm trying to protect you both. One of us needs to be there for him, Gabriel. He needs one of us. If I can make the sacrifice, then that is what I'll do."

I grew desperate. "You promised me we'd both go home to our son after all this is done. Do not make yourself a liar."

Tension mounted between us. I knew now was not the time to hash out my frustration with her reckless behaviour, but I worried she might not have another time for me to do so.

Instead of fighting back, instead of being the sassy, stubborn woman I had fallen in love with and expected her to be, she gave me a sad smile and gripped my arm with her hand. "There has to be a world left to go back to, Gabriel," she said gently.

There is no world for me without you.

The other warrior Angels had caught up to us now, their swords held high in front of them, ready to do battle. They did not immediately charge the building. Rather, they waited for my instructions, something I appreciated.

Dear Lord, please let this not be the end. I'm always willing to sacrifice my own life for the good of the people, but not Kadie's. Not the mother of my child's.

I drew a long breath, attempting to calm the thunderous racing of my heart. At least Kadie was not running in there. At least she was giving me a chance to vocalize my concern.

I turned to her. She looked at me with big, beautiful eyes. They were filled with shimmering hope. Not necessarily hope that everything would end well. Rather, she was hopeful that I would have faith in her, that I trusted her enough to let her do this if it needed to be done.

"All right," I said finally, nodding once. My eyes never left hers. "Let's do this together then."

I could trust the Angels to do the right thing, but I hated the fact that Kadie may get hurt. I did not want to protect her, not when I knew she could defend herself and not when I was well-aware that I needed to be focused on eradicating Demons from this world. But I wished things were different. I wished my loyalties weren't drawn down the middle with me straddling the thin line. I wished this was more simple.

Two white Angels flung open the door and an inferno blazed. Heat seared our faces like we'd opened the very gates of Hell. I winced, narrowing my eyes due to how bright and how warm it had become. Dread piled up inside of me, heavy like an anchor tied to my gut and dragging me down into despair.

This is the place.

Kadie grabbed my arm and held me back while the others rushed inside, searching out an enemy we didn't know how to defeat. All we knew was to kill, kill, kill. Every Demon was a threat and needed to be put down, no matter what.

I grabbed my sword and stepped forward. Kadie coiled her fingers around my wrist, stopping me. I turned, furrowing my brow, imploring her for some sort of answer.

"We have to do this together, Gabriel," she said in a voice that made everything seem obvious. "You already said that. We're meant to fight by each other's side."

I nodded, my arms trembling with the effort it took to hold onto my sword and not grab Kadie and sweep her off to safety. Not to grab her face and kiss her one last time. I looked into her determined face and tightened my grip on my weapon. She was right.

Then it hit me, swift and immediate. As if the realization came from a higher power.

Kadie wasn't my weakness, she was my *strength*. She was my *reason* to fight, and for her, I could win. I was sure of it. I would not cower or worry with her by my side. I would be grateful for the chance to fight with her, to be with her in this way.

Screw it.

I pulled her into my body with my free hand and kissed her passionately, absorbing her love and giving her mine. I wanted to lose myself in the moment, to forget that there was a Hell on Earth and I needed to help take care of it.

But I had to draw myself away. I had to refocus my attention on the task at hand.

When I pulled back she stared up at me with an understanding that only my soulmate would know. We didn't know what would come from this. We did not know if we were going to survive. But we were together, and we were fighting for the greater good. And that was what mattered.

Together we surged into the dark building, the heat on my spine so intense I wished for snow to soothe it.

"This way," Kadie yelled, taking a sharp left turn and pushing open double doors. I did not understand how she knew such a thing, but I would not question her. I trusted her.

When the doors opened, we stepped into a huge room filled with Demons. I was not afraid of anything, not even this amount of Demons. My grip on my sword tightened and I narrowed my eyes, trying to come up with some sort of strategy on how we should handle this.

Angels to either sides of us rushed forward, slicing at the Demon monsters and carving a path through middle of the cavernous space.

At that moment, something came over Kadie, something strange, almost ethereal. I couldn't explain it, even if I wanted to. It was like she knew, she knew what she could do and she had every ounce of faith in her abilities to do it for herself.

Suddenly, I was aware what happened. She understood her powers. She embraced the uncertainty rather than ran from it.

Kadie lifted her arms and screamed as she blasted the Demons with her white light. I fought by her side, admiring the strength of my lover. She was magnificent. So strong and powerful. I was honored to be her partner.

I wanted to hug her, to tell her I knew she had the ability within her if only she just believed in herself. Instead, I focused on the task at hand.

Far away, at the other end of the enormous room I could see the doorway to Hell. It looked exactly the same as the one from the castle. My shoulders nearly sagged with relief. At least we had the place where they were coming from. We'd found it! The pathway. The source of this evil.

Unlike the pathway at the castle, this one was much larger, which meant more of the demons could pass through it at one time.

"They must be linked in some way," Kadie shouted over the noise of the battle raging around us. It was as though she could read my thoughts.

I nodded once, agreeing with her assessment.

The Angels fought beside us, the cries and groans of their efforts echoing in the immense room. I longed to re-join them, but I paused, flicking my gaze over the pathway, hoping to perhaps decipher any of its mysteries, to understand how to destroy it.

"Yes, but the question is, which one can shut both of them down?" I asked.

And how? What do we need to close them up?

A huge, yellow, fire Demon came at us and Kadie blasted him without a care. She was getting used to her powers.

Good girl.

Another snuck up behind me and I whirled to take him out. My blade sliced through him and turned him to ash.

Kadie moved closer to the massive, gaping hole in our dimension. Part of me was eager to see what she could do, but another part of me worried what might happen if she got too close. Could someone grab her and pull her through? Suddenly a human man came out of nowhere and stepped close to the pit of darkness.

I continued to look at the man. There was something familiar about him. It niggled the back of my mind. I should know him, but from where? How?

I squinted through the sweat that rolled down my face. Another Demon stepped through the hole, ignoring the man standing by the entrance. I waited. Was this human good? Probably not, or the Demon would have seen him as a threat. Kadie destroyed the Demon with a single blast.

She's getting damn good at that.

I was glad she had had a better handle on her gift. I knew she had been concerned about that.

A Demon grabbed me from behind and pain filled my back. I whirled around and sliced him in half, ash flying everywhere. I turned back to the man, wanting to keep an eye on him. Wanting to figure out how I knew him.

Then it hit me. It was the same man who'd taken Kadie's blood in the room at the castle. The one who had started this. I narrowed my eyes. Who the hell was he? What was he doing here? What did he want?

CHAPTER SIX

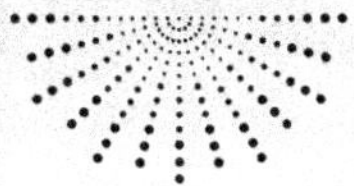

The man's grin was unnerving, too sharp, too evil. His laughter was maniacal, high pitched and indicating he was enjoying himself far too much.

His eyes were lit with a dark, evil intent that I could not even fathom. And what was worse, this man was human.

"You've lost, Angel," he said, stepping forward.

It took everything in me not to stagger back. I had not realized he had noticed me, but his eyes, now on my form, were penetrating. It was as if he had some special powers that saw straight through me. I had never felt so exposed, especially in front of a human stranger.

The human growled as he spat out the words, "You know you've lost. Soon, New York will be a wasteland, and the rest of the planet will follow. The Demons who've come through the portals will not stop until every soul in this city is under their control. And when we're finished here, we'll go elsewhere and do the same until the world is under our control."

"You're wrong!" I shouted back, a roar to my voice. And he was, in so many ways.

Any soul killed unjustly by a Demon would go straight to Heaven. They would ultimately be safe.

But what of those left on Earth? Would there be any civilization left after the Demons had finished with it?

If they completed their task. I had to remind myself that just because he had the upper hand in this moment did not mean he had won. I would not allow his success to happen.

"You'll never be able to close the portal. You're all done for," the man yelled, his eyes glowing a fiery red to match the Demons nearby. The Demons continued to step out, not even looking at the man. It was as though he did not exist to them.

I shifted my weight from foot to foot and gripped my sword tightly. I brought it up, ready to strike if I needed to. I didn't want to kill a human, but this one was definitely a lost cause. He was responsible for this. I saw no remorse in his eyes, no regret for all of the damage he had done. He would do it again and again if given a chance.

I ran forward and lifted my sword. Pain hit me like a burning iron through my chest.

The man before me cackled like a Witch as he threw red, burning light at me, very similar to Kadie's white magic. "You can't stop me, Angel," he said. "You have no powers, to speak of."

I cried out against the pain squeezing my ribs and crushing my lungs.

I couldn't breathe.

Couldn't think.

He was right.

I was a fool.

How could I have assumed he was a mere human who had the ability to control Demons? I should have prepared myself better. I should not have made any assumptions. My arrogance would be my undoing.

My fingers loosened around my sword and it clattered to the ground. My throat began to close up, my head swimming in a vision of black and silver stars.

Then I was free of his evil grip, falling to the ground in a painful heap.

I lifted my head to see what had happened to change my path of death.

I could barely hold my eyes open. The second I was able to, I sucked down breath, trying to reinvigorate me, to fill myself up with life.

When I was finally able to look up, to see what was going on, my heart stopped. Kadie was blasting the male Witch with her magic, both arms outstretched, white light blasting into his red.

The man groaned as the tide began to turn. The stream of white light powered by Kadie began to move closer and closer to the male Witch.

I nearly grinned, but doing so was difficult for me to do. At least I could fight. At least I was still able to do something, thanks to my little Witch.

I grabbed my sword from where it had fallen and dragged hot air into my aching lungs. I needed to breathe. I needed the energy if I was going to do this.

Kadie screamed out in anger as her power flowed faster. I watched in awe as white began to overpower red. Beads of sweat appeared on her forehead. Her temples started to pulsate as a telling headache began to form. I wanted to help her, but I could not. Not right now, in this moment.

I staggered to my feet in time to watch the male Witch fall backwards, Kadie's white magic pummelling into his chest, leaving him gaping and gasping like a landed fish.

This was my opening.

I ran forward, lifted my sword above my head and sliced through the flesh and bone of the evil Witch with ease. The vibration of death shivered along the metal, leaving a nasty taste in my mouth.

The man slid to the floor in a pile of blood and bone, his crazy smile still plastered across his ugly face.

Regret pitted itself in my stomach. I wished there had been

another way, but after watching him, after hearing all he had to say, I knew his fate was written before I had completed it.

I turned back towards Kadie, forcing the regret of the murder I had just committed away. I could not lose focus over an evil, broken Witch. "We need to do something," I told her, my voice raw. Speaking felt like embers and glass on my throat.

"I'm the key." Kadie whispered and fear rippled along my skin like the hand of death on my spine. She said it like she was still trying to wrap her head around it, like she couldn't quite believe what she was saying.

"No… Kadie…" I reached out for her but she side-stepped my grasp.

I knew what this meant, but I did not want to let myself believe it.

"We can't let them destroy everyone… everything, Gabriel." She stepped over the corpse of the man I'd killed, and walked closer to the crack. "I can't continue to live in a world where I could have made it better but didn't for my own selfish reasons."

Another fiery Demon stepped out into the daylight and Kadie held up a palm.

White lightening sizzled from her skin and blasted the Demon apart. She didn't even seem winded. Before, her magic exhausted. But now, it was as though she and her magic were as one, united. If her magic was strong, she was strong, and vice versa.

I heard an exclamation of awe behind me, but ignored the Angel who was obviously watching what my Witch could do.

She stepped over the Demon's pile of ash and moved closer to the opening, her intent obvious.

"No. Kadie you can't do it!" I shouted. I could not allow her to sacrifice herself. I could not allow her to throw her life away, not when there was still so much I wanted to do. Not when there was still so much I wanted to tell her. To experience with her.

She was going to throw herself into that gaping hole, and I couldn't let her.

I took off, flying right at her. My wings screamed, still in pain from the Demon touching it, still strained because of all the use I had put it through. I did not care. I pushed even harder and I reached her in an instant and grabbed her arms. We'd figure out another way. Anything but this. I attempted to pull her up into the sky with me, away from all of this.

She pressed her still sizzling palm to my arm and lightening shot up into my shoulder, exploding through my spine.

I fell back down to Earth, landing flat on my back.

I was so shocked, I couldn't even speak. I couldn't even cry out in pain.

"I'm sorry Gabriel," Kadie whispered calmly as she moved even closer to the gateway to Hell. "I mean you no harm. But I cannot let you stop me from doing what I must do."

How was my girl so calm? So brave? I didn't know a single Angel who could step into Hell with so much courage in his heart.

A single tear rolled down the side of her cheek, but her eyes were determined to see this through. I was in awe of her. If I was not surrounded by other angels and Demon ash, I probably would have fallen to my knees.

"No! Kadie! No!" Tears streamed down my face as the inevitable end to this story began to unfold. I wanted to go to her, to reach for her, but my body stalled. I could not stop her. Even as I shouted at her, I knew my words would do me no good.

She had fought beside me as Jasmine had predicted. And as Tabitha had also foretold, Kadie was the only one who could end it all.

There was nothing I could do that would stop her.

I rolled onto my side and pushed up with my good arm, the one Kadie had struck, crippled at my side.

Another Demon turned to ash as Kadie stepped closer to the vortex, tugging at the bandages covering her neck.

As the blood-soaked material fell to the ground, Kadie's life force began to flow once again, rivulets of red running down the side of her neck.

Before she moved any further, she stopped and regarded me with one of her soft smiles. The twinkling mischief was back in her eyes, and it made my heart swell just seeing it.

"Tell our son that I love him, more than anything in this world." A soft smile quirked up the sides of Kadie's beautiful mouth, deepening it. This smile, I recognized. This smile was the one she reserved solely for me. "Well, almost as much as I loved you…"

My heart cracked in half.

I looked at her helplessly, my faithful weapon useless, the tip scraping the floor under my feet. I was surprised I hadn't released my grip completely, especially nothing else mattered anymore. Not when Kadie was going to sacrifice herself, was going to leave me and our son.

"No…" I hauled my body forward, reaching out with my good arm as Kadie flung herself backwards.

Right into the fiery embrace of hell.

I watched, my mouth open, my eyes wide. There was nothing for me to do. She was gone. The blackness had swallowed her up, and I could not save her.

I couldn't speak. I could barely breathe and it was not due to the smoke and the sulfur that permeated this building.

"No. No. No!"

I didn't realize I was shouting until my voice echoed back to me. I was numb and yet I felt a hot searing pain rip across my chest through every inch of my body, from the crown of my head, all the way to my toes. I moved forward but I nearly fell. I was not in control of my body, not in the way I used to be.

I had to save her. She couldn't do this. Not alone.

She was falling into the abyss and I couldn't get there. I couldn't. My body was so weak… so much pain…

The portal began to close up, swallowing Kadie.

She was dying. A sacrifice for us all.

I crawled closer to the crack, dragging myself across the ash-covered earth. My body was coated by the remains of Demons. I felt awful, unsure, disgusted with myself. The last thing I wanted was any of these vile beasts clinging to my form, but there was nothing I could do to wash them away. The only thing I could do was ignore them for the time being.

I had to get to Kadie.

When I got closer to the fissure in our dimension, I reached out to her. The hot wind covered my face. Then the jagged opening suddenly snapped shut, as though it had never been there.

I reached around and up, extending my hand into the space where the gaping hole had once been.

It was gone.

"No!" I cried out, slamming my fist into the ground and feeling Kadie's wet blood on my skin, soaking the ground. "No! That is impossible. Give her back! She isn't meant to be down there. No!"

I was talking to ghosts, ghosts who laughed at my anguish, who relished in my misery. This could not be her fate. Certainly there was still something I could do.

The image of Kadie's beautiful face surrounded by fire, burned into my mind, torturing me in a circular hell.

She was gone.

There was silence surrounding me as the remaining Demons began to wither and die. The Angels slashed at the final flames, but it wasn't necessary. They were extinguished, their link to this world severed by Kadie's sacrifice.

We were safe. The Angels, the humans, the Witches. There was no Demon left to fight, not after Kadie's sacrifice.

The Demons weren't meant to be here, and thus, they returned to whence they came. The magic they had relied upon to keep them here, their tie to Kadie and her blood, was now gone.

There was a great cry of triumph around me as the legion of Angels cheered the disappearance of the Demons who had come to claim the land as their own. In my anguish, I had forgotten they were present. Which meant they had witnessed my pathetic cries. They witnessed me crawling on the floor, trying to stop Kadie, trying to save her.

I felt no shame, only anger that they had done nothing to help her.

Why should they, Gabriel? my mind asked. *They are Angels, as you once were. They do not feel the same way you now feel.*

The cheering continued. I should be happy as well. Kadie would want me to rejoice at the fall of the Demons, at the safety of the world.

But there was no rejoicing in my soul. Only a deep, dark hole that would never be filled again.

"Gabriel! Gabriel!" Titan yelled as he ran to me.

He was covered in black ash, part of his face burned, and yet the pain he must be feeling did not dim the smile on his face. "We won! They're gone!"

"I know," I said, pushing up from the ground, the feeling in my arm returning. I pulled myself into a seated position. The pain that had permeated my body was numb. I would feel it all a hundred times more if it meant that I would get to see Kadie. Even if I could not be with her, I would do anything to know she was alive.

The world was saved, and mine was over.

My son…

"Where's Kadie?" Titan asked, his gaze darting around me as though waiting for my diminutive human to appear out of thin air. He mustn't have seen who'd actually won us the day.

I assumed wrong, then. The Angels did not see what Kadie did for us. They were not aware of her sacrifice.

"She's gone." My voice croaked, as though I was some sort of frog. I pressed my lips together. I did not want Titan to see me so emotional, but at that moment, I could not be bothered to care.

I didn't want to elaborate, but my fellow Fallen Angel reached out and grabbed hold of the arm Kadie had shocked. I could feel it now, in a strange, tingling sort of way. It was her way of stopping me, her way of keeping me distant so I would be unable to stop her from doing what she had done.

"What do you mean, she's gone?" Titan asked, his voice curious but also tentative. "Did a Demon get her?"

Some of the warrior Angels who had been fighting with us walked closer. Michael had a sad look on his face that indicated that he'd seen what had happened.

I looked away. The last thing I wanted was Michael's pity. I would rather have him insult me, I would rather have him order me not to get so entirely emotional over a human. But he continued to look at me with sad eyes.

I hated him even more for his sympathy.

"I need to get to my son, Titan." I turned my attention back to the other Fallen Angel, so I would not be able to say anything I would later regret.

He's all I have left.

Quite honestly, I did not want to be alone. And even though I was surrounded by fellow Angels, I was hollow, a void, searching for someone to hold onto.

Being with my son would make me feel better.

"What happened to your woman?" Titan repeated, his voice harder and more serious than I'd ever heard. It did not seem he was ready to let go of this. I did not understand why.

"She…"

My throat closed up as though someone had wrapped a hand around my neck. I did not understand his incessant desire to know what happened to Kadie. Certainly he could see how difficult it was for me to speak about it. And still he waited. Still he pushed me with the intensity of his gaze. I cleared my throat. I would get no reprieve if I did not explain. If I wanted to see my son soon, I needed to get this over with.

"She… sacrificed herself for us. She threw herself into Hell… She…" I clenched my teeth together. I couldn't say any more.

Titan's hand fell away as his eyes went wide.

"I'm sorry." His words were cryptic. Not sympathetic but I knew from his sincere tone, he meant them.

This gutted me more than I was willing to say. Titan understood I wanted no sympathy. Despite our troubles in the past, he respected me enough to give me that.

I took a step away from them all, my eyes blinded by the tears that gathered and fell down my cheeks. I did not want them to see me cry.

Michael, who was nearby, caught my eye, and instead of looking away as he always did, he bowed his head and put his hand on his heart—a deep sign of respect.

I nodded at him. It was better than his sympathy. I spread my wings out around me. The pain pinched, but I barely noticed it. There was too much raw pain in my heart for me to understand the pain in my chest. I needed Nathaniel. I would fly to Tabitha's, despite the damage my body had faced through the battle, despite my tattered wings who needed to rest, needed to heal.

The pain in my muscles couldn't compete with the pain in my heart, and as I slowly made my way up into the air, my damaged wings beating as hard as they dared, the scream inside my head grew.

She's gone.

Kadie's gone.

I lost her.

We might have defeated the Demons, but the cost was too high.

And there was no way I could live without her.

CHAPTER SEVEN

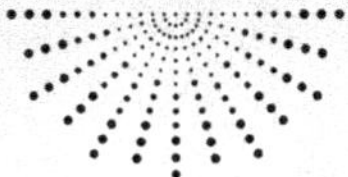

The sky was clear. The sun was slowly starting to set, causing a stream of beautiful colors to stream across the sky. Bright orange, red, and yellows lit up the sky, with dashes of soft purples and pinks. This was the definition of beautiful, this peaceful sunset that offered everyone who looked upon it a symbol of hope.

And yet, my heart ached just looking at it. Because Kadie was not here to see it. I was unable to share something like this with her.

I never would be able to share something with her again.

Night was just starting to touch the world. Under other circumstances, night was predatory, dangerous. Night was when Demons came out and claimed souls, when Guardians would prepare to hunt, to fight, to kill.

But this night promised peace and solitude. This night promised stillness and serenity.

But for me, this night promised nothing more than mourning.

I reached Tabitha's house before I knew it, so lost in my thoughts I was. I barely felt the wind in my hair, scraping against my cheeks, tousling my wings. I barely felt the earth under my feet as I landed.

I needed my son. My arms felt empty, and I needed to rectify that as soon as possible.

Before I stepped inside, I did a quick cursory glance. Nothing seemed out of place. There was no damage, nothing that would indicate something was amiss here. For that, I was grateful. As far as I was concerned, my son was all right. My son was safe and unharmed.

"Tabitha!" I pushed open the door to my Agent's home.

She was ready for my return, already loaded with buckets of water in her arms. I did not know how she knew. Then again, Tabitha always seemed to know something, always seemed to know what was going on even before I did.

"Come into the bathroom," she instructed, her voice nothing more than a whisper. "The baby is asleep."

Even though I knew Nathaniel was safe, to hear the words from her lips made my heart swell with joy and relief.

I staggered to the room she indicated and stripped the clothes from my exhausted body. I had a moment to clean myself off, to remove the stench of darkness, of death, of evil, from my body before I could face my son again. I did not want him anywhere near me until I was clean, until I had scrubbed everything off and could be as clean and pure as I was able to.

Tabitha poured cold water all over me. My wings, my shoulders, even over my head so that the screaming inside my mind began to ease as the pain subsided. The water felt surprisingly soothing. My wings sang as the water ran through them, a balm to ease the discomfort and torment I had put them through. Instead of constricting because of the unexpected burst of coldness, my muscles eased under the water. In fact, I was so comfortable, I did not realize my eyes were filled with tears until they started rolling down my cheeks.

That was when the sobbing began. My shoulders jerked up and down, my back curved forward. I needed to sit soon or my knees would give out.

I couldn't control it. I could not control my emotions. I knew this made me pathetic. I knew this made me weak. It stripped the very essence of what being an Angel meant and we differentiated ourselves from being human, but I did not care. My heart was broken and there was no way for me to put the pieces of it back together.

Deep. Dark. Soul-wrenching sobs that couldn't be contained and racked my body to its core.

I tried to clamp my hand over my mouth. The last thing I wanted was for my son to hear his father cry, to hear his father so broken and inconsolable. I did not want to scare him. I did not want to wake him with such terrible, desolate sounds.

Tabitha stroked my head and said soothing things that I couldn't distinguish. I could not bring myself to listen to her. And I didn't care what she was saying. No matter what she said, Kadie was not coming back. Nothing was going to fix this now.

"She's gone," I managed to get out as Tabitha continued to stroke my hair. The gesture itself was soothing, but it had no effect on me. I barely noticed anything she was doing, though I did feel more settled than I had before coming here.

"I know… I know…" Tabitha's calm voice finally broke through to me. She said nothing more, nothing about how I still had Nathaniel, nothing about how I should feel good at what Kadie and I and everyone else had accomplished. She did not tell me it was going to be all right. For that, I was grateful. The last thing I needed right now was my angel agent lying to me.

I allowed my breathing to slow down and my body to ease into the healing flow of the water. My muscles began to sag forward. It was difficult to hold myself up. Not because of my sadness, not anymore. More because I was weak. I was tired.

Eventually my head cleared of the bright red cloud of anger. The screaming inside my mind stopped and all that was left was a dull, black emptiness. I was like a melon that had all of its center scooped out.

There was a thin cry in the air and Tabitha left me to tend to Nathaniel. I should go to him, to hug him tight to me and assure him that I was still there for him, but I couldn't. Not yet. I wasn't ready. I did have to get up and out of this bath. I didn't want my son to see me like this. I scrubbed my face with my hands and pushed myself to a stand.

I grunted as I did so, the water rushing off of me. My muscles burned. I wanted nothing more than to collapse. But I did not. I held myself together and craned my neck to both sides, stretching it out.

The water had washed away a lot of the physical pain. After a moment of standing, my legs were strong and sturdy beneath me. When I stepped out, I was confident my knees would not shake and I would not fall.

I towel dried my body the best I could and tucked my wings in to my side to heal. My nakedness didn't bother me normally, but at this totally vulnerable moment, I needed something solid around me. I needed to shield myself from prying, knowing eyes.

Soft footsteps filled my ears. I heard Tabitha before I saw her. I straightened when she walked back into the bathroom, grabbing a towel from the rack so it offered some sort of small reprieve from the fact that I could not find any clothing to cover myself.

"Here's Daddy. Daddy's back," Tabitha walked back into the room with Nathaniel and I wrapped the towel around my waist, tying it tightly.

I wanted our bed. I needed to crawl into the warmth of the last place Kadie had slept and never get out. I wanted to breathe in her scent so I could never forget it, so it surrounded me and seeped into my skin like a tattoo.

"Here you go," Tabitha handed me my son, whose chubby hands were reaching for me as he attempted to climb out of Tabitha's arms.

At first, part of me worried that something would change, that knowing Kadie was gone would change the way I loved him, the way I held him. But the second he was in my arms, it was as though everything else fell away. The thought of forgetting how to love when my only love had been stripped from me felt foolish with Nathaniel in my arms.

"Come here, beautiful boy," I murmured, gently touching my forehead to his much smaller one.

I cradled my son in my arms and pressed my lips to his head. His warmth filled a small part of my heart with happiness and I let out a huge sigh that I'd been holding in. The night was still dark, certainly, but Nathaniel was the lone star shining.

I closed my eyes and wished the world away. Wished for things to be different. Wished Kadie was here, holding our beautiful child, and murmuring things to him.

"Come into the family room and tell me what happened," my Agent instructed me, and I did as she bade. There was no use arguing. If anything, it felt good to be told what to do. Orders, I could follow.

We moved into the living space and I collapsed onto the couch, cradling my jumping boy who was still smiling and moving about like his world hadn't ended. His eyes were filled with such happiness when he saw me. I knew he was too young to rationalize that his mother should be here as well, but it felt amazing, seeing that he knew me, that he recognized me as someone important to him.

His innocence made my throat swell and tears re-emerge in my eyes. How was I going to tell him that his mother was gone? How was I going to tell him that I had been right there, but that it didn't matter? That there was nothing I could do to save her?

Maybe I didn't have to, a cowardly part of me suggested. Tabitha could raise him for me, when I was gone. I'd be nothing more than a memory.

Before I could allow myself to head down that dark road, Tabitha gently cleared her throat. I was suddenly grateful for the interruption, not sure I wanted to find out where my mind wanted to lead me.

"Tell me what happened, Gabriel," Tabitha said again, this time with a tone that brooked no argument.

I sighed, ripping my eyes away from my child so I could focus the attention on her..

"We fought, all of us," I began. "The Fallen Angels. A legion of true Angels. The Witches. Some died, I'm not sure of the numbers. I don't know if I know any of the Fallen, except…" I let my voice trail off, refusing to finish that sentence.

"And Kadie?"

It would seem Tabitha did not care for my hesitation. She wanted me to face my sadness. I almost hated her for it.

Yes… Kadie.

"Kadie realized, well she guessed correctly, I suppose… that the only way to close the gateway to Hell was to sacrifice herself," I said. My face got hot again. The grip I had on Nathaniel tightened, but only slightly.

I continued to bounce my standing son on my knee, unable to look at Tabitha while I spoke.

"She threw herself into the crack, and everything stopped," I said. "The Demons practically disintegrated on the spot. Everything stopped at that moment. The war was over. There was nothing left to fight."

There was silence in the room. The only interruption was Nathaniel's beautiful baby babble. How could a sound bring me so much joy and so much sadness simultaneously? I didn't understand it.

"So, our premonition about Nathaniel being the savior was incorrect," Tabitha said, breaking the silence in her no-nonsense way. I was almost grateful for how indifferent her voice sounded. It reminded me that my emotions were useless, that they would not help me understand what had transpired any better.

I nodded my head, my vision blurring with fatigue. *I hope so.* I couldn't go through all this again in a few years when he was fully grown.

"I think so," I said, though I could barely speak at this point. "Looks like his mommy was the hero after all."

I couldn't hold him anymore. Nathaniel's eyes were his mothers, his lips…

"Take him for me, would you?" I said, standing up. "I know you've already watched him for a while and I know you probably need your time. But I can't… I'm going to go to bed."

"Bed?" Tabitha furrowed her brow, cocking her head to the side as she regarded me with an unapologetic gaze. "What do you mean? You don't sleep."

"Then I have centuries to catch up on, don't I?" I handed the baby to Tabitha and she took him with practiced ease.

I was grateful for the break. I needed time to myself, time to process everything that had happened. I was glad to see Nathaniel was okay. I was happy that he was healthy. But I needed to mourn my loss. If I did not, if I pretended everything was fine, I would be unhappy deep down. And I would resent anyone I felt I needed to hide my true emotions to.

I stumbled away to the bedroom where Kadie had slept for the past month. The room was still enchanted with her fresh smell and as I closed the door and fell between the sheets, her scent enfolded me like a blanket.

The tears and fell and my heart broke once again.

I placed the pillow over my face to conceal the sobs that racked through my body. It wasn't just my eyes that cried, but my entire body shook with emotion, emotion I could not control.

And no one was around to see it, for which I was glad.

I indulged my emotions. I let myself cry without lecturing myself on the uselessness of them, or the fact that Kadie would not want me to be so sad.

I did not care about any of that.

I cried and cried until I could cry no longer, and that was when sleep finally took me.

The hole inside my heart grew bigger with each passing day. After Kadie sacrificed herself, I knew life would never be the same. I just had not wrapped my head around the concept that I would be living without her. It sounded silly, but I thought somehow, Kadie would come back to me. Perhaps she would fight her way out or perhaps there was some sort of miracle from God that would bring her back to me. I just did not think I would have to do this on my own.

The truth of the matter was, besides the love I had for my son, I did not know how to be a parent to him. As such, I began to worry that he might do something – with no intention to do so – that would shift my feelings for him.

I still went to bed each evening and thanked God for my son, for his health, for his presence in my life. I reminded myself that Nathaniel was a part of Kadie and I loved him even more for being that.

But it was not enough.

After a month of torture, my future was decided. I could no longer stand to live without her. Even though Nathaniel was happy and thriving, I was not. And the last thing I wanted was to get in my own child's way because of a selfish desire that I could not change.

The gnawing blackness inside me would only spread, and I couldn't continue to be around my innocent son without infecting him with my misery. Nathaniel was happy. He knew naught of his mother. He did not understand all she did. He should not have to be punished or resented for his ignorance. What kind of father would I be to do that to him?

I was dying inside. Slowly, and painfully.

It didn't matter how many Demons I killed. How many innocents I saved. It was all a fruitless journey to nowhere. And I was dragging my son down with me.

Each time he smiled at me, each time he babbled and insisted I play with him, it felt more forced and more trying than the last.

Night came, and as darkness fell I said my goodbyes. I picked up my sleeping son, his thick eyelashes fanning out over his plump cheeks. God, he looked so much like Kadie. It broke my heart. As much as I was disappointed with this life where she was not in it, it almost felt as though I was leaving her behind again.

"I will love you for as long as the sun and moon rise and fall," I promised him.

I placed him back in his crib, content with the parent I had inadvertently chosen for him. He would be safe with Tabitha. And I knew she would do everything for him.

I hoped she understood. I hoped she knew I did not want to abandon any of them. It was just too painful to bear on my own.

Instead of wallowing, instead of allowing myself to become a victim, I had to do something about it, even if that meant leaving.

At least I knew he would be safe, and loved. Understood and guided by another half-Witch, half-Angel. He would thrive with her, and not wallow with me.

"You're leaving, then?" came Tabitha's harsh tone as I snuck through the house. I almost made it to the front door when her words sliced through me the same way I sliced through Demons.

I stopped, my fingers grazing the doorknob. My shoulders sagged forward. This was what it must feel like to be caught by a parent sneaking out of the house.

I turned slowly, pulling on my jacket as I did so. My wings rustled behind me as I pushed them further into my back. Though they were still in pain every now and then, they had healed to nearly their full capacity.

"Yes." I gave her a nod. "Demon hunting in the Bronx tonight."

A final goodbye to Kadie's home and I'd find a nice pack of Demons to commit my final fight to. Despite closing the portal, there were still a few that managed to escape. I did not know why they had not turned to ash when Kadie closed up the portal. I did not actually care.

"I can't stop you from doing this, Gabriel, but I must advise against it," she said, keeping her voice low so she would not wake up Nathaniel. I was appreciative of her consideration in this matter. I did not want to have to say goodbye to him when he was awake, when he did not understand why I was leaving.

"I don't know what you mean," I lied, wanting out of this conversation. I looked down at the carpet, clenching my jaw. I hated how clearly she could look at me, as though she could see right through my armor, see through all the misery and lies I had surrounded myself in so this very moment would be easier to handle.

Tabitha rolled her eyes and crossed her arms over her chest, clearly not impressed. "Oh, please, don't insult me," she said, clicking her tongue against the back of her teeth. "I know what your plan is, and I don't want you to go through with it. Nathaniel needs you, I need you. The world, and all its victims needs you. Do not allow yourself to wallow, Gabriel.""

I looked away from her impassioned face.

"The Demons barely cross over to follow anyone anymore, Tabitha, you know that," I pointed out. "I've had what... two Targets to protect in the past month? What purpose do I have anymore?"

The attacks on Witches had stopped and the list of Targets was way down.

Either the evil bunch was mounting forces for another attack, or their side had taken a massive hit when Kadie had severed the connection to them. I liked to believe it was the latter. For all Kadie did, I would be furious to know her sacrifice meant nothing if they could regroup and attack again.

"Gabriel, please. Don't." The pain in Tabitha's voice was unbearable. "You ask what your purpose is. Is being a parent not enough?"

I backed away from her, towards the door and the living world, where Demons resided. I did not want to hear about her disapproval.

"You have been a wonderful friend for a very long time, Tabitha," I said through gritted teeth, trying to be careful what I said. I did not want an argument to be the last thing we shared together. "Please look after my son. I trust you with him."

Tears streamed down her pale face. "He still needs you, Gabriel," she insisted.

I smiled as I reached for the door handle, oblivion not far away now. If anything, I felt good about my decision. It felt right.

"You will be a wonderful mother to him, Tabitha," I said. I risked looking at her, scanning her one last time. I did not want to forget the woman who always had my back. "Just make sure he doesn't forget us."

She sobbed and wrapped her arms around her body as though to hold in her breath. "I will..."

I turned away from her and opened the door, the cool breeze on my face the best I'd felt in too long. I breathed in the air and my lungs expanded, giving me an extra boost of energy I hadn't been expecting.

Not long now.

I would see Kadie again. I would see her soon. That was something to be excited about.

I extended my wings and flew towards the Bronx slowly, my damaged wings barely able to hold my weight. I did not care. Despite the pain, there was a smile on my face.

I'd lost so much in the recent battles, I could easily justify this choice. It was a choice I finally got to make on my own.

I was no use to anyone, broken and beaten as I was. I could not be a father, not the sort of father Nathaniel deserved.

This was the right thing to do. And I would go out in a blaze of glory. I was sure of it.

CHAPTER EIGHT

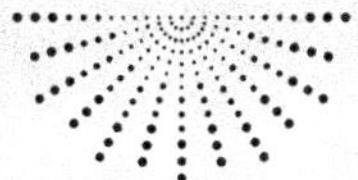

Sulfur and brimstone pierced my nostrils as I landed. I followed my instincts and chased down a large group of Demons rallying together not far from Kadie's home.

They were terrorizing a young woman and as I got closer, the heat on my spine was as familiar to me as an old friend.

A smile lifted my lips when my feet hit the courtyard and it lit up with the orange and yellow fire of the Demons. It was like a beacon calling me home.

I drew my sword and folded my wings into my body so tight that it seemed as though I would be fighting as a human. Everything about my movement felt natural, felt good. This was right.

The woman they tormented screamed inside her home and ran for her life. I could hear her footfalls on the tiles as she hid in another room. I was not going to allow them the satisfaction of harming another innocent. They took my Kadie. I would take them until they were all ash, every last one of them. That, or I would die fighting. Either end scenario was acceptable to me.

"Come on," I said. "If you want me, you're going to have to fight for it!" I yelled the last sentence, hoping to draw their attention to me and away from their victim..

There were five of them. I could take out a few before I folded. Surely. My wings were still hurt, but I might even be able to take out all five of them. Who knew what I could do, now that I had nothing to live for. Now that I had accepted the fact that there was a good chance I was going to die.

One last good deed before the end.

I charged forward and sliced at the first two Demons, taking off their heads and arms, loving the disintegration of their beings as they burned to ash before me. It was almost too easy. I wanted a challenge, a real fight before I was killed.

Three others appeared as though by magic. I laughed as I spun in a circle and collected two more heads.

Did they know of my plan and wanted to help out?

Whatever the reason, I was glad they were all here. If they wanted to help me, it was one good deed they would be able to participate in before they died or I did.

My heart raced as I parried and thrust my sword into each Demon, the heat of their bodies surrounding me and making sweat roll down my face.

I started laughing but nothing was funny. It was maniacal, a reaction I could not control because it bubbled up inside me and left me no choice in how to respond.

I didn't concern myself with my reaction. It didn't matter. None of it did.

Then the heat burned my wings as one grabbed me, and the other scorched my shoulder.

I cried out and swung my sword wide, hoping to connect with one final Demon, but then my sword was gone. They managed to rip it away from me – something that never happened. When I held onto my sword, it was like an extension of my arm. It was unable to be pulled away from me.

Concern knit my brow, but I stopped myself. This was what I wanted, did I not?

The Demon had knocked my sword out of my hand. Flung across the yard.

Should I reach for it? Or should I surrender?

Even thinking that word made my chest constrict. Surrender was not a word I had in my vocabulary. I refused to go down unless I was fighting. As such, I needed to get that weapon back. I needed to take more Demons out before they killed me.

I dove for it and was blocked by a mountain of fire. I grunted.

I pulled myself up onto my knees and stared the Demons in the face as they surrounded me, their dark holes of eyes boring down on my helpless body. I could not be sure, but it seemed as though they were smiling.

I panted hard, my heart thundering in my chest in these last few moments of my existence.

I'd lived well, and loved the most beautiful woman I could. I had a glorious son who would grow up with a loving, caring mother in Tabitha.

My time on this Earth was done.

I closed my eyes, the heat of Hell on my face… oblivion was in reach.

And then it was gone.

A cool breeze passed over my skin and my eyes popped open to see a bright white light in place of the yellow fire.

I furrowed my brow, trying to get a grasp on my surroundings.

Had I passed over? Had I been granted access back into Heaven despite my transgressions?

Impossible.

I looked around the backyard and my mouth fell open as my heart began to gallop in my chest like a racehorse.

"Kadie…"

But that was impossible. Kadie was gone. Kadie was the reason I was here in the first place, to get to her. How could Kadie be here?

And yet, somehow, I knew she was. I felt her in my body, in my very soul.

The white light I'd seen was shooting from her hands was taking out every last Demon still standing.

But how?

They were all reduced to a pile of ash around me.

I blinked. And blinked again. I had to be dreaming. This made no sense. It was impossible – unless another Witch had her powers?

I doubted it, but I could not be sure of anything anymore.

But even as my eyes adjusted to the light, I saw her, still standing there before me. A vision in white. With black wings…

I knew it was her before I saw her face.

Hang on a second.

"Kadie?" I repeated, pushing my weary body to its feet. "Is it really you?"

I had to be dreaming… or this was a trick Hell was playing on me to drive me truly insane. This made more sense than Kadie saving me, than Kadie being here.

I didn't care if it was the latter. I'd get to feel her again. I reached out both hands, needing to touch her.

She came forward and slapped harshly at my fingers, the pain shooting through my body like a knife.

I dropped my hands away and stood up straighter. If this really was Kadie, that was not the response I would have expected from her.

She glared at me, the angelic glow around her shining even brighter now.

That look, I definitely remembered. If this was a façade the Demons were trying to use to drive me insane, they managed to capture the look she seemed to reserve just for me down pat.

"Don't give me that!" she exclaimed. "Of course, it's me! But if you seriously thought I'd just rush into your arms when you were planning on killing yourself, then you've got another think coming!" She stamped her foot like a toddler. "How dare you even think about it? Let alone come this close to achieving it." She swept her arm out to encompass the ash on the grass. "Don't you remember our deal? One of us had to survive for Nathaniel. You survived, and yet, here you are, ready to give him up as though it's so easy, as though our son is so easy to give up."

My heart rate began to slow and a strange euphoria settled over my body. I could tell her annoyance was turning into frustration, but I did not care.

"I'm dead, aren't I? Is this really how Heaven looks?" I glanced around, waiting for things to shift and change. I remembered Heaven being a lot more majestic than this.

Another harsh slap to my shoulder had me turning around to look at her once again.

"No, you are not dead," she snapped as though I was daft just suggesting it. "And no this is not Heaven, this is New York City." She rolled her eyes and her lips lifted up into a semi-smile. "The city of Angels."

"That's L.A." I pointed out and she smacked me again.

I rubbed my shoulder as the pain vibrated along my tired muscles.

I'm definitely not dreaming this.

I had another look at her, not quite believing what my brain was concluding. So, I went through the list once again. Slowly.

She shone like an Angel from Heaven.

She had black wings like one of the Fallen.

She had powers like a Witch.

"What happened to you?" I asked, my senses still totally overwhelmed. "If this is not a dream, I mean."

"Come over here." She took my hand and led me over to a bench seat in the courtyard.

The shiver of invisibility moved over me and it wasn't mine.

I looked around, my mouth hanging open like I was a fish. "How…?" I did not even know how to finish that sentence, so I didn't.

Kadie took a deep breath. "Okay," she said, settling beside me, as though she knew I was going to ask this question and had prepared for it already. "Well… after I broke the connection of Hell to Earth…"

"By throwing yourself into Hell and basically killing yourself," I finished for her, surprised at the amount of anger in my voice.

She stared at me for a moment, seeming to absorb my feelings at the same time.

I cleared my throat and tried to calm down. That had come out of nowhere.

"Yes, Gabriel. I had to, and you knew that," she said. Her eyes flickered away. "If there was a way I didn't have to…" She cleared her throat. "But there wasn't. No use getting upset over something that's already done."

"It may not have worked, you know. And you would have died for nothing."

She reached over and grabbed both of my hands, squeezing them tightly with her own. "I know… but it did work, as I knew it would. I'm sorry I had to put you through such a terrible ordeal." She smiled. "I'm glad you trusted me, Gabriel."

"I can't live without you, Kadie. I thought I could, I hoped Nathaniel would be enough… but…"

She jumped at me, wrapping her arms around my neck, sliding onto my lap like she used to. I held her as tightly as I dared, pulling her into me and praying to God that this wasn't a dream.

She laughed softly in my ear as she moved slightly away so we could look at one another. "I'm not a dream, quite the opposite. We are both very much alive and on Earth. Together."

"How?" I still did not understand this. I knew I was not supposed to understand miracles. Miracles were God's business and His alone. But there was something so spectacular about Kadie being here, being alive, that I wanted to understand, to ensure it could not be stolen from me later.

I'd never heard of anything like this before. Not in the millennium I had lived in both Heaven and Earth.

"Well, as I was trying to tell you before, after I threw myself into Hell, I was transported up to Heaven, of course. Having never killed anyone, and you know…" She let her voice trail off and nudged me with her shoulder, subtly telling me she was trying to make a joke.

"Saving the whole world with your selfless act?" I finished for her. I should have thought about that, but I'd assumed once Hell had her, they wouldn't relinquish her. I tried to smile in return but it came out like a grimace.

It had never occurred to me that a human could be turned into an Angel.

She looked away, her embarrassment obvious in the slight shrug and redness in her cheeks. "Yeah… well. Anyway, I got to Heaven and they wanted to just leave me up there to enjoy whatever they do." She ran her hand through her hair and brushed it away from her face.

"And you didn't like that idea?" I asked, the humor of the situation finally getting to me.

I could just see her, marching up to those in charge, demanding to be sent back down again. A request that would be denied to ninety-nine-point nine percent of people. I nearly laughed at the thought.

"Of course, I didn't like the idea of frolicking around Heaven for God knows how long, waiting for you all. My son was just born, and I'd left him already!"

My heart fell like a stone beneath the weight of the water. "Nathaniel is beautiful, just like you. I know he's missed you," I managed to say, though my chest seemed to be under the weight of an elephant's knee.

Kadie's hands moved up my arms, across my shoulders and came to rest upon my face, where she cradled my jaw and looked into my eyes. "Gabriel, I didn't come back just for Nathaniel, I came back for you," she said, her voice quiet but insistent.

My hands tightened on her waist, pulling her closer. "What do you mean?"

We'd had so little time together to express how we truly felt. Although I'd declared my love for her, I'd never been quite sure if she loved me the same way.

Kadie leaned forward ever so slightly and kissed me upon my lips. The lightest of touches. So gentle, it was almost as though I imagined it.

"I love you," she whispered against my skin, and my heart sang in rapture. "I begged for the chance to come home to you both, not as a human, who will die all too soon, but as an Angel who could fight alongside you. Live as long as my son will. My ultimate dream."

She pulled back and I stroked along her back where her feathers would protrude.

"You know your wings are black, like mine?" I asked, my voice soft.

She grinned at me. "Yep, of course I do. They refused to send me back initially, of course." She rolled her eyes and flicked her wrist dismissively. "They said I could become an Angel in Heaven, but to go back to Earth, I'd have to break one of their eternal rules."

My stomach dropped at the light in her eye. "What did you do?" I asked. I wasn't sure if I wanted to know. What could she have done to get herself kicked out of Heaven? Would it change my perception of her?

My mind was imagining so many terrible things. There was only so many things you could do to be thrown out of Heaven, and it usually involved murder.

"I may have stripped naked and started a fire in the Great Hall," she said, her eyes looking away.

My mouth fell open. "You what?" I asked, my tone flat.

"Well, I know it wasn't some big adultery scheme or anything, but I was running out of time," she said quickly. "I'd been watching you, and I knew you wouldn't last much longer."

"But… but, how?" I asked. I still did not understand. "Fire is forbidden in Heaven."

A light blush stained her cheeks. "I… ah, got some help." Her gaze met mine. "From Teramea."

Oh, fuck.

"No, it's okay," she said, seeing the look on my face. "She was lovely, actually. She could see how much I wanted to get back to you and our son, and she offered to help me. I think she feels guilty about what she did to you."

I just nodded, unable to understand the weird and wonderful ways of the female mind. I contented myself with just holding Kadie once again.

"I thought I'd never see you again," I said, running my fingers through her hair and breathing in her scent.

She threw her arms around my neck and squeezed tight. "You can't get rid of me that easily."

I laughed, my heart light and carefree. "So, where to next, my Angelic one?" I asked. "I think I prefer calling you my little Witch."

She jumped from my lap, grabbed my hand and extended her wings. "These things take a while to get used to, don't they?"

I chuckled. "Yes, they do."

She took my hand once again and looked towards the sky. "Take me home, Gabriel." She brushed her lips across my knuckles. "Take me to our son."

I nodded and extended my wings, guiding her through the air, and back to our son.

Kadie had fought Hell and Heaven to get back to us, and as we flew towards Tabitha's dimension and I was still very much a Fallen Angel, I realized my quest was no longer to ascend back to Heaven.

My purpose in life was to defend those who needed me, and to have Kadie fighting by my side. A powerful Witch and a mother to our son.

The next in line to rise as a warrior and protector of our people.

THE END

SISTERS OF THE COVEN PREVIEW

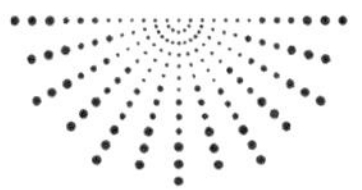

If you enjoy Fated Mates, and magical goodness, you should download and read my FREE first in series- Sisters of the Coven. Download from all retailers:
https://books2read.com/u/me9KM9
Or read on for a sneak peek into Chapter 1.

1

AVA.

If Mother knew the cause of her strange illness, she refused to tell us. That was just like her—treating my sisters and I like small children, right to the very end.

My gaze flickered over my mother who lay in the middle of her bed, frail and willowy. Her pale blue eyes—slightly milky now with her sickness—looked up at me. We'd tried everything to save her. Bella had scoured every book we owned. I'd tried every spell I knew. Nothing worked. My magic was exhausted.

I didn't want her to die. My mother was my only parent, my whole world. I didn't even know what was wrong with her.

Guilt gripped me. I had to look away.

My heart clenched.

"What can I do, Mother?" I did my best to control my voice, to make sure it didn't shake. "Tell me."

My mother's blue eyes brimmed with tears. It was a strange sight. She wasn't one for outward displays of emotion, especially not in front of her children.

"You need to help them, Ava," she said, her voice steady. Even on her deathbed, she had more control over herself than I did.

By "them," she meant my two younger sisters, Bella and Courtney.

Bella was a classic middle child with wallflower tendencies. A bookworm who'd spent every waking minute of the last two years since Mother got really sick, looking for a way to help her.

Courtney was the rebel of the family. The baby. She'd struggled the most when Mother got sick. Going off for hours at a time by herself, flipping the house upside down with her rage.

Meanwhile, I was the one who had to be dutiful, responsible… perfect. The curse of the first born. We were sisters filled with clichés and topped up with magic.

I leaned forward and smiled as bravely as I could.

"Of course, I'll look after them, Mother," I said. "I always have."

She reached out with her fragile, thin fingers and I stared at the paleness of her skin. The way the veins shone blue against the white. Like thin spider legs against a wall.

I resented her for how hard she was on me and for the pressure she'd heaped on me. She drove me half mad sometimes with her expectations of perfection.

But this woman was my world. My *everything*. She'd taught me every lesson worth learning, and some that weren't.

Her skin was cold to the touch as I gripped her hands, and I cringed at seeing the last signs of life leaving her. No matter how powerful she was, or how much strength my sisters and I had, we could not save her.

We had tried. And we had failed.

"Things are going to change, Ava," Mother said, swallowing hard as she struggled to breathe. Her voice sounded foreign to my ears.

I hadn't expected to be at this life-altering juncture for many years. Yet here I sat, not much past my twenty-third birthday, watching my mother take her last breaths.

"I don't know what we're going to do—what *I* am going to do— without you."

As I said the words meant to make my dying mother feel better, the truth pierced me through the chest like a well-aimed arrow. What *would* we do without her? I didn't have a clue.

"Ava, you will have… nothing." She gasped for air, and then coughed loudly.

I looked down, not wanting to watch as the sickness consumed her. My gaze was drawn on the plush carpet and the well-worn throw rugs in her room.

I forced my mind back to the last thing she'd said. "What do you mean, we'll have *nothing*?"

We had a house, a beautiful house. Servants. Our health. A vast yard where we could be free to practice our magic.

She wasn't making any sense. If she meant we had no family, no friends, no one outside our little world we could trust, then yes, we had nothing. But that had never bothered us before. Not too much, anyway. We had each other.

"Everything around us, Ava… the house, the land—it's all magic." She paused, coughing. "A conjure. It's not real."

An eerie coldness crept up my spine. She was delirious. She had to be. The disease had taken hold of her mind and she was saying things that made no sense.

"What do you mean, not real?" I asked.

Part of me didn't want to entertain her words. How could one person produce so much magic, such a façade, for two decades?

"I mean, there's a reason I don't leave the realm anymore," she continued. "Not since I built the house after my last babe was born. My presence is what keeps the house erect. The servants visible. It is all an elaborate spell."

My breath caught in my throat. "It's… what?"

No. Impossible.

Mother wheezed again, louder this time, and I reached for a glass of water and held it to her lips. "Hold on, Mother. Just hold on a minute more."

My blood boiled with anger. How dare she wait until her deathbed to tell us this? Why did she not prepare us for what was to come? How could she lie to us about something so important?

Something flickered in my peripheral. I blinked. The elaborate wallpaper faded, as though aging a hundred years in only a few seconds. The rich carpet beneath my feet shrunk away. The whole house shook, as though the very foundation on which it was built on was disappearing.

Fear raced through me, my heart pounding hard and every sense coming alive. What was I going to do?

I swallowed. My throat was too dry. My skin tickled, crawling with premonition. We were all in a lot of trouble.

"Just hold on, Mother." It was strange, me telling her what to do rather than the opposite. "Until Bella and Courtney come."

I hoped hearing their names would move her, would make her stay with us a little longer.

"Give me the locket, Ava," she said. "Quickly."

I reached for the necklace that hung from my neck, the ancient gold warm against my skin. I hesitated. I pulled it over my head and handed it to her.

My mother opened it with trembling fingers and lay it on her chest as though she wanted to wear it.

She pinned me with her gaze, strong and steady despite the shaking of the house around us. "No matter what, Bella and Courtney must be your only priority. Build a home of your own on the land nearby. Stay there as long as you can. Aunt Alison is the only one you can trust… in the village. If they find you…"

My sisters burst into the room in a cloud of noise, a look of sheer horror on Bella's face as she held up a beloved book.

"What's happening to the house?" she asked, as though she couldn't—or wouldn't—see our mother lying on a bed, helpless, my locket on her chest. "My books are falling to bits."

She held out the book as the papers crumbled away into dust in her hands. She let out a squeal, her eyes wide and full of tears.

There wasn't time for explanations. Not now, anyway.

"Quickly. Come." I waved to them and my sisters rushed over to the other side of the bed, grabbing our mother's hand. Bella sobbed as she put her head to the bed, and Courtney's eyes filled with tears, but she didn't make a sound.

Mother gasped as she looked at each of my sisters, her eyes soft and filled with love.

"I'm sorry for leaving you," she said. Then her gaze swung around to me, wildness and panic clear in her gaze. "You cannot search for him, Ava. You mustn't."

So unfair.

I pulled in a deep breath. I didn't like when my mother got the best of me, but then I realized I wanted no part of being bitter. *Mother is dying.*

I clenched my teeth against the command that had held me prisoner for too long. My mother's prohibitive magic had stopped me from searching out the other half of my family. My father.

And once she was gone, her hold on me would be gone, too. I could make my own decisions. Figure out what was best for *me*.

"You never told us." I said. "Why can't we search out our father?"

When I was ten years old, my mother revealed to us who our sire had been. Our father was the strongest, most powerful warlock in the universe, and he lived in the Magical Realm. It was a place she had forbidden us to go, so we had complied.

"Because… if *they* find out…" She tried to speak, but she was fading.

The light in her eyes was disappearing.

"If who finds out, Mother?"

She didn't answer me.

I narrowed my gaze and grabbed her arm. "Who?"

Her eyes widened and she stared at me like she didn't recognize me.

I squeezed. "Tell me! Please. If you want me to save my sisters, you need to tell me everything. I can't prepare myself if I don't understand what we're to face."

"The Council… they arranged his marriage." Her voice sounded raw. Each breath was a wheeze. "They…"

She was disappearing, like an ethereal ghost before me. I reached out for her again and my hand passed through her like she wasn't even there. My stomach dropped with dread. It was happening. The ground beneath our feet began to shake like an earthquake was ripping through the land.

My sisters shrieked and clung to the bed. I tightened every muscle in my body.

Oh, God. We're going to die.

I tore my concentration away from my mother and focused on saving us. It was difficult to do so, what with the ground shaking and Mother dying, secrets floating between us like ghosts.

I gathered my magic and released a breath. I opened my eyes, murmuring a protective spell I'd learned many years ago from my mother.

I threw my magic out and around the bed like an impenetrable bubble. A shield, protecting my sisters and myself as well as my mother from the crumbling house, as they cried out in terror.

"Mother!" I yelled down at her.

She met my gaze as her eyes glossed over, and becoming a milky white void. "The Council... the assassins. They'll kill you if they find out who you are..."

My heart cracked wide open as my mother continued to disappear. It was difficult to maintain my anger when she couldn't even speak sense.

"Take the locket. Quickly." Her voice was a whisper, but I didn't think she meant it to be. She gestured toward the locket that still lay on her chest.

The middle of the gold locket, where a picture should be, glowed purple. Violet, like the flecks in my mother's eyes.

I had to let go of the spell as I reached out and grabbed the locket, throwing the chain back around my neck so I didn't lose it in the maelstrom that was heading our way.

"Mother!" Bella screamed, her face raining tears. "Don't leave us."

And in a second, she was gone. Before my very eyes, before my sisters, my mother faded into nothing.

In the blink of an eye, her physical body was ash and dust, trailing off into the vibrating wind, leaving the three of us on our own.

A sob wracked my body and I reached for her, or rather where she should have been. I was met with air. I did not know what else I expected.

My sisters sobbed, leaning into each other.

I couldn't dwell on the hole in my heart for long, though. I was the oldest, after all. It was my responsibility to protect us.

The bed my mother had been on vanished. My sisters shrieked.

I grabbed the girls up in my arms. This was going to be horrible, but we would get through it if I concentrated properly.

I began the protector incantation in a low voice. A spell that would at least save what we had on our persons. Our clothes. Jewelry. If nothing else.

The protection spell coiled around were we huddled together, shielding us from the chaos that surrounded us. I continued repeating the words over and over as my love for my small family beat with every pulse of my heart.

Courtney and Bella clung to me.

All around us, the house we'd lived in our whole lives crumbled, like a giant gingerbread house that had been dropped and stomped on. It was fragile, something a gust of wind could have destroyed. How had my mother been able to maintain such a thing?

Our servants, Gemma, Elinor, and Henry, all people I thought I knew, all people I considered part of our family. The flowers Courtney had planted, the drawings Bella had created and insisted we showcase like she was an artist. All disappearing.

The lush curtains crumpled and the roof began to cave in. Sunlight from outside—the real sunlight and not one Mother had created for us—surrounded us. I was forced to squeeze my eyes shut, not used to the brightness.

"Ava!" Bella screeched as she grabbed tighter to my arms. "What's happening?"

I continued to hold on to my sisters.

"Hold on," I said. "Don't run. Don't leave this circle. I've got you."

The roof fell on top of my protective bubble, making a sound like thunder. It vibrated through my body.

Courtney dropped to the ground, screaming. Both her hands clutched her ears. I bent over so I could grab her hand in mine before she disappeared along with the house.

"Don't let go!" I shouted.

Courtney got to her feet, tears streaming down her face. My sisters continued to cling to me, and I wrapped my arms around their shoulders, pressing their heads to my chest.

I was almost afraid they, too, were part of the façade my mother had created. But they couldn't be. I loved them too much.

Their sobs rang in my ears as the house slowly but surely fell away. I didn't even care that my ears pinched with pain because of their screams. At least it reiterated the fact that they were as solid as I was. That they wouldn't be leaving me, too.

The noise coming from the crumbling manor was the hardest thing to block out. The farm we loved was no more.

The sounds of shrieking wind, of ripping fabrics, of a building crumbling to the earth echoed in my head. Stone hitting grass. Ash fluttering in the sky.

Finally, it stopped.

I opened my eyes, keeping the protection spell around our bodies and enforced as strongly as I could manage. It sounded like the devastation was over, but I couldn't be sure.

There was nothing left. Nothing but a vacant plot of land. The farm we'd grown up with, nurtured and loved, was gone. The animals we raised as beloved pets were no more.

A ringing silence hung in the crisp air. Encompassed by space, encompassed by silence. It was a straightjacket I could neither see nor feel.

After a moment, my sisters' sobs faded as well.

Not a speck of my mother's magic lingered. She was truly gone.

Finally, I could let go of my spell and took my first breath of clean air. It was a bittersweet moment. I'd lost my mother. I'd lost my home. I'd lost everything I knew to be true.

And yet, now I was free to find the man who'd sired me and hopefully everything Mother had worried about was untrue.

From now on, I was free to make choices. I was free to do as I wished.

We were three adult witches standing in a field, clinging to one another for dear life, and I had no idea what the next step was.

Download here: https://books2read.com/u/me9KM9

www.ingramcontent.com/pod-product-compliance
Lightning Source LLC
Chambersburg PA
CBHW070755190726
48292CB00002B/536